DOLPHIN DAYS

Charlotte Milne

The story contained within this book is a work of fiction. Names and characters are the product of the author's imagination and any resemblance to actual persons, living or dead, is entirely coincidental.

Cover Design: www.selfpubbookcovers.com/Shardel

ISBN-13: 978-1979129152
ISBN-10: 1979129150

Acknowledgements

My patient husband who never fails to encourage me.

Claire Anson, Trudi Murray, Charlotte Mackenzie Crooks,
Sue Prag, Carol Plunkett and Emma La Fontaine Jackson for their
encouragement and constructive criticism.

The New Writers Scheme and my Romantic Novelists Association
readers, without whom I would not have persevered.

Hilary Johnson, who not only edited, but taught and corrected with
the greatest good humour.

And finally, Rose, who in 1992 said,
"What you need now, Mrs M, is a denouement."
With my apologies for taking 25 years to provide one.

CHAPTER ONE

"**W**ait. Let me see it properly!" Melissa wished she understood the man's mixture of Greek and English better. "I can't buy without seeing it first."

She reached across the taverna table, with its clinical covering of thin plastic, and picked up the heavy book. "I'm not going to part with thousands of euros without having a good look."

The dark, hairy little man almost prevented her from taking it.

"Not here. You think I cheat you?" She looked up sharply into his unreasonably aggressive face and felt a pang of real disquiet. Her instinctive dislike of him gave her voice a new authority.

"Cheat me? I think not. But I won't buy without examining it. There's no one else here."

She unwrapped the huge book, almost sure there was something wrong, and brought all her limited training into play.

But he didn't appear to be cheating, and the book seemed to be genuine. It was by no means the best she had seen, but it was still extremely beautiful. The bindings were unbroken, but worn with long usage. Dust lay dappled and ingrained in the tiny indentations of the leather. The unpolished gems were all in their rough silver claws.

"It is good, yes?" He still sounded aggressive.

"Quite good," she said neutrally. "There is damage and wear. I must examine it further." She used her jeweller's loupe to check the settings, finding them unscratched, the grime and dust the same texture and colour throughout.

Opening the book, she checked that no pages had been removed. The leaves were vellum, unevenly cut, but with no

1

sign of damage. Some of the ink had faded towards the edges, but most of the illuminations were fresh and rich, intricate and inspired.

The fat man was trying to rush her, moving his hands impatiently on the table. Taking out her calculator she began to work out sterling to euros, frowning in distaste at the commercialism of the transaction. When she named her price Mr Rambiris looked at her incredulously, as if she had made an outrageously improper suggestion, and laughed, his black eyes without humour.

"You joke? For this? You foreigners! You think because we are a poor country we do not value our national treasures?"

His agitated hands described his indignation, and the harsh guttural English became increasingly more obscure. He seized the book and began to rewrap it, but she guessed, and fervently hoped, that it was all part of the negotiating routine. He quoted his own outrageous figure. Shaking her head, she redid her calculations and produced a slightly higher offer than her first.

"I will make a loss. I am not a fool, to give this away!"

She quoted valuations and pointed out the damage.

"I have limited financial authority. Clive Mann will not authorise a higher price, especially in view of the wear to the bindings."

Mr Rambiris became more agitated. He had many eager buyers, the rich exploited the poor, the greedy west pillaged the helpless. He lowered his price, she refused it, but increased her offer again. He raised his arms and his voice and announced his final price. It was still far beyond her instructions and as a young and inexperienced employee of Clive Mann Antiques she didn't dare to offer more than her boss had sanctioned. She sighed, shrugged and stood up, not offering her hand.

"I am sorry I cannot pay your price. I cannot go against Mr Mann's instructions."

Fifteen minutes later she left, the bible safely in her big shoulder bag. Her triumph hardly diminished by his irritation that all the relevant export forms would have to be retyped due to the unbelievably low figure, a give-away price, that he had allowed her to have it for, and on her part the nervous knowledge that she had paid Mr Mann's maximum price.

The triumph lasted through the rest of that long, hot Friday, and in the evening, as she sipped a glass of white wine on her tiny balcony, she examined her treasure again, running her fingertips over the thick tooled boards and delicate silver-gilt. The sheer euphoria of having achieved it, of having stood up to that horrid little man, the feeling that it was worth what she'd paid, gave her a heady joy and made her laugh aloud. She sent Clive Mann an email which she doubted he would read until Monday, and posted an upbeat Facebook message attaching a photo of blue sea through olive groves and Mediterranean pines. For the time being she shelved the two shadows on her mind: the price, and the bible's security.

The thought of leaving it in her room, protected only by a flimsy lock, while she went to the beach or on one of her long walks, made her uneasy, but the bank was closed for the weekend and the police station unmanned. She gazed round her little room, coolly white-washed, shining tiles on the floor, two beds, with a pine bedside table between them, a few hangers on the back of the door and three open shelves. The shower room was devoid of hiding places, wet or dry. Her landlady, Nina, changed the sheets and towels and cleaned daily, and everything was spotless but basic. It was either a case of taking the heavy bible with her wherever she went, neither practical nor safe, or leaving it inside her soft travel bag. She chose the latter, wrapping the book carefully into the bubble wrap, and then into several plastic carrier bags, finishing with the thickest heavy-duty carrier in the design of the Union Jack. She then placed the whole package inside the travel bag on top of the shelves. The likelihood of this humble little room being burgled was extremely remote, but she still felt uneasily responsible for such a valuable object.

The following morning, having checked the book was still safely in place, she set off with backpack and water to climb up to the old earthquake-ruined village. Round the corner, two young men sat smoking in the shade of a garden wall and she smiled at them.

"*Kalimera*. Is this the right way to the old village, *Chora*?"

They looked oddly startled and one of them pointed upwards. "To the right, between the olives and the orchard. Then follow the track uphill."

She felt their eyes following her as she walked on, and hoped that it was only their eyes and not the rest of them. She had no desire for company or conversation.

The day was perfect, the sun spring-bright, with a breeze to temper the heat. Scarlet poppies and white cistus still studded the olive groves and roadsides amongst the seed heads of a myriad earlier flowers and grasses. After a long hot ascent, she explored the ruins of the hilltop village and then scrambled down to the sea on the other side, for a brief and chilly swim at a deserted pebbly beach. With a familiar twist of sadness and guilt, she thought how her brothers would have loved this place. By the evening she had walked miles, and after an early supper of bread and taramasalata, sank into her bed and an exhausted dreamless sleep.

She woke late on Sunday morning, still drugged with sleep and sun. Something odd about her travel bag niggled at her subconscious as she glanced at the shelf, but the memory of the triumph of her purchase, and the congratulations awaiting her in London warmed her, like the gentle Sunday morning sun she was about to walk in, her bikini under her shorts and shirt. As she had done the previous day, she stepped on the chair to check that the bible was still safe in the bag before she went out.

Her hand felt not the hard block shape, but only the flat canvas, the buckles and the straps. Stomach lurching, brain refusing to believe, she lifted the bag down to ensure it really was safely there, but this time the panic gripped her throat. The bag was light. Light and empty.

The churning, sweating sickness of disaster swamped mind and body in numb horror as the full impact hit her. The bible was gone, without a shadow of doubt. She had taken the little white room apart and now the enormity of her loss, her vast stupidity and depthless naivete struck her physically as she crouched on the edge of the bed, the debris of her tidy life strewn in chaotic disarray, useless and disregarded because it did not include the one object which mattered. She felt physically sick, completely helpless, an indescribably frightening aloneness. Ahead loomed the questions she would have to ask Nina, the explanations to the police, the telephone calls to England, Clive Mann's fury, the repayment of several thousand pounds, the loss of her job, the humiliation of having allowed—no, caused—this disaster to happen. She let herself fall sideways on to the lumpy flock pillow and wept.

CHAPTER TWO

Three hours later nothing had changed for the better. Nina's English was limited to domestic nouns, but she had been distressed to see her guest's tear-swollen face and had searched again in a puzzled compassion for the 'book', proudly finding passport and novel and crestfallen that they were not the right ones.

Numbed by disaster, Melissa stumbled down to a quayside taverna where she knew the waiter spoke good English because he had flirted outrageously and told her how beautiful she was. He helped her find the number for the Skiathos police, and sympathetically warned her that they would have to come by hydrofoil, and today being Sunday, there wasn't one until tomorrow morning. At that moment, she felt more desperate than ever, for there was no answer from the number he had looked up for her, and she savagely supposed that Greek police didn't work on Sundays. She sat miserably at a table, drinking the filthy Metaxa three-star brandy he had given her free to make her feel better, and gazed blindly at the bright sea and the boats sucking lazily in the gentle swell at the harbour wall. A tall, bronzed, good-looking man effortlessly carried boxes of supplies on to a yacht. In happier times she would have found him extremely attractive, in spite of his severe, forbidding face.

The brandy spilled from her shaking fingers. Mr Rambiris of the hairy hands was the only person who knew she had the bible. He also knew Nina's name and the location of her room. She had thought nothing of it at the time, it had just been a conversation about a town that he knew quite well, and he was trying to discover exactly who Nina was—he had a friend who was married to a Nina, perhaps it was the same one? He had promised the Export Forms on Monday at noon at the same taverna. Some hope, she now thought

6

bitterly. On her insistence, he had scribbled an indecipherable receipt and, to add to all her other stupidities, she had placed that receipt, along with all the relevant documentation, with the bible inside all the wrappings. To keep it safe. In case her shoulder bag was stolen. A sob escaped her, and she took another gulp of the cheap brandy. Mr Rambiris, or his associates, had watched her movements; her visit to the Old Village and the beach. Now she remembered those two startled young men and thought bitterly that they were probably waiting for her to leave her room. How easy to open the flimsy door lock, how easy to search that small space without making a sign. There were not, after all, many hiding places in that room. So easy, they must have laughed. Such a silly, trusting girl. She felt herself flush with humiliation, sick with the horror of it. Now she had no proof of purchase, and there had been twenty-four hours before she had discovered its absence.

When had he done it? The last time she had checked had been yesterday—Saturday—morning. She had been criminally negligent, she realised.

The man on the yacht carried two large empty terracotta plant pots on board, and put some bags of rubbish on to the quay. One of the taverna owners crossed the road and they exchanged a joke, the man throwing his head back in laughter, his even, white teeth lighting up the dark, harsh face. She didn't feel she would ever laugh again and gulped some more brandy. Turning away, she dialled the number in Skiathos again. Again, it rang endlessly, and she was about to cut the call when suddenly someone answered shouting in Greek. She winced and established that it was the police.

"Police? *Ne!*"

"Do you speak English?"

"English? *Ochi!*"

There was another flood of Greek, interspersed with 'wait', but she was not now listening. A carrier with several empty plastic water bottles sticking out of it lay on the quay by the yacht. A distinctive Union Jack carrier, red, white and blue, trumpeting its Britishness on a Greek quay. Her heart thumped like a pile driver while she told herself that those bags might be unusual, but were surely not unique. Where had she got hers? She couldn't remember. She did remember that the outer bag she had wrapped the bible in had had a Union Jack design. She found she had bitten her lip and drawn blood.

Her phone yapped at her in Greek again, and she glanced at it in consternation. Even if she could make them understand, they wouldn't get here until tomorrow, and the yacht was leaving, she was sure. She cleared the call without taking her eyes off the rubbish bags on the quay. A thin plastic one from the so-called supermarket, and the distinctive Union Jack bag. The boat now looked deserted, but she was unsure and wished she had paid more attention to the man's movements. He was definitely not Mr Rambiris, whose short heavy figure was embedded in her memory, but she had had an impression of purposeful efficiency, a man probably in his thirties, attractive, confident, but somehow dangerous. She looked at the unfamiliar vessel, noting the sail covers were off and no awnings were rigged. Was he Rambiris's partner making a quick getaway? Could he have been the thief? It all seemed extremely unlikely, except for that Union Jack bag discarded on the quay.

Leaving the brandy on the table, she allowed her long hair to swing across to hide her face and walked slowly along the front, ostensibly looking at the assorted boats. She could feel nervous sweat running down her body. The yacht was anchored from the bow with a stern rope attached to a ring on the harbour wall. All the other boats within twenty yards on each side of it were little fishing caiques. There was no sign of anyone on board and the blue and white Greek flag sagged in the heat. It was called *Ioanna*. There was no label saying, 'Stolen Bible Aboard'.

Panic made her shiver. By tonight the boat could be anywhere. The police would never find it.

She could wait for the owner to return and ask him. Excuse me, have you stolen my bible and if you have please could I have it back? A Greek, with no English. Either a criminal and therefore dangerous, or entirely innocent and unhappy at the accusation. Guilty or innocent, he would deny it, get in his boat and sail away. Guilty, he'd have plenty of time to dispose of the evidence; innocent, he wouldn't have to.

She could get on the boat now, search it, find her property and leave, disappearing into this great metropolis of eight hundred Greek souls and a few tourists, before he could miss it. The fantasies of the novel. Behind her were four or five tavernas filled with locals with nothing better to do than watch every movement of every human, especially female, and then to talk about it. If he wasn't on his boat already, he was probably having a last drink at the bar directly opposite, and watching her watch his boat.

She shivered again in the scorching sun, feeling eyes boring into her back and pressed her fists into the sickness in her stomach. Turning, she slowly made her way down the steps and on to the harbour beach, sinking down against the wall out of sight of everyone.

She could swim to the yacht, but the man might have already come back on board. For a moment, she prayed that that would be the case, and she'd have to swim right back again, but then the equally awful thought of Clive Mann, and the loss of her job and career, swept into her mind, and she knew that she couldn't go home without trying to redeem herself. If she swam close behind all the boats it would be unlikely that she would be seen from the shore, but the harbour itself was not at all a common place for swimmers, with boats going in and out. She tried to shut out the nightmare thought of getting sucked in to rotating propellers. Of all the ghastly scenarios, it was possibly the least likely.

She screwed up her courage, and got to her feet, aware of the rising wind. Slipping off the shirt and shorts to the bikini beneath, she rolled them up with her money belt and phone

9

in the middle and placed them carefully against the wall, placing her flip-flops on top. Walking slowly into the sea, a wave slapped chilly water against the bare skin of her midriff, and her stomach contracted at both the chill and the fear. She stopped, her toes curling on the pebbles. This was utterly mad, and dangerous and stupid. No book, however valuable, could be worth it. He would catch her, beat her up, kill her, and dump her body out at sea to be eaten by the fish. Stop it, she told herself sternly.

She stood irresolute, remembering now that she had nothing waterproof to put the bible in even if she should find it. Would she brazenly step on to the quay clutching it to her, or could she possibly swim back with it held above her head? She tried to make herself think it through, but her mind could only shout 'Hurry! Hurry! He'll come back before you get there!'

Perhaps she would swim along anyway; a perfectly innocent, if stupid, thing to do. She could bang on the hull and ask for some fictitious friends. If he was there, she'd apologise for the mistake, and hope that he didn't know what she looked like. Perhaps he might even ask her aboard. If he wasn't there, she could search the boat. Surely there would be a plastic bag somewhere she could wrap it in, and if necessary one of the little fishing boats would provide a temporary haven for a package under a pile of nets. She suddenly felt more confident and launched out into the sea.

The beach swimming area was sandy and clear, but the harbour section on the other side of the jetty seemed less desirable. The flotsam and jetsam of a working fishing community floated by her: a plastic bag, pieces of string and plastic, bits of octopus and dead fish. She shuddered, trying to avoid the debris, trying not to think of all the things in the water let alone what floated on top. She swam under the anchor ropes and cables, occasionally hanging on to catch her breath and get her bearings, but the water no longer felt cold, and the numb horror that had gripped her mind earlier no longer paralysed her thinking.

The yacht stretched her clean slippery crescent before her, and glancing up at the quay she thought it unlikely that anyone would notice a stray swimmer. Further down the front, a fuel lorry started filling someone's tanks, and simultaneously a motorbike engine shattered the air. She held on to the anchor chain to study the boat. Access might be a problem.

Squeezing between the hull and the adjacent fishing boat she came to the stern, which, to her relief and surprise, had a short ladder and a sort of ledge just above water level. Sitting on the ledge she was hidden from view, but standing on it she could be seen from any quayside taverna. Glancing round she felt like a moth in a torch beam, and fully expected several people to leap from their beers and descend on the boat, shouting and waving their arms, but not a soul moved, not a head turned. Rather unnervingly, she saw the two rubbish bags had gone.

"Hello! Anyone at home?"

She felt amazingly silly, as well as frightened, cleared her throat and tried something louder.

"Anyone aboard? Hello?"

No one replied, and no one advanced across the concrete; no one moved at any of the tables across the road.

She climbed quickly into the boat, past an enormous steering wheel, streaming water which she hoped would evaporate quickly from the textured rubbery floor. The cabin loomed dark from the open companionway and the blood thudded in her ears. Descending rapidly to get out of sight, she found an orderly disorder of open crates and boxes, some obviously domestic provisions, and some not so obvious. Two bunks were tightly covered in brightly patterned Greek fabric and at the sides were little cupboards with sliding doors and railed shelves below them. Ahead of her a narrow door, and on her right a navigation table and various instruments. Behind her, on each side of the steps, were two more narrow louvered doors.

11

Squinting nervously out to the quay, she saw only empty sunshine, with the odd tourist crossing in front of the tavernas. No one had seen her illegal entry. Turning her mind firmly back to the urgent search, she realised with dismay that finding even a large book was not necessarily going to be straightforward. She started by the table and worked her way back, breathless with nerves and her thumping pulse deafening. A table with long drawers contained only charts. There were tools, first aid, cards, paper, binoculars, oilskins, manuals, CDs and shelves of Greek and English books; but not her book. How long had she been here? Ten minutes? Her heart was still racing, sweat running into her eyes. The first louvered door turned out to be the tiniest loo and shower, the second a single unused cabin under the cockpit. She cautiously opened the door at the far end, almost expecting him to be having a siesta, but the double bunk was untidily made, obviously in use, the shelves occupied with the detritus of everyday living: cigarettes, a lighter, receipts, a used Spiralette. Hairbrush, pocketknife, clock and books. Above, there were photos, pinned with rusty tacks; people and buildings. She averted her eyes, feeling both the intrusion and the onset of panic. The cupboard contents were sparse; a couple of shirts and a pair of chinos hanging up, and at the bottom a plastic briefcase. Just the right size and shape for a large book. At last! The blood thumped even more loudly in her head as she placed it on the bunk with trembling hands.

Although there was a combination, it stood at 0000 and the case opened and revealed, not her book, but rank upon rank of tiny sealed plastic envelopes. Each with a small amount of white powder in it. Each with a tiny label printed in Greek: writing and numbers. At one side a compartment contained vacuum packed syringes and needles, and on the other side several rectangular tablet boxes. A sob of fright escaped her tight throat and her knees nearly gave way. Snapping the case shut, she pushed it back in the cupboard— she had not thought of drugs as being part of this story and the danger she was in became frighteningly clear.

The light came from a small skylight above the bunk, cracked slightly open. She thought it would be a possible means of exit should he come aboard and down the companionway. Standing on the bunk, she raised it right up, unsure if she could even squeeze through it. In fifteen or twenty minutes, she hadn't found the book and it probably wasn't here anyway. She was burgling a drug smuggler, or drug dealer, or at the very least a drug user who might return at any moment. Fear shafted through her again. There wasn't anything more she could do, apart from getting into serious trouble. She must leave.

As she stumbled forward towards the steep steps of the companionway she saw, in one of the cardboard boxes, a thick packet, placed vertically alongside soap powders, spaghetti and tins. Bending down, she slid it out. She couldn't see the book itself, but sealed inside two thick waterproof polythene zipped envelopes, the type that ramblers used to carry their maps in, was a thick heavy object swathed in bubble-wrap.

Triumph sang through her at the same moment that the boat rocked as the stern rope was hauled in. Clutching the package, Melissa bolted like a rabbit for the forward cabin, eased the door shut behind her and leapt on to the bunk. She eyed the gap between the deck and the wire rail and knew she could slide under it, if she could squeeze out of the hatch. The book, sealed in its wrappings, would even float, she thought. She could see no one from her eye-level view, and slid the package on to the deck behind the hatch and waited, her heart thudding and her whole body shaking. The boat rocked and swayed again and then she heard footsteps on the companionway. With terror lending her strength, she thrust herself through the hatch, not feeling the scrapes and cuts on her arms and body from the metal surround and latch. Adrenaline flooded and she pulled her flailing legs up, every second expecting them to be grabbed from below.

What she didn't expect was his voice above her.

CHAPTER THREE

She felt as if an electric shock had gone through her, draining her of blood, paralysing, obliterating rational thought.

He spoke again, the Greek sharp and incomprehensible except for the anger. He stood on the cabin roof above her, tall and dark against the sun.

She froze, her muscles turned to water.

He spoke again, forcefully, obviously a question, and after a moment of her continued mute terror, moved purposefully towards her. She heard herself say, stupidly, "Don't!"

"English?" he said incredulously into the ensuing silence. "What the hell are you doing?"

There didn't seem to be any possible answer, so she said nothing.

"Who the hell are you, and what the hell do you think you're doing?" The English was perfect. He sounded more incredulous than angry.

"I—I'm sorry—I didn't know it was your boat." The inane remark came out as a croak. After a slight pause, he said, "And whose boat did you think it was?"

She forced the terror down.

"I thought it—I thought it belonged to friends of mine." Silence. "I'm so sorry. I've made an awful mistake. I thought their boat was called—er—*Joanna.*"

"Did you." It somehow wasn't a question. "Certainly, you seem to have made a mistake—and a somewhat mistaken exit." He hesitated a moment. "But perhaps you know my wife?"

"No. No, I don't." She couldn't fathom that question.

"And your friends' name?"

14

"Oh!" Her mind went temporarily blank. "Campbell. Peter and Vanessa Campbell. I'm really sorry about this mistake."

"I'm sure you are," he said. "I don't know of any Peter and Vanessa Campbell, but if I could give you a piece of advice, I suggest that when you do find them, you do not go aboard their yacht uninvited, nor drip salt water through their cabins, nor try to depart through an extremely small hatch. It looks very odd indeed. Would you like to leave by the quay or the way you came?"

She became aware of her still damp body and extremely brief bikini and the fact that from above, she must be revealing a great deal of bare flesh. The package lay behind her, and she didn't think he had seen it, but neither could she think of a way of taking it with her. She felt the sweat of fright and embarrassment trickling down her face, and her hands were slick on the metal hatch frame.

"I'm terribly sorry—I never thought—I've never been in a boat—a yacht—like this before. I was expecting to find my friends, so I went down—it's lovely—fascinating—I mean, so neat."

"And your chosen exit?" His black eyes hardened.

"Oh. By the quay, thank you. I'll follow you."

"Actually, I'm not leaving, you are. Would you like me to pull you out of the hole you seem to be in?"

She searched helplessly for something to persuade him to look elsewhere.

"I'd like to find my friends. Would the harbour master know where they're moored?"

He didn't move, but his face became grimly taut. "What a very curious girl you are," he said slowly. "And I wonder why you are frightened rather than embarrassed. I also wonder why you appear to be so reluctant to leave. Have you left your job half done? A camera or recorder not quite ready, or perhaps seawater has got into the works?"

The admission of his guilt astounded her.

15

"Of course not!" She tried to make the protestation into a laugh, but knew he could hear the high pitch. "And I am embarrassed—very—but you also gave me a fright, creeping up on me like that."

He didn't respond. She swallowed. "I realised when I was downstairs—below—that it couldn't be the Campbells' boat."

Rather unexpectedly he said, "And how did you know that?"

"Oh! Er—there were none of their things around."

"None of their 'things'. I see. You've never been on their boat, but you would still recognise their 'things'. What 'things' were you expecting?"

Her brain was working in slow motion. "Um, well, clothes."

"So you normally go through people's cupboards in their absence, do you?"

"No! Of course not!"

"You didn't go into mine then?"

"Certainly not!" she lied defiantly. Then suddenly remembering the books, clung to faint hope. "I saw Greek books. They don't read Greek—wouldn't have them on board. And Vanessa is terribly untidy. She leaves her clothes all over the place, and there weren't any, so I knew it was the wrong boat. And I hoped to leave without—"

He suddenly stepped towards her, impatient with her thin story, and as he did so, he saw the package on the deck. For a second he checked, astonished, then rapidly bent and picked it up.

"So, you hoped to leave with a souvenir of your visit. Not quite what I was expecting, I must admit. You couldn't obtain what you'd been sent to get, so you thought a memento of your visit was a deserved perk, is that it?"

She stared at him stupidly, not understanding. "I don't know what you're talking about!"

"No?" he said grimly. "Well, maybe you're just a sneak thief."

16

"I'm not!" she croaked. Her throat felt as if he had his fingers round it.

"No." he said slowly, his eyes thoughtful. "No, on reflection I don't think you are an opportunist thief. I think you knew exactly what you were looking for. Who sent you to steal it? Who told you where I was?"

Confusion almost overwhelmed her. "No one sent me. I don't know who you are."

"That seems truly unlikely," he said, and then glanced up at the flag fluttering at the masthead. "I want the wind" he said curtly, "and I have an appointment to keep. I'm not going to waste more time here, but I'm damned if you're going to walk off scot-free to continue your freeloading lifestyle. You'll come with me until I get the truth out of you, and then I'll decide what to do with you."

His abrupt statement terrified her.

"You can't! I mean don't! Please, let me go—I'll forget the whole thing, honestly I will."

"No."

"If you don't let me go, I'll scream."

"Scream away." He gave an unamused laugh, the black eyes cold. "And I do hope you won't forget the whole thing. I'll do my best to help you remember. Now, come along and let's see if you've left something behind in the excitement of absconding with my property."

With which incomprehensible remark he leant down, seized a wrist and hauled her ungently off the hatch, inflicting several more scratches and grazes on her legs in the process. Propelling her in front of him, he marched her straight down into the forecabin.

"I knew someone had been here. I left the hatch down, and when I came back it was open. You needed a quick getaway if I happened to come back and come below, didn't you?" His voice was contemptuous. "So, what did you put in here? A camera?" After a pause, he said, "You had better tell me, you know. I'll find it anyway. My temper is unreliable. I'm sure my wife told you that."

Her voice cracked. "I don't know your wife. And I didn't put anything in here. I don't know what you're talking about."

They were standing in the minute U-shaped space at the end of the bunk, his height at close quarters overpowering. Suddenly he turned.

"Perhaps this is going to take a little longer than I thought. I shall put you somewhere safe for a little while, and then we're going to have a proper chat, you and I."

He pulled her back to the tiny cabin in the stern, opened the door and pushed her in. She heard a slide-bolt grate.

"You can't!" she gasped frantically. "Let me go!"

"I can. If you damage anything, you'll regret it. Don't try kicking the door down."

She didn't think he was joking and remained frozen, immobilized by shock.

The boat rocked slightly as he moved about. There were noises of cupboards and doors being opened and closed, of boxes being moved, of metal clinking on metal, mysterious soft thumps. He must be looking for whatever he thought she had hidden and checking on his drugs, she thought distractedly. A little later, she saw glimpses of his feet in the cockpit through the narrow horizontal window, and felt the vibrations as he moved over the coach-house roof. It had all happened in a matter of a few minutes; she was being abducted by a criminal and would probably be murdered unless she did something. She tried the door, which looked flimsy but was rock solid. It didn't even rattle. The cabin was completely empty except for the bright cover on the bunk. She had to do something; she couldn't just let him sail away with her without doing anything. She shouted. She shouted and yelled and screamed. And absolutely nothing happened. She felt faint from panic.

The engine suddenly coughed into life. Her stomach knotted at the realisation that he really was abducting her and she covered her mouth with her hands on an involuntary sob. With a sudden rattling the anchor chain came up, and then the boat swung, mastheads came and went in the narrow window and water began to rustle down her sides. Melissa stopped yelling and banging on the door; she put her head against it and closed her eyes tightly on the panic.

It was hot and airless, and the window was locked with an outside catch. A few minutes more and they would be well outside the harbour. She became aware of heavier seas, and the floor unsteady under her feet, so that she had to brace herself against the unfamiliar movement. At the same time, the minutes raced towards the moment when he would unlock the door and demand explanations, and her brain felt as if someone had stirred it with a spoon. She heard him come down into the main cabin and found herself backing away from the door and stumbling to the farthest corner of her tiny space, but he ignored her and more time passed with unidentifiable noises and occasional returns to the companionway steps, perhaps to check his course. Then he spoke.

"I hope you're sorting truth from lies. I'll be wanting it very soon."

He went up on deck again, and in a few minutes the floor beneath her tilted, the engine died, and she heard water and wind and realised they were under sail. The minutes dragged on and the little cabin became hotter and more airless.

Her grandmother Mops's words of warning about the dangers of the business world, and business men, a legacy of her grandparents' bankruptcy, had all come to pass and Clive Mann had sent her literally into a den of thieves. She tried to review what had happened, and how she could persuade this man to take her back to Perissos. Despairingly, she knew he didn't believe her thin story of looking for friends, so the truth about her search for the bible was the only feasible one. If he could be persuaded that she wouldn't, and couldn't, expose him as a thief perhaps he would let her go. As a drug smuggler, his anxiety about a camera or recorder made sense. Perhaps Rambiris was part of that, and had paid for drugs with the book. Did he think she was a police agent or that

Rambiris had double-crossed him? And why did he think she knew his wife? And who was he, with his perfect English and faint Greek accent? The questions chased round in her clogged brain, going nowhere.

The bolt slid back and she instinctively wedged herself into the corner as he looked at her grimly.

"Come up on deck."

He disappeared as rapidly as he'd come, and she stood in the cabin door and stared at the four small drawers in the galley. She'd found knives in the top one during her search, but she could not get at them now as he would see her opening the drawer from the cockpit. As if in answer to the thought, he jumped lightly up on to the coach-house roof and went forward. She crossed the gap in an instant, slid the drawer open and there they were, held in little slots. She dithered over the big knife or the five-inch blade; the latter would be easier to hide, she decided. She slid it, blade down, between the top step and wall, and then on an impulse took the remaining two, sliding the big knife down the side of one of the bunks and the little one on the opposite side of the cabin behind some books. He was still on the coach-house roof. Nervous sweat trickled down her face and between her breasts as she went slowly up the steps and stood irresolute at the top of the companionway, bracing herself against the angle of the deck and the snatching movement of the yacht. The sun streamed down, but its heat was tempered by the wind; open sea behind, choppy and sparkling, the occasional wave top chipped to white. The empty wheel moved sluggishly and she wondered vaguely how the boat steered by itself.

"Sit there," he said brusquely from above her, indicating where he wanted her, "and put that on," he dropped down a life jacket, "just in case I push you overboard. At least you'll float for a day or so." His voice was humourless and the sinister statement instantly conjured up a vision of torture before being fed to the fish. She sat down and put her hands between her knees so he couldn't see them trembling.

20

"I've got friends—they're expecting me. If I don't turn up, they'll raise the alarm."

He looked at her with contempt. "More friends! What a lucky girl you are to have so many!"

She could see land, Perissos she assumed, hazy and already receding on the horizon. Turning her head to the taut white sails, she could see only water beyond them.

"Please, take me back. I won't tell anyone, I promise."

"I'm not taking you back and I want an explanation."

"But I must go back! I can't do you any harm, so please, take me back. You could drop me on some remote beach and be miles away before I even reached the town. Please."

"Forget it," he said sharply. "You should have thought of the risk before creeping on to yachts just leaving harbour."

He went behind the wheel, his body muscled, very brown. "So, are you a habitual thief, or what?"

What indeed. Mr Mann would sack her when he knew what had happened. If she survived.

"I'm not a thief," she said defiantly. "I was sent to buy that book."

"Who sent you? My wife?"

"No!" She was bemused. "My employer sent me."

"But you didn't buy it, you stole it from me—or you tried to."

"I didn't steal it." She took a deep breath to steady herself.

He shook his head. "'Your employer'" she heard, but did not understand the contemptuous sarcasm, "sent you, not to buy, but to steal. You knew where to look for me and what to look for, didn't you?"

She shook her head in confusion. "No, I bought it from a dealer, on instructions from my employer."

Fleetingly she thought of those instructions, and how she hadn't even questioned them.

"And finding it already sold and you were too late, you decided to steal it, thereby avoiding all those trying financial negotiations? I suppose you then intended to hand it over to your 'employer' explaining what a fortune you had spent on it, and getting reimbursed for your 'deal'. Quite a clever idea, I suppose, if it had come off."

"No! I did buy it!" she said, despair beginning to overwhelm her.

He gave her a derisory look. "I think not, but it's quite easy to ascertain for sure. Who is your employer and how much did you buy it for?"

She hesitated; she felt some further frightful train of events would start if she answered all his questions. This man was obviously a criminal and she should not be telling him anything.

"Who is your employer?" he said again. "My wife? A newspaper? Newspapers don't normally employ such inept newshounds in my experience, and they certainly wouldn't have any interest in that book. And if entrapment was the idea, the last effort, though tacky, was more professional—she looked good and at least she came with a camera."

She stared in incomprehension. "No! Honestly, you've got it completely wrong. I don't work for a newspaper. I've no idea who you are, so you're perfectly safe."

"How very kind!" he said. "I feel so relieved by your assurances. But my dear wife is one hell of a bitch, and your incompetent efforts are not going to please her at all, are they?"

The wife sounded terrifying, and Melissa's confusion and alarm rose.

"I don't know your wife."

He laughed without humour. "I bet you don't," he said, "but I do."

"I don't understand what you're talking about. I'm prepared to forget the whole thing—I told you—I won't tell the police anything. What can I tell them anyway? I've got no proof, and you'll have disappeared. Just take me back to Perissos and I promise I won't try to follow it up at all. Please take me back."

He was unconvinced, the dark eyes hard. "I'm not taking you back to Perissos, so stop bleating. Now, my name is Nicholas, as you probably know. What is yours?"

After a small silence, she said, "Melissa."

"Melissa." He seemed to taste it, repeating it with a hesitation after the first syllable and a slight emphasis on the second.

"Melissa what?"

"Scott-Mackenzie."

"What a very Scottish name. And do you hail from a long line of thieves?"

"I'm not a thief." She hunched her shoulders.

"Not a very good one, certainly. Who told you I was in Perissos?"

"Nobody did. I was in Perissos to buy the bible."

"For your employer."

"Yes."

"Who is?"

There didn't seem to be any point in not telling him, whether or not he had stolen the bible, or even if he was a drug smuggler.

"I work for Clive Mann."

He frowned. "And who is he?"

"An antique dealer," she said reluctantly.

"Ah. Things become ever so slightly less opaque. And where does Clive Mann, antique dealer, have his empire?"

"In London."

"Who were you buying for?"

It seemed an extraordinary question and she frowned in confusion.

"I told you. For Mr Mann."

He shook his head. "I don't think so. How long have you worked for him?"

"A year."

"And does Mr Clive Mann normally send junior employees of one year's experience to retrieve little bits of the ancient world for him?"

His ironic tone reminded her that despite her pride and pleasure in being given this chance, a part of her had been surprised that Mr Mann had sent her alone to a foreign country for such a valuable object. She said nothing.

"I suppose your silence means 'no he doesn't'. How very odd. And who were you meeting in Perissos to buy the book from?"

"A dealer." He waited. "A man called Rambiris," she said hesitantly, unable to calculate whether her answers would help her or not. There was quite a long silence while the man stared at her thoughtfully.

"And is Clive Mann a friend of Mr Rambiris?"

"No—that is—I suppose he's a business connection," she said unhappily.

"And what about you? Have you dealt with him before? Is Rambiris a friend of yours, or a business connection?"

"Neither. I met him for the first time on Perissos, as instructed by Mr Mann. He sold me the bible. On Friday, as I'm sure you know." Anger surfaced through the nervousness. "And then he stole it back—or you did."

"He sold you the bible on Friday." He repeated the statement sarcastically. "Actually, I didn't know, and neither do I believe it. I have been in correspondence with Rambiris for some weeks and I bought the bible from him, quite properly and legally, yesterday, Saturday, afternoon"

She stared at him in frustration and disbelief.

"You can't have! I had it yesterday!" But there had been twenty-four hours before she had checked again, this morning. How could she have been so criminally careless! The churning guilt made her feel sick and she pressed her fists into her stomach.

"But I did. I have a receipt to prove it. But if you thought you bought it no doubt you have a receipt, too." She said nothing. "Don't tell me," he said with dry irony, "your receipt has disappeared as well. How very inconvenient—or perhaps convenient—for you. How much did you pay?" He laughed into her silence. "I'm assuming you won't tell me because you didn't pay for it and have no idea what it's worth. You don't have proof of purchase because you never bought it. Maybe you intended to, maybe you didn't, but it was sold to me and you decided to take a short cut and steal it instead."

Goaded to anger by his contempt, she told him the figure.

"You and Rambiris cooked this up between you, didn't you? Making sure that I would have to wait until Monday for my forms and a proper receipt," she said bitterly. "Well, there's nothing I can do about it, so I suppose you've won. Why did you bother with bringing me out here when it was perfectly obvious I couldn't interfere with your nasty little dishonesties?" His eyes hardened and she went on wearily. "He wrote me a receipt, and I put it in the same package with the bible. And don't tell me how stupid that was. I do realise. You've got the bible, and no doubt destroyed my receipt. You made sure that although I paid over my employer's money I have no proof of purchase and no goods. I don't know who you are, so why can't you take me back to Perissos, or at least leave me somewhere within reach of a telephone? I've got no clothes, no money and no passport. I can't possibly do you any harm."

He shook his head. "You're not going back to Perissos until I get the truth. It seems to me that you knew exactly where to find me and that book, courtesy of Rambiris, and were waiting patiently for a chance to sneak on board and steal it."

Suddenly furious at his disbelief, she took a deep breath to steady herself. "No! I didn't! I bought it on Friday. I had it yesterday morning and when I checked today it was gone. I'd wrapped it in bubble wrap and plastic bags, and the outer bag had a Union Jack design. The police station on Perissos is closed, so I went to the taverna on the front because the waiter has good English and I needed help to ring the police. I can't manage a Greek phone book, and the waiter got the number in Skiathos for me. But they didn't speak English and then I saw you put the bag on the quay, with rubbish in it, and I thought you were about to leave and I dropped the call."

"And in an instant, you decided to search my boat, find your treasure and abscond without me knowing a thing about it." His mouth had hardened in scepticism.

"I had to at least try to find it—to get it back before you disappeared. I knew it was wrapped in that bag when it was taken. I saw the bag on the quay, and then I found the bible on your boat. It was proof you'd stolen it."

"I'm afraid it isn't." He tilted his head slightly, considering her. "Which taverna, and which waiter?"

"What?" She looked totally blank. "I—I don't know. The one on the corner."

"And the waiter?"

"This is ridiculous! I've no idea—he was just a waiter. I suppose I would recognise him again."

"So, you can't tell me where you were, or who helped you telephone, which does make me wonder if your imagination isn't at work again. And you say the police didn't speak English? That's rubbish. Of course they speak English. And Italian, and German, and French, and probably every other tourist language in the book."

"They didn't," she said, becoming angry again. "The first time I tried, it rang and rang and nobody answered, and I was so upset, by that, and everything, the waiter gave me some of that foul brandy, and then I tried again and they answered and I asked if they spoke English and he said—" She stopped suddenly, her memory confused. He looked at her gravely for a moment and then began to laugh softly.

"Oh God! I don't believe it! *'Ne'*. He said *'Ne'*, didn't he? So you put the phone down. Some things do ring true in this farce."

"I don't think he did say *'Ne'*," she said unhappily. "I asked if it was the police and he said *'Ne'*, and then I asked if he spoke English and it was different. I'm sure he said *'Ochi'* and then 'wait'. Then I saw the carrier bag and I cut the call.

What could I tell them? And they were in Skiathos and the waiter said they'd have to come by hydrofoil and there wasn't one till tomorrow, and I didn't have any proof of ownership—the story was going to be pretty unbelievable, a point you've made already, several times," she said. "And it looked as if you were leaving."

He moved suddenly, decisively, and she shrank back fearing he might touch her, but he swung down the companionway and a few moments later she heard his voice in a sharp Greek exchange on the radio. Her eyes pricked with tears of apprehension and she rubbed them away. She could see him perched on the galley counter, one long muscular calf braced against the chart table. The flood of Greek came from him now, with an occasional shout coming back. He jotted notes on a pad and she looked at him more carefully; there might come a time when she would need to identify him. A tall man, his age hard to guess, between thirty and forty perhaps, compact and muscular, the face strongly boned, but not by any means the classic Grecian ideal. Good-looking, but not handsome in the fashionable sense. There were deep lines around his eyes and mouth which gave him a look of severity, even anger, but now they crinkled in brief laughter, the teeth even and white in the tanned face. He brushed away a lock of the dark straight hair from his eyes, and she saw that his hands looked very strong, the fingers long and tapered.

He finished his conversation and came back to the cockpit carrying two bottles of water.

"You'd better drink something." he said, handing her one of them. "Where were you staying in Perissos? A hotel?"

She shook her head. "A room."

"Where? Whose?"

"I don't know the address. The lady was on the quay with a Room to Let sign when the ferry came in, and I just followed her."

27

He made a sound of irritation. "And? Describe where you went. What was her name?" Melissa remained silent and after a moment he spoke again, slowly and emphatically.

"You are not helping yourself. If you want to get out of this mess you had better start co-operating."

She shivered involuntarily at the menace in his voice.

"She's called Nina." She described the location as loosely as she could, remembering that Nina knew about the bible going missing, and that she might be endangered by the knowledge. The dark eyes pinned her and she gripped her hands between her knees again.

"How long were you there?"

"A week."

"Describe, accurately, starting from the ferry port, the exact route to your room. Not too difficult after a week, I don't think."

She didn't have the courage to resist, and he listened carefully to the directions, then went down to the cabin and made another radio call.

She thought she heard him mention the name Nina, and wondered if he might be trying to confirm her story. On the other hand, as a criminal, he might be doing something far worse. She wondered if she had put Nina at risk.

The yacht mysteriously sailed itself onwards, towards land which gradually became clearer, pine trees on the steep slopes down to the sea. Light reflected blindingly, briefly, from windows, but the building remained hidden in the trees. Their destination, she supposed apprehensively. Ahead she could make out a small motorboat moored at a jetty, and a track winding up the hill.

The man came up from the cabin and throttled back the engine. He then took her below and without explanation locked her once more into the cabin, hot and claustrophobic.

Peering from the little horizontal window she could just see a figure emerge from the trees and walk down the track, and the boat slid gently towards the pier. As the figure came closer she realised it was a woman, walking with a noticeable limp. A few moments later the man came into view walking up the hill towards her. He carried the black plastic case.

Melissa watched them meet, the case put on the ground, embracing, kissing on both cheeks, the woman gesticulating generously with hands and shoulders. Then he took papers out of his pocket and gave them to her, and she handed over an envelope. Melissa knew that it must contain money. She also knew that now no proof of his drug dealing existed, and she had no clue about the location of this island. The couple talked for some minutes, then embraced again and parted. She, carrying the case, and he his envelope.

He didn't unlock the cabin door until the island had sunk into the afternoon haze behind them, and then she sat silently in the cooler air of the cockpit, the engine vibrating under her feet like a menacing heartbeat, while he made more incomprehensible calls on the radio. Her previous brief hopefulness had evaporated and she now felt only a deep lassitude edged with a headache brought on by hunger and anxiety. The sun had sunk low, almost in the sea, and the air felt cool. She shivered slightly, glad of the protection, however small, of the buoyancy jacket.

Land came closer, but she could see no town or village, or even a house. The yacht, with no one at the wheel, headed straight for bare rock punctuated by the odd stunted tamarisk. Wafts of fennel and thyme filled her nostrils. He's going to crash the bloody boat, she thought hysterically, and I'm going to be tipped into this cold black water and he'll push me under and drown me. She clenched her fists to squash the thought, relief flooding her as he finished speaking, climbing leisurely into the cockpit and behind the wheel. Even then, another thirty seconds elapsed before he reduced speed and the yacht sighed softly into a tiny bay, a white beach in a cul-de-sac of tumbled red rocks to the left and a rough low cliff on the right. The stern anchor clattered interminably until the yacht came within a few feet of the shore. He came forward, dropped a bow anchor and went gently into reverse before cutting the engine. In the silence, he did efficient things with ropes and sails before returning to the cockpit to stand looking down at her with that considering, speculative stare. She tensed under his eyes, deeply uncomfortable, cold in the gathering twilight.

"Where are we?" she said, aware of the tremor in her voice. He heard it too and laughed a little.

"A waterless and uninhabited island. I'm debating about leaving you here." She shivered.

He toed off his plimsolls.

"Take that jacket off and make yourself useful getting some food ready while I have a swim. I'll show you where everything is—though of course you've had a good look round already."

She flushed at the sarcasm, but said nothing, following him down to the galley. He retrieved the ingredients for a salad and some cold meats from the little fridge, directed her to a crate for some fruit, and then unhooked a towel from the shower as she went into the galley.

"And the knives are here," he said, leaning over the counter and pulling open the slotted drawer. He was suddenly still.

"Or they were. Oh, Melissa." That soft emphasis on the second syllable was like a caress, but infinitely terrifying.

"Where are they?"

She didn't answer. She had entirely forgotten about the knives and for one long, awful moment she simply couldn't remember. She felt the sheen of cold sweat on her skin. As they stood there staring at each other she knew he took her silence for refusal. Then the slow change that she saw coming into his eyes sent terror prickling through her and propelled her into flight. She turned and leapt up the companionway in a hopeless desire to escape, and stumbled into the cockpit. He came up after her, unhurried and sure-footed.

She gasped for breath, her heart crashing. "Don't. Don't touch me. Leave me alone."

He said nothing, but caught her arm. Dragging away from him, she fell heavily against the wheel and the pain in

30

her side obliterated her fear and replaced it with outrage. His hand was within reach of her teeth and she sank them viciously into his knuckles.

CHAPTER FOUR

In due course he retrieved his knives, anointed his knuckles with antiseptic cream, and passed the tube to her for her grazes. To her surprise, his mood changed for the better and there was almost a sense of humour in the atmosphere. He gave her bread and tsadziki, allowed a shower and locked her into the forward cabin, this time opening the narrow window on to the cockpit for ventilation.

Restless and wakeful all night long, she must eventually have fallen asleep for an ungentle grip on her bare shoulder shook her into heart-stopping wakefulness again.

With a suppressed groan, she rolled on to her side and half sat up. Groggily, she took in Nicholas, dressed as yesterday in faded denim cut-offs, long, lean and brown. He leant easily against the doorframe, a mug of coffee in his hand.

"How did you contact Rambiris?" The suddenness of the question, seconds after he had shaken her awake, made her gasp. She lay clutching the duvet to her neck, feeling utterly vulnerable under the cold steady gaze.

"Mr Mann gave me his mobile number. I rang him from Skiathos."

"And arranged what?"

"He told me to come to Perissos. Last Friday was the earliest he would meet me."

"When were you due to fly back?"

"This Wednesday." Her eyes dropped. "Look, you know I can't prove I bought the bible first. I won't involve the police—I've got no evidence to give them. But I must go back."

He shook his head. "Too late. You won't make your flight and the police are already involved." Jolted to full awareness by this statement, her eyes widened. "And

32

discovering you've made an unfortunate mistake is not going to help you much. I arranged that meeting some weeks ago, and have the correspondence. I came, I saw, I bought. Legally. End of story, I thought. And then you arrive," his voice took on a steely grimness, "dripping into my yacht, wearing less than nothing; you go through all my possessions, you steal my rather expensive acquisition, which you are then fully prepared to destroy by dousing it in the sea." She tried to protest at that, but he went remorselessly on. "You tell some immediately obvious lies, and then crown the lot by the most unlikely story outside a novel. From antique dealer to picking through rubbish bags. And then you expect me to believe that you aren't working for Rambiris, don't know who I am, and didn't know where to find me, my boat, or the book. Frankly, Miss Scott-Mackenzie," he emphasised her name with biting sarcasm, "you insult my intelligence by expecting me to believe any of this pathetic trail of incompetence and lies."

He left her, speechless with mortification, and only with a severe effort of will did she prevent herself from crying.

When she went on deck he was unlashing the mainsail from the boom.

"Can I eat something?"

He nodded. "You know where everything is. Don't go hiding any knives," he added as a sarcastic afterthought.

She took herself and her flushed face below, and had bread and honey and made more coffee. The noise of the sea as it hissed down the hull was ever-changing and yet monotonous. Wishing she had a hairbrush, she went slowly up into the cockpit, taking the towel with her to protect her shoulders from burning. She didn't want to ask Nicholas anything, but her mind seethed with questions.

He was sitting at the stern, one long leg stretched out to the wheel, a foot wedged against a spoke. In his hands was a small complicated-looking piece of equipment which he was either mending or oiling, or both. His knuckles still had plasters on them, and she hoped they hurt. The sea was calm and almost windless and the engine powered the yacht through the water at what seemed to her considerable speed. There were land shapes on almost every horizon.

"Where are you taking me?"

She had to speak quite loudly, to overcome the engine noise and the rushing water. He glanced at her but didn't answer, apparently concentrating on the metal gadget in his hands, and her heart sank.

His glance took in the towel draped over her shoulders. "You were wearing clothes, I assume, before you took to the sea. Where did you leave them?" His foot moved the wheel a fraction.

"On the beach. By the harbour wall."

"What else was there?"

She thought for a moment.

"My phone. My wallet."

"With how much cash?"

"About fifty euros."

"Mr Clive Mann's? This was an all-expenses paid trip I assume?"

"You assume wrong," she said coldly. "The office paid my travel because I was doing business, but I had to cancel my summer holiday in July and take it now, and I'm paying."

He smiled faintly at the last phrase.

"Did you travel alone?" She nodded and he looked sceptical.

"Most people don't holiday abroad alone."

"I was coming with a friend in July, but she couldn't change her plans."

"So Mr Mann wanted you to come now? To buy the book? Why did you agree if it spoilt your holiday plans?"

"He said he was too busy to come and the others in the office needed to take time off in the school holidays, and therefore I had to come now."

She sounded a wimp, but was not going to confess to being flattered by the opportunity Mr Mann had offered. She cursed him for putting her into this impossible and dangerous situation, and cursed herself for agreeing to do it, knowing that she wasn't experienced enough. It had been pride. Coming before the fall.

"Look—I never thought I'd be cheated. I never thought the bible would be stolen." He flicked a glance at her but said nothing, apparently concentrating on his bits of metal. "There is no police station, and the bank was closed, so there was nowhere to leave it safely. The nearest police are in Skiathos—so useful for depositing valuables." He glanced up again at the bitter tone. The dark eyes were bright, but she couldn't tell if it was amusement or malice.

"There's no point in holding me. I've got no money, and I can't prove Rambiris cheated me, or that you did. I only know that one or both of you did. What's the point of bringing the police into it when you have the bible and, you say, a valid receipt? Not that I've seen it, of course."

His hands became still on his gadget.

"The point is that I have made certain charges against you. They still stand." His tone was cold. "They are unlawful entry—coming on board my yacht without authority. Trespass and theft. The fact that I prevented you from getting away with it doesn't alter the fact that you were stealing. And maybe we could add grievous bodily harm, if not intended murder to that little list."

"That's ridiculous! I only wanted to protect myself!"

He ignored her protest. "And oddly enough, I dislike my privacy being invaded. By invitation only, in other words. And finally, you wouldn't even leave when I gave you the opportunity. I would have let you go to avoid the hassle if you hadn't tried to take the book with you. Stealing from an unoccupied boat is dishonest; trying to steal in front of the owner's nose is dishonest, incompetent and a bloody insult. And now you have the nerve to ask what is the point of bringing the police into it. Well, I'll tell you, Miss Scott-Mackenzie. The point is that you'll be charged, arrested and locked up until you either pay a fine which you might just get away with, as a foreign national, or pull some diplomatic strings to get you out of prison. I very much doubt if the people who sent you will lift a finger to help you. That's why they always get someone else to do their dirty work. I hope for your sake that you were paid in advance, because they won't pay you anything now." He bent down to an inset ring in the rubber flooring and pulled up a section of decking.

She stared at him incredulously, her fingers clenching till the knuckles whitened.

"What do you mean? I don't understand."

"Don't you?" he said. "What exactly don't you understand? Perhaps I can clarify for you. Arrest means—"

She interrupted angrily. "I don't mean that! What do you mean by 'getting someone else to do their dirty work'. And 'paying me in advance'? I'm paid a salary, not commission! And Mann's weren't getting me to do their 'dirty work'—this was a perfectly normal business deal; nothing underhand or dirty about it." It sounded as if he knew something about Mann's which she didn't and the possibility made her even more nervous. "You don't have to make those charges. This whole thing could be cleared up by a few telephone calls."

"I've made them," he said, dropping to one knee and inserting the piece into some bit of machinery below. "Yesterday. I see no reason for withdrawing my charges. The police are on their way and they can interview you at my house. They will then remove you and after that I will be left in peace. Hopefully without being knifed or bitten and with my possessions still intact."

She gulped in a ragged breath. "Remove me—where?"

He shrugged. "I don't know or care. Custody anyway."

"But you *can't* do that!"

"Why not?" he said conversationally.

"I didn't—it doesn't! Oh God! Look, I didn't do any harm—I didn't damage anything—I didn't take anything—and the only thing I tried to take was mine, something I thought you'd stolen from me. It's not fair—I've apologised. I'm sorry."

"I'm sure you are. Life is seldom fair according to our own perceptions. Explain your reservations to the police, not to me. In any case, I can't stop them coming now, even if I wanted to."

"Which you don't."

"Which I don't," he agreed calmly.

In the face of his self-assurance she was becoming less confident that he had stolen the book. Perhaps Rambiris was the only criminal involved. Except for the matter of the drugs, he just might be an innocent client. She stared at him wordlessly, all her muscles tensed. There didn't seem anything else to say. There was no point in screaming at him, or cursing him. Abuse was hardly worthy of this catastrophe and would only serve to antagonize him further. She got up and made her way carefully to the prow, as far from him as she could possibly get. There was no shade anywhere, and she felt as if she was burning even under the towel. Time passed in a thoughtless limbo and the sun climbed higher. The yacht was like a knife, slicing the indigo water into bleeding white foam. In the distance, the silver reflection blurred into a darker matt area, and a rippling shiver touched the surface. The engine faded and stopped and she heard him move up behind her and the noise of ropes and the crackling of the sail.

"Wind's coming," he said laconically. "Go aft."

"I'd rather stay here." she said, without turning.

"I dare say you would. But I'd rather you didn't."

There was a small silence. She was unmoving, but he was still preparing the sail. When he spoke again there was only a hint of steel in the casual manner.

"If you'd prefer to be moved forcibly it can, of course, be arranged."

She got up slowly, feeling the stiffness behind her knees where the edge of the deck had caught her, and went aft without looking at him, down into the hot shade of the cabin. The wind came. How did he know? He sailed his yacht without reference to her, as she sat bracing herself

37

uncomfortably on the bunk, first tipped forward and then when he changed tack, tipped backwards, the hard edge of the shelf digging into her back and rubbing the tender sunburnt skin. Her headache had returned with a vengeance. Twice he came down for a tumbler of fruit juice, ignoring her completely. She had the impression he had forgotten her existence.

The movement of the yacht gradually changed. Instead of the steady forward movement there was now the unpleasant sensation of being sucked back and then thrown forwards. She began to feel distinctly queasy and stumbled up the steps to the fresh air.

The yacht was sailing between two islands and the sea had that extraordinary shine on it again, as if the surface was covered with a sheet of satin, binding in the living creature that heaved beneath it. And how it was heaving! A huge swell chased them, rearing high above the stern, then lifting and overtaking the yacht, sucking and hissing as it passed. Behind, a fresh monster mountained up and the yacht seemed to be moving backwards; then it, too, reared, lifted and surged past, the yacht planing with it, yawing in the sea's fingers. She stared, fascinated and nauseous, and he watched her from where he stood behind the wheel. She had been burnt despite her efforts with the towel and perched uncomfortably on the top step, trying to keep out of the sun, but in the wind. She felt extremely sick.

Suddenly he locked the wheel and hauled her unceremoniously to the side, holding her head firmly over the gunwale and pulling her long hair back from her face. After a few minutes he left her there, retching and sweating, and returned to the wheel.

"There's always a big swell here, but it won't last long," he said, not unsympathetically.

It was the only bout of sickness she suffered, although the nausea stayed with her. Much worse was the humiliation and indignity of being manhandled by him. Later the swell lessened and dropped away, the wind came from astern and the two sails were set on opposite sides. In the exhilarating speed she almost forgot him, revelling in the power of the sea and wind. It was he who broke the silence.

"We've got company."

There were four dolphins, sleekly grey with paler underbellies; their curved ephemeral leaps broke the smooth swell only to return in a different pattern. Their beauty and perfection fascinated her; these great smiling creatures seemed to be playing with the yacht, enjoying its speed and shape. They leapt and dived, were lost, and reappeared; they turned away and she saw them leaving to leap and play elsewhere, and knew a sudden loss. And then they were back and vaulting with their great white playmate again. Eventually they were really gone and the sea was empty. She said nothing, because words were superfluous.

The wind strengthened and he broke the silence again.

"Go and drink water. You've lost fluid and I don't want dehydration problems along with everything else."

Coming below himself, he cut off two hunks of bread and made two plates of cold meat and salad. Melissa ate with fierce concentration, not hungry, but grateful that it wasn't just bread. He returned to the cockpit and sailed his yacht as if she didn't exist.

"We'll be there in about ten minutes," she was later informed. "Clean up the galley and pack your suitcases."

Her heart started to thud and she nervously washed and dried the few dirty items, putting them carefully away. Going up the steps she saw land ahead.

"Will they be there?" she asked uncertainly. He raised his eyebrows.

"Will who be where?"

"The police. Wherever we're going."

He smiled his faint mocking smile.

"I doubt it."

She stared at him in frustrated dislike.

In due course the sails were lowered, the yacht's speed dropped, and he moored efficiently, stern on to a little concrete jetty.

"Make yourself useful and pass up the boxes," he said crisply. "Then empty the fridge into that box and pass it up, too."

Melissa complied silently, and the cabin emptied steadily. She saw high above her, on a rocky point at the top of the cliff, a white building with a domed roof. A house, or perhaps a church. At the end of the jetty, there was a little shed, into which he stacked most of the boxes, and a pathway led to steps up the cliff face. Telling her to carry the box containing the food, he picked up the remaining two and started up the steps. He climbed rapidly, fit and undisturbed by the heat and she followed more slowly, the sun beating at her off the reflecting rocks, the rough stone pricking her bare feet.

He was waiting for her at the top and led her across a terrace and large sitting room into a kitchen, the pale granite counters spotlessly clean. A decorated pottery bowl was piled with fruit, and a heavy chopping board lay on the counter. A yellow earthenware bowl stuffed with herbs stood on the window sill.

"Wait here," he said brusquely, and disappeared through another door.

Three vast decorated plates hung on the walls and on the central pine table was a bowl of roses. Fresh, scarlet and yellow, their leaves large and shiny. The house was silent. Where was the hand that had cut and arranged those flowers? Melissa found herself tensing for a slammed door, the clack of heels on tiles. She shuddered and longed for some garment to put on over the bikini which she now loathed for its mortifying brevity. Her thoughts ranged over what sort of explanation she might give an irate and astonished wife. Would she even speak English?

What would he do with her tonight if the police didn't come? Lock her up somewhere? She didn't think he would be very hospitable. If the police came to take her away tomorrow, what would she wear? Would his wife lend her something? Was there a wife here at all?

He appeared at the door. "Follow me please."

He led her through a wide hallway, and opened a door, ushering her inside. "Unfortunately, I have nowhere else to put you. This house isn't designed with inclusive punishment cells, but only with guest bedrooms, so much against my inclination I am having to house you in some degree of undeserved comfort. You can make your own bed up. You will stay in this room until I fetch you."

He closed the door firmly behind him, and after a few moments she went to the windows and opened the shutters on to an astounding view. Far below was a beach and the sea was so bright a turquoise it almost hurt her eyes.

She couldn't see the jetty or the yacht, and realised this room must face a different way. On the wide balcony, suspended over space, was a white cast-iron table, two matching chairs and two sun loungers. On further exploration, she discovered she was sole proprietor of a large bathroom, furnished with expensive toiletries and bottles of water, a double bed and acres of cupboard space with nothing to put in them. Bedlinen and a bath towel and, joy of joys, an enormous grey T-shirt were on a chair. After a shower, which stung both sunburnt skin as well as the cuts and grazes and bruises, she made up the bed and lay down, unable to think clearly about her predicament. Unwanted tears came sliding silently from the outer corners of her eyes and coursed, one by one, down her temples and into her ears. Half waking dreams brought back the old recurrent nightmare of metal screeching on metal; the void, the fall, the screams, the flames. The silence.

CHAPTER FIVE

During that afternoon, after he had made enquiries in London and Athens, his mind drifted back to Melissa. He remembered the narrow wrists which had fitted so easily within his hand, the fine bones, the heavy fall of hair which turned a startling shade of deep red in the sun and the grey-green eyes, wary and angry and afraid. He wondered how she would look when she smiled. He wondered if Marie Claude had sent her or whether she might be telling the truth.

He regretted his decision to bring her here. It would perhaps have been better to have turned her off the yacht, and left her in Perissos. Or even better to have left her, as he had mockingly threatened, with food and water on that uninhabited island for the police to pick her up. With hindsight, he recognised that his decision had been the result of anger and suspicion, not common sense, and now he had started the ball rolling and couldn't stop it.

The internet had produced a website for Clive Mann Antiques and his London office had confirmed that Marie Claude was believed to be in Skiathos. A distinct feeling of unease made him more than usually bad-tempered, reducing Melissa to nervous quivers when summoned from her room. He had asked a good many personal questions and it gave him some satisfaction as she moved from evasion to wary anger.

"I don't believe my private life is any of your business," she said coldly.

"Oh, but I think it is. Everything about you is my business. You intrude on my private life, and I'll intrude on yours."

"I haven't. I didn't," she protested.

"Yes, you did. Only by the grace of God did you not spoil a beautiful relationship. What if my wife had been on board? A lady of jealous inclinations, you might have put me in a very awkward position. Perhaps you still will. I think it was your intention, your instructions, wasn't it?"

"No! It wasn't!" She shook her head, the tumbled hair flicking into her eyes.

"Well, you arrive on a remote Greek island all on your own. You stay two weeks to do one day's business. I call that pretty strange for a start." His eyes probed hers. "You stayed in Skiathos on your way to Perissos, and my guess is you had an appointment there with someone. And maybe someone, perhaps the same person, met you in Perissos. And maybe an appointment in Skiathos was made for your return journey, to hand over the book, no export licence needed?" She denied it vehemently. "Where exactly did you stay in Skiathos?"

"I rented a room near the front, just for one night, and I can't tell you exactly where, though I'd probably be able to find it again, and I didn't have an appointment with anyone until I met Rambiris in Perissos."

"Do you have a receipt for the Skiathos room?"

She looked despairing. "I paid cash. She didn't give me a receipt. I got the first ferry to Perissos in the morning."

"All very convenient." His scepticism was unfair, he knew, because all rental rooms were cash only, and no one gave receipts.

"You know I've checked your flight arrival and when you arrived in Perissos, don't you?" Not that it had helped him.

"Check all you like," she said furiously. "You'll find that I've told you the truth."

"What is truth?" he said. "You have failed to account satisfactorily for the hours between your flight arrival and the ferry departure. You had plenty of time to meet people, to find out about my appointment with Rambiris and to organise, or at the very least, take instructions for stealing the book."

She slumped miserably in her wicker chair.

"But I didn't." Her fingers plucked at the striped fabric of the cushion. "How can I account for that time? I found a room, I went out and walked around the old town, I took photos—Oh!" She sat bolt upright. "I took photos. On my phone. My phone will have the date and times."

"Your phone," he said, with withering derision, "is on a beach in Perissos, you say. It may or may not be retrieved. Did you take photos every few minutes for the entire time you were in Skiathos? Perhaps there are portraits of your dining companions?"

She shook her head, deflated.

"So, you arrive in Perissos. There isn't much to amuse the average pretty girl in Perissos, but getting to know the natives, preferably those with a yacht, is easier without a man in tow, I expect."

He thought her startled amazement and anger were probably genuine.

"How dare you? If you think I was trying to pick you up, let me tell you that my preferences run to men within my own generation, not someone old enough to be my father." The insult was enough to needle him.

"You're quite pretty. I wonder what you look like in clothes. Odd, isn't it? Mostly men wonder what girls look like without their clothes." His enjoyment of her embarrassment was cut short because suddenly the telephone rang.

He leant against the kitchen counter answering the police queries, writing in rapid hieroglyphics, spelling out her name. The call ended and after putting the phone down, he continued to make notes for a moment or two, glancing at her anxious face with a faintly mocking look.

"Tell me, Miss Melissa Scott-Mackenzie, if there's anything you think you can do competently. So far, the record isn't impressive: trespass, burglary, theft, sailing—"

"I'm good at my job," she flared. "Until I come up against thieves and criminals."

He ignored the comment.

"Not very good at the buying bit of it, or is that just lack of experience?"

"I certainly won't make the same mistake again," she snapped.

"I'm relieved to hear it," he said. "And I daresay your employer will be, too, if he ever gives you the chance to try again." He thought for a moment. "Do you, for instance, bid at auctions on your own initiative, or have your own clients?"

"No, neither," she said, obviously puzzled by the question.

"Do you advise other people? Mann's clients for instance?" She frowned. "Well, yes, sometimes, but only very basic advice."

"So not valuations?"

She shook her head.

"Why were you buying the Perissos Bible? For a client, or for stock?"

"I don't know. I assumed for stock."

"Had you identified it was on the market, or had Mann?"

"Mr Mann told me about it. I had no idea."

"He doesn't normally buy stuff like that to have in stock, does he? He deals mainly in furniture and porcelain. I've checked. That is so, isn't it?" She thought about it and didn't deny it. "But he will buy to order, for clients. So, this was to order. I want to know who ordered it. Someone else knew about the sale and wanted Mann's to obtain it for them. Would you have known about something like that?"

She looked at him uneasily. "I—I don't know. If it had come on the market surely lots of people would know? Manuscripts are very desirable, especially to institutions. If it was for a client, he didn't say so. Normally he tells us if a client wants a specific item. I suppose he might not—if the client didn't want it known. I don't know, and I didn't ask."

"I see. And this Byzantine treasure, for which apparently paid a lot of money, you were prepared to immerse in the sea."

"I wasn't," she protested. "It was in a sealed bag."

He gave her a speculative stare.

45

"You didn't know that, or you shouldn't have. Rambiris knew, because he saw me put the whole package in that bag. Which makes me wonder if he told you it was safe to swim in, and swim out again without damaging it." She shook her head despairingly. "I get the impression," he continued, "that somebody told you that you were to prevent me from having it at all costs."

She looked bewildered and he heard desperation in her voice.

"I needed it _back_ at all costs. My job depended on it—it still does. With no proof of purchase, no receipt, and no book, Mr Mann could accuse me of stealing from him. I thought even a damaged manuscript was better than nothing."

"Your trouble was you didn't think at all," he said crushingly, and after a pause, "Do you want to go home?"

She swallowed, her voice a thread. "Yes."

He walked over to the big windows and looked out in silence for some time. Then he turned to face her and said abruptly, "Tell me the name of the client who instructed Mann to buy the manuscript."

"There wasn't one," she said, sounding weary. "Or if there was, he didn't tell me. He heard it was on the market—I assumed Rambiris told him—and he sent me to check it was genuine, and its condition. And he gave me the funds to buy it. I can't tell you a name, because I don't know. I really don't."

He was beginning to think she might be telling the truth.

"Even if I promise to withdraw all my charges and send you home? No police, no arrest, no fine, no prison?"

Her eyes were enormous. "I don't know. I can't remember something I never knew," she said, choking on tears. "Tell me the name of the person you suspect is trying to get the bible, and I'll tell you if I recognise it."

He half laughed. "Good try, Melissa, but not nearly good enough. Go through the names of all the clients you've ever heard of, and hope that one of them rings a bell with me."

"I can't do that!" She looked horrified. "It's confidential information."

"Tough. I'm not going to repeat it. Start."

"No. I've no guarantee that you won't, and in any case, it's unprofessional."

He looked at her for a long, appraising moment. "OK" he said. "The offer stands until they take you away."

"Was it the police you were talking to? When are they coming?"

"Yes, it was the police. They'll come tomorrow or the day after. They've been trying to check your story and get your belongings back. It appears that some of it anyway is true, but I'm afraid it doesn't prove your innocence." He looked at her anxious face. "You see, Melissa, I know I didn't steal the Perissos Bible, and I can prove exactly where I was last weekend, and I also have documentation, receipts and correspondence. I also have you, the evidence of my own eyes and a story which doesn't add up very well at all. I know I'm not the thief, but I'm not convinced that you aren't." He watched her face, disquieted by what would happen to her because of his lack of conviction.

She was silent, her hands balled into fists.

"So, you won't tell me about Mann's clients, because it's 'unprofessional'. How ethical." He mused for a moment. "What does your father do? Does he have any money?"

She got up abruptly, the T-shirt falling loose and shapeless. The thin fabric draped her slight frame so that her breasts and hips were more than hinted at. He had enjoyed seeing her in the bikini from a purely aesthetic point of view; the firm body, slender, well-shaped legs and taut young skin, and now, seeing her in his over-large T-shirt, covered chastely from throat almost to the knee, he was aware of her again. He suppressed the awareness by remembering Marie Claude.

"I don't have to tell you anything." He heard an odd anxiety in her voice. "I don't even know your name or where I am. I'll tell the police what they need to know. If you're going to be responsible for putting me in prison, I don't see why I should give you information about my family."

"Temper, temper!" he said. "How sensitive you are to a not very difficult question. The reason I asked is that life in Greece can be handled reasonably well if you have money. Money is part of a corrupt bureaucracy here. It might give you segregation with other women at the very least. It might give you access to paper and pencil or even to a lawyer."

He didn't really know why he was being so brutal. None of the implications had hit her, and he wasn't sure that she was taking in what he was telling her now. "You will have to make sure that your family know that, and provide for your needs accordingly."

Her face closed on him, but not quickly enough to hide the panic.

"I see." There was a short silence which he did not try to break. "And can you give me some idea of what sort of figures we're talking about?"

"You mean a monthly budget? I'm afraid I have insufficient knowledge of the judicial system to give you a figure. I suggest you ask the police when they arrive."

Nevertheless, he gave her a rough figure which widened her eyes in dismay.

Her presence suddenly aggravated him. He wanted a coffee and a cigarette and peace, not the image of this young woman swamped in one of his old shirts, her fingers clenched into anxious fists. An image distractingly appealing.

"Could I telephone home now? England is two hours behind."

"No," he said. "You've nothing to tell them anyway. Until the police arrive and you know more, there's no point."

He sent her back to her room, and sat on the terrace smoking. He thought again about Marie Claude and what they had both done, and about his unwelcome guest and her misplaced timing. If indeed it was misplaced. He still wasn't quite sure. He wasn't sure whether she was an excellent actress who had misjudged his reactions and found herself in deeper waters than she had bargained for, or whether any of her story was true. He disliked being unsure; he disliked being made a fool of even more.

He knew that he was going to have to explain to his housekeeper Zena what this girl was doing in the house, with just a bikini to her name. Zena, along with all her generation, disapproved of unchaperoned single girls, and especially of exposed flesh. He went back upstairs to his office, making phone calls which got him no further forward in discovering how she had found him or why. Or why, beyond greed, Rambiris would sell that book twice in three days, if he really had. The risks were surely too great. Unless it had been just a case of two buyers being there at the same time and the chance was too good to miss, especially if the book was in her room, and she was out. After all, the likelihood of her finding it again was remote. And that, he reflected, was the problem. It was so remote that she must have been told where to find it. Where to find him.

CHAPTER SIX

He rapped on the door and walked in without waiting. She was on the balcony and he saw her head turn towards him nervously.

"You'd better have some food," he said. "You can get it yourself in the kitchen. There's yoghourt in the fridge and bread in the terracotta jar. Bring it back here to eat it." She nodded.

"And when you've eaten you will stay here. Zena is the maid and she will collect your tray. She doesn't speak English."

"OK," she muttered.

He went back to his office and tried to work until he heard Zena calling out to the cats as she came down from her house. He went downstairs slowly and prepared coffee. Zena eventually came out to him on the terrace, calling her greetings and telling him three days' worth of island news. In return, he gave her the Perissos gossip and the news that they had a temporary and unwelcome house guest. She gave him a sharp look, hearing the resigned irritation in his voice.

"A girl? What sort of girl?"

"English. Young. Too young to be climbing on board other people's yachts uninvited."

Zena was indignant.

"What was she doing?"

"At first, I thought she was Marie Claude's latest effort to discredit me, hiding a camera or recorder, but I couldn't find anything and she seems a most unlikely candidate. She turned out to be stealing, undoubtedly set up by Marie Claude."

Zena looked dumbfounded. "Stealing? What was she stealing?"

"Something valuable that I'd just bought."

"Why did you bring her here then?" asked Zena, now cross and bemused. "You should have left her there for the police. Why bring a thief here? Madame will not be pleased."

He shrugged uncomfortably, thinking that his mother would indeed not be pleased. "It's nothing to do with Madame. I wanted to question her and there was no way I was going to hang about Perissos and let everyone gossip about it. I've told the police and with any luck they'll be here today and take her away and if she is telling the truth, which seems unlikely, they'll send her back to England."

Zena was not convinced. "You were a fool to bring her here. Marie Claude will get to hear of it and then you'll be in trouble. And bringing the police into it! You're crazy!"

He shrugged, knowing she was right. "Maybe. If she's just a thief she deserves to be locked up. If Marie Claude hired her, she ought to be taught a lesson. Either way, the police can deal with it. She'd been prowling all over the boat, but I was going to let her go until I realised what she was stealing, and then I was damned if she was going to get away with it. What else could I have done? She says I stole it from her and she was trying to get it back, which of course is just the sort of accusation I can do without just now."

Zena's mouth had dropped open. "She said you stole something of hers? What is this thing?" He shook his head.

"I'm not telling you. You'd tell Madame and I don't want her to know yet."

She looked hurt. "I wouldn't if you said not to!" He put a hand on her shoulder with an affectionate smile.

"You know perfectly well you would."

"Well, you should have left her in Perissos for the police, not brought her here."

"I couldn't," he said, angry that his reasoning was in fact the same as Melissa's. "There was nowhere to put her. The police would have taken twenty-four hours to get there. I would have had to wait for them, and the whole town would have known by that time. I brought her back because I didn't know what the hell else to do with her. If I'd let her go, think of the news flying round Perissos—and Greece. And I had that delivery for Isabella. Anyway, it's done. She's here. With not a stitch of clothing to her name, until the police bring her luggage. If they do. I've put her in the small guest room."

Zena was a study of disapproval which was still apparent when she collected Melissa's tray. The brown wrinkled face was set in uncompromising hostility, but the black eyes took in the fact that the girl was wearing a familiar T-shirt, which came practically to her knees. She noticed that the bed was neatly made, and that, unlike their normal guests, she had made no impact on the room at all. She might have just gone in to look at the view.

*****

Melissa supposed the police would come to take her away today—to what? No one knew where she was. She had no money, no passport, no clothes, no shoes. She would be accused of offences she could not disprove and locked up or fined, or both. Her stomach cramped with anxiety and she tried to force her brain to think positively. Greece was a member of the European Union; it couldn't possibly be as bad as this man made out; he was only trying to frighten her. Days, possibly weeks, but surely they couldn't imprison her for *months*. She failed to be reassured.

She gazed out at the turquoise and indigo sea, seeing only the barrier of the water, her isolation and helplessness overpowering.

She would be allowed to make her phone calls, she supposed. But what was she going to tell Mr Mann and what would be his reaction? Her grandparents would help with money, with lawyers, getting the British Consul. But even as she thought it, she knew she couldn't tell them, both because of their health and the bankruptcy. Mr Mann was the only hope, but she doubted that he would be supportive after learning how much of his money she had lost. Her fears heightened.

She could remember the telephone numbers of Clive Mann and her grandparents, but all others eluded her muddled brain. If she was ever reunited with her possessions, her phone had all the information. If she was going to be in a Greek prison for weeks, or even months, her grandparents would have to be given some plausible explanation for her absence which would not alarm them. She would have to explain fully to her brother Johnny, even if he was jobless and his marriage was coming apart at the seams.

Should she give notice on her flat? The rent was high and would be a huge drain on her resources, but how would she move out of her flat *in absentia*? And what if she let it go and then found herself back in London after a few days, or perhaps a few weeks? Infinitely worse, the thought of her explanations to Clive Mann loomed over her, like some personal Nuremberg Trial.

What did Nicholas do, that he could live here in near isolation? And what was the rest of his name? It was oddly uncomfortable not knowing. If it hadn't been for the evidence of the drugs, she could have believed that he was a discredited politician or businessman; it could account for his paranoia about cameras and journalists. Where was the wife he had spoken of? A wife who didn't appear to live here with him. Was he divorced? He was rich; the house and yacht and his manner all proclaimed it; she had learnt to recognise the arrogance of money at Clive Mann. Her thoughts returned to the Perissos Bible, and she wondered where it was and why he wanted it. There was no evidence of antiques that she had seen, the furniture was modern, and she'd had an impression of good contemporary pictures. There were sea urchin shells and little bunches of dried grasses—trophies a child might have brought home. She found herself astonished at the thought of a child. Perhaps this house was only a summer home, an escape from the heat of Athens. Was there a house in Athens full of priceless *objets d'art*?

The door opened suddenly and Nicholas stood in the doorway. "The police are here. Come through to the sitting room."

Her heart banged in her chest with shock. She looked at herself briefly in the bathroom mirror. Her hair was tousled and her eyes strained and there was nothing she could do except splash water on her face. She would have to endure this terrifying interview dressed in a bikini and an old shirt. The sudden summons and the future unknowns made her tremble. She went slowly out of her room and towards the voices. There were only two men on the terrace and when they saw her, the conversation stopped. She felt their eyes on her and wanted to sink through the floor. The policeman was older—sixty perhaps—slightly heavy, but hard-muscled as many Greeks were, the short-sleeved grey shirt with its confusing rank epaulettes almost as sinister as the holstered gun on his hip. His eyes were hidden behind dark glasses and the hands, one of which surrounded the ubiquitous Mythos beer, were wide and strong.

"This is Inspector Kiprionidis." The cold voice was crisp. "He has some questions for you and has asked me to translate. We'll go to my office."

But Melissa had seen the most welcome and pleasant surprise and had no intention of going anywhere except to her room.

"Not till I'm dressed," she said firmly. She walked over to her bags and picked them up. "Five minutes. It's not going to make any difference, is it?"

If there was any reply she didn't hear it. She returned almost within the allotted time, wearing slacks, short-sleeved shirt and leather flip-flops. Her hair was brushed, and so were her teeth, and she had on a minimal amount of eye make-up and lipstick. She felt considerably more protected, and if not completely confident, at least able to hold her own.

There was silence for a brief moment as they stared at the transformation and then he said something which made the policeman smile, before leading the way upstairs.

They passed several doors on varying levels as he led the way to the top of the house and ushered them into what he had called his office. It was a big circular, domed room, walled with curved sliding glass doors giving access to a circular balcony. The balcony and balustrade were made entirely of glass and the view was literally panoramic. She gulped and prayed that she would not be required to walk on air.

She had an impression of an array of office machinery and of a big cluttered desk. On a table lay the source of all her problems, the Perissos Bible, together with a batch of assorted papers held together with a big paperclip. He indicated chairs for her and the inspector and went behind his own desk. She saw his hand reach out and press a button on one of the machines as he sat down.

"Inspector Kiprionidis has heard what happened from my point of view, and he has some questions for you. You can speak directly to him, but you must give me time to translate."

"What did you switch on just now?" she asked, suspicious.

"A recorder." His tone was mild. "Have you any objection? It will prevent any misunderstanding in the future about what was or was not said."

She struggled briefly with whether she thought it was a good thing or a bad thing, but doubted that what she thought would make any difference anyway.

"How do I know you'll translate accurately?"

"You don't." His amusement was unsettling.

The policeman wanted the entire story, beginning in London. He let her tell it, waiting patiently through the even-voiced translation, only occasionally asking for expansion or explanation; he took notes of names, details of people involved, the location of Nina's rooms and the taverna she had telephoned from. She described the two men outside her room, the waiter, and which bureau de change she had used. It was the inspector who asked her if she had had a receipt

55

for the money transaction, and she confessed that it, too, had been with the paperwork in the bag. Nicholas rolled his eyes. The policeman's interest in Rambiris was sharp, but if he was disappointed that she could give him no details of the connection with Clive Mann he didn't show it. He produced an envelope from his briefcase in which were her tablet, mobile phone and all her papers: passport, ticket, letters and euros. She signed a receipt for them which was typed in Greek and English and everything was put back into the envelope which went into one of the desk drawers. She found the policeman's dark glasses disconcerting; there was no way of telling what he was thinking.

Zena had brought coffee upstairs and Melissa drank as if it might be her last. The two men had further discussions over her head, the policeman calm, matter-of-fact and firm, but the effect of his words was clearly having an unsettling effect on Nicholas. The policeman obviously wasn't going to change his mind and the younger man stopped speaking with a shrug of acceptance.

"What are you saying?" she asked nervously.

"He is on his way to Skyros in the coastguard boat to pick someone up. You would be in the way—in other words there isn't room on the boat for you—so he's leaving you here for the moment and will pick you up later. I am being made responsible for you until they can collect you. Another two days probably." He looked at her rather grimly. "As you may imagine, I am not at all pleased about that." He poured himself some more coffee. "Secondly, you will have to post bail. If you don't, you'll be taken into custody. You'd have to stay at an agreed address, at your own cost, until your court appearance."

She gripped her shaking hands together. "How long will that take?"

He shrugged. "How long is a piece of string? What you don't want is to be taken into custody."

Panic was overwhelming her ability to think straight. "What am I being charged with?"

"Trespass and theft, and at a guess, conspiracy to steal." He translated for the inspector, who nodded and made further comments. "If you are found guilty of conspiracy as well as the charges I've brought against you, there will likely be a prison sentence, but if the conspiracy charge is not found it could be reduced to a fine. I guess if you don't pay you'll end up in prison."

She said nothing into a silence which stretched until the policeman broke it again and the other man translated.

"We'll ring Clive Mann at 11.30, London being two hours behind. The connection isn't good enough to Skype. After that, you may ring your parents if you wish to."

Last night he had told her what it might take to make life bearable in prison; now she had been told what it would take to keep her out of prison. Both were beyond her reach. She dug her nails into her palms in an effort to control herself, but found, shamingly, that her eyes had blinded with moisture. She wished, at that moment, to stop fighting and let them do what they wanted.

"Would you ask the inspector," she said, so softly that both men had to strain to hear her, "what will happen now, so that I can inform my family. I should like to know where I'll be taken, and when and where I'll be in court. And I don't know your name and I'm going to need it."

"I don't see why." But he had a discussion with the inspector before turning back to her.

"You may call me Nicholas Richardson. You'll be taken to Volos. Contact with your family and lawyers can be made through the police headquarters there. He will provide the relevant details before he leaves. Court appearance will be in Volos. He has no exact idea about the length of time any of that will take. I think you could safely assume some months."

She felt extraordinarily cold, as if someone had put her in a refrigerator, and her vision blurred as the floor rose towards her. The inspector leant forward, flicked her sharply on the cheekbone and pushed her head between her knees. Her vision cleared as he spoke angrily to the man across the desk, who shrugged his shoulders in an anger of his own. Conversation raged past her, meaningless, interspersed with telephone calls, and emails sent and received. She flinched when she was eventually addressed.

"I'm ringing your office now. Let's hope your Mr Mann is sympathetic."

Now that the moment had come to explain to Mr Mann, her nerve utterly failed her, but the policeman was expressionless and the man dialling international enquiries was implacable. He checked the number against the one she had given and then dialled it on the landline, switching the telephone to loudspeaker.

Under the bleak cold eyes of one man and the impassive black gaze of the other, she stumbled her way through the miseries and disasters of the past days, on an open conference line, the cause of all her grief listening in unemotional silence. Mr Mann was not only unsympathetic but extremely angry. He stopped her confused explanations to clarify what she was saying.

"And then you left the receipt with the bible! You must be out of your mind—why the hell did you trust Rambiris—surely you could tell he was a typical bloody Greek dealer, you stupid girl!"

She recoiled from the malignancy.

"I had the bible, Mr Mann." she interrupted desperately. "I didn't think he could possibly not come back with the forms—he needed them, too. It was Friday—he had to wait till Monday, he said. It seemed reasonable."

"You had the bible! But you bloody well didn't hold on to it! Why the hell did you leave it in your room? You thought! Ha, bloody ha! God knows the last time you had a sensible thought! Of course it wasn't reasonable!"

The explosion of fury made the telephone crackle. She was concentrating on her tightly interlaced fingers, the shame and humiliation of this public conversation making her unable to lift her eyes.

"And they haven't caught him? Par for the course! Have you even told the police? Have you made a proper complaint to them?"

"The police are here now, Mr Mann. An Inspector Kiprionidis from Volos."

"Volos? Where the hell's that? Why not Athens? What are they doing about Rambiris?" He was unstoppable. "If they don't find him that bible will be on the international market again and I'll have lost it, and you'll be liable for the money. Are they even looking for it?"

"No—they don't have to," she said unhappily. "The bible is here, but—"

"What?"

"Please let me explain. The bible is here. Rambiris stole it back from me and immediately resold it—to someone else. Legally. The buyer has the papers—"

"Have you seen them?"

"What? No! But he assures me—" She cast a desperate look at the man across the desk. He indicated with his eyes the paper-clipped documents under the policeman's hands. From where she sat she could see the text.

"He tells me he has them. They're in Greek."

"He tells you he has them." He was separating his words with ironic malice. "And of course, you believe him. And of course, he is a perfectly innocent member of Joe Public and doesn't know Rambiris from Adam, and just happened to be passing and bought this nice book on a whim. None of that matters, for God's sake. Who is he? Have you told the police about him?"

She raised her eyes briefly again and saw no change of mind. He was just listening and waiting.

"He's called Nicholas Richardson. He called the police."

"He called the police? Not you? What the hell is going on, and what the hell is wrong with this telephone? You sound as if you're in water or something. Where is this guy, and has he got that damn book?"

59

"Mr Richardson is here, and the book's here, and the police are here." She took a deep breath. "I thought he had stolen the book and hidden it on his yacht. I went on board to get it back, but he—er—found me. He's charging me with theft and trespass. He's doing the translating. I'm in his house."

She had at last succeeded in silencing him, but only briefly.

"You did what?" It was so explosive that all three of them flinched back from the loudspeaker. "Is this a joke, Melissa?" After a brief suspicious silence, he said, "Are you under arrest?"

She glanced sideways at the policeman, who sat with his head against the back of the chair. He might have been asleep. Nicholas was not. His brows went up and he nodded faintly.

"I think so, Mr Mann. And, no, it's not a joke. Mr Richardson says he bought the book from Rambiris and it was arranged in advance. He says he has correspondence to prove it. He doesn't believe that I was only trying to get back your property which was stolen from me. He thinks that either you or I or possibly both of us are in some sort of deal with Rambiris, and he won't believe anything I tell him."

"I'm not bloody surprised!" he shouted. "I can't believe any of this myself. In a deal— You've managed to lose a great deal of my money and to lose the manuscript as well. And to ruin my reputation in the process. I should have known better than to take a stupid girl on. You've cost me a fortune one way and another. You are fired, Melissa. F I R E D." He spelt it out, letter by letter. "Do you understand? FIRED!"

"Mr Mann! I understand, but you can't just leave me here!"

"Why the hell not?"

"You sent me—Rambiris is your connection—"

"I didn't send you to make this sort of balls-up!"

"I know. I'm sorry—I'm really sorry. I know I made mistakes, but I'm not a criminal—they're arresting me on

60

charges of attempted theft and trespass and I've got to put up bail, and at the very least there'll be a fine. I haven't got any money, and I'll get put in prison if I can't pay it, and I don't understand Greek—I don't understand what's going on, but I need help—now. Please."

The humiliation of having to plead with him in front of the two men was so great that she had gone white under the tan, her fingers bloodless as they gripped together.

"You have to be joking!" He sounded genuinely amazed. "On top of a plane ticket, the loss of the book and the price I've paid for it, you then expect me to hand over more money to you and pay bail and fines? Apply to your family, my dear. It really is not my responsibility. I believe I have carried sufficient of your folly to last me a lifetime. I'm giving you your contractual month's notice with effect from today, and your last pay check will go towards some of the debt. A drop in the ocean, alas. On your return, you can apply to me for your P45 and we'll make the arrangements for repayment at that time."

He broke the connection abruptly, and she found she was aching from tension, her muscles taut, her mind a swirling confusion in the ensuing silence. It was broken by the man across the desk.

"Well, well! What a cross boss! Not at all sympathetic."

She looked at him sightlessly. The conversation had been worse than she had ever imagined, but now that she knew there was no possibility of help from that quarter, she felt a certain recklessness. It didn't really matter now. She didn't have to beg or plead any more to anyone. The policeman spoke suddenly and a lengthy conversation ensued. She supposed some form of translation was going on, and it allowed her time to regain some equilibrium.

She thought of all the things that now needed organising: her flat, her non-existent job, her savings, her friends. Things she required: a good bilingual lawyer, a lot of money, power and influence. If only the policeman spoke English, she could ask him how to contact the British Consulate, but they would only ask the questions that she had no answers for. Where was she? Who was he?

A silence fell and she looked up nervously. The policeman spoke, a short abrupt sentence. The other man glanced at him thoughtfully and dialled another number.

"This is the number you gave for your home. You can speak to your parents now."

"It's my grandparents' home."

Her grandmother answered. Rushing in breathless from the garden, full of English rain, and the washing getting wet, and how she must walk the dog, Brig never seems to bother these days even though the doctor had told him the exercise was good for him. And dogs did need their routine, even when the world fell in, life must go on. Melissa waited patiently for her to remember that her granddaughter was on holiday in Greece, that there was life beyond their little circle of sadness. Again, the telephone was set to conference monitor but she knew that this revealing of her family's privacy was part of her protection; she hoped it could only show innocence, much as she disliked it. Eventually Mops ran out of home news and asked whether it was raining in London.

"I don't know about London, but it's not raining in Greece," she said.

"Greece? Oh! Yes, of course. How silly of me! You're on holiday, aren't you? I remember we went to Corfu years ago, when Brig could be persuaded to take time off. Are you in Corfu? I expect it's changed in sixty years. Can't remember where we stayed, but it was rather nice. Are you having a lovely time—with your teacher friend, aren't you?"

"No. I did tell you, she could only come during the holidays and I had to come now—on a business trip."

"Darling, it sounds so grand! A business trip! How did it go?"

Melissa winced and avoided Nicholas's eyes. "Not very well, I'm afraid. I'm calling to say it's been extended— possibly for quite a long time. I'll be somewhere very remote—no telephones—so you won't be able to ring me. I'll ring you whenever I get access to a phone, or send a message. It might be through the British Consulate or whatever they are, so don't be surprised."

Her grandmother was understandably dismayed.

"Extended? British Consulate? Good gracious—what is Mr Mann thinking of? Where are you staying? Surely hotels have telephones?"

"I won't be in a hotel." Nicholas was laughing silently. "I'm sorry, Mops, it can't be helped. It may be several weeks."

"Weeks? Darling, you can't, you really can't. Mr Mann must be mad, sending you off alone for weeks. Are you alone, or is there someone from the office with you?"

She sighed, knowing what was coming. "No, there's no one from the office. And you won't be able to contact me through the office, so please don't ring them. I want you to promise me that you won't ring the office."

"Why not?" She immediately sounded suspicious.

"Mops, I'm on someone else's phone and I haven't got time to explain. Just promise me, because I've got to go now."

"I don't understand, but I must have some contact number. Brig might—either of us might—get ill, or fall. Brig is so clumsy these days."

"Johnny must cope." She sounded hard. Brutal.

"He can't—you know how hopeless he is. It's not like you to leave us in the lurch like this. You're too young, and a girl alone in Greece! It's dangerous and—and—" Melissa knew that the word 'immoral' was hovering on her lips, "something could happen. They're not civilised, those people. A lone girl is asking for trouble." Another thought seized her. "Melissa, you're not going off with some man, are you?"

Melissa shrank. At least she was enlivening the morning for her host. "No, I am not going off with some man, and I will be perfectly safe. I will be escorted throughout, I promise. Please tell Johnny and Sarah I won't be back for some time, but I will write. The post is terrible from Greece, so don't expect anything soon."

Her grandmother sounded as if she was crying, and Melissa's nails dug into her palms again. "Is Brig all right?"

"No. No, he's not. You know he isn't. Melissa, please don't do this. It's really very selfish. We need you here. It really isn't fair of Manns to send you, or of you to accept. It's not like you. How can you do this to us?"

"I've got to go. I'm on someone's private phone. I'm sorry, but there's nothing I can do. I'll get back as soon as I possibly can."

She couldn't trust her voice any further and reached out, cutting the call on a further protestation. Her hands were shaking violently and her face running with moisture. Tears or sweat, she couldn't tell.

Neither of the other two said anything either; the policeman was perfectly still, and Nicholas tapped the tips of his fingers together, his eyes surveying her thoughtfully. His amusement had passed.

"You didn't tell them the truth. Why not?"

"That's my business."

"You didn't mention your need of funds."

"Also my business."

A flash of anger showed in his face. "Melissa, you obviously don't quite realise the trouble you're in. You need to make some effort to raise bail. Your grandmother is right. You're too young, and Greece is a dangerous place for lone young females. You absolutely do not want to be in custody."

"I don't have the money," she said bluntly. "And you've put me in this position. Don't tell me you're suddenly acquiring a conscience."

"I'm certainly not acquiring a conscience, especially as you've got yourself into this mess, not me." He opened a drawer and took out a wad of euros. "I'm not overflowing with the milk of human kindness towards you just now and the inspector is insisting on an insurance policy. He doesn't want me drowning you, or dropping you over the cliff.

Equally, even though I am the aggrieved party, he doesn't want me having a sudden change of heart and letting you go before he gets back. I'm not paying your bail, but I'm having to pay to make sure you don't sprout wings and fly. When he returns, and finds you in one piece, I'll get my money back." He smiled, a charming, delightful smile that did not reach his eyes. "What he doesn't know is that sometimes I don't mind losing money."

She had no idea whether he was extremely angry, making a joke, or trying to frighten her. Or all three. She swallowed nervously. He turned to the inspector and there was another long incomprehensible conversation before he spoke to her again.

"He'll take you in to local custody in Volos, and if they're satisfied with your story, and if they can get anything out of Rambiris if or when they find him, he doubts if a custodial sentence will be the only option. A fine, probably reduced if you pay it in cash, probably larger if you don't. Wiser to pay it. He thinks about five thousand pounds."

"I can't raise that sort of money," she said slowly.

He sighed with weary patience. "You must. Sell something. Borrow. Ask the bank. Beg from friends."

She looked at him with loathing. His dismissive arrogance filled her with rage.

"I can't ask my friends for money."

"You'll dislike the consequences of not asking them," he said, leafing through the papers on the desk. "Go downstairs and get us some more coffee. I want to talk to the inspector."

"As it's about me, I want to be here."

"And when," he said, "did your Greek improve so dramatically?"

Smarting from the sarcasm she took the tray downstairs and Zena made another jug of coffee, emanating silent disapproval. She had no idea how she could raise five thousand pounds.

When she took the coffee upstairs there was obviously some deal going on—a lot of heated discussion, a lot of paper, together with the bible and a large wad of notes.

He looked across at her, standing nervously by the door, with that assessing black stare. "Put it there and go to your room. And stay there."

She didn't understand how he could be so unreasonably rude. Never in all her life had anyone been so ill-mannered for so little reason as this man. Fury washed into the humiliation and she carried the tray over to the table and dropped it from about two inches.

"'Please'," she said with deceptive mildness into the silence after the crash. "And even 'thank you' wouldn't go amiss."

As she went down the circular marble stairs, holding on tightly to the polished rail, she could have sworn she heard a crack of laughter. If so, the policeman must have had a sense of humour.

She unpacked her belongings, putting them carefully into spaces previously unoccupied, clothing a few hangers with her existence, making this alien space hers in a defiant gesture of residency. Surprisingly, the clothes which she had left on the beach were also in the bag.

She sat down on the edge of the bed and tried to clarify the whole extraordinary situation in her mind. Nicholas could have drowned her, or left her to die on that island, but instead he had involved the police. His comments about the media, and spying and entrapment had appeared to be an admission of guilt of some sort, but he did not, on the face of it, seem to be a likely drug smuggler, although she was hardly an expert. There were other areas of criminal activity, but his involvement of the police would seem to indicate either total innocence or at any rate no worries about possible investigations. She was no longer at all certain about his guilt.

She heard the two men come downstairs and tensed, expecting some retribution for her earlier defiance, but there was no contact, not even for food. She was not hungry, but had a hunger headache. Later she heard Zena leave, the back door clacking on the latch. Melissa sat down at the balcony table with a pad and began to sort out her life in lists of things to do, people to contact, by telephone and by letter.

She wrote down 'Jeremy' on her pad for the second time, staring at the word, drawing a box round it. As her boyfriend, surely he would help. Concentrating fiercely, she managed to retrieve his office number from her scrambled brain. Her mobile was locked in a desk drawer upstairs, but if she could telephone him without Nicholas listening, perhaps he could do something. As a stockbroker, he knew about money and always seemed to have plenty. She opened her door a crack and strained her ears to hear their voices. She realised that the policeman was leaving; they were on the rock stairway, their voices blurring on the wind. In a panic, she wanted to rush out and beg the policeman not to leave, not to leave her here with this unspeakable man who enjoyed frightening her out of her wits and might possibly do worse than that. She left her room and crept through to the main terrace. They were descending towards a black powerboat, its inflated sides festooned with silvery equipment and double consoles in front of vast twin outboards. The coastguard could move fast, she thought.

Going quickly back to the kitchen, she picked up the telephone and dialled Jeremy's office, impatient at the time it took for the national codes to click through. Frustratingly, she discovered that he was due back from a meeting but hadn't arrived. She couldn't leave a number because she had no idea where she was or what the codes were. In any case, the thought of Jeremy's return call being answered by her host made her shiver. She went out to the terrace again, but was unable to see where they were. When she redialled, she must have made a mistake, for the unobtainable tone bleeped. Her hand shook as she tried again, visualising the inspector back on board and Nicholas coming up the steps two at a time and catching her red-handed. But with strange, hollow clicks the call connected and in huge relief she heard Jeremy's voice.

"Hello, darling—how's tricks? Is gorgeous Greece hot and sunny? It's belting with rain here and perishing."

She interrupted. "Jeremy, listen. I've got to be quick. I'm in trouble and I need help."

There was a strangled noise from London.

"In trouble? Darling, what's happened? Have you had your passport nicked? I'm not exactly convenient!"

"Listen! *Please.*" She managed to silence him sufficiently to give a shortened version of what had happened.

"Mel, for God's sake don't pay anything, you'll never get it back! Tell the consul and let them sort it all out. They're only trying it on, trust not the Greek and all that. Call their bluff and they'll back off, honestly."

"It's not bluff. The police are involved." How could she make him understand?

"It all sounds quite extraordinary and my guess is that they're all greasing somebody's palm, and threatening you to try to make you cough up backhanders. I don't think you should pay a thing—they'll all probably go away if you just shrug and say you've got no money."

"I haven't got any money, and this thing won't go away. He's furiously angry about the whole thing and absolutely terrifying. He won't tell me where we are, or anything and I think he's a sort of high-class criminal, maybe dealing in antiques or drugs or—"

"Mel, I'd help you if I could, but honestly, it's madness. And it's really complicated and the market is right down. I'd lose a lot if I sold shares now. Couldn't your wretched brother help? What about Clive Mann? They sent you out there—it's their problem. They're used to sending money abroad. I haven't a clue about that sort of thing." He sounded relieved and pleased with his solution. "Get onto them and tell—"

"I already have. They won't." She was cold with the hopelessness of this conversation. "I had no proof of purchase and the book I bought was stolen from me."

"Mel, look, I'm sorry, but I really can't. It's too risky and selling shares just now is not on—very tricky. I just can't afford to risk losing it. You do understand, don't you?" His voice trailed off a little, embarrassed for them both.

She sounded brittle bright. "Of course. I shouldn't have asked you. I must go. Don't know when I'll see you. Don't worry about it—I'll sort it out somehow."

She put the receiver down numbly and went quickly back to her room, shutting her door quietly. So much for friends. Well, one of them. There was a list of much better and more faithful ones, but they were mostly impecunious university friends.

*****

He had shaken hands with Kiprionidis, who had made some unwelcome observations about his assumptions and attitude, and had walked along the beach. Stripping off, he went swimming for half an hour, shedding his anger through physical exercise. He had no certainty that the policeman's undertaking of discretion would protect him from the story leaking out. He saw Melissa doing him a good deal of damage in the long term. The fact that he had probably made another severe error of judgement only made him angrier. He could probably have dumped her in Perissos quite safely. He could probably have left her anywhere and she wouldn't have damaged him. Probably. But he still wasn't quite certain. And Marie Claude was probably in Skiathos, and that probability was much too close for comfort.

He thought back to those two telephone calls which had been so appalling in their different ways. His certainty about her guilt was fading rapidly and he knew he was behaving extremely badly. His temper fired again.

He looked at the yacht's moorings and checked that all was secure before returning to the house. After he'd showered and changed into clean shorts and T-shirt he took a beer back to his office. The tray was still on the table where she had dropped it, a puddle of spilt coffee drying on the glass. He gave a half grin of remembrance and then frowned as his eye caught the little red light blinking on the recorder. He had forgotten to turn it off after the interview had finished, but it shouldn't be blinking unless a call had been made or received. Going slowly to his desk, he lit a cigarette and jabbed the playback button.

He found her sitting on the balcony, paper and pencil on the table, looking out over the sea. She turned her head and met his eyes apprehensively, the now brushed coppery hair framing her faintly uneven features in a straight silky waterfall. A more than acceptable face, but a long way from Marie Claude's beautiful sculpted bones and expensive haircut.

"You need to make some more phone calls. Come up to the office."

It wasn't an apology, but he managed to be slightly kinder as she went through her mobile contacts for the painfully humiliating process of asking her more prosperous friends to lend her money. As she again struggled through her explanations and requests during the afternoon, he found her efforts to raise the finance scratching at his conscience like some particularly virulent insect bite.

Restlessly he went out on to the glass balcony. Gazing down at the empty beach and the empty sea, he remembered Marie Claude's negative reactions the one time he had ever brought her here. A wave of grief and regret for the irreversible thing he had done washed over him. Now this young woman had brought with her the unforeseen complications of bureaucracy, as well as being the source of yesterday's row with Zena, which clearly still rankled with the old woman, and had had her muttering about Madame's reaction to all these 'goings on'. He didn't wish to tell Madame, but he knew perfectly well that Madame would hear about it. It would be better if he told her before Zena did.

The yacht jibbed at her moorings, and he saw a grey haze on the horizon. A wind was coming, if not a storm.

Melissa had managed to increase her pledged money to nearly two thousand pounds, promised in varying degrees of generosity, suspicion or grudging agreement. Her last call, to the bank, was a foregone conclusion, because they asked if her employer would guarantee an overdraft. By the time he brought the phone session to a halt she was stiff with tattered pride, her hands trembling from tension. He sent her back to her room and went to check the windows and shutters, bringing in the chair cushions from the terrace as the day darkened and the wind came. With the wind came lashing rain which poured off the terracotta tiles and into the downpipes feeding the water butts and underground water cisterns. The ill temper of the day cooled with the air temperature and in a more pleasant frame of mind he went to the kitchen to inspect Zena's provisions for supper.

He called Melissa out to the kitchen while he cooked. She looked neat and tailored and came up to his chest. Marie Claude was as tall as he was, wore her loose, casual clothes with flair and elegance and stiletto heels with everything.

Taking a bottle from the fridge, he poured her a tumbler of wine and touched his glass to hers.

"*Yammas.*" He took a slow swallow, regarding her speculatively, aware of her uneasiness. He continued to prepare the meal, then asked abruptly, "Why did you telephone your grandparents and not parents? Are they divorced?"

"No."

"So why didn't you ring them?"

The look she gave him said mind your own business. The question was quite mild, yet he could see apprehension, almost panic, in the grey-green eyes. It was making him very curious.

"Has there been a major family row? Are Mum and Dad missionaries in Kazakhstan? Or in prison? Or on the dole?"

Or possibly, for some reason, not alive.

"No." He heard the cold affront at his impertinence. "They're dead."

So, the unlikely possibility was a fact.

"How?"

After a moment she said, "An accident." It was quite casual, but he saw her fists were clenched.

"You may be relieved to hear," he said, "that pity is not in my repertoire of emotions at the moment. Brothers or sisters?"

"A brother."

"Younger or older?"

"Older." It was like extracting teeth, he thought.

"So, why can't you tell your grandparents that you're in trouble?"

"He has a heart problem."

"You were speaking to her, not him," he said, more gently.

"She'd tell him, and he's in no fit state to take another shock."

"The first being the accident?"

She looked evasive and this time he didn't insist, but changed tack slightly.

"Who are Johnny and Sarah?"

"My brother and sister-in-law."

He was silent for a while, considering all this rather imperfect information.

"You are twenty-three, according to your passport, and you didn't ask your grandparents for help you badly need. You have an older married brother. Brothers might normally be expected to help out a younger sister."

"Johnny hasn't got a job. So, no money."

The wretched brother had been accounted for. She wasn't going to get any family assistance by the sound of it, he thought wearily.

"Well, we don't seem to be making huge progress towards getting you the money you need." He made an effort to sound less unkind. "What's the boyfriend going to say? Mightn't he help you out?"

She shook her head, negating the suggestion of a boyfriend.

He raised his eyebrows. "No boyfriend? I'm surprised. I was thinking that a stockbroker would be useful—at least there might be a whiff of filthy lucre. They usually have a fat bank account."

Her eyes dropped. "No."

She looked very vulnerable and he felt a distinct twinge of conscience.

"OK. No boyfriend. You're left with other friends, if you have any, your savings if you have any, rich godparents, a kindly uncle. Or a combination of the lot. Three people at £1,000, six people at five hundred pounds, twelve people—"

"OK! I'll think," she snapped. "It'll mean a lot of telephoning."

"The telephone bill may be the least of your worries. It will certainly be the least of mine."

"Can I use the telephone in the kitchen?"

"No, you may not. I gave an undertaking to Kiprionidis that any calls you made would be in my presence and recorded. You'll have to make them upstairs. If he hadn't had to go to Skyros first, you'd be in police custody, but as it is, I'm unwillingly responsible for you. I deposited a large amount of money to that effect and, despite what I said this morning, I don't intend losing it. You need to concentrate on raising the remainder of these funds before Kiprionidis comes back. So, after you've eaten you can do some more phoning."

She looked appalled at the thought.

"Is Nicholas Richardson your real name?"

He smiled, but not unpleasantly. "No."

Again, she went through the painful experience of begging, of trying to explain the unexplainable, of being truthful and insane instead of making up a more believable untruth and obtaining the necessary funds. Eventually he couldn't stand the lack of progress and stopped the proceedings.

He had, he thought, extracted quite a lot of information from this bloodless stone.

CHAPTER SEVEN

"Have you got deck shoes? You've got to negotiate the steps."

She looked miserable. "No. I really don't want to come. I promise to stay in my room."

He looked at her with deceptive mildness. "If you stay, you'll stay in the only place I've got with a lock on the outside. It's full of logs, mosquitoes and possibly snakes and it has no electricity and not much ventilation. Your choice."

She obviously wished that she hadn't embarked on that small rebellion. Her eyes dropped and he saw the shoulders droop, too.

"And you might be dead when I got back, and then I'd lose my deposit." She didn't hear the amusement in his voice.

It was a threat he had no intention of carrying out, for the good reason that Zena would release her the moment she yelled, but his unease about Marie Claude was increasing. He wanted no uninvited visitors from Skiathos meeting his unwelcome guest and the best way to avoid that danger was to remove Melissa from the premises.

"Go get your things—don't forget a hat—and don't be too depressed: you might possibly enjoy it."

He carried Zena's basket of provisions down to the jetty and saw that Melissa eyed the choppy sea and cracking canvas rather nervously.

As usual, when he was sailing, his mood changed for the better and his questions were conversational rather than interrogatory. He could see she enjoyed the sailing, watching how he handled the yacht, how the sails snapped and filled as he changed tack, enjoying the tilted hull and hissing speed. He thought it was rather like having a cat on board, initially wary, but gradually beginning to believe that a shoe would not be thrown at it.

"Might the dolphins come again?" she asked, searching the wind-driven expanses.

He smiled. "They might. It depends whether they find a nice source of fish, or just feel like playing."

She hooked back the chestnut hair behind her ears. She had none of Marie Claude's elegant sophistication, nor Marie Claude's awareness of the effect that her body had on others: jealousy and envy in women and desire in men. He smiled a little bleakly at the thought of Marie Claude sailing with him, and again uneasily wondered where she was.

"Tell me about Clive Mann. What's he like? Was he a nice boss until he fired you?"

She thought for a moment.

"I thought he was really nice when he interviewed me. It was only later I realised he wasn't quite what I'd thought."

"In what way?"

"Well, he'd given me the impression that they would train me—teach me about antiques, and the antique trade. But I was mainly used as the office dogsbody and coffee-maker. I even had to collect his shirts from the laundry. I didn't mind doing office work and typing—I could learn quite a bit from that—but some of it seemed—" She broke off, frowning.

He probed. "Seemed what?"

"—a bit, I don't know. Sharp. Not dishonest or anything. He's a good businessman, I suppose."

He looked at her thoughtfully and when she glanced up she flushed and turned her head away.

Changing tack as a sharp gust of wind hit them, Melissa lost her balance moving from one side to the other. He caught her against his chest as she stumbled, holding her trapped between his body and the wheel, and looked down at her surprised and embarrassed face.

"Girls who throw themselves at men," he said teasingly, "are just asking to be kissed." His head bent until his mouth was just touching hers and she jerked away from him.

"I'm not! I didn't!" she gasped. "Let me go!"

76

He felt unfamiliar laughter bubbling in his throat and moved his hand lightly on the bare skin of her collarbone above her thin top. Her muscles tightened in a strenuous effort to evade his touch. He was amused by her indignation and tightened his grip, but her hand came up like a snake and slapped him sharply across the face. He released her and rubbed his cheek ruefully.

"I get no thanks for having saved you from a bruised bottom. A kiss ought to be preferable to concussion, but I have a feeling you don't agree. Hold on next time, if you don't want me to catch you." There were tears of anger sparkling on her lower lashes and his amusement was faintly apologetic. "I was only going to kiss you. There was this nice mouth, under my nose as it were, and it just seemed the obvious thing to do."

He had, he realised, just thrown a shoe at the cat, and the cat had used her claws.

The wind dropped early in the afternoon and the combination of Melissa's silent discomfort and his dislike of motoring meant that he brought the yacht back to the island early. There was no sign of any visitors.

At the house, he deposited the basket in the kitchen, and went upstairs to shower and change, pondering on how Marie Claude would use the fact of Melissa's presence here, if or when, she discovered it. If she didn't know already. If she hadn't orchestrated it. He was now virtually certain that Melissa herself was ignorant of any plan of Marie Claude's, but that was not to say she wasn't being used by her. His wife might not be an academic, but she had an innate shrewdness which had ignited into fury by what he had done. He had learnt the hard way that Marie Claude's fury could take a very dangerous form.

His sympathy for Melissa dwindled as he visualized the damage she might do him, unwittingly or not, and the idle thought occurred that he might just as well be hung for a sheep and seduce her. No one, least of all Marie Claude, was going to believe that he was an innocent lamb. She was attractive to look at and, despite the accusations of stupidity, obviously intelligent, and he was surprised by the spark of desire he felt for her. He discarded the idea. Seduction might not be that easy to accomplish, he conceded, and in any case, would be a dangerous game for him just at this point.

He was unaccustomed to natural innocents; a girl who used clothes to protect herself rather than one who took them off to indulge, seduce and manipulate. A girl for whom money was a private problem rather than public greed, and a girl who very much disliked being under any obligation to anyone. He had felt a genuine sympathy for her as her efforts to raise the money came to virtually nothing. As a rich man, the amounts had seemed trifling, and it had been a faint shock to discover with what difficulty trifling amounts were raised. He wondered what she would do now, and whether that pride would crumble in the face of having to raise a great deal more.

*****

He had told her to come up to his office after showering to continue her fund-raising calls, but as she stood at her window towelling her hair dry, her eyes were drawn to the horizon by a tiny movement. A black speck that moved imperceptibly nowhere and yet enlarged and came nearer. The police launch. Her heart lurched. He had said they would not come today and she was mentally quite unprepared, rooted horrified to the spot.

The inspector must have tried to telephone again while they were out sailing. The nightmare moment had arrived much sooner than anticipated, and her stomach cramped in shock.

To calm herself she changed into slacks and trainers, and methodically put her possessions into her bags, placing them beside the door. She would be ready and calm.

The boat had disappeared from her sightline and she went through to the main terrace. The speck was now a boat close inshore, and anything less like a police launch was hard to imagine. It was in fact a large luxury motor cruiser—one of the 'gin palaces' that island-hopped with jet-set passengers. Melissa's stomach lurched for a different reason as she realised her mistake. These were visitors, friends 'dropping in'. He wasn't expecting them, she was almost certain, and now a little demon nibbled at her mind. He was upstairs and was possibly unaware of their arrival. They might blow a whistle or whatever boats did to attract attention, but she wasn't going to warn him. She could possibly get her bags down to the jetty and explain her situation, ask to come aboard, to be taken to safety. In the same instant, she knew it wouldn't work; whoever this turned out to be, it was unlikely they'd take her on board and sail away without first asking a great many questions of her host, and her host wasn't going to be pleased about that. Could she get her passport and money out of his desk, and then stow away on this boat? But if they stayed overnight she would be caught and the thought of it made her shiver. She stood, uncertain and undecided as the huge boat turned in a welter of white foam and reversed on to the jetty, neatly avoiding *Ioanna*, which bobbed up and down in the disturbed water. Various figures in white uniforms moved about efficiently and tied her up to the rings set in the concrete. A railed gangplank was lowered from the stern and a graceful figure in red stepped ashore.

Melissa picked up the binoculars that hung on a hook just inside the terrace doors. The glasses focused in alarming and intimate close-up first on the jetty and then on an extremely beautiful woman walking with rapid grace towards the rock steps. Her face was disturbingly familiar, classical in its golden, oval perfection, framed with a shimmering hood of dark hair in a sharp, shaped cut which would need restyling every second day. Great hoops of gold swung from her ears, and her wrists and fingers gleamed with gold. All of her was mesmerising grace, and she was dressed straight from some designer in a thin floating trouser suit of scarlet chiffon. The beautiful face was unsmiling, almost flinty, and though Melissa was seeing her foreshortened from above, and her eyes were hidden, there was an aura of angry determination. She turned to call back to someone on the boat and the impression was of a powerful, dominant woman. The wife, Melissa guessed. And with the guess came the immediate instinct that this was no lady to beg any favours from. The woman turned to look with frustrated irritation at the cliff path, and with infinite grace, despite her scarlet high-heeled sandals, started to climb it.

Melissa went back to her room, taking the binoculars with her and contemplated her two bags before putting them out of sight beside the armchair on the far side of the bed. Leaving the room as devoid of her presence as it had been on her arrival, she stood uncertainly at the foot of the stairs looking up towards his office before turning and leaving the house. She climbed the slope up past the garden towards Zena's house and on into the shade and shelter of the pines beyond. The jetty was hidden from view by the bulk of the house and the angle of the cliff, and there was no sign of anything unusual from the house itself. She sat for a few minutes on a huge boulder, and then she saw Zena apparently chatting peacefully with her husband in their little garden where the pair of them inspected the vegetables and fruit. Zena's voice came clearly up to Melissa, with her husband's deeper tones interjecting and Melissa was unsure if they could see the jetty and the boats from their house. Her uncertainty rendered her indecisive. Was this visitor really his wife? If so, would he be pleased and was this visit as unexpected as she thought? Had she come to stay—it seemed to Melissa highly likely. A divorced wife wouldn't come at all, and at no time had he given her to understand that he was divorced. He had spoken about his wife being jealous, and how angry she would have been to have found Melissa on the yacht. How much angrier would she be to find her in residence in her house. Melissa shivered in the heat. If this woman had just come home after a shopping spree, or a visit to some other house, or whatever ploys the rich and beautiful got up to, she would undoubtedly be staying home for a while. That meant that Melissa would have to face them both at some stage. She couldn't sleep out in the open, and she would need food and water. And the problem of her passport remained.

Various scenarios passed across her brain. 'Mr Richardson' having to explain to a jealous wife why he had a lone female staying in the house. Though it was ridiculous to suppose that anyone so beautiful and sophisticated could possibly be jealous of someone as young and gauche as Melissa.

A furious husband—or ex-husband—accusing his wife of trying to entrap him with a young girl, and a furious wife—or ex-wife—denying it. Or not denying it. Despite the heat, she felt cold inside. Perhaps this was not his wife at all. Perhaps she was his mistress. Perhaps his obsession with keeping his identity secret was because he had this beautiful mistress and thought Melissa would tell his wife. That seemed a far more likely situation, and fitted much of the questioning she had endured. No wonder he had wanted her off the premises and safely locked away, and no wonder that he was so angry at the police's delay. It would explain why he had suspected her of carrying a camera, or a tape recorder—the jealous wife must have her suspicions and be trying to prove it.

Melissa lifted the binoculars and studied the house. It remained blank and apparently empty, sleeping in the sun. She got up and slowly made her way through the trees parallel with the shore until she could see the length of the beach and the two boats at the jetty. One white and graceful, the other dark blue and somehow shocking in its huge luxuriousness. Was she just going to walk back in and let him do the explanations? His mistress might be the jealous one and depart in a passion. Melissa thought uneasily of being left to the tender mercies of Mr Richardson.

The solution suddenly hit her. She would go back to Zena's house and firmly stay there, language problems notwithstanding. Zena would have to inform him she was there, and he would have to decide what to do. She felt a huge relief, and finding a more comfortable boulder, turned the glasses back to the blue motor yacht. After a time, her perch in the shade became uncomfortable and she was thirsty. The yacht looked cool and air-conditioned. Full of cold drinks and attentive stewards. A modern heroine would have swarmed up the anchor chain with a spare passport tucked into a waterproof pocket in her bikini. She sighed, recognising her cowardice, and set her mental sights on Zena's house. He would have to be faced, and probably this beautiful, contemptuous woman would have to be faced too. She got up, but as she did so, she saw a gleam of scarlet on the cliff path. Pulse racing, she lifted the binoculars again. The woman was alone, descending carefully, but rapidly. There was an impression of clipped anger in the way she moved, but her face was hidden. Then the path turned and she was facing Melissa. Her beauty almost made Melissa gasp, it was so perfect, and again the face seemed familiar, although anyone that beautiful could never be forgotten once met. The mouth was generous, even if anger had tightened it, and the eyes were enormous under perfect dark arched brows. The binoculars brought her within touching distance and Melissa recognised extremely expertly applied cosmetics, although the face and body would have been perfection without either designer clothes or the artistry of make-up. She was leaving, and Melissa would have given a good deal to know whether it was because of her. Had she discovered her bags? Had he confessed to having some strange girl in the house, with the result that she had walked out on him in a fury? She couldn't be going to get her luggage, as either the men on board would have carried it up, or Nicholas himself would have gone to fetch it. Without the binoculars, it looked like a drop of blood oozing down the cliff face. Then the woman was on the jetty and moving rapidly to where the men in white had leapt ashore and were waiting for her. Using the glasses again, Melissa saw that she went on board without hesitation and without looking back. The gangplank was brought inboard and the boat almost immediately drew away. She watched it until the vessel was only a dark speck on the water, the wide V of her wake lost in the desert of the sea, and then she walked slowly back to the house.

She was reluctant to face him so she sat on a stone bench in the garden. She did not see Zena come out on the terrace, stand for a moment staring at her, and go back in again before finally stumping back up the hill. She heard his voice, above her on the terrace, clipped and cold.

"Come up here."

Apprehensively, she went up the steps. He was standing in the middle of the sitting room, a tumbler of whisky in his hand, and he watched her place the binoculars back on their hook.

"Where the hell have you been?" he demanded.

"Not far. I didn't go out of sight of the house." She paused. "I saw you had a visitor and I thought you might not want me around."

"Did anyone see you?"

"No." He was obviously concerned about this and she had a desire to unsettle him. "I don't think so."

"You don't think so." His black eyes bored into her. "So, you didn't go down to the jetty? I assume you intended to thumb a lift. What happened?"

She said coldly, "There was no point in going down to the jetty as you had my passport and money. In any case, I thought it was the police coming."

"No one in their right minds could have mistaken that for the police."

"I saw it on the horizon—just a speck. I went to pack."

"Oh yes. You packed. And where are your bags now if you didn't put them on the boat?"

"In my room."

"They are not." He had, after all, checked, and so had Zena.

"They are."

For a moment, they stood silently facing each other. She was perfectly calm and he was not. He marched her down the

83

passage and threw open the door on the tidy empty room. The glass balcony doors concealed nothing; the empty cupboards and empty bathroom were just that, and he could see all the way under the bed to the rug on the other side.

"They are not."

There was such satisfaction in walking round the bed to the chair and lifting the two bags off the floor behind it. She placed them gently on the bed.

"You can't have looked," she said. There had been no previous moments of triumph and she was going to enjoy this one, however minor.

His mouth tightened and he ushered her back to the sitting room.

"Why didn't you come back upstairs and tell me?" Proven right, she had knocked him off balance.

"Why should I? I assumed you knew they were coming and hadn't told me on purpose. When I'd finished packing, I went back to see where it was and it was tying up and I realised it wasn't the police at all. I thought the lady might be your wife."

As an explanation, it was concise. He glared at her.

"I imagined you'd be grateful," she said. "Did you want to have to explain what I was doing here? I assumed I was doing you a favour, but obviously not." She had also wanted to give him a few uncomfortable minutes, and by the look on his face he realised it. "I thought you meant to give me a shock, not telling me they were coming."

"I see," he said. "And you assumed the lady was my wife. I wonder why. Could it possibly have been that you recognised her?"

Melissa hunched her shoulders. She *had* looked vaguely familiar. "I don't know who she is," she repeated.

"Did she see you?"

She realised that the time for fencing, for scoring points, was over. It obviously mattered very much whether Melissa had been seen, and whether she had recognised the visitor. He wasn't afraid, just very angry and rather weary.

84

"I wasn't close," she said, hearing her own voice sharpen. "I had the binoculars. I thought at first she was your wife, but I think you're afraid I've recognised your mistress and might blackmail you by threatening to tell your wife. But I didn't recognise her, and I don't know you from Adam, or your mistress, or your wife either. If you think your wife has set me up to spy on you, you're wrong. I have no interest in whatever sordid little liaisons you've set up here, wherever 'here' is. I came to the islands to buy the Perissos Bible, and that is all. I'm sorry to have interrupted what was obviously going to be an idyllic love nest, but frankly, that is entirely your own fault, and if you've had a lover's tiff because of me, I can't say I'm madly sympathetic. I did my best not to advertise my presence, but you haven't been very grateful, and I can only imagine you told her I was staying in the house, and she jumped to all the wrong conclusions."

The result of this outburst was extraordinarily satisfactory. He remained standing, his glass half way to his mouth, apparently struck dumb. Melissa seized the opportunity and stalked back into her room, where she savagely unpacked her bags and put all her clothes away again.

85

CHAPTER EIGHT

Although he had been expecting Marie Claude's visit, he hadn't expected her to come in the afternoon, and had been alarmed by her unannounced arrival. She had stood in the office doorway and gazed at the apparent chaos on the floor. Walking in, she toed a pile of drawings with a slingback stiletto that looked as if it had diamonds on it and which he hoped were only rhinestones.

"Darling, some things just never change! I suppose that maid never gets her hands on this mess!" She picked her elegant way through the paper to the centre of the room. "Are you surprised? Your ever-loving wife has come to visit you. Aren't you pleased to see me? No? You look just the tiniest bit cross, and here I am, come to relieve your loneliness and boredom." She tilted her head and shifted her weight on her hips as if she was on the catwalk. He leant back in his chair and smiled.

"Hello, Marie Claude. What a very kind thought. A little bird told me you were in Skiathos."

"Checking up on me, darling?" She turned elegantly and surveyed the rest of the room. "You are reduced to working! You really must be lonely, my poor love. I thought you'd have found someone to keep you company, but obviously no one has taken up the offer. What a shame! Perhaps you didn't offer them enough—you really should learn to be a little more generous, darling."

He smiled again. "I'm much too busy being generous to you, my sweet." He looked appraisingly at her outfit. "I bet you paid Versace on my account, not yours."

She turned gracefully, professionally, showing the lines of the trouser suit. "I did. What a good eye you have, my darling."

"Not really. It's quite recognisable."

She made a derisive miaowing sound. He rose from his desk and crossed to the balcony to look down at the yacht at the jetty.

"But it seems that you have a rather more generous friend than me. That's quite an expensive toy down there. A present? Or only a loan? Bait, perhaps? I'm sorry I didn't hear you come or I'd have provided a welcoming party from amongst my guests."

She shrugged her extremely lovely shoulders. "Jean Paul is certainly generous, but you'll be glad to hear I haven't brought him. I know he isn't your favourite man. And don't worry about the lack of a welcoming party, I truly wasn't expecting it." She made a little ironic moue.

He wondered if Melissa was already on the boat. Perhaps she and Marie Claude had met each other on the steps, acknowledging each other in passing. The employer, the employed. But Marie Claude was usually incapable of the mental discipline required for subterfuge—her acting ability was reserved for emotional scenes. On the other hand, she was extremely devious by nature and he was wary. In this case, proof of adultery, or near enough, would certainly help her in the divorce court.

He said, "But I don't suppose you climbed all this way just to show me Jean Paul's new toy or Donatella's new outfit. Is there a reason for this delightful interlude in my working day?"

"Darling, of course there's a reason!" She looked again at the papers on the floor. "It's such a shame you're toiling up here when there's that nice beach down below, but I expect you get some sailing in sometimes, don't you? Have you got someone nice to crew for you?" He didn't react, and she made a graceful gesture towards the garden. "Why don't you put a pool in up here? So much more convenient."

"Because there's a perfectly nice one down there, thank you." He indicated the Aegean Sea and wished she were at the bottom of it. "So, what is the reason for this visit," he asked again, "or do I take it that it's just my charm that draws you?"

"No, no, darling! It certainly isn't your charm. You had rather inconveniently forgotten to tell me that you were going away and there is the issue of a not very nice letter from your lawyers. I'm getting particularly bored by only communicating with you via a lawyer, but no one seemed to want to tell me where you had gone."

"But you discovered," he said.

"I discovered." She smiled her extremely lovely smile. "And conveniently it was moth to the flame, and my flame is actually in Skiathos for some sun and sea—and me of course—and he lent me his little boat to pay you a visit because it seemed a shame to be so close and not to come and visit you. Are you going to offer me any refreshment or is that outside your list of my allowances?"

He took her downstairs. The house was silent and cool, and she stood with her back to the fireplace contemplating the room.

"It's pretty basic, but nice enough, I suppose. I can't think why your mother is so passionate about it."

"No, I'm sure you can't." She didn't react to the irony. "Are you on or off alcohol at the moment?"

"Off, darling. I'm in Milan next week. No thanks to you. I do take my job seriously." He knew she did. He gave her a chilled tomato juice. "Weight isn't an addition I can afford, whatever the cause, my figure being my fortune as it were, and my fortune was recently nearly lost because of you." Her eyes were hard. "I can't afford a lot of things, Nico," her voice became as hard as her eyes, "because of you."

"Ah!" he said. He reached across and ran a finger down the fine cheekbone. For a second she held her face to it, and then jerked away, but for a moment he held her chin between a hard finger and thumb. "My dear, you can actually afford anything you like, legal or illegal, and I really do rather resent having to pay for the illegal. You earn a fortune—which I certainly don't—and apart from that you manage to live very successfully off your friends. I know a lot of parasites, but you're by far the best. If you want to negotiate you'll have to deal with that letter and the lawyers." His voice was as hard as hers, and he wondered again, savagely, where Melissa was.

Marie Claude suddenly seemed a little less confident.

"You're being totally unreasonable, darling, and I thought we could talk things through, just the two of us, without all those stupid lawyers. We could come to an agreement, couldn't we, and then just tell them what we want?" Her voice had become less angry and defiant, but this time, he thought, he was not going to be seduced by it.

"Nico, it's over. It isn't working any more. You don't love me and you want the one thing I just can't give you without wrecking my career. And you bloody well nearly did wreck it, damn you."

"Not can't. Won't. No, I don't love you any more, Marie Claude, especially now. I have no desire to live with you—not that you've been near me for months." He lifted a hand to stop her speaking. "But the settlement is in your favour only if I divorce you. If you want out, you'll have to divorce me. You're greedy and selfish, and you've taken advantage of me once too often and for something I am definitely not going to bankroll you for. If you hadn't done that I might have been more amenable, but this time you've bitten off more than you can chew, and I'm going to make sure that you choke on it. I'll meet you in court with all my evidence."

"You planned it," she shot at him. "It was all your fault and you know it. You knew my career would be ruined, and you set out to do just that, and you very nearly succeeded. You owe me for that!"

He dealt with his anger in the same cold, controlled way he always did.

"I owe you nothing. And nothing is what you're going to get. That letter isn't guesswork—I have proof. You've broken the law and I'm going to cite it in court if you force me to. You might well end up in prison, unless you buy your way out of it, which will cost you both financially and socially. It's not going to go down at all well even in the depraved circles you move in."

"You're the depraved one! What you did is also against the law."

"That's rubbish, and you certainly can't prove it, not with your adulterous reputation. You want my money, but you'll find you have an expensive fight on your hands to get any."

She glared at him in frustration, and then he saw her eyes change and soften. He knew what was coming; it happened whenever they met, and he guessed it happened to every other man that she met, too. Her arms went around his neck and pulled his head down to her mouth. She was exquisite and a bitch, and she still exerted a power over him which he had to fight to resist.

"Make love to me, Nico. I'm still your wife and you still turn me on, damn you."

He moved against her, slowly, sensually, and she moaned as her mouth opened under his. Where the hell was Melissa?

"You didn't give me any warning," he murmured into her ear. "I'll have to shift the girl out of my room first."

"There isn't one. I looked." She was moving her body against his in a way which was liable to make him lose his ability to think clearly.

"You looked? Already? What a busy lady!"

"Mmm. *Bien sûr.* It's not a big house."

The house door opened and then shut with its distinctive snap of the latch. Marie Claude stiffened and he released her.

"Who's that?" she said sharply.

"The girl, of course. You must surely have found some evidence of her in your explorations? Young. Pretty. Not quite up to your standards of beauty or sexiness—you're a hard act to follow, sweetheart—but she has youth on her side, of course."

Zena stumped down the passage and into the sitting room. Her black dress, with an ancient worn apron on top, gave her bulk the solidity of a monolith, and in the brown wrinkled face her mouth looked like a slit envelope. The hostile black eyes took in Marie Claude but ignored her.

"I saw you had guests. Do you want a meal? Yiannis has fresh squid."

His relief made him laugh aloud. But where, oh where, was Melissa?

"Thank you, Zena, but my wife will not be staying." He reverted to French. "Zena is offering to make a nice dish of calamaria. She's nicer than me, because I'm withdrawing the offer."

He would have liked to ask Zena where Melissa was, but he was always careful about what he said in Greek in front of Marie Claude. Over the years, she'd picked up enough of the language to get the gist of most conversations, and could make herself understood by using words rather than grammar. Zena stumped out and Marie Claude looked furious.

"Very funny, Nico. One of these days you'll make a mistake. You've never lived like a hermit and I don't believe you do now. You can't keep your hands off a woman."

He made a little tutting sound to annoy her. "And there I was thinking it was the other way round! You were so available, my sweet, of course I couldn't keep my hands off you—and nor could anyone else. You're a very high-class whore, as everyone agrees, but even caviar can get tedious if you don't have anything else with it, and you, my darling, have very little else to offer." His voice hardened. "But I'm warning you, Marie Claude, I have proof of your serial adultery and I will use it." He moved to the terrace, looking down towards the yacht. "Of course, your adultery will be chickenfeed compared to what I have on you now, so be careful. Your ideas for my money may well backfire on you."

He turned back to face her. "If you'd like to see that interesting video footage we informed you about, you could contact the lawyers in Athens. I'm afraid I keep them there as I am getting a bit paranoid about prowlers, reporters, sexy girls, thieves and sundry other devices to trip me up." He was watching for a reaction and saw the quick evasive, sideways glance. "Jean Paul is a bit pathetic, isn't he? All mouth and money, but he looks less good underneath his Armani suits and St Laurent shirts, I noticed. We could have a movie show in court, though it's a bit of an insult that you left me for him, I must say."

She looked curiously wary. "It's not your style. I don't believe it exists." But he knew she wasn't sure.

"Good," he said with a smile that got no further than his teeth. "Nor is it my style to go on bankrolling you and your lovers. You should use what passes for your brain, darling. If you come here unexpectedly, hoping to catch me with my pants down, as it were, you should have come with a photographer. Are you sure you've been right through the house? Did you check for undies in the bathroom? No, it's not my style, but sometimes it's a case of needs must, and I am not, emphatically not, going to let you go on making a fool of me as well as walking off with my money. Just think about what will happen when the latest evidence is aired in court."

"You're bluffing. They'd never admit it even if it was true, and it's not."

He really did laugh this time. "Of course it's true—and we have proof—and they have already admitted it. I have it all. And a lot of photographs. That won't help your career, *chérie*, along with everything else, even though it's bitch eat bitch in your business. Don't make the mistake of thinking that I can't change my style. I can if I have to. You're not the only one who can use entrapment and cameras, and money talks in the dirty tricks department, doesn't it? You should know. And sympathy will be on my side, not yours."

He put a hand at the back of her neck and drew her towards him, his other hand drifting down her throat into the valley between her breasts.

He forced his knee between her thighs and she sank against him, suddenly soft and fluid and unbelievably sexy.

"Oh shit, Nico! There's never been anyone but you, no one comes close. I don't want anyone else but you and I don't want to fight you. Let's go to bed."

"Darling," he whispered, running his tongue along the top of her ear and down to the lobe, "there's been plenty besides me, and they all come close, and you want every bloody man you can lay your hands on. Who do you think you're kidding?"

He held her wrists in one hand behind her back, having no desire to have her nails rake down his face. "And as far as I'm concerned, *chérie*, you're just another tart—a high-class one, I grant you, and your favours don't come cheap—not any more. Not cheap enough."

He tightened his grip on her as she struggled to free herself, and ignored her furious swearing. "I don't want you, Marie Claude. Is that clear enough? I don't want you, third, fourth or fifth hand. Looking good isn't enough, though it was at the beginning, when you were younger and firmer, when I thought you just might agree to a baby. But you never would, and now it's my turn to say no. I'm not going to pay you a penny more than I have to. You can use the media as much as you like because it simply doesn't bother me. Do you think anyone, even your silly coterie, believes these infantile stories of repression and poverty and rape?" His voice changed subtly. "Just try me, Marie Claude, and see what your boring husband is capable of when you push him too far."

She looked up into his face, infinitely menacing, and was shaken by his intensity.

"Let go. You're hurting me, Nico."

"Good," he said, and his grip remained as tight. The years of pent-up anger and hurt, of public humiliation and private misery, had breached the dam of his normally controlled emotions and he couldn't have stopped hurting her even if he'd wanted to. He knew it wouldn't really help. Marie Claude saw only in terms of winning or losing, and so he was going to make sure that she lost, even though he had lost, too.

"Shall we make this our last goodbye, my dear? I really don't think I can be bothered with you any more. The ball is now firmly in your court, and you can do your own thing with lawyers and divorce proceedings. Just remember what I have on you, *ma petite*. It could make quite a sensation and maybe you'd like that, but don't forget that your career is a very short-lived one, and you're not quite as young as you were." He avoided her teeth and overbalanced her as she tried to knee him in the groin. "And you could find it rather expensive—I think my resources, in the long run, will be greater than yours, but I think I will still apply to the courts for a part of your very high income."

She was spitting with rage and frustration.

"I loathe you, you bastard, you'll be sorry—you'll wish you'd never laid eyes on me."

He laughed without humour. "I'm already sorry I ever laid eyes on you, or indeed ever laid you. You don't excite me in the slightest, darling." The endearment held such a wealth of contempt that even she noticed. "And 'skin deep' has taken on an entirely new meaning since I met you. Goodbye, Marie Claude. Don't come again—I may be less welcoming next time, and don't bother with sending any more girls with cameras and recorders, or thieves, or any other of your pathetic attempts to annoy me. Would you like copies of my videos, by the way? I'd be delighted to give you, and various others, an evening or two of entertainment." He paused and held her away from him. "Don't underestimate me, Marie Claude. I've been extraordinarily patient for a long time, but my patience has run out now, and this last episode is the final straw. I will not tolerate your behaviour any longer and I think you could safely say that your future, in every sense, lies in my hands. Go away. Your lover awaits—enjoy him—you may not have too many more this side of prison."

He turned her and forced her across the terrace and down the first few steps of the path. She looked back at him with hatred.

"You'll regret this, Nico. I'll take you for everything you've got."

He smiled his cold, charming smile. "Can you see yourself out?"

He waited until her high heels had clacked off down the path, and then he turned and strode down the hall. Melissa's room was empty, the cover on the bed, the mat neatly squared on the marble tiles. Not a shred of her, her belongings, or her personality. He threw the bathroom door open and surveyed the empty white space before opening the wardrobe doors and finding it empty, too, the padded hangers in a neat row on the rail and no Melissa hiding inside. He swore aloud and went upstairs two at a time remembering that he'd left the office unlocked. To his relief, he found the envelope containing her passport and all her documents still in the drawer.

In the kitchen, Zena was scrubbing fiercely at the already pristine hob.

"Where the hell is she?" he demanded.

"I don't know. I didn't know what to do. She wasn't in her room. It's empty."

"I know that," he snapped. "And all her clothes are gone. Why didn't you warn me? You must have seen them coming."

"I didn't see them," she said, her tone sour. "I was at home and when I did see, I came as quickly as I could."

"Well, she's done the damage now and I daresay is about to regale Marie Claude with tales of abduction and brutality. I'll wring her little neck when I catch up with her." He gave her a sharp look. "How's your French, Zena?"

The old woman gave a ghost of a smile. "It wasn't necessary to translate your conversation, Master Nicholas."

95

"God! Women! What have I done to deserve all this! You'd better go home. There's nothing to be done about it now."

She insisted on staying and in a sense he was glad she was there. Somehow the house was still ringing with their mutual malice, and he could hear the pointless arguments and taste the bitterness of what their marriage had become. The whole wretched episode had left him weary and depressed and raw, as he had known it would even before he'd given in to the temptation to hurt her. He wondered how she would treat Melissa and how she would use the girl's story. A strange and unaccustomed feeling of regret and disappointment flooded through the anger as he poured himself a stiff whisky. Zena came to the door.

"She's here. In the garden." Their eyes met and Zena spoke severely. "She is only young. Don't treat her like you treated that one. She can't have spoken to her."

She indicated with her head towards the steps, the boat, Marie Claude.

"Go away, and don't interfere."

She cast him a dark look and he heard her bang the house door as she left. He went out on to the terrace and looked down at Melissa.

As Zena had suspected, his relief did not make him feel any more charitable towards her and he saw how she flinched from his verbal savaging.

He had another whisky to relieve his feelings and several cigarettes and eventually his sense of proportion began to return. Melissa had apparently done no damage, and he had perhaps been rather hard on her. If she hadn't had the wit to clear her room and disappear, Marie Claude wouldn't be going back to her lawyers empty-handed. After simmering down, he prepared the calamaria and went to Melissa's room to find her sitting on the balcony in the gathering twilight. Dragging her unwillingly out to have some food, he saw her eyes were puffy and red.

"Crying on an empty stomach is bad for the digestion," he said. "I have cooked you a delicious supper to make up for being nasty to you."

"I'm not hungry," she said. "And I'm not crying."

"You were crying, and you will be hungry. You thought you were paddling, and now you've fallen in over your head. These are dangerous waters."

She lifted her head and looked him in the eye.

"Hindsight is very useful, isn't it? Anything would have been preferable to this situation, and I can hardly wait to get to my next destination. It will be a greater relief to me to be out of your house than it will be for you."

His mouth twitched. "I doubt it, Melissa, I doubt it. As days go, this one will be truly memorable."

That evening the police rang. She would be collected the following afternoon. He thought sourly that twenty-four hours earlier would have made all the difference.

Inspector Kiprionidis came with a lesser uniformed officer, who was dispatched with her bags to the launch. His glance took in Melissa's strained face before she was sent to her room while they completed the paperwork.

It was quite a long time before Nicholas opened her door and shut it again behind him as she turned slowly to face him. Crossing the room, he stood for a moment looking down at her.

"Goodbye, Melissa."

He bent his head and kissed her, and as she reacted violently away from him, he savagely forced her mouth open beneath his, one hand holding her head to his, the other behind her shoulders, pressing her to him. After a few moments, he kissed her more gently until he felt her body weakening against him. At last he lifted his head, tilting hers back so that he could look down into her face.

"I'm taking repayment, Miss Scott-Mackenzie," he said softly. He touched her lips again with his, lightly, gently, and his thumbs ran slowly under her eyes wiping away the angry tears. "Paid in full."

He put a hand on her back and propelled her out to the sitting room. The inspector took a slow look at them both, shook hands with his host and ushered Melissa down the steps in front of him.

CHAPTER NINE

She was tired, as she often was these days. The London rain came in misting gusts and although she had an umbrella it wasn't worth trying to use it in the wind. It always seemed doubly cold after the restaurant doors had swung shut behind her. It wasn't a long walk, because she had chosen carefully when hunting for this second job, knowing that she'd be on the streets late at night. It was Friday night, so a sleep-in beckoned for tomorrow. The restaurant was a good one and in the five months she had worked for them they had been good employers, with high standards, and there was always good food at the end of the shift.

She walked quickly back to the flat, head down into her coat hood. After a hot bath, she wrote a 'Please do not wake me up' note for her flatmates, turned out the light and sank into oblivion.

The morning brought more wind and rain, dismal grey skies and puddled pavements. Melissa woke late, drugged with sleep, queued for the bathroom with a strong cup of coffee and washed her hair. Her mobile rang and the voice said, "Melissa?" and she knew instantly it was Nicholas. The way he said it was unmistakable: the sensual first syllable, the hesitation at the second.

"Oh God!" she said, appalled, and then put her hand to her mouth at the blasphemy. She heard his laughter.

"Not God—nearly, but not quite. I'd like to see you."

"No!" she said, struggling to control her breathing. "You can't—I mean, it's not necessary. How did you get my number?"

He ignored the question. "I'll be with you in an hour."

"You will not!" she said. "I don't want to see you, and all I need is your name and address."

"What on earth for?"

"To send you the money."

"Money? What money?" There was an indrawn breath. "Ah. That money. You're fully paid-up. Forget it—I have."

She winced at the reference to being fully paid-up. "Well, I haven't forgotten and I want to be rid of it. It's not all of it yet, but it will be. Your name and address are all I need."

"No it isn't."

"Yes it is!" she said. "Or if you're still so shy about your name, your Sort Code and account number will do. But I don't want to see you, and I don't need to, and I won't see you."

"Yes. Please. In an hour." The please didn't sound like a request.

"No—look, you can't." She felt desperate in the face of his insistence. "I have to go to work. You really can't. Just give me those BACS details and leave me alone."

There was a short pause. "Work? On a Saturday? OK. I'll tell you when I see you. And I'll drive you to work."

"No—"

"Yes. One hour. Outside your flat." He cut the connection.

"Bastard!" she yelled at the phone. "Bully! You're an arrogant, overbearing, horrible bully and I hate you."

She stood paralysed, holding the hairdryer like a gun, her heart thumping with anxiety. He must have kept her mobile number and address from Greece. Was this how it felt to be stalked? 'I'll drive you to work'! He simply could not know where she worked. Could he?

She thought back to the day when that policeman had collected her. The long journey in the police launch, the Greek being spoken around her, but no one speaking to her, hunched in a pit of misery and apprehension. Hours later, to her confusion, they had arrived in Skiathos, not Volos. She was shut alone into a small hot room at the airport, and later again Kiprionidis escorted her on to a small Olympic Airways hopper. Puzzled by only hearing a loudspeaker reference for

Athens, she queried it with him as he buckled himself into the aisle seat beside her.

"Yes, this is the Athens flight. Didn't the gentleman tell you?"

She stared at him. His accent was strong, but his English was fluent.

"No. He didn't. Inspector, I thought you didn't speak English?"

"Did you?" His face was expressionless behind the black stubble of a long day and his dark glasses.

"Yes, I did. You gave me the impression—and he did, too, that you—What was the point of all that translation?"

"I like to hear both sides—one gets to the truth quicker sometimes."

She was rendered speechless while she tried to remember what had gone on during that appalling interview.

"Oh!" she said eventually. "Why didn't you tell me today you spoke English?"

"It wasn't necessary."

"But it is! I don't know what's happening, where I'm going to be, how long for, or anything. And now you say we're going to Athens not Volos. Do I go to court first or straight to prison? Do I get a lawyer? How do I let my family know where I am and what I need?" She kept her voice down with difficulty. The inspector turned towards her.

"He told you nothing?" He seemed surprised. "You're going to London, Miss Scott. Not to court."

"London?" Her shock was such that it took several seconds to sink in—for the hope to start surging into her mind. "Why? I mean how? I thought—I haven't paid—was the fine cancelled or did you get Rambiris and the money? Tell me you got the money back—I might even keep my job!"

He shook his head. "No, we haven't found Rambiris, and I doubt that the money will ever be recovered. You should be more careful about your business associates, Miss Scott, and remember that some, if not all, of the bureaucratic process exists to protect you, and to prevent just such dishonesty. If you had completed the legal paperwork properly you would not have had these problems. I suggest that you do not return to Greece again for such purposes."

The rebuke hardly penetrated through her bewilderment.

"Am I going back to England in police custody? Has the fine got to be paid in England?"

"No, Miss Scott, you are only in custody until I have escorted you off Greek territory. After that you are a free individual. If you had been a Greek citizen you would possibly have had a criminal record, but as you are a British citizen and the penalty has been paid, there is nothing more for you to worry about."

"What do you mean, the penalty has been paid?" she said.

"The gentleman has paid the fine. It has been lodged in the Athens courts by his lawyers."

She pressed her head back into the seat and closed her eyes fiercely. 'I'm taking repayment,' he had said. 'Paid in full.'

"Inspector, how much was it? And his name, and address?"

He shook his head. "You don't need to know, D*espinis*, and he doesn't wish it."

"But I must repay it! His lawyers? Couldn't it be sent there? Or his bank—just the bank and an account number would be enough, wouldn't it?"

"Miss Scott," he said patiently, "you would be wise to accept your good fortune, and go quietly home. The gentleman has influence and is a rich man. It's paid. Forget it. If he chooses to pay the fine incurred by his own charges, that is his business, and I would advise you to leave well alone."

She got nothing more out of the inspector, and was left to her own thoughts. She understood then why he had not allowed her to make any more phone calls. He had left her to suffer nightmares of apprehension, but at least had prevented her from giving notice on her flat. She should have felt grateful for that, but didn't. But to pay that fine! She didn't allow herself to even think about that kiss. It brought on a thumping pulse and her whole body flushed.

In Athens, she had sat in another hot little room and had eventually been escorted into International Departures, where her passport, papers and money were handed over. It was a scheduled flight and she assumed he must have paid for that, too. An inconvenience disposed of with as little fuss as possible.

And now, for some inexplicable reason, he had tracked her down. The memory of that kiss flooded back and her stomach cramped. She put on careful make-up, dried and French-plaited her hair, gathered up the 'Richardson' account statements, and put them with her cheque book in her bag. She took a deep breath and went downstairs. Why, if he didn't want the money repaid, had he contacted her? There had to be a reason, but she couldn't think of one and it made her extremely uneasy.

He was waiting in a dark blue Jaguar, right outside the flat. She heard the electric window whine down.

"Hello, Melissa. Punctual to the minute. Get in the front."

"No, thank you," she said. "I only have to write you a cheque—and I can do that here—so if you'll tell me who to make it payable to, that would be helpful."

"You're getting wet, and the ink will run. You can do it in the car."

"I'd rather not."

He looked at her ruefully. "You've made that clear, I think. However, you're getting wet, I'm getting wet and I have things to say to you. I'm not going to abduct you, so don't look so nervous; once was quite enough for us both. Get in, or I'll get cross. You don't like me when I'm cross."

"I don't like you, full stop," she said tartly. "As you still seem unwilling to give yourself a name I'll leave the payee blank and you can complete it yourself. But I want to know where I can send future payments—this is only six months and I want to pay it monthly."

He looked at her gravely for a moment. "This is really quite important for you, isn't it? Repaying the money?"

"Yes. Yes, it is."

"OK. You win. You can write me a cheque. Now, get in, and let's keep this wretched rain out."

She went slowly round to the passenger door. Who had won? The car was warm, comfortable, luxurious. She sat stiffly, sliding the scarf off her hair, and took the papers out of her handbag.

"OK. We'll get the business end straightened out first. You can leave the payee blank." A thought struck him. "Are you trying to repay Clive Mann as well?"

"Yes. The monthly amounts are the same. I'm sorry, otherwise I could pay you twice as much."

"You're mad," he said, twitching the statements out of her hand and taking a rapid look. "I didn't want it back, I didn't expect it back, and I told you that you'd paid in full." His elbow was on the back of the seat, and he was half turned towards her. The rain was making the windows mist up. He didn't smile. "Didn't it occur to you that I was fairly nasty to you?"

She blinked and shrugged. "It did occur to me. You stated your reasons."

"And you thought they were good enough reasons to warrant having you locked up, and humiliation generally?"

She was confused, uncertain where all this was leading.

"No, I didn't, but what I thought didn't make any difference, did it? You were hung up on trespass, burglary and theft."

"I'm sorry" he said quietly. "There was a reason—is a reason. But I am very sorry, and I would like to try to make restitution. Well, partial restitution anyway. I'd like you to come to a special event in a fortnight—the evening of Saturday 23rd."

She was taken aback and embarrassed both by her previous rudeness and his apology, but relieved that she didn't have to lie.

"I'm sorry, but I can't. I waitress in the evenings, including Saturdays. It's kind of you, and quite unnecessary, but I actually can't. But I need to know where I can send the money, and I still don't know your name."

He frowned. "You have a full-time day job as well?"

"Yes."

"Which is?"

"HR. For a software company," she said impatiently, wanting to get to the root of her anxiety. "How did you find me?"

"I had your address and phone number in Greece, remember? I'd still like you to come that Saturday."

"I can't. I told you. Saturday's a very busy night and I'm not going to let them down. And I must go to work now, so if you don't mind—and Nicholas *what?*"

"I like the French plait." He was smiling as he turned the ignition on. "I'll drive you. Which restaurant?"

"Thank you, but I'll walk."

"Melissa, it is now pouring. Which restaurant?"

She gave up and told him where it was and the car moved out into the traffic.

"I promised someone I'd bring you and I can't let them down, can I?"

His assumption that she would fall into immediate line astounded and enraged her.

"This is my life you're picking up and dropping—you've done it before and I'm damn well not letting you do it again. Let me make it very clear—I'll pay that debt just as quickly as I can, but I never asked you to pay the fine in the first place and I never wanted to be in your debt. I don't know who you are or why you want to mess up my life. If you've got all this money lying about you could have let Mann's have the bible and gone and bought another—there are Byzantine books on every corner." She was aware that this wasn't a sustainable argument, but didn't care. "But I haven't got money lying around, and I work for every penny I earn. I've no intention of losing a job I both need and like just because you come breezing in and think one date is going to compensate for all the damage you've done. Forget it, Mr Nicholas Richardson, or whoever you are. I may be the first girl who didn't dance to your tune of money and bullying, but just put it down to experience and try someone else."

"OK. If you choose not to, I can't make you, but if you really insist on paying this money back I promise to give you all the information you need then. Bank, account number, name, and we'll put it on a proper footing. I'll pick you up from the flat in two weeks at six-thirty."

"You will not!"

"—and it's a concert. There'll be an event, a celebration afterwards, and something you'll be interested in. Wear your smartest outfit and the Crown Jewels, or at any rate your best tiara." He grinned at her, teeth white in a still tanned face. He switched off the engine.

"You are unbelievable!" she said. "Who the hell do you think you are? Even if I had free nights from here to eternity, I wouldn't be seen dead in your company."

"Ah well! You've got a couple of weeks to decide. It will be a family affair, and as I said, there will be something there you will be extremely interested in. And somebody who wants to meet you."

"Your wife, I suppose. Was that your wife or your mistress who came that day?"

"It was my wife. But she won't be there. It's not her that wants to meet you."

"I don't care *who* wants to meet me. I don't want to meet them."

He shook his head. "I'll tell you my name. I'll tell you how to repay this non-existent debt as well. Melissa, this is not another exercise in humiliation, I promise you. It is part explanation, part apology, but you need to be there to understand it. Go to work. I'll see you in two weeks at six-thirty."

The big blue car eased into the traffic leaving her standing on the pavement in the rain. Of course, she wouldn't go, but she did have a certain curiosity. Why should she have to be there to understand? What explanation? Who was he? Did he live in London or Greece? Who was this person who wanted to meet her? How was she going to rid herself of this awful debt unless she went and found the answers? Apart from anything else, he knew an unnerving amount about her, and if she didn't turn up, what would he do? From past experience, she had no desire to be on the receiving end of his annoyance, and though she despised herself for her cowardice, her initial injection of courage gradually evaporated into a miasma of indecision. He had been conciliatory. He had apologised. He had promised that it was not an exercise in humiliation. He was very attractive. But he had not explained a black case full of drugs.

She arranged the evening off from work and eyed her wardrobe in despair. Even if she went to this event, whatever it was, there was nothing she possessed which gave her any feeling of security. And the Crown Jewels were a joke.

She decided on a silk dress bought from one of the smarter second-hand clothes shops in Putney. Her jewellery was minimal, but real. She still wasn't sure if she had the courage to go. Or the courage not to go. Eventually, tense and nervous, she did her face and hair very carefully indeed. Perhaps he just wouldn't turn up. But the bell rang on the dot of six-thirty and she went downstairs quickly, not wanting him to see either the flat or to meet her flatmates, curious as they were, and as she opened the outer door he stepped inside. He took a rapid comprehensive look before helping her on with her coat and ushering her into the car. As he closed the umbrella and slid into the driver's seat he commented, "Understated elegance. You look great."

She sucked in a breath. "I just want you to know that I'm not here willingly. If I'd had the guts, I'd have gone to the cinema hours ago." He said nothing. "I don't want to come to whatever this thing is. I don't want to be involved in any family party." She swallowed. "I really don't want to come tonight."

He leant forward and started the car.

"So why didn't you go to the cinema? Or out? Or you could have just stayed in the flat."

"You know why," she said, not bothering to keep the bitterness from her voice. "You promised to give me the information I need and that's the only reason I'm here."

He was silent for a moment, gazing out at the rain, his face blankly unreadable, before moving out into the traffic. When he spoke, it was as if their previous words hadn't been said.

"We're going to a charity fund-raising concert, and afterwards you'll meet my mother and stepfather, and my brothers and their wives and we're having dinner together. It's my mother's birthday."

"Why are you taking me along to this?" she asked. "I'm a total stranger. I don't even know your name. They won't want me, and I don't want to be there. You and I can't stand each other and an evening of Greek family jollity is my idea of purgatory."

He laughed. "My mother is Greek, but the language will be English. And my mother would like to meet you. You're attractive to look at, intelligent and hard-working, so you'll hold your own without any bother. And you blush delightfully," he added, taking an amused sideways glance. She put a hand up to her hot cheeks.

"You may not think this is an exercise in humiliation, but it is for me. And how can your mother possibly want to meet me? She doesn't know me from Adam!"

"Ah, but she knows about you, because I told her. I had to really—the house in Greece is hers, and Zena would have told her anyway. However," he continued, "I haven't yet told her what our—misunderstanding—was about, and you will understand why as the evening goes on. All she knows is that you were trying to get back something that was stolen from you." He glanced again at Melissa's apprehensive face. "Please don't worry. This is restitution for you. Part of my apology."

Not much of this conversation was making sense. Which bit of that horrible episode could be classed as their 'misunderstanding'? Her attempted theft? Rambiris? His wife? Drug dealing?

"So it wasn't your house at all, and you've amused your entire family with my—with what happened. And you now expect me to—what? Be the butt of their jokes all evening?"

"I haven't amused any of the family. They truly don't know anything about it. My mother certainly wasn't amused by me." He hesitated. "They know I've invited you because it's to do with her birthday, but they won't ask awkward questions, I promise you."

"Oh." She was now confused and uncertain. What exactly did he tell his mother? And why would no one ask questions about her because it was his mother's birthday?

"She seemed to think your behaviour was entirely normal, which only goes to show that women think quite differently to men. She was very cross with me."

He didn't look much like a mummy's boy, she thought, hearing the laughter in his voice. He can be charming, but underneath he's a bully.

He manoeuvred her skilfully through the pre-show crowd, introducing her where appropriate, and moving on naturally after a brief word or two. There were a good many Greeks, and she realised why he had advised her to dress up. In terms of designer clothes and chunks of diamonds, this was a showcase. The champagne was free. She was introduced briefly to a cheerful, pretty sister-in-law called Sophie who was heading purposefully in the opposite direction carrying all before her in the form of an unborn baby.

"Hi, Melissa. Nice to meet you. I'll see you later, but I absolutely must go to the loo this minute. The baby is doing a jig on my bladder. I expect I'll be up and down like a yo-yo all through the best bits."

Melissa felt heartened by her friendliness and normality amongst the smart crowd and, despite her nervousness, she enjoyed the concert. The Greek singer, Galina Molinaris, wasn't a young woman, but she was beautiful. The structure of the jutting bones and high planes gave her face an ageless quality and she exuded the professionalism of a true entertainer. There was a vague teasing familiarity about her.

The concert finished to a lengthy ovation. Both singer and musicians came down into the small auditorium afterwards to greet friends and receive congratulations and the singer was followed by a good-looking young man who gathered up all her flowers for her. As she drew level with Nicholas, sitting in the aisle seat, she looked penetratingly at Melissa for a moment, then she smiled and bent to speak to someone in the row behind, one hand touching Nicholas's face as she passed. The caress was patently tender and he seemed unsurprised by it, taking the hand in his and kissing it briefly before she withdrew it, sliding it up his cheek and moving on.

Melissa experienced an odd jolt. It had been an understated caress between two people who had no need for overt statements or gestures; long-time lovers perhaps, secure in a relationship. She was surely older than him, but neither of them was easy to put an age on. It was only a tiny incident, but it made her curious – and something else she couldn't quite recognise.

She allowed herself to be escorted, moved, introduced; heard herself responding, knew that she smiled and listened and did everything that was required of her. They had gone steadily upstairs, and arrived eventually in the balcony bar which had a large 'Private. No Entry' sign on the doors. A tall, silver-haired, elegant man welcomed them.

110

"This is my stepfather, Richard Newington," Nicholas said, "Richard. Melissa Scott-Mackenzie."

Richard Newington smiled with old-fashioned charm, one hand still holding hers in a strong friendly grip. He chatted briefly, easily, his eyes kind. She was aware that he was putting her at ease, and was grateful. He must be seventy, she guessed, but young at heart. However, if Richard Newington was a stepfather, she was no nearer to knowing Nicholas's identity. Nicholas introduced her to several people already in the bar. A Greek aunt called Isabella with a beautiful but worn, tired face who seemed somehow familiar as she rather inexpertly juggled a stick with her champagne glass. There were two sisters-in-law and three brothers, one of whom, Will, was the young man who had been collecting Galina's flowers. In her nervousness, she immediately forgot all their names. They appeared to take her presence at a private family occasion entirely in their stride. Did they think she might be a girlfriend, she wondered? One of the brothers, Michael, whose heavily pregnant wife Sophie she had met earlier, was crippled with an appalling limp, but he was astonishingly good-looking and more importantly, genuinely interested in other people. Melissa warmed to both him and Sophie, and found herself sitting at a small table with them, discussing arts funding and the peccadilloes of the Tate Gallery.

Nicholas was being helpful, pouring champagne, chatting easily, a word for everyone, but Melissa thought there was a remoteness, a separation between him and the rest of the family. He had none of their light-heartedness. She also wondered who their mother was and was puzzled at not having been introduced.

Melissa felt confused by the plethora of siblings who all seemed to be called Newington, although Richard Newington was Nicholas's stepfather, and in a kind of desperate recklessness, said so.

"Hasn't Nicholas explained?" Sophie laughed as Melissa shook her head. "Hopeless man! I'll start at the top. Richard

Newington had two children by his first marriage: Michael, who is my husband, and Anne, who's in America. Richard's wife died of cancer. Galina—or Madame as we call her—had Nicholas by her first husband Alexis Thauros, and Alexis died of a heart attack when Nicholas was eight. Richard and Madame then married and had Oliver who's a publisher and Will who's at uni. The five of them are a perfect muddle of halves and steps, but we're all Newingtons except for Nicholas who is Thauros. Michael is married to me, Nicholas is—" She hesitated. "Nicholas is married to the model Marie Claude de Rimanac, Oliver is married to Ruth, and Anne and Will are footloose and fancy free."

The conversation moved on, but Melissa only half heard it, just as she had not taken in much of Sophie's explanation. However, some things had clarified. The singer, Galina Molinaris, was Nicholas's mother, not lover, although she didn't look old enough to have a son in his thirties. The name Thauros meant something; it jangled on the edge of memory but she couldn't place it. She asked Sophie where her mother-in-law was.

"Oh, she'll be here any minute, I expect; she'll be chatting to people downstairs." She turned to Will, who had returned with the champagne bottle. "How are you doing, Will? Nose to the grindstone?"

He grinned at her. "No. You know me!" He transferred the grin to Melissa. "Did you enjoy it? The concert?"

"Yes," she said, "enormously. I thought it was wonderful, and your mother has the most gorgeous voice. It made my hair stand on end! What an amazing talent."

He was delighted with her pleasure. "Madame—we all call her that, for some reason—was seventeen when Alexis Thauros heard her singing, fell in love and married her. Has Nicholas told you all this already?" She shook her head. "Alexis was much older and frightfully rich. Alexis made Galina's career, but then he died and two years later she married Richard who had been ambassador to Greece. Today is Madame's fifty third birthday." He grinned again. "Clear?"

"Well, clearer!" Melissa couldn't help laughing. "What do you all do? Have any of you followed in her footsteps?"

Will laughed. "Nope. Michael's a doctor, Nicholas is an architect, Anne works for an American pharmaceutical company, Oliver is in publishing and I'm at Oxford. And none of us can sing!"

The doors opened and a crowd of people appeared, led by Galina Molinaris and Richard Newington. There was an eruption of clapping and wolf whistles and shouts of 'Happy Birthday'. The introductions went on, a blur to Melissa, and every now and then she was aware of Nicholas's glance.

Richard Newington spoke at her shoulder. "Come and meet my wife. She's talking to Sophie, my very pregnant daughter-in-law, and no doubt filling her up with more Greek old wives' tales. Have you met Sophie? She's quite mad."

His humour put Melissa at ease. "Yes—I thought she seemed quite sane, but I'm sure you know best."

He chuckled, tucking her arm into his.

"Her house is full of creatures. Her own, and other people's children; dogs, cats, rabbits, fish, hamsters. God knows what. Tell me about you. You don't look old enough to know all about Byzantium, but Nicholas tells me that you do. I've always had a secret passion for Theodora, festooned in her jewels. I think she was an actress with a rather grimy reputation, but I have a soft spot for performing artists, as you may have noticed."

Melissa laughed. "No, I don't know much about Byzantium." Nicholas had told him something. But how much? And what? "I've always thought Justinian must have been a bit of a romantic. She was much younger than him, wasn't she?"

He twinkled at her. "That's nothing! Here's Galina, who is nearly twenty years younger than me and I suspect is directly related to Theodora. It's a good thing we live in a different culture." Galina and Sophie were in a group of friends by the bar.

"My darling, I've brought Nicholas's friend Melissa to meet you."

With practised skill he extracted Galina and ensconced her and Melissa on a red velvet bench by the wall. Galina's blue-black hair was swept up into a smooth chignon, emphasizing the high cheekbones and straight narrow nose. The mouth was full, sensual and mobile. A strong face, dominated by huge dark eyes.

"You must be exhausted after the show. I enjoyed it so much." Melissa said. She felt inadequate and shy. This woman must hear such adulation every day; how could anyone possibly compliment her?

Galina looked at her thoughtfully. "I'm so glad you did. I don't suppose you expect to enjoy much of the rest of this evening, but I hope it won't be nearly as bad as you think it will." She had a strong Greek accent and was smiling, laughter lines crinkling the corners of her eyes, seeing Melissa's embarrassment. "Nicholas told me that you were very reluctant to come tonight, because he had been so unkind to you, but for some reason it was important that you were here. And I wanted to meet you as I understand that you were an unwilling guest in my house on Mixos, due to some misunderstanding—on both your parts, I think?" Melissa flushed and nodded. She hoped Nicholas hadn't told her the full extent of her reluctance to come; it made her seem ungrateful and rude, and however badly he had behaved, Galina had had nothing to do with it.

"I was reluctant because he said it was your birthday, and a family occasion. As a complete stranger, I feel I am intruding on your privacy. I don't understand why he was so insistent."

"I don't either, but we are delighted to have you. I expect all will be made plain. How did he persuade you?"

Melissa drew in her breath sharply at both the words and indeed the way she said them. There was curiosity, yes, but more. An anxiety? An unease. About her, or about her son? Melissa wondered if she thought Nicholas had lured her with

114

the bait of meeting a celebrity and in sudden distaste at the thought decided to tell her the truth.

"He had to lend me some money—a result of our 'misunderstanding', and because he wouldn't tell me who he was, I couldn't repay it. Then he rang up about tonight. I refused, of course, but he still wouldn't tell me his name. He said if I came tonight, he'd tell me how to repay him. If I didn't come, he wouldn't tell me. He'd just disappear and this horrible debt would hang over me for ever."

Galina looked amazed. "But why didn't you just forget the money? He has plenty!" She looked at Melissa's face and the mobile mouth twisted in sympathy. "Oh, my dear! Female pride! He won't make it easy for you, you know. I know he feels guilty about whatever it was that happened, and no doubt would like you to accept the money in compensation for treating you badly." She sighed. "I can imagine that he was very disagreeable. If it is of any comfort, you did not suffer alone, but there were reasons which I can't go into. May we leave it there, my dear? I would like you to relax and enjoy the rest of this evening and the rest of our friends and family, who I am sure you will like to the same degree that you dislike Nicholas."

Melissa felt wretched and coloured uncomfortably. "I— I—no. That is—I don't know him well enough—I mean, it doesn't come into it." She was floundering and the older woman was half laughing. She put a hand on Melissa's arm.

"You need not be polite! He warned me that you were much too well brought up, but that I would read everything in your face. And he is quite right. Naturally you do not like him! He told me he was utterly and unforgivably unkind and I don't imagine he has really apologised either."

She was spared having to respond to this unexpected plain speaking by Richard Newington appearing armed with a bottle with which he refilled both their glasses. Galina sipped her champagne, thoughtful eyes on Melissa.

"I heard from Zena that his wife visited the house while you were there and that you managed to make yourself invisible." She lifted a hand as Melissa began to protest. "You don't need to explain to me why you did that, and Nicholas assures me you were not 'another woman', but you saved him, and indeed the rest of the family, from some unpleasant consequences." She smiled faintly.

Melissa said nothing. She didn't understand what Galina was saying and there didn't seem any possible comment. She looked down at her tense hands as the older woman continued.

"I would like to apologise for him, my dear, and I hope you will find yourself able to accept it on his behalf, and possibly even to forgive him in time. He is my son and I love him."

Melissa raised her eyes. There was a wry plea in the dark ones regarding her. "Thank you, Madame." The form of address came spontaneously. "Of course I accept. You certainly don't need to apologise to me." She swallowed rather painfully. "He did apologise—sort of—today. Also, it wasn't altogether his fault. I did something very silly and—wrong; I made a lot of mistakes, too."

"But you are young." Suddenly Galina was cheerful again. "We all make mistakes. A life without mistakes would mean that we never fail, and to learn about failure and how to deal with it when we are young is one of the most important lessons in life. What really happened in May I don't know and don't need to know, though of course I am curious, being female." Her eyes crinkled in a smile. "Now, we are all going to have dinner at the Greek restaurant next door, and I will place you as far from Nicholas as I can."

Melissa felt liberated, and the evening became a pleasure. Every now and then she was conscious of Nicholas's eyes on her, and his faint, wry smile, but she no longer felt at such a disadvantage. The dinner was in a private room and the food was delicious. She was seated between Will and his brother Oliver, both of whom were delightful and entirely uncomplicated, and Melissa found herself sparkling in response.

116

When the coffee came, Richard Newington placed a large parcel in a cleared space on the table in front of Galina, and the conversation died to a murmur. Everyone was smiling, grinning. It was obvious the family knew the contents, and equally as obvious that Galina did not. She was like a child, gleaming with anticipation, curious, her eyes shining with love and laughter as she glanced round the table at her family.

The gold paper was removed, the tissue paper, the bubble wrap, more tissue paper. Richard Newington slid it all away onto the floor. Melissa suddenly knew what was coming and felt the blood drain out of her face and then surge back again, pumping in her ears. The last layer peeled away from the heavy object, and the Perissos Bible lay gleaming in its gold and silver and jewelled glory on the white tablecloth.

She looked at Nicholas down the length of the table, sitting next to Galina. As if he could feel her eyes, he glanced up at her, and gave the faintest shrug. 'If you tell them, I'll kill you,' she said to him silently. He smiled and shook his head fractionally. Then he turned to watch Galina. She lifted the great book in her hands, reverently, as if she was holding a newborn child.

"Perissos." She said it very quietly, and her voice sounded thick. The family were all smiling at her; delighted, silent, thrilled. Into Melissa's numbed mind came an awareness that there was more to this birthday present than she understood. Galina was silent, too, staring at the book in her hands and suddenly Melissa saw that her eyes were bright with tears, and as she watched they spilled over, hesitating on the long lashes, swelling and falling.

"Oh! My darlings! You are all simply wonderful. How did you—? What a miracle!" She put the book on the table, touching the jewelled cover with her fingertips, and then turning, flung her arms round her husband, and then around Nicholas, holding him against her for a long moment. Then the others got up and hugged and kissed her and the table broke up into noisy good wishes, and excited conversation.

Melissa discovered that she'd been holding her breath and gulped in air. She got up shakily and went to the cloakroom, taking her time. Sophie came in as she was putting fresh lipstick on.

"Are you OK? Nico said you didn't look very well. You're rather pale."

"I'm fine, thanks."

"I needed the loo anyway—again, so I said I'd check you were all right. Wasn't that lovely? I assume you know why Madame is so tickled with her birthday present?"

"No. No, I don't," she said unsteadily. "It obviously has a special meaning for her."

Sophie disappeared into the loo, but continued the conversation at a louder level. "It's a bible, very old, from three hundred and something and it comes from a monastery on a Greek island called Perissos—where Madame's family come from. There's been a member of the family in the monastery for generations and generations—can you imagine? Simply awful I'd have thought, but there you are—very Greek. Her uncle is there, but the monks get older and die, and no more young ones go in these days. You can't blame them, can you? And so the monasteries are dying—as a result of having no new blood. In Perissos there are only four monks left, including Great Uncle Georgio, and they couldn't afford to keep it going—you know, repairs and all that, and growing stuff in the garden—jolly hard work, poor old things." She reappeared and started brushing her hair.

"Ah. That's why they sold their bible?"

"Yep. And Madame heard about it and was terribly upset—it's very valuable, but it's much more than that, it's been there for ever and she felt it was wrong, selling it. For her, and I expect for the monks too, it's not just a valuable antique, it's part of their faith, their love for God, the continuity of a worshipping community. She was really, really upset when she heard they'd sold it. She would have bought it herself, if she'd known, I think."

118

Melissa said nothing, wondering how Mr Mann had heard about it.

"She didn't know it was sold until Uncle Georgio wrote and told her," Sophie went on. "By then it had gone and the monastery had the money. I don't know how long it'll last, even that amount. I think she gives a lot of money to them anyway. It's rather sad, isn't it?" She clipped her bag closed. "Shall we go?"

As they made their way back Melissa said, "So was she expecting it? The present? She looked so surprised."

"Oh no! It was sold, and she had no idea where it had gone, and was really quite distraught. Nico found out and bought it, darling man, and we all chipped in a bit—not much I suspect, in terms of what it must have cost him. Anyway, the boys kept that bit fairly quiet. Nico's had a rotten year and been like a bear with the proverbial, but he got the bible even though that awful Marie Claude was trying to get hold of it so that he couldn't have it, just to spite him. At least I think that's what was going on. We don't really know. She's—ugh. Can't tell you."

Melissa, astounded by this revelation, made for her seat, but Richard Newington called her over and put her into his place.

"Come and tell Madame about this thing we've given her. Nicholas tells us it's Byzantine, and you, my dear, are Justinian's spokeswoman."

Galina's intelligent eyes looked at her thoughtfully; both of them now knew why Nicholas had been so insistent that Melissa should come tonight. She gave him an uncertain sideways glance, but his face was uninformative.

She answered Galina's questions, explaining about the different gemstones and their symbolism, how the silver gilt was applied and hammered, how the boards were covered and stitched, about the vellum and how it was prepared, and the threads of gold wire, twisted with strengthening silver, what ink they had used and how the illuminators worked. She noticed that it had been expertly restored since she had examined it with Rambiris. Gradually she was aware that there was silence around her, and stumbled to an embarrassed halt, conscious that the entire table was listening to her.

"I'm so sorry. How awful of me. I never meant—" Richard put a hand on her shoulder from behind.

"My dear, please don't be sorry. We are all fascinated—I can assure you that nothing normally stops the Newington clan from talking, and their silence is probably the greatest compliment you'll ever have. You've made Madame's birthday present very special for us all and we are very grateful, and we would love to hear more." But Melissa was not to be persuaded and the conversation again gathered impetus until he brought the evening charmingly to a halt.

Galina gave a brief speech thanking them all for coming, and she thanked Melissa personally for making her present even more special. At last the farewells were all made and coats collected.

Nicholas took Melissa's arm as he walked her to his car. "Kissed and dismissed," he said smiling. "Did you like her?"

"I did. Who couldn't?"

He laughed rather grimly. "My wife and mother loathed each other. Two prima donnas in one family was one too many." He waited for the lights to change before escorting her across. "I hope I left you enough space to enjoy yourself. You did seem to get on better without me." His dry tone wasn't unkind, but it irritated her.

"I would have enjoyed it more," she said evenly, "if you had given me some information in advance. Like your name. Like who your mother was. Like what you were giving her for her birthday."

"Don't be absurd. You'd never have come. And she would have missed out on that perfectly wonderful exposition from my very own tame Byzantine expert. But I'm sorry you got such a fright. You went sheet white and I really did think you were going to pass out—I sent Sophie to pick up the pieces. I didn't intend to give you such a shock, but I did want you to see where the Perissos Bible was going and I wanted to explain the significance of what we gave her tonight."

"You don't need to. Sophie explained. I understand." She felt weary now and a sense of anti-climax filled her with sudden depression. "You don't need to drive me back. A taxi will be fine."

"It will not. My car is right here. Did you enjoy any of it?"

"Yes, of course. Your mother is—what is she? Astonishing, delightful, charming, kind and a brilliant entertainer. Your family mostly ditto. But it was very uncomfortable, as you knew it must be. To be dropped into that with no background information was embarrassing and aimed, I think, to make me look and feel a fool."

He opened the car door for her. "No one thought you a fool—the very opposite in fact." She noticed he didn't deny her accusation. "Everyone was fascinated, myself included. Did Sophie tell you about why the bible was sold in the first place?"

"Yes. But I wasn't to know that last May, was I? And I had a job to do for my employer. No one's in business to be sentimental, however sympathetic one might feel." She knew she sounded petulant and changed her tone with an effort. "What will Madame do with it now? Give it back to the monastery?"

He shrugged. "I would think so. A beautiful thing to be locked away from the public gaze for perhaps another millennium, though I doubt it. There are only a few monks left in the monastery, and when they have gone the government will undoubtedly claim and display it."

"Sophie said something—"

"She does speak on occasions," he said encouragingly as Melissa left the sentence hanging. "What did she say?"

"Something about your wife trying to get hold of the bible to stop you getting it, to spite you. Is that why—is that what you thought I was doing, buying it on her behalf?"

121

"Something like that," he said. "That is in fact what you were doing."

Shock jolted through her.

"I don't believe this! I was not. I promise you I wasn't!" She was shaken by his accusation, after all this time.

"You didn't know. I came to believe that you didn't know." He didn't want to admit to recording her telephone call to Jeremy. "But Clive Mann knew, and that's why he sent you out to do the dirty work, rather than someone more experienced, and that's why he didn't go himself. If he hadn't known there was something odd going on, he wouldn't have sent you on your own. My wife, who is nothing if not devious, got Rambiris to retrieve it back from you."

"But why? Even supposing this fantastic story is true, why? If she was trying to prevent you from getting it, she wouldn't have told Rambiris to steal it back. It doesn't make sense."

"Yes it does. She just hadn't calculated that Rambiris would do another double-cross and sell it again—to me. She herself had no interest in the bible. She knew I wanted it so she got Mann's to buy it from Rambiris on her behalf before I could. I would never have discovered what had happened to it, or if I did find it at Mann's, the price would have doubled. *Un point* to Marie Claude, *nul point* to Nicholas. If you had brought it back to London, she would have owed Clive Mann the money, but if you came home empty-handed she wouldn't have to pay anything, so she suggested to Rambiris that he should steal it back from you."

"But she had no way of knowing that it would be in my room. Something like that would be put in a safe deposit."

"What safe deposit, where? As you so rightly pointed out to me." he said. "Rambiris was quite happy to double-cross Marie Claude, and Clive Mann and you. I daresay me, too, if the opportunity had arisen."

She was silent for a moment, thinking. "But you said you'd arranged with Rambiris weeks before—what if he hadn't been able to get it back?"

"He'd have just disappeared before our appointment, and I would have been left licking my wounds. Any old way, Marie Claude and Rambiris would have achieved their objectives."

"I still don't see what they were trying to do," Melissa said. "What was the point?"

"Rambiris was making as much money out of one item as he could. Quite clever really."

"And your wife? What was she trying to do?"

He shrugged. "Oh, scoring points, I guess. Anything to irritate or annoy."

She had a distinct feeling that there was more to it than he was saying.

"Why couldn't you have explained all this?" She felt confused and hurt. "I assume you realised I was telling the truth while I was still on Mixos, otherwise you wouldn't have paid my fine or the plane ticket."

"I didn't know for sure, but Kiprionidis was quite stuffy about sending young women to prison, however silly they've been. As for explaining," he exhaled sharply, "I'm afraid I just didn't feel like it."

His offhand tone angered her. "Well, I don't intend to owe you anything, and I want to deal with it as quickly as possible. You promised to give me your name and address so that I can repay you."

"Well, my name is Nicholas Thauros, as you've no doubt discovered." He took a small notebook out of his pocket, and at the next red light scribbled some figures down before tearing out the page and giving it to her. "And these are my bank details. You're a fool to do this, Melissa, but I hope you're satisfied."

Any residual pleasure she had felt from the evening drained away, and he drove in silence and deposited her back at the flat.

CHAPTER TEN

The weeks dragged on, cold, windy and wet. The long working days were tiring in themselves, but the extra work in the restaurant was wearing her down, and gradually she was getting more colds and coughs.

By December the inevitable happened and the restaurant had to take on a new waitress who didn't cough. At least she could come home from work and not have to go out again, but the relief that this brought was offset by less earning power. She contemplated her bank statement and the interest charges on the so-far small overdraft, and knew that she would have to write to both Clive Mann and Nicholas Thauros to request a reduced payment until she could get another job. The thought of this humiliation made her cringe.

Will Newington rang, for by no means the first time. He'd asked her out on several occasions, but she'd seldom been able to go and ridiculously she worried about Nicholas finding out. Will was cheerful, amusing and unthreatening. They made a date for Saturday lunch and she would go down to her grandparents in Hampshire in the afternoon.

He took her to a proper pub in Barnes, which had a roaring fire and wonderful steaks, but by that time she looked, sounded and felt thick with cough and cold.

"Will, I'm really sorry. I shouldn't have come. I've sneezed so much I've probably given you whatever bug it is."

"I doubt it," he said comfortably. "Madame had a filthy cold last week and I haven't caught that."

"Poor Madame. I hope she didn't have any singing engagements." She sneezed into her handkerchief for the umpteenth time. "Do tell me about your mother—she

124

fascinates me. She looks incredibly young to have all you grown-up children. Or is that being too curious?"

"Curious? No, of course it isn't. She fascinates me, too. I sometimes wonder how on earth we can be her children; we're so English and she's so Greek. Well, her family came from an island in the Aegean—not at all wealthy, but Grandfather Molinaris owned his own fishing boat so they were better off than most, I think. When she was seventeen Alexis Thauros came to the Sporades to set up a ferry connection."

Melissa's memory clicked. The ferries coming in and out of the Sporades islands had 'Thauros' painted on them.

Will was still explaining. "Apparently he heard her sing in the taverna and fell in love with her! He was thirty when she was born! I've never been able to fathom it. Can you imagine? He'd had two wives already and there's a nightmarish mass of Greek sort of half cousins nearly a generation older than us. Anyway, he fell for her, paid a vast bride price to the Molinaris family and married her. She had Nicholas nine months later."

"Did she love him, do you think?"

"She says she loved him as much as an uneducated and ignorant seventeen-year-old could love. Alexis was very kind to her and developed this gorgeous voice she had. He educated her and gave her voice training and created her career. There was money pouring out of every seam as you can imagine. He could have created her career even if she hadn't got a voice. Then, when she was twenty-six or so and Nicholas was eight, he died of a heart attack. He left her several houses, and a socking great yacht, and God knows what else. All this after looking after his two previous families, mind you. He was rich, but he was also damn generous. Then, at a concert in Athens she met Papa. She was twenty-seven and he was forty-five. She's always said he was a boy compared with Alexis. I suppose some women just suit older men. His wife had died of cancer and Michael was about twelve."

125

"He's very young at heart."

Will grinned. "He's great actually. Good fun. Wise old bird, too."

"What happened to Michael? Was it an accident?" She was suddenly anxious, feeling she might be prying. "Sorry—do you mind me asking?"

"Michael? Oh, his leg? He was on hols with his parents, and he got polio. He was very young; five or six I think. One minute he was swimming and mucking about and the next he was paralysed. Unbelievable really. He has a caliper. I think sometimes it makes his back ache and he gets grumpy, but Sophie's amazing. Anyway, he's never as bad as Nicholas, and Sophie's amazing with him, too."

This was dangerous ground and she should avoid it, she knew, but her curiosity got the better of her.

"What do you mean 'he's never as bad as Nicholas'?"

He rocked his beer mug thoughtfully. "Sophie just has the right way of saying things—or not saying anything, and she's quite—um—brisk. You know, she'll shove a cushion behind him or kick a stool under his leg while saying something else. Not sugary. No 'Are you all right, darlings'."

"And Nicholas?"

"I dunno really. She just doesn't take offence. And God knows Nick gives it! Oh!" He looked comically contrite. "Hope you don't mind me saying that. Do you like him?" She laughed till she coughed, waving her hand as if to fend off the very idea. Will looked relieved. "Don't get me wrong—Nick can be great. He's just ultra miserable and unpleasant at the moment—has been for ages. Anyway, Sophie kind of absorbs it without getting uptight, while the rest of us back off. Can't explain really. The thing about Sophie is, she hasn't any hang-ups about herself, so if she hasn't caused Michael to be grumpy, or Nick to be foul, something else has, so she doesn't have to apologise or feel it's her fault. No, I haven't quite got it. I'm not an analyst. She has a very strong faith—maybe that's it."

He hadn't really told her what she wanted to know, which was why Nicholas was so bad-tempered. Her throat was now very sore and it hurt to swallow and to breathe.

"I can see why Michael could be grumpy—but why should Nicholas be so—" she hesitated. "So unpleasant?"

"Well, it's not surprising really, is it? She's been so perfectly awful, you know, you can't blame him. But sympathy doesn't go down a bundle."

"Am I being amazingly thick, and should I know? Sympathy about what?" She knew she was being disingenuous, and felt guilty, pumping this nice boy for information. Will looked rather uncomfortable.

"Oh Lord. I imagined you knew. Everyone else does. It's been all over the glossy mags for months—years even."

"I don't read them," she said rather shortly. Will looked amazed at this information.

"I thought all girls read glossy mags. What do you do in the hairdresser?"

"I hardly ever go to the hairdresser." She laughed, hoping that she didn't sound stuffy and pompous, and ended up coughing. Will blinked in surprise.

"Ah. Right. OK. Well, his marriage is falling apart. He married the French model Marie Claude de Rimanac when he was twenty-four and she was twenty, and as far as I can make out it was a disaster from the start. My parents tried to prevent it, and I suppose their disapproval made him more stubborn. He sure is stubborn. Madame went all Greek and body language and my father went all British and stiff. Frightful ructions. It was a horrible time. Nick was supposed to be training in architecture, but often trailed round the world in her wake trying to keep her on the rails, and it was all perfectly awful. It was obvious to everyone that she just wanted his money, and he simply wouldn't accept it." He paused to drink some beer. "She slept with every celebrity around, but he was furious if anyone accused her of being a gold-digger and a nymphomaniac. All very humiliating." He fiddled with his beer mat. "Mind you, she *was* gorgeous—still is come to that—and rather exciting. Madame never had make-up teams, and hairdressers and designers and dressers and photographers and God knows what else. The lifestyle was lavish and Nick provided it." His mouth twisted slightly. "He doesn't like the endless social round and she does. He's private and she's very public. In the end, he did put his foot down and stopped bankrolling her—she earns a fortune of her own—and he stopped chasing round after her. She accused him of deserting her, even though he had a job which he'd virtually abandoned. The whole thing has been a complete nightmare. We all loathed her, which didn't help, and then quite suddenly last year Nick became totally impossible—horrible really. The parents told him to go and lick his wounds in their house in Greece, as he was quite unbearable here. He bit everyone's head off. No one would speak to him except Dad and Sophie. Well, I exaggerate a bit, but you know what I mean."

Melissa looked at him aghast.

"When did all this happen? I mean, when was he in Greece?"

"Oh. Last summer. He disappeared for about six or seven months, came back in the autumn. Marie Claude was livid—deprived of her rows, I suppose—and never stopped hitting the headlines with some new man or other. Nick just kept his head down."

"But she knew where he was?"

"Oh, I suppose so. The house is no secret, as he built it. Madame invited her once, for Nick's sake, but it definitely wasn't her sort of place. Not smart enough. No jet set. I bet she never bargained on how angry he was, and how tough that made him. She accused him of having affairs, deserting her, beating her up, depriving her of money, taking her cars away, throwing her out of the house—which was ridiculous as there are several houses, and she was hardly homeless. You name it, he'd done it. The tabloids adored it."

She wondered if any of Marie Claude's accusations were true. Will was obviously very fond of his half-brother, but she

128

wondered if he knew that Nicholas was involved in drugs. She thought Will would defend him to the hilt whether any of it was true or not.

With appalled understanding, she thought of her experience in Greece. Of all times and of all people to have chosen to tangle with!

"You said he built the house?" she said, before remembering. "Of course, he's an architect."

"Well, he designed it. He gave it to Madame for her fortieth birthday present. Sort of an apology for Marie Claude, I think. It's lovely, a traditional Greek house built on a cliff above a beach. It's on an island in the Sporades, where her family came from. We used to go for family holidays on the island, staying with aunts and uncles, and then Nick built the house for the parents. Madame and Richard usually go several times a year, when they want peace and quiet, but this year Nick was there from about March and we were all told to leave him severely alone until he'd sorted himself out. I don't know that he has really, although he is much better. They're getting divorced, thank God, and it's all rather nasty." He glanced at her uncomfortably. "I think I've been a bit indiscreet. I shouldn't have said all that. You won't go blabbing to anyone, will you? Nick's had enough problems without me adding to them." A sudden thought struck him and he looked suddenly apprehensive. "Melissa, you're not a reporter, are you?"

"For goodness sake!" A sudden laugh caught at her throat and made her cough again. "Of course not! And I won't mention it to anyone, I promise you. I'm sorry I was so curious, and I shouldn't have asked. It was just that you all assumed that I knew things, and I didn't, and it was a slightly awkward situation."

She was nervous that he might now ask her what she was doing at Madame's party, and how she had met Nicholas in the first place and as she had no idea how to answer, a change of subject seemed desirable. She turned the conversation to safer and wider channels until her coughing was so painful that she asked him to take her home.

His anxious concern for her was rather touching and she promised that she would go to bed and postpone going home to her grandparents until the morning. Bed was certainly the best place to be. By the time she got back to the flat she felt shaky, and hot and cold by turn. Every cough hurt her chest, and her whole desire was to sleep. After phoning home to postpone her arrival, she swallowed two paracetamols and went to bed.

Sunday morning found her drugged and aching, nose running, throat glands swollen, sweaty and coughing. She dragged herself into the kitchen for a coffee, felt ridiculously wobbly and retired back to bed and to sleep.

The doorbell rang, ignorable and of no interest, and after a time her bedroom door opened.

"There you are, pet." Her flatmate's delectable Geordie irony dropped into her consciousness. "Sleeping Beauty. I don't think she'll be very chatty."

Melissa opened her eyes reluctantly, to find Nicholas Thauros standing, hands in pockets, looking down at her with concern in his eyes.

"Oh dear, oh dear. I do pick my moments, don't I? You certainly don't look your normal elegant self."

Melissa looked at him blankly and then at the clock. She groaned and grabbed her phone, only to find the battery flat.

"What are you doing here?" Her voice was a croaky whisper. "Please go away." He ignored her, sitting on the edge of the bed and laying the back of his hand on her forehead.

"You, my girl, have one hell of a temperature."

"Go away." Her breathing rattled.

"No. You need a doctor and probably antibiotics. Your mobile wasn't working and Will thought you might have died in the night. He told me that you intended to stagger out to Hampshire on the train, which didn't seem very sensible, and asked me to make sure you didn't."

"How dare you?" She heaved herself up on one elbow in astonished outrage, which was less effective as a whisper, and coughed painfully, clutching her breastbone. "Don't you try bullying me again. Go away. If I want to go home, I'll go home, with or without your permission." The whisper died away to nothing.

"For heaven's sake, Melissa! You're not really considering it, are you? You'd pass out in the street." He obviously wasn't being unkind, and his concern overcame her defences. She lay back, defeated.

"What's their phone number? I'll tell them you're ill."

"Oh God! Don't you dare!" She choked on a half laugh that was near to tears. "Don't even think about it. A strange man ringing to say I'm ill? I'd never hear the end of it." The whisper failed again and the idea was so appalling that tears, to her shame, pricked at her eyelids. She shut them tightly.

"You idiot! I'm not that tactless! Come on, what's the number. You've got no voice and your phone's dead. Don't be irritating about it."

She gave up and told him the number. He grinned encouragingly at her anxious face. Melissa reluctantly admitted to herself that he told the most effortless and flawless lies. He was Dr Michael Newington. She hadn't just got flu, but pneumonia as well. If she was to go home, it must be by private ambulance or fetched by car. She must go to bed for a week. He would prescribe antibiotics. It would be better if she stayed where she was, in the warmth. He would be looking in regularly. Nasty thing, this flu, everyone seemed to be catching it. Could Mrs Scott-Mackenzie look after her granddaughter? Oh dear, her husband not well, he was so sorry. Flu and heart problems were not the best of bedfellows of course, perhaps it would be wiser not to. He understood. If she became worse he would let them know; no, he didn't think Melissa should try to speak; she had no voice for a start, strain on the lungs, not a good idea. Yes, pneumonia was quite nasty, but modern drugs effective. Hospital a possibility if she didn't respond. His telephone

131

number, of course." He gave them Michael's practice number.

"Such lies!" Melissa whispered. "You make her out to be a lousy grandmother, and she isn't. She has awful problems."

"Well, don't let's add to them," he cut her off briskly. "I didn't make all that up. Your chest is gurgling like water going down the plug, and any minute now you'll drown."

He dialled another number, and apparently got an answering machine. "Michael, it's Nico. A convoluted message from Will who took Melissa Scott-Mackenzie to lunch yesterday and thinks she's dying of pneumonia. Please would you go and see her on her death bed armed with some miracle drug. I suppose I'm doing his dirty work because he thinks you'll send the bill to me." He gave Melissa's address and mobile number and plugged her phone in.

She felt extremely ill and out of control. "Who was that you rang?"

"My brother. He's a doctor."

"You can't do that!"

"I can't do what?"

"A private doctor—I can't afford that! You must stop him. Oh! Ow! Damn this cough."

"Melissa, stop fussing. I'm leaving, you'll be glad to hear, as I've no desire to catch whatever you've got. Will was genuinely very worried about you, but didn't know what to do. I'm sorry to be so bossy, but you really are quite ill. Please don't be childish about a bill. I know you can't bear to be in my debt, but it's your problem, not mine, money being something I have, like a large nose, or two left feet. Unfortunate, but you just have to learn to live with it."

She tried for some extra oxygen.

"I wasn't looking forward to going home, but I honestly don't think I need a doctor." She held his gaze with an effort. "Please cancel your brother. And tell Will—" she stopped and coughed.

"I'll tell Will that you wish the flu on him for his indiscretion, is that it? It wasn't his fault; you hadn't actually

132

told him that you thought I was the most poisonous man you'd ever met. Next time he takes you out you can."

"He won't, I won't," she muttered. For Nicholas to think that she considered him poisonous made her feel despicable. She knew her face was scarlet and hoped he'd think it was the fever.

Michael had come later in the morning, cheerfully sympathetic and efficiently wielding stethoscope and thermometer. He turned her embarrassment at having his Sunday with the family interrupted by saying that he was glad to be out of the madhouse. In any case, he said, grinning, he made his living by it, and there was no one he'd rather send a bill to than his brother. He listened to the wheezing lungs attentively, made her take a double dose of pills under his eye and made her repeat the subsequent dosage to make sure she had taken it in.

"If it isn't pneumonia now, it nearly is. Stay in bed, keep warm, plenty of liquids. You go nowhere for at least a week. OK?"

"A week? I've got a job! Surely I'll be better before that?"

"No, you won't. You'll feel like cooked spaghetti. If you get up too soon you really will develop pneumonia and end up in hospital. I'll do you a note for the boss. Now, take the pills, drink lots, don't eat junk food, and stay in bed. I'll look in tomorrow."

"Oh! No, you mustn't!" she said, positively horrified. "I promise to do all that, really, I will, but you mustn't come again."

He grinned and got up from the bed, clicking his caliper straight. "You sound like Sophie promising to rest when I know she has no intention of doing so. I can be terribly fierce, I warn you. Can't your parents come and fetch you home? There's nothing like a mother clucking round to encourage a speedy recovery."

"She doesn't cluck," she whispered, unable to face explaining grandparents, "and he's got a heart problem."

"Well, you're better off here then," he said pragmatically. "I'll see you tomorrow."

The week was punctuated by Michael's visits, Will's phone calls, and a prompt delivery of fresh fruit, vegetables and meat from Waitrose. No one owned up to this, and her suspicion that it must have come from Nicholas was unprovable. Her flatmates had had no qualms about cooking the food, and helping to eat it, and Melissa perforce had had to eat it, too. The flu subsided gradually, and when her voice returned more or less to normal she shakily took herself back to work.

If the flu abated, other problems did not, and the financial demands on a reduced income became heavier by the day. Her job seemed more tiring, and the personnel problems more complicated. There was no time to look for a second job, and in any case, she still felt utterly exhausted when she got back to the flat.

There was very little she could do to reduce expenditure. Already economising at almost every level, clothes, food and travel pared to a minimum, Christmas now loomed with extra spending for presents whichever way she looked at it. She viewed her overdraft and iniquitous interest and bank charges with dismay. The letter to Clive Mann, explaining some of her difficulties and asking to reduce the standing order by half was a sweat-inducing lesson in humility, and the prospect of writing a similar letter to Nicholas Thauros was equally difficult. She had already forced herself to write thank you notes to him for both Galina's birthday party and for Michael's medical attentions, which had had to be sent via the only relevant address she could find, which was Michael Newington's Sloane Street practice.

She was strongly tempted to reduce the standing order without informing him, guessing that he was unlikely to check his bank statements, and even if he did would he care if a negligible monthly repayment was reduced to an even more negligible amount? After all, he had never wanted repayment. She remembered, however, her avowed intentions of full reimbursement and shrank from his real or imagined contempt. He had not attempted to contact her again; a fact which was both a relief and, surprisingly, a disappointment. There was a subconscious desire to see him—but not quite subconscious. The memory of his mouth on hers and his hands touching her, those casual caresses of a man accustomed to women, would slide into her mind and cause her breath to shorten and nerve ends to flare. It was odd, she reflected, occasionally leafing through a magazine in the stationers, how you never saw a photograph or heard a name until it was familiar, and then it never ceased to shout from the page. Marie Claude de Rimanac featured prominently on the catwalks and strutted the pages of every fashion magazine. Nicholas Thauros featured not at all, but then a man who dealt in drugs would probably not seek the public eye. The continuing itch of him in her mind worried her. But whatever her wandering thoughts, the unpalatable problem remained: the repayments would have to be reduced.

In the meantime, Christmas was only a week away. She sent Christmas messages to as many friends as possible on Facebook and email, and finished wrapping the few and inexpensive presents for her grandparents and, separately, for Johnny and Sarah and Sam.

On the face of it, Johnny couldn't have found himself a better wife than his pretty, no-nonsense, hard-working, competent Yorkshire Sarah, and it still hadn't worked. Would it have worked if his twin hadn't died?

She shook herself back from the past, took a pad from the table and began to draft the letter to Nicholas once more.

Dear Mr Thauros. Mr Thauros had kissed her.

Dear Nicholas. Nicholas had been so weary of her silly scruples.

Dear Mr Thauros. Mr Thauros had been very kind when she'd had the flu.

Dear Nicholas. Nicholas had had a case full of drugs and syringes.

She looked at the first word in faint horror. Could one begin a letter 'Mr Thauros' and leave out the 'dear'?

Later she put the stamped envelope in with a Christmas card to Sophie, reminding her of who she was, asking after the baby, mentioning what a happy evening her mother-in-law's birthday had been, and would she be very kind and forward the enclosed envelope to Mr Thauros as she didn't know his address. Hoped she had escaped the beastly flu and do have a Happy Christmas.

Her grandparents had, she realised, gone to a lot of trouble to make it a good Christmas. They played family bridge and she and Johnny walked on the Downs, discussing their grandfather's bankruptcy and frail health, the selling of the house in a bad market, the pros and cons of moving them.

They both stayed the full week, to be with Brig and Mops over the anniversary of the accident. It was always the worst time in the entire year.

Clive Mann had not responded to her letter asking to reduce the monthly payments, and nor had Nicholas Thauros.

She had not told Nicholas that she had decided to terminate the payments, that his wholly unasked-for interference was now placed in the Recycle Bin. Past, forgotten, ignored. No more contacts, humiliations or embarrassments.

Oh no. She hadn't done that. She hadn't swallowed her pride and got rid of the whole thing, finally and forever. She was like some beaten wife perpetually returning for more abuse. She tried to imagine how she would feel now if she had written a different letter and her insides felt like a crow's nest. But it would only have stung for a little while, surely. Broken pride simply couldn't be that painful.

CHAPTER ELEVEN

Irene, the receptionist, had buzzed him to say Miss Scott-Mackenzie had arrived and now he finished signing his letters and shuffled the drawings vaguely together. He took a thin file out of his briefcase and opened it. On the top was her letter, written just before Christmas, but which had reached him about mid-January, with a scribble from Sophie on the back of the envelope. 'Sorry' heavily underlined. 'Came with Christmas card and got buried. Hope not urgent.'

He studied the letter again. How long had she struggled over it, he wondered? Those considered phrases never dropped spontaneously from Miss Scott-Mackenzie's keyboard. The signature was firm and clear—no apology for its length. He found himself exasperated again by both Melissa and himself, puzzled by his own motives and by hers, in prolonging this—connection—if that was the right word for it. Was it just pride that prevented her from letting go of this bone? And why did the memory of her keep disturbing his thoughts; the coppery hair and greeny-grey eyes, the feel of her collarbone under his fingers, his mouth touching hers. He wondered whether to be pleasant or unpleasant. It might be easier to persuade her to let go of the bone if he was pleasant. So, he would be pleasant.

She was studying the information brochures in reception and he watched her for a moment before she became aware of him. She had dressed carefully, in a suit which was neat and businesslike; not cheap, but not expensive either. Make-up redone after a day at the office, that weighty gleaming hair clipped neatly at the nape of her neck. He suppressed an urge to slide his hand under it. Clean shoes. Thinner. Nervousness disguised under a faint belligerence. He smiled, but neither shook hands nor proffered the social cheek.

"Hullo, Melissa."

She didn't like the chair. It was too big for her; too deep. She sat forwards, her legs neatly slanted sideways, back straight, hands resting in her lap.

"Thank you for coming. I hope it wasn't too short notice."

"Not at all," she said politely. "It's March and I wrote in December." Was that sarcasm, he wondered?

"I'm sorry. Sophie buried your letter. She's usually quite efficient, but what with a new baby and Christmas, perhaps it's understandable." He didn't add that he hadn't replied for well over a month. Irene brought coffee and he wished her a nice weekend. The file lay closed on the table, and he permitted a short silence.

"You wanted to terminate our financial arrangements, I think?"

"No" she said. "No, I didn't. I wanted your—I hoped just to have your permission to change them. For a while." She hesitated under his unchanging expression. "Just until—"

"Just until when?" he asked gently.

"Until I can—um—clear my overdraft. It seems so stupid to be paying the bank interest, when I could be paying you."

"I see. So, you clear your overdraft, and then start the original payments again?" She nodded. "Won't the same thing happen all over again?"

She looked blank for a moment. "Oh. No. I hope not. I'll have another job by then."

He raised his eyebrows. "Another job? What happened to Human Resources then?"

"No, no. I've still got that one. I mean, I'll have another job as well."

"Waitressing? What happened to the last one? I hope it wasn't me taking you away on a Saturday night?"

"No," she said hastily, "of course not. I got ill and they had to replace me."

"I remember. So, like before? Waitressing?"

138

She nodded. "Possibly. Maybe something at the weekends."

"I see," he said again, and continued in the same reasonable voice. "And then you'll have some more wages and pay off some more debt, and you'll have no time off, and you'll get exhausted and ill and you'll lose the job and then you'll write me another letter. Is that it?"

She looked horrified. Rendered speechless. He regarded her steadily.

"Melissa, this is ridiculous. Can we dispose of it once and for all? I don't want repayment, I never did. I'm a wealthy man—the amount is negligible to me, but not to you. You are twenty-three, in your first job—"

"Second."

"Earning a reasonable salary, but one which cannot possibly sustain what you are proposing if you are to live the normal life a young woman should be living. If you have a second job you will have no friends, no social life, no enjoyment, and you will be exhausted and get ill again. You have to forget it. Write it off to experience."

"I can't," she said angrily.

"You could. Don't be so stubborn. What is this? An exercise in masochism?"

"No! Of course not!"

"Well, I certainly don't understand, but not for want of trying. Why can't you just close this chapter? Is it to annoy me, or to prove some particular point about your ethics being on a higher plane than anyone else's?" He was aware that the pleasantness was slipping.

"Just let me pay back what I can," she said.

"No."

"I shall just alter the amount then."

"And I shall instruct my bank to refuse the payments."

"You can't," she said, rather uncertainly.

"Of course I can. In my business, I have to be able to prevent illegal payments. Otherwise I could be accused of accepting bribes."

"This isn't a bribe!" She flushed with indignation.

He closed his eyes briefly and repressed the laughter.

"No. Of course not. At least, not a very big one. Look, why don't you think of it as a loan, and pay me back when you're a millionairess?"

"It's not a joke to me."

"Nor me, I can assure you. How about it? I can even have it put in writing if you like."

"I don't see why you won't accept regular repayments. If the bank won't accept them I'll just send them here. I know the address now."

He laughed. "I'll tear up the cheques."

"I'll send cash in the post."

"Do you think I can't tear up cash?"

"That," she said flatly, "is up to you. I will have paid it anyway."

"God preserve me from stubborn women!" He couldn't prevent the smile. "I think I'm having to admit defeat." He thought for a moment. "All right. You want to pay something monthly, but less than at present, is that it?"

"Yes. Please."

"Then I will accept that, but I have some conditions of my own."

"Conditions?" she said, wary. "What conditions?"

"If you impose conditions on me—after all, you insist on owing me the money—then I have the right to impose certain conditions on you. Is that fair?"

She was still wary. "I suppose so."

"Well, do you accept?"

"I don't know what they are." He just waited. "I suppose so," she said again, uncertainly. "All right, what?"

"You may repay me on condition that you deliver fifty pounds in cash during the first weekend of every month, to me in person, at a place and time designated by me."

To his considerable satisfaction she was so taken aback she couldn't think of anything to say.

Eventually she took a breath. "This is ridiculous! You can't possibly mean it! And fifty pounds a month! I'll be a pensioner before I'm done!"

"I do mean it. Those are my conditions, and if you insist on a repayment plan, that's the plan. You need not agree to it, in which case you must drop the whole thing. I did take my payment, you know, and I did tell you that I considered it paid in full. Or had you forgotten?"

"No," she said in a small voice, and flushed redder. "Look, I've got a good job and I really can manage more than fifty pounds a month. Fifty pounds a week wouldn't be difficult."

"No. Those are my conditions. It's either pay up or forget it. Of course, you can stop at any time, but if you do, you can't start again."

She looked disconcerted and stared at him wordlessly.

"It'll take longer," he went on, "but at least you might eat in between. And you won't have to get another job. And you might even get some social life. I take it the unhelpful Jeremy has gone the way of all things. Is there a new boyfriend?"

"How do you know about Jeremy?" Her eyes were suspicious. "I never said anything about Jeremy."

"Your fund-raising conversation with him from Mixos was recorded. I was having a spot of bother with my wife at the time, and all phone calls were recorded just for safety."

"How underhand can you get?" She was mortified and angry and he was apologetic.

"The recording wasn't directed at you. Well, is there a new boyfriend?"

"Not really."

"What does 'not really' mean?" Her eyes said 'mind your own business' and he laughed.

"My conditions stand. Do you accept? Yes, and you pay it off at fifty pounds a month, no and you forget the whole thing. I know which one I would advise."

141

He knew she was out-manoeuvred. "I suppose so. Yes, I accept. I don't understand—you can't want—why in person?" He ignored her question and got up.

"Come along, Miss Scott-Mackenzie, it's the end of a hard week. Our business negotiations are finalised, I think." He shrugged on his jacket.

She got up, too. "Why can't I send it? I mean, why do I have to bring it?" He ushered her out into reception, holding her coat for her.

"Punishment, girl," he said quietly. "But you don't have to come, you know. If you insist on paying, you must pay in person, that's all."

She was obviously bewildered by the lack of alternatives, and he propelled her into the lift, into the small underground car park and finally into his car. Ignoring her protestations, he drove her back to the flat, through the March rain flurries, asking where she'd spent Christmas, how her grandparents were. Sophie's baby was a girl, Michael must feed it neat brandy because it slept so obligingly.

Her street was full of parked cars and he stopped in the middle of the road, blocking the traffic both ways.

"Look," she said desperately, "I can't—"

He was brisk. "See you at six-thirty pm at my office on the first Friday in April. In exactly two weeks' time. Or not, of course,".

There was a cacophony of angry horns and he left her standing helplessly in the doorway.

She felt as if she'd been hit by a tornado. Five minutes of his time and—what? She changed into jeans and allowed herself to be furious and insulted and grateful as she slumped into one of the ancient armchairs. He had made it clear that he considered her behaviour childish, and now she thought it was, too. Why should she make such a fuss about something which he obviously had not considered worth even thinking about? She had been a blip on the end of his Friday, to the extent that he'd deposited her back here as if she were too incompetent to find her way back on her own. On an impulse, she ran back downstairs and along the street to the off-licence for a bottle of wine; by the time she got back the brown paper wrapping was sodden. She cracked the screw top trying to feel cross, but instead felt a flutter of anticipation.

A fortnight later she took her fifty pounds to his office. He gave her a small package in a Jiffy envelope which he said was a receipt, told her when and where to come next time and disappeared. The anticipation died into anti-climax. The exchange had taken less than thirty seconds. She was left staring at the package, reluctant to open it on the spot as the reception area was still busy. When she got home she tore the seal cautiously and withdrew a little ceramic dolphin, at the point of leaving the water, the glaze an incandescence of fuchsia and raspberry and black. There was writing on one side. '£50 Received' and the date. The writing did not rub off. He had written it before she brought the money. It was beautiful.

Towards the end of April, she put fifty pounds in an envelope and sent it under confidential cover to his office to arrive on the due date. It came back in the following Monday's post. The notes had their numbers cut off. There was a business card paperclipped to them with 'Last chance' scrawled across it, and underneath 'Sat. 2nd June 7pm here' with an arrow pointing to an address which wasn't the office. She nearly cried at the waste.

On June 2nd at precisely seven o'clock, she stood on the wide stone threshold of an enormous house in Eaton Square. The door was intimidatingly black and the doorbell one of those ceramic marbles set in an expanse of polished brass. She pushed her thumb hard on to it in a last-minute bid to maintain the higher ground. When he opened the door, he eyed her jeans and jacket, ignoring the envelope she held out.

"Come in."

"I only have to give you this," she said, hoping to sound firm, but in fact sounding apprehensive. "Coming in wasn't part of the deal."

"It is now. I'm not going to eat you, so don't look so nervous."

He sat her in his elegant, rather French drawing room, and gave her a gin and tonic without asking her. She coughed at the strength of it. A cat came and sat on her knee.

"He's called Cat." He poured himself a whisky and sat down opposite her. "You look better," he commented. "A bit."

"Better?" She was startled.

"Less thin."

There didn't seem to be anything to say to that, so she continued stroking the purring animal, and he was silent, watching her. She wanted to leave, but the tumbler sat on the coffee table, accusingly full.

"Don't you like gin and tonic?"

"It's very strong."

"I thought you'd want it strong. You looked as if you needed it. Dutch courage sort of thing." The tumbler was further diluted but full again, and his voice had a smile in it. "You looked like a Greek cat, standing on the doorstep. One false move and you'd have run."

She took a healthy gulp and glanced up at him. He was relaxed in his chair, the tumbler balanced on the arm. His eyes were amused, not unkind.

"I nearly did." She smiled faintly.

"That's better," he said. "More smiles, please, otherwise we'll have a very grave evening."

"Evening?" She was alarmed. "I'm not staying—just this drink and then I'm off."

"There's the Greek cat again. What were you expecting?"

"I was expecting," she said, "to deliver that envelope and go home, which is what I intend to do."

"Well, it's not my intention. I told you it was a punishment, so you must take it like a man. Woman rather. My intention is to take you out for dinner. Fishbones for the cat, if you take my meaning."

"But I can't. I mean I'm not—" She looked helplessly at her jeans.

"No, I can see you're not. Well, it can't be the Café Royal, they won't let you in. It'll have to be more downmarket this time. Wear something more festive next time."

She was horrified. "There won't be a next time."

"You won't come? Well, that was my original suggestion, if you remember, which you turned down flat. So not coming again is pure cowardice." His teasing didn't amuse her.

"But you can't! I mean, that's not fair! You said I just had to bring it, and I have. You can't go on adding conditions."

"Indeed I can. It's hardly unreasonable. You have to eat after all, and as it happens, you'll be paying for it." She was momentarily silenced by his weird logic. She took refuge in the gin and tonic.

"I think you're—you're despicable." She had a sudden inspiration. "Anyway, I'm going out tonight."

His eyebrows rose in mock astonishment. "Have you only just remembered? What a perfectly hopeless liar you are. I noticed it the first time I met you! I think you're quite extraordinary, Miss Scott-Mackenzie. I'm going to take you for a meal, not seduce you. Most girls would be suitably grateful."

"Maybe." She refused to respond to the teasing. "I'm not most girls."

"You most certainly are not. I never normally have this trouble. You don't know what you're doing to my self-esteem. Here I am, a perfectly ordinary man, no white socks; I don't drink Babycham or drive a Lada, and you say I'm what? Despicable? Now who's being unfair?"

"Oh, stop it!" She didn't know whether to laugh or be angry. "Look, I wasn't expecting this, and I was going to meet some friends at a pub. It's very kind of you—the drink and everything, but—"

"Kind? Wherever did you get that idea? You insist on paying me money which I don't want, so I'm just making you

145

suffer for it. Don't be under the misconception that I'm being kind." She wished at that moment for cheerful, uncomplicated Will, and the thought of an evening in the company of this sharp and dangerous man was infinitely alarming. She found she had finished her drink and he had given her another. She looked at it in dismay and wondered if he was trying to make her drunk. She had another sip and mentally straightened her backbone.

"I don't understand you at all, but as usual you seem to get your own way. If you intend to take me out for a meal I expect it will be rather more tedious for you than for me. I just can't imagine why, that's all."

She looked him straight in the eye, and he smiled again, lazily.

"The gin has injected some fight. I thought it might. Now, what will be the result of some decent food and wine, I wonder? I never did think you were very compliant. There were odd little signs of the bitten biting back."

"That's not quite right."

"No? What about a very hard slap and a very hard bite, not to mention a dropped coffee tray?"

Her face felt hot. "I meant the expression."

He grinned and got up.

"How deliciously you blush, Melissa. And how onomatopoeic that is. Delicious Melissa, the little Greek cat."

He watched her, smiling.

He had made it a very enjoyable evening. The restaurant was casual, comfortable and expensive and the teasing was gentle. Later, she realised that he had somehow managed to make her very ordinary life seem interesting. By contrast, he had told her absolutely nothing about his personal life, although they had discussed architecture and modern taste, sailing and shipping, art and politics. He never referred to their time in Greece, or to a delivery of drugs to some woman on some island. He never spoke of anything which might have caused the colour to flare in her cheeks again, and he gave her a receipt in a Jiffy bag.

146

It was to do with age, she thought crossly, staring across her bedroom to the table where a second dolphin, cobalt and sapphire and ultramarine, leapt with its playmate in the dark. He was a sophisticated man who knew how to put naive young things at ease, but it was still a total mystery as to why he had imposed this penance on himself, and it was an even greater mystery as to why he should have bothered to make it enjoyable, which he had. He didn't care about the money, that was obvious, and perhaps he thought that demonstrating his lack of interest would be more effective than telling her. Her mind vaguely calculated how many days she could feed herself for what that meal had cost. No, it hadn't been a punishment at all, and even his parting shot had been robbed of unkindness as she tried to thank him. "No, no. No need to thank me. You paid for your own meal!"

A sudden thought—a suspicion—leapt into her mind. Was he, in fact, trying to seduce her? A meeting, once a month, something for her to look forward to, an evening of gentle humour, civilised talk, soft lights, wine? Was that the punishment he had in mind? Tonight, after the coffee, he had driven her back to the flat. As usual the bottom door was unlocked for her, and he had said, "See you in July, Melissa, same place, same time. Goodnight." And had put the package into her hand. Was this the softly, softly approach, to be gradually refined over the coming months? See you in July! The assumption that she'd be there, unable to break away from the pride which insisted on paying this stupid debt, unable eventually to break away from the good life he was introducing her to, the temptation of an expensive night out which might develop into a taste for luxury. Letting her see how little it mattered to him, how big an issue for her. Was he intending the enjoyment to lead to a further and final humiliation—a seduction and then a rejection? Serve you right for being so stubborn, so childish.

So. She wouldn't go in July, or ever again. It was every month or not all. Do what he wants, she told herself. He doesn't want a monthly reminder, the effort of entertaining

147

some gauche young thing. It might give him brief amusement but the tedium will quickly outweigh the novelty. She would not go in July, and two dolphins were enough for anyone.

She went out with a group of the fast-track young professionals from the office. They hadn't asked her before and she wondered why they asked her now. After a few drinks at the pavement table in June warmth, one of them told her.

"Miss Haunted, we called you. Mizzy Melissa. Efficient, but, oh boy! Touch me not!"

"Oh!" She had stared at him in surprise. "Really? Well, I'm very sorry. I had no idea."

"So what changed? The man came up trumps?"

She looked at him blankly.

"For heaven's sake Melissa. If it was a love affair, are you off or on limits?"

She put her head back and pealed with laughter.

"Well?" he said, sounding as if he wanted the answer quite badly.

She considered him. He was good-looking. His suits were well cut. He was the Investment Division Manager. It sounded good, even if there were several financial divisions, and each one had a manager, and each manager had a director. And they reported to the Finance Director, who reported to the Managing Director, who reported to the Board. Shut up, Melissa.

"Oh. On limits, of course. It was a financial crisis, not a heart crisis."

He grinned with relief. "I can cope with that. Dinner? Tomorrow?"

She smiled in response. "OK."

CHAPTER TWELVE

In July she had gone to Eaton Square on the appointed day, in spite of her intentions not to. She found herself looking forward to it. Nicholas took her to the National Theatre and she paid fifty pounds towards her ticket and dinner.

"Tell me about the latest boyfriend," he said when they had ordered. "What's his name?"

"Ben."

"Have you moved in with him?"

"No. We're not an item, exactly. I mean, he takes me out, but he's not the only one."

"Not head over heels in love then?" She shook her head.

"Once bitten, twice shy?"

She frowned. "What do you mean?"

"Well, Jeremy didn't really come up to scratch, did he? He let you down when you really needed some help." She looked at her hands, remembering how disillusioned she had felt. "Having heard that phone conversation I would have hit him if he'd been within reach. Selfish bastard."

She looked up at him in astonishment at this revelation.

"Maybe he'd have hit you if you'd been within reach!"

"I'd have hit harder!" They both laughed, and Melissa felt a warmth spreading through her.

"So. Not in love. Or not yet. And one of several all vying for your hand—or bed. Safety in numbers?"

"Something like that," she said, smiling. "Men can become frightfully possessive otherwise. And of course, they always know best."

He lifted his eyebrows. "That sounds like a warning shot across my bows."

She tried to look ingenuous. "No, of course not! After all, you've never tried to tell me what to do, or given me the benefit of your advice, have you?"

149

His eyes glinted. "I'm learning not to even attempt it." He topped up her wine glass. "So, what does he do to amuse you?"

"Well, we went to the semi-finals of the English Sumo Wrestling Association a couple of weeks ago."

His mouth opened slightly. "How dull of me not to think of that! Is he, by any chance, a sumo wrestler himself? Do you get lost in folds of flesh? Have you learnt the correct responses? Aaiiee! Hachaka!?" His laughter was infectious and she giggled.

"No and no."

The evening had been genuinely pleasurable, and when he opened the bottom door for her he gave her the little package and kissed her on the cheek.

"See you in August, unless you're on holiday."

The third dolphin was emerald and sea green. They arced through the summer heat and Melissa lay in bed, revelling in the colours and remembering the feel of his lips.

*****

Ben was much addicted to sport, but not much to art. After a day's racing and his efforts to explain the betting system, she announced her intention of going to The Glory of Constantinople exhibition at the Victoria and Albert Museum.

"I'm exhausted," he grumbled.

"Don't come then," she said briskly. "Go home and sleep off your winnings." For an investment guru, he had done badly.

But he came to the V and A, although she knew he found it uninteresting. She was crouched down by a glass case to study some carving and when she got up she looked straight into Nicholas Thauros's eyes. He smiled a disturbing, slightly mocking smile.

"Hello, Melissa. This must be your sort of exhibition."

"Uh. Yes. It is."

His gaze slid to her companion.

"Won't you introduce me?"

She turned and looked at her escort and for an instant could not recollect his name, but after a moment she performed the introductions reasonably enough. Ben, Nicholas Thauros. Ben Melbury. Nicholas commented pleasantly on the exhibition and because Melissa was suddenly and inexplicably silent, appeared to be interested in Ben's description of their racing successes. Then he excused himself politely, leaving them, as he said, to enjoy the exhibits in peace. See you soon, he said to Melissa, and smiled to see her flush.

Exactly two weeks later she went to Eaton Square. She was more nervous than usual since seeing Nicholas at the museum and suspected that he would tease her. She was right.

"I didn't know you were the betting type," he commented as he put her drink on the coffee table.

"I'm not. I won eleven pounds ninety purely on the name of the horse."

"Which was?"

"True Scot. Out of Honesty and Robert the Bruce."

He laughed. "Feminine intuition! Perhaps you could dispose of all your financial problems with your winning streak."

"Eleven pounds ninety isn't going to make me a millionaire," she said, stroking Cat who was making happy clawholes in her skirt.

"Is Ben?"

"Is Ben what?"

"Going to make you rich. So that you can pay me off." He was teasing, but there was a faint sharpness in his voice.

"No," she said shortly.

"Pity. Won't he come to the point?"

"Come to the point? What point are we talking about?"

"Heavens, you sound cross! Why are you all upset?"

151

"I'm not upset. Why on earth should I be? I just don't know what you're talking about. I went to Epsom with a friend. What's wrong with that?"

"Nothing at all. Except that you're screeching."

"I am not! What rot you do talk!"

He grinned and her annoyance evaporated into laughter. She noticed that he was very tanned.

"You've been away somewhere hot and sunny since I saw you. Greece?" He shook his head.

"No. I helped a friend crew a boat out to the West Indies. You wouldn't have liked it."

She pretended to be affronted. "And why wouldn't I have liked it?"

"Half of it was dead dull with no wind, and the other half was a howling gale. The West Indies were full of people you would have disliked on sight, so you see, you would have hated it."

"Well, it was lucky I wasn't asked then. Certainly, the last sailing excursion I had was rather disagreeable."

"The sailing or the company?" He was provoking her.

"The company," she snapped. "Oh, Nicholas! Do stop it!"

"Sorry." He sounded apologetic and ran a hand down her cheek. It took a real effort not to turn her face into the caress.

"I hope you don't find Ben's company so bad."

"No, I don't. He's quite amusing." She took an unladylike gulp at the glass of white wine he'd given her.

"So, Ben takes you to the horses, and you take him to the culture." He said it in such a way that there didn't seem any possible response, so she said nothing, twisting her wine glass uneasily in her fingers. This evening was getting off to a bad start.

"And what else does he do?" He said it quite mildly, but in her sensitive state the question took on overtones of derision.

"Do you mean what does he do for a living or what does he do with me?" She closed her eyes in irritation at having put her foot where her mouth was.

He couldn't resist it, and his grin got the better of him.

"My goodness, we'd better stick to the social conversation level I think, and not get too personal. I meant what does he do for a living? Is that safe, or am I hitting below the stockbroker belt again?"

"Very witty," she said. "He works in the same company."

"Ah! The office love affair! I hope he has a romantic job like designing computer games and isn't a financial whizz kid like Jeremy."

It was so unfair of him to put his finger on a sore spot. Ben had frequently tried giving her financial advice, especially since she had unwisely admitted to a financial crisis.

"Perhaps," she said with dignity, "we could leave my private life alone? He's a friend, he happens to work at the same office, he occasionally takes me out. I occasionally like to have some fun."

"I'm very glad to hear it. After all, if it wasn't for my insistence you wouldn't be having any, would you? You'd be up to your elbows in greasy washing-up water and handing out plates of spaghetti bolognese." His tone was still infuriatingly mild. "I'm delighted you've got a boyfriend. I was only trying to take an interest."

"You weren't. You were being—"

"Being what?"

"Being patronising." The wine was making her unwisely reckless. "It comes in the same category as this summons every month. The amount is an insult, my having to come here is an insult."

"But you don't have to come, and you don't have to bring anything. I'm not insulting you, you are."

His mildness was enraging her.

"I'm not. I was brought up never to have debts."

He stopped teasing. "Actually, it's just an excuse to be stubborn. Was I to let you be locked up in a Greek prison to oblige your sense of duty? I didn't have much alternative really, having seen your efforts to extricate yourself from your debts." His tone became less mild. "You see what happened in terms of your own innocence. I saw it from an entirely different perspective, equally compelling. I came to regret my mistake—if it can be called that—and tried to make amends. As it turned out, you weren't as innocent as you thought you were, and I wasn't as mistaken as I thought I was. Being brought up never to have debts may be a fine theory, but it doesn't appear to teach you how to cope when things don't turn out according to your lofty ideals. You're behaving as if I shouldn't have saved you from a fate worse than death! Did you really want to pay that fine, or indeed go to prison? That was the alternative, wasn't it?"

"I didn't mean that! You know perfectly well what I mean. I want to pay back a debt, and you're not letting me—this will take years, and I have to come like some tame poodle dancing on its hind legs—of course it's an insult!"

"Don't exaggerate! And I really am not making you dance like a tame poodle! You are, on the whole, paying for your entertainment, though perhaps you wouldn't call it entertainment, so you're not living the parasite. My God! I was married—am married—to one of the highest-earning women in Europe. She never, before or since being married, paid for anything that she didn't have to, so you are, I can assure you, a complete revelation to this particular husband. You insisted on this course, not me, so you must live with it now. Come on, finish your wine, stop being so stroppy and put your fists down. We're going to Covent Garden."

The wine had made her slow. There was something wrong with the logic, but she couldn't work it out. His irritation had again been deflected into mild and reasonably kind amusement, and she was frustrated by being out-manoeuvred.

"Covent Garden?" That sounded way too grand.

"We're going to the ballet. I hope you like it, otherwise you're going to have an even worse evening than you thought you were."

Her body stiffened in annoyance.

"I don't know whether I like ballet or not. I was taken once, as a child, and I remember not one thing about it."

His eyes glittered. "Would you like to pay for the interval drinks now, or at the bar?"

She opened her bag, removed the envelope and dropped it on the coffee table. Her hand was trembling slightly and the tiny movement caused it to plane off like a paper dart, hitting him on the knee and falling to the floor with a pathetic little crack. As he picked it up and stowed it away in his inside pocket, she busied herself with glass collection and cushion-plumping while she recovered her equilibrium.

She was apprehensive. Nicholas seemed suddenly remote and rather cold. He had given her a programme, which she had not read, and as the evening progressed she developed a headache. In the interval, she put down her wineglass, and muttered that she was going to the Ladies. Back soon.

In the harshly lit mirror above the basins she saw her face was pallid and strained. On returning to the lobby, she found it full of noisy people squashed elbow to elbow, impossible to get through. Anyway, get through to where? Nicholas was nowhere to be seen and he usually could be because of his height. She looked left, towards the outer doors. The squash was definitely thinner there. A bell sounded and a faint human eddy started towards the auditorium. She took a deep breath and plunged in the direction of a taxi.

Nicholas was outside, smoking. He threw the cigarette down and put a gentle hand on the back of her neck. It felt cool against her hot skin.

"No rush," he said. "That was only the first bell."

How had he known, she wondered helplessly? Was her state of mind that obvious that he had come out here just waiting to catch her trying to run away?

155

She tried to remember what the first half of the programme had been. All white tutus and white satin shoes, and rows of dancers in lines doing the same impossible and dangerous acrobatics to music from heaven. Music which was as familiar as the present music was not. There definitely wasn't a connection between this ballet and the previous one, or at least only in physical agility. Here the impression was of war and battle, of heroism and terror, of dirt and exhaustion. It was so strong she felt like crying. Perhaps one didn't have to understand, just to feel. The curtain came down on muted khaki death and to her astonishment she found her eyes had blurred and filled with embarrassing moisture. She stared straight ahead, hoping strenuously that they would dry out before the lights came on and Nicholas could see her.

He took her to a fish bar afterwards and told her about Ballet Imperial, and Requiem.

"Glad you stayed?" he asked.

"Yes." She glanced up at him, feeling herself flush. "An extraordinary experience. How do you know so much about classical music, and ballet, and opera? I feel so incredibly ignorant."

He grinned. "My stepfather is an addict and after a bit we became addicted, too." He asked about her holiday plans.

"I don't think I can organise anything. There's an offer on the grandparents' house and I'll have to help Mops declutter and pack up."

"Is there a lot of clutter?"

She nodded. "Years of it. It's a big house, and they moved with everything after—" She caught herself. "It was too difficult to sort it all, and we were too young to help. There's horrible Victorian silver plate, sets of stained tablecloths and napkins, garden tools and machinery, dreary prints and pictures, acres of unreadable books. And every single thing has history, and a story, and simply cannot be disposed of, or not without tears and misery."

She gave him a wry grin in an effort to make light of a disagreeable job.

"And do they realise that it will all have to be pruned to move into a smaller house?"

"In theory, yes. In practice, I doubt it. It's going to be a tough call. Mops is amazingly stubborn. Sometimes it makes me laugh, but sometimes I'm so frustrated I feel like crying."

"Like?"

She looked at him doubtfully. "Do you really want to know?"

He nodded. "Yes. What makes you feel frustrated?"

She thought for a moment and then laughed.

"Well, for instance in April the winter chair covers come off, and are washed because it's cheaper than cleaning, so the shrinkage remains unnoticed until October. Then we have a true trial of strength when the clean covers are stretched round the sofas and chairs. Despairing poppers spring apart, cast-iron hooks straighten like fuse wire. Much mending goes on. The same thing happens for the summer covers." She shook her head despairingly. "No other family on earth has two sets of chair covers dating back to the eighteen hundreds."

He put his head back and roared with laughter.

"What else frustrates you?"

She thought. "The ornaments. Collecting dust, taking up a great deal of space. All my life they lived in a glass cabinet, untouched by human hand, but they've all been bombarded by meteors from outer space; not one is unbroken or unchipped. They wouldn't even be accepted by a charity shop, but she won't let a single one go."

"They make up the good memories."

She flicked a glance at him. The curl of attraction was overlaid by something more surprising. Affection? Gratitude?

"What sort of housing are you looking for? Do they need care?"

"They may not need care yet, but it's on the horizon. They are in their eighties. He says Mops wouldn't live in a bungalow, but actually it's him that's appalled by the thought, though sheltered housing would be a much better option for them both." She realised with a jolt that she had revealed more than she intended after an evening which had started so uncomfortably.

Later, she unwrapped her receipt slowly, dropping the paper into the waste basket, running her fingers over the smooth glaze, the colour of fire. Four leaping dolphins played in the grey night. Lying uneasy and wakeful in her bed, she remembered his hand on the back of her neck, his lips gentle on her cheeks. The ache within her was dolphin coloured: red, orange, yellow, white.

CHAPTER THIRTEEN

On the first Friday of September she was ten minutes early at Eaton Square, three buses having appeared all at once just as she got to the bus stop. She imagined Nicholas's comments, 'Can't wait to get here, I see. Very keen to get on with your night out', and sat down in the sun on his very wide and very clean doorstep. After five minutes, the door opened and Nicholas came out with an extremely elegant lady with a dark and delicious tan wearing a sundress which Melissa would have given a lot for, all cut on the bias and swinging from the hip. She smiled at Melissa, who rose to her feet.

"Your appointment seems to be here already, darling." She had a strong Greek accent.

"So it is," he said. "This is Melissa Scott-Mackenzie, with military punctuality, as always." He introduced her. "Angeliki Thauros, my cousin. You met her mother Isabella at Madame's party." He kissed Angeliki on both cheeks. "Goodbye, *Kopelia Mou*. Come again soon and give my love to your parents." With a final word to her in Greek he turned to Melissa and said, "Come in."

"Sorry," she said awkwardly. "I didn't mean to be early—the buses—"

"Come in," he said again. "It's too hot for doorstep conversations."

He had mixed Pimm's, full of fruit and mint and borage.

"How delicious," she said, sniffing the herbs. "Where did you find borage? Or do you grow it on the balcony?" She gazed through the open doors on to the wrought-iron balcony, which was smothered in scarlet geraniums. "No, I can see you don't."

"A hundred yards down Elizabeth Street. Now, what have you been doing? You look like a bag of chewed chicken bones."

159

She sat up rather straight. "How rude! Not everyone can have a figure like your cousin. She was—is—I mean, very beautiful—and gorgeously brown."

"Angeliki is an international lawyer which is why she wasn't at the party. Beauty and brains—very unfair. You, however, are not gorgeously brown. You look as if you've been living in a cave or under a stone."

"Thanks for the slug description."

"Last month you said you were going to organise a holiday."

"It didn't happen, for various reasons. I will take some leave soon."

"When?"

She shrugged. "I don't know. Maybe in a few weeks."

"Well, I'm pleased to hear it. Where are you going?"

She was taken aback by the continued interrogation. "Oh! I don't—I haven't quite decided yet. Cornwall perhaps."

"Or Southend. Or Bognor Regis?" He was gently teasing and watched the blush. "And who with? Cornwall doesn't sound quite like Ben's cup of tea."

"Ben isn't involved." She tried to turn defensiveness into a joke. "Look, why the cross-examination?"

"Oh dear. He's gone as well, has he? That didn't take long—what was it—three months? A short-lived office romance."

She got up abruptly and took her tall Pimm's glass over to the open balcony doors, where she leant against the frame, facing the scarlet geraniums and taking nonchalant, but too frequent, sips.

"Sorry," he said. "I hope you ditched him and not the other way round. How about coming to Greece with me instead?"

"Very funny." She was relieved when he changed the subject.

"How did the house sale go? Have your grandparents got used to the idea of moving?"

"It didn't happen." She turned from the window. "The buyers withdrew the day before exchange and we've had to start all over again. It was one of the reasons I couldn't go away." Her mouth tightened. "How can somebody do that to vulnerable elderly people? I could have killed them. Poor old things—it's like giving them neat arsenic, then taking it away and giving it back slightly diluted. It just makes the whole thing more painful and more drawn-out."

She swung back to face the flowers again. He said nothing further and she knew it must be uninteresting to him. She couldn't think of a single thing to say. The silence lengthened and eventually she turned around and came slowly back to the sofa. He was lying back in his chair, his long legs stretched out to crossed ankles, just watching her.

"Would you mind," she said quietly, "if I just went home—now? I really rather would. Please."

He didn't move at all, not even his eyes, for ages.

"Yes," he said at last. "I certainly would mind. The pussycat really does need feeding tonight. Tell me what happened to Ben-from-the-office. What was he called?"

"He still is called. Melbury."

"Did it just fade out?" She shook her head. "A row?"

"Mmm."

"Why?"

"Honestly! The questions you ask! Mind your own business!"

"Go on. Tell me. His boring racing and your boring art?"

"No. Well, that was part of it. I wouldn't sleep with him, if you must know."

"Oh, ouch! Poor guy! Why not? Wasn't he attractive?"

"Not enough." Her spirits were lifting a bit.

"A fearful blow to his self-esteem, no doubt. Men do like to think of themselves as being irresistible; I know from experience." He was smiling. "Is there anyone else beating a path to your bed—door?"

161

"Hundreds." She grinned at him. "So far invisible. They'll come, of course, when they hear I'm available. No, not available, that has all the wrong connotations. Free—No!"

"Unencumbered, perhaps."

She put her head sideways, considering the word. "In Scotland they'd say," she put on a mock genteel Edinburgh accent, "Are you catered for?"

"Would they indeed! What else would they say?" He looked amused.

"Well, Miss Jean Brodie would say, 'I am here to put auld heads on young shoulders' and the Morningside ladies would say, 'We will have tea at sex'" The accent made him chuckle.

"I expect poor Ben had sex at tea more in mind! Now, what are you wearing? It looks suitable for dining *à deux chez moi*. What do you think? Or shall we go and eat lobster at The Seashell?" She was alarmed by the prospect, and he pounced. "Aha! It's a long time since I took out a girl who's never eaten lobster."

"How do you know I haven't? I might be horribly allergic to them."

"You will be if you have lobster plural. We'll soon see—you can be sick in the gutter—it won't be the first time I've held your head over the edge."

She took a sharp breath, remembering.

"What an unromantic thought," she said lightly after a moment.

He gave her a reassuring grin. "I'm not here to be romantic, I'm here to make you suffer, so we'll have lobster at the Seashell."

You do a most peculiar mixture of the two, which is just plain confusing, she thought, glancing sideways at him. She liked the teasing when it was not unkind. Does he watch everyone like that? It was like two sides to a coin, an abrupt kindness and understanding as if it could be the real man but he wanted to hide it, and then an equally abrupt shift to some unkind remark. She shivered in the heat.

"What's wrong?" he said.

162

"Nothing's wrong. Except for the lobster. Are they swimming about in a tank like in Greece, and you choose one?"

He sat upright and reached for the nearly empty Pimm's jug on the table.

"They are. Then a great big hairy arm comes down into their peaceful prison, seizes the victim," he tilted the jug back and forth, "struggling and snapping in a desperate and vain attempt to escape, the knowledge of the torture to come—"

She had sat upright, too. "That's ridiculous! It can't have any idea!"

"It knows something nasty is going to happen to it, especially as it sees an enormous seething cauldron steaming below it. Melissa, for goodness sake, what's wrong?"

"You know what, you horrible man! Stop it!"

He stopped. "Sorry." He was having difficulty controlling his laughter.

"Is that true?"

"I don't know. I've never been a lobster—especially a cooked one." He removed her empty glass and kissed the tip of her nose affectionately.

"You're the pits," she said, wishing the kiss was on her mouth.

Let him give me lobster, she thought defiantly. It's not a crime to be twenty-four and never to have had one. By the end of this evening, I shall be twenty-four and expert in the ways of lobsters, and I am not a squeamish little miss. She took the envelope containing fifty pounds out of her bag.

"What are you thinking?" he said, holding out his hand for the envelope.

She said untruthfully, "How far that will go towards a lobster. A claw?"

"Just about. Here's your receipt. Will it fit in your bag? Shall we walk? We'll need a good walk to work up an appetite." He collected jacket, keys, wallet. "Have you got comfortable shoes?"

The door closed with a rich thunk behind them and he put his right hand on her left shoulder across the road. The hand was warm and firm and she regretted its removal at the pavement. They walked down Elizabeth Street.

"There's the borage" she said, as they passed a bucket of soft grey fuzz. "Such a lovely blue. It ought to be borage blue, not cornflower blue."

"Why?"

"It sounds better. Borage blue has a poetic ring to it."

The Seashell was two doors down from the borage.

"I didn't need comfortable shoes for a pathetic hundred yards," she said, laughing.

"Lots of girls think a hundred yards is more than enough. Do you like walking?"

"Yes, I do. I walk a lot and London is rather fun on your feet. It's studded with milestones. Some of them are Roman, most of them are just Victorian." She put on a semi-dramatic expression. "There are pictures in cast iron, and stories in carved stone; there is history galloping on war horses and festooning obelisks and plinths, there are kings and generals, and boys swimming with dolphins, and little blue plaques commemorating the oddest people, and even those awful green and white things the heritage people put up. Nicholas Thauros lived here."

"No. Melissa Scott-Mackenzie ate her first lobster here. Or she will. Come and choose a screaming victim."

"Poor lobsters. You have no heart."

"You'd be surprised. But it doesn't run to not eating lobsters. What else did God make them for?" Their table was beside the open door into the back garden, and a waiter duly appeared with a bottle of white wine. "Would you like a starter?"

She slid her fingers through the cool beads of moisture on her wine glass. "You must be joking! Where would I put it?"

"I'm not quite sure," he admitted laughing. "There's not a lot of you."

164

"That's unnecessary. I'm not thin and I eat like a horse."

"When you eat. Which I suspect is only with me since Ben-at-the-office went the way of all things."

She would have liked to be rude back, but decided it wasn't worth it.

"How do you eat lobster? There seems to be such a lot of armour-plating."

"They go at them with a machete. It's terribly physical."

In the event, it wasn't at all physical. It was presented in a helpful half and he showed her how to pick out the claw meat. She leant back in her seat.

"I'm exhausted. And full. It was delicious. I think I feel less sentimental about them now. My grandfather kept pigs— little ones—years ago. They rootled around in the woods and squealed adorably. It took me ages to realise that we were steadily eating them, and then only when my little Wilbur disappeared." She remembered the sadness.

"Wilbur? Why Wilbur?"

"As in *Charlotte's Web*. The very fine pig." He was still looking blank. "How very badly read you are," she said severely. "I'll give it to you. You can't go all your life without reading one of the beacons of English literature—well, American literature."

He nodded slowly, smiling. "Do that. What else did he keep besides pigs? Was this after he retired from the Army?"

"Yes. He kept geese. Instead of a lawnmower. He was full of cost-saving ideas. They were terrifying, though my brothers pretended not to be scared. Hissing and beating their wings at us when we collected the eggs. I don't blame them. I'm sure I would have done the same."

"I can just see you hissing. Not so sure about the wing-beating, though." He gave her a penetrating glance and she realised that she had said 'brothers' again, plural. Not brother Johnnie, singular. "How about something sweet and fattening. Chocolate mousse, crème brûlée, a plate of double cream?" His eyes slid past her, not hearing her reply.

"Damn," he said softly. "Don't talk, please."

She was aware of a presence directly behind her and then a woman's voice.

"Nico! How nice to see you out and about again. How are you?"

"Probably as well as can be expected." He gave whoever it was a slightly wary smile. "If you stand there, I can't introduce you. You'll give poor Miss Scott a crick in the neck."

He put a hand out and drew her round to his side of the table. His eyes touched Melissa's and seemed to carry some sort of warning.

"Don't I get a kiss, or would your companion mind?" There was just the faintest of hesitations round 'companion'. She bent with a laugh and touched her cheek to his with a little moue. But she was looking at Melissa, not at him; a tall, confident and thin-faced woman, her hair as dark as his, shaped sleekly in an enviable cut. She straightened gracefully, allowing him to make the introductions. Melissa took in a beige silk two-piece, expensively casual, and a lot of gold, along with the fact that the expensive silk lady was called Diana Goring, and she herself was, a little surprisingly, Lissa Scott.

"How do you do, Lissa? We haven't met, have we?"

"How do you do. I don't think so." She was polite and inwardly amused because Diana Goring had that slightly avid look that wondered if she was Nicholas's girlfriend.

"I doubt you've met," Nicholas said. "Not unless you've taken to buying antiques, and as far as I know you're a singularly modern lady."

Melissa kept her face smooth. He was giving her some coded instructions which weren't clear as yet. She wondered if Diana Goring was a friend or relative of his wife's. Fleetingly, and tardily, her brain registered that if he didn't want to be seen with strange women because his wife might hear of it, he shouldn't be asking her to come to his house, nor should he be taking her with him into public places. Or perhaps Diana Goring was the lady of the moment.

"Oh?" Ms Goring lengthened it out. "Ohhouu? How fascinating. Antiques for dinner? Not antique fish I hope."

It was such a pathetic remark, that Melissa couldn't help her expression, which twitched her eyebrows down, and pursed her mouth. Nicholas saw it and gripped his lower lip between his teeth.

"We had lobster," Melissa said, and contrived to be repressive. Diana Goring sharpened.

"Lobster! My dears! How delicious! The antiques must be something special to be worth a lobster dinner. It sounds terribly expert, antiques—how very clever to be so expert so young."

"Thank you," Melissa said, and said nothing else because Nicholas had put his foot firmly on hers and it hurt.

"And you're with Christie's? Or Sotheby's?" Her eyes drifted down speculatively to the man beside her.

"Neither, Diana. Stop snooping. I'm not telling you who she's with or what I'm buying. You'll only mention my name and the price will miraculously double. And she's not telling you either. Have you had coffee yet?"

"No darling, I was only visiting the Ladies when I saw you. We're upstairs."

"Well, order me one and I'll come up and join you. Miss Scott and I have finished our business."

Diana looked surprised and oddly disappointed. "Darling, I don't think poor Miss Scott—"

But he squeezed her hand and smiled at her. "Won't be five minutes. Black, please."

He hailed a taxi, and laughed rather grimly into Melissa's bemused eyes. "You were quick on the uptake, Miss Scott. Well done. We'll have better luck next time. I'm afraid she is a journalist. I'm a bit cautious of journalists at the moment."

"Try avoiding them then," said Melissa. "Thank you for the lobster—and the crème brûlée."

He looked slightly abashed and gave the driver her address and a twenty-pound note.

Her receipt was a fifth dolphin. It had a blue green glaze overlaid with deep turquoise and there were pale turquoise flecks on it, like bubbles. She gazed at it for some time, her memory replaying the fleeting beauty of the dolphins around Nicholas's yacht. That memory was swiftly followed by another. His hands holding her between his body and the wheel. His fingers on her skin, his mouth touching hers. Her stomach curled and she pulled her mind sharply back, putting the dolphin on her dressing table with the others. She might be attracted to him physically, but unlikely or not, he still dealt in drugs.

Other than feeling she'd been packed off to bed when the grown-ups had arrived, the following week improved radically. On Monday afternoon, the estate agents rang to say there was another prospective buyer, and on Wednesday, according to her grandmother, a sharp little man in a sharp little suit came and looked over the house in complete silence.

"Come on, Mops! He must have said something!"

"He didn't. Frightfully rude. Oh, he asked how much land there was." She went on, "I think he's a builder and he's going to pull the house down and build lots of ghastly bungalows all over the garden."

"He wouldn't get planning permission. I'm afraid it doesn't sound very hopeful. Don't count on that one."

But on Friday the sharp little man returned with a surveyor who stuck skewers into walls and floorboards and stood ominously silent over the wiring.

After that there was a week's silence. Her grandfather rang, sounding brisk.

"They're property developers. They want to buy the house, but won't be selling it on yet. Nice man. Sensible. Friendly. Said they'd want a caretaker—preferably living in. To keep the house in good condition, and if there was anyone locally who might be interested, to let them know. Said there wouldn't be any rush to move."

Too good to be true, she thought. She went home for the weekend, and read the dry legalese of the offer from a

168

company called Cathedral Properties whose name seemed vaguely familiar. Surprisingly, the offer was nearly the amount they were asking. Completion negotiable and mutually agreeable. She went to see the estate agent. Speculator, he confirmed. Free money, buys at the bottom, sells high. When did she want to complete? I'll let you know, she said. Finding something to suit the old people wasn't proving very easy.

It transpired, after rather feeble argument from Melissa, that caretaking was exactly what they wanted to do. What was more, they'd be paid for doing it. Melissa, who felt the whole thing was getting more and more curious, had no support from her brother.

"They don't need to move, Mel, and though half the value will go to the creditors, Mops will have the other half and we can look at alternative housing in our own time. It was only the running expenses that were so impossible and the small print says two thirds of the oil and the electricity will be paid by Cathedral Properties to prevent deterioration. Brig and Mops will be responsible for one third."

Melissa was astounded. "There has to be a catch," she said. "It's too good to be true. We must send the agreement to the lawyers to have them check it."

The house negotiations moved at an alarming and unusual pace.

"I have this feeling in my bones," she told Johnny, "there will be a disaster. Some problem will come up and the whole thing will fall apart again."

"Shut up, Mel, or you'll be a self-fulfilling prophecy. The lawyers checked it, nothing will go wrong. Why should it?"

But she was convinced that the buyers would back out, and they would have to start all over again. There was no question of organising a holiday as there was only just over a week before she had to present herself and her fifty pounds at Eaton Square again. Unless she stopped this painful process which at the present rate was going to continue for years to come. However much she was attracted to Nicholas, it would only compound the misery every time she saw him.

169

He was out of reach, out of her league, in the middle of a very public divorce. He would not wish to get involved with anyone let alone her. And he was involved, somehow, with drugs.

She should see no more of Nicholas Thauros; no more dangling on a line, puppet on a string, being laughed at, fed, watered, patronised. He could pay the wretched fine if he wanted to, and her pride, which wasn't pride at all, but just plain stupid stubbornness, could be dropped in life's dustbin, where it belonged. And she could take leave when it suited her, including the first Friday of a month.

Her boss, Mr Emmett, came in to say he was going home, but finding her at her desk looking thoroughly despondent, instead knocked down the arguments against a holiday one by one. Not arranged, nowhere to go, no one to go with, family crisis, etc. etc.

Organise a week, preferably two, he had said firmly. When she got back to the flat she sat in the springless armchair feeling dazed. She was past thinking.

Her phone rang and her stomach lurched on hearing Nicholas's voice. Had she got her dates wrong? Was it payday this weekend?

"I need to see you," he said. "I'll pick you up in an hour."

"No. Definitely no. I'm shattered, I've just got in from work. No. No. No. I can't." She was aware that she sounded tense.

"What's wrong?"

She fended him off with worries about the house and her grandparents, and how tired she was. For a while he was silent then said, "OK. Tonight's menu is off. But I do want to talk to you, so tomorrow instead."

"No."

"Yes. Please don't argue. Eight o'clock tomorrow."

"I'm busy tomorrow. You can't just reorganise my life and demand to have me on parade. Of all high-handed—"

"Melissa! Are you going out tomorrow?"

She hesitated just too long. "Yes."

170

"You're a hopeless liar," he said, sounding amused. "Wear something gorgeous and I'll pick you up at quarter to eight."

The affection in his voice disarmed her. "But why? I mean—you're such a bully, and I'm exhausted. If you need to say something why can't you just say it? I'm not going to let you give me another nasty surprise."

He laughed. "Surprise maybe. Not nasty—at least I hope not, and I promise to bring you back not too late. But I bet you need dinner and I want to ask you something. See you tomorrow."

CHAPTER FOURTEEN

He was having to work hard to persuade her.

"What's preventing you from coming if you've been sent on holiday? You've already admitted you've got no plans, nowhere special to go, no one to go with, and you don't want to go home."

"I need a holiday. Not a working nightmare."

"You'll get a holiday. I won't be working all the time, and there'll be times when I won't need you and you can take yourself off to see friends or do whatever you want to do." He knew that wasn't altogether his intention. "But you know Scotland and I don't. And I need a driver."

"Why? You like driving your fast cars."

He hesitated, unwilling to explain this particular predicament of being unable to drive. "I need to work. In the car."

"You could hire a driver."

"That's what I'm trying to do. And I need a PA."

"You just need a competent secretary and you could hire one of those, too."

"A driver/secretary/PA all rolled up in one takes up less space. And you take up very little space. Anyway, as you very well know, it would be virtually impossible to get someone like that at short notice, and I've been given no notice at all for the Fife proposal which means I really will have to work on the way north." He had put on a hang-dog pleading expression. "Please, dear Melissa, you would be the answer to my problems. I need you, I'll be nice to you, or as nice as I know how. I'll pay you the going rate on a proper company invoice, I won't bully you, and you can have time off to visit your alma mater and all your old friends and have that holiday. What on earth would you do for two weeks all on your own, and where would you go? You'd be bored to death in London, or thoroughly frazzled with your grandparents. Be honest."

"But I need to be within reach of them—the house—something could still go wrong with this sale," she objected feebly.

"It's only Scotland, not the Australian outback. They have your mobile number; you can text and ring them ten times a day if you want to. Nothing dreadful will happen if you're not on the spot. I mean, they're not totally incompetent. Or are they terribly upset by it all?"

"Well, no, they aren't, rather to my surprise," she admitted. "They both seem rejuvenated by the prospect of having 'a job', as Mops puts it."

She'd told him about the speculator. He'd been amused, hearing the details from her point of view, and less than comforting about the prospects, until she realised he was winding her up again.

"It seems so odd. Why on earth would anyone buy a house, and leave the ex-owners as—sort of sitting tenants?"

He shrugged, thinking about it. "Wasn't there some sort of caretaking agreement? If they're being paid to do it as a job, there must be a contract or something?"

"Well, yes," she admitted. "I sent it with all the papers to our lawyer to check and he said it was all right. They'll have three months' notice. But I still think it's most peculiar."

He grinned. Melissa was not daft. "Cautious girl! Quite right, too. It's thoroughly sensible to check these things out. But it's not that peculiar, you know. It was probably just convenient for them that the sellers were willing to stay; usually they'd be moving to another house. It saved them the trouble of advertising for caretakers, hiring, taking up references, showing them the ropes of a house they don't know either. You just can't imagine anyone having enough money to invest in property over an extended period, waiting for house prices to rise. It happens all the time. The recession hasn't bottomed out, but it probably will soon, and for those who can wait to sell, there will be a booming market in maybe one, two or three years' time. He'll make a killing. He's probably doing it all over the country."

Which all sounded so logical that he could see Melissa felt heartened.

"I think you're one of the lucky ones," he went on, "and when the money's in the bank, you'll be laughing."

She'd made a dry little grimace and he guessed there was a big mortgage to pay off.

"Well, you should be laughing." He changed the subject back to his proposal.

"Be brave, I won't eat you! And I promise not to shout at you when you're driving," he teased, and saw her shoulders lift defensively.

"You're such a bully," she said crossly. "You don't even think about whether I want to or not, you just make all these assumptions to suit whatever whim you have at the time. Even if I was mad enough to consider it, you haven't told me what you're doing, where you're going, what I'm supposed to be doing! Where would I be staying, for heaven's sake?"

He sighed. "All these questions! Does life have to be so pre-organised?"

"Yes. Semi-organised anyway. I'm not sleeping in the car or—"

"Or? Or what?" The lighting was too dim to see, but he guessed she was blushing. "I have to visit a man in Fife who's thinking of turning his house into an exclusive retirement-stroke-nursing home, some work on an initial feasibility study for that, a bit of sight-seeing. Is there anything to see in Edinburgh?"

"Of course there is! It's the most beautiful city in the world."

"Really? And here am I, misled with tales of Venice and Vienna, of Prague and Constantinople and Athens and—"

"Nicholas! Don't be horrible! It's a lovely place, full of history and lovely houses and the castle is sensational and Holyrood reeks of Mary, Queen of Scots and blood and love

174

affairs. Anyway, it's my city—where my roots are. Obviously I think it's beautiful!"

He laughed. "I'll really need a native guide then, won't I? And we'll be staying in perfectly respectable hostelries which have been booked by the company—and my expenses include travel, accommodation, office equipment and staff and whatever else I need to carry out my work. Anything outside of work is at my own expense. After Fife, we go to Glasgow."

"Do we?" She turned up the amazement. "And what do *we* do in Glasgow?"

He ignored the sarcasm. "Glasgow is two projects. A hospital which is half finished and as usual behind schedule, and a children's hospice which my company is building. I've never been outside Glasgow on my previous visits and that seems a pity, so I thought you might like to show me around. Loch Lomond. Ben Nevis. That sort of thing."

She stared at him disbelievingly. "Why," she said suspiciously, "do you want me to come? You must have a motive, and I know quite well it can't be any of those spurious reasons you've tried to fob me off with already. I really can't be your idea of the ideal companion, so what is going on?"

"Why can't you be my idea of an ideal companion?" He was quite irritated. "Go on, tell me why not?"

"Well, I'm too young, for a start—not classy enough, and even though it amuses you to make me uncomfortable, I can't believe that you'd enjoy it for two weeks—you'd be bored after half a day."

He wished she wouldn't denigrate herself and raised his eyebrows. "Really?"

Scepticism was written all over her face.

"I know that you're trying to set me up for something. You think I've been really stupid about what happened in Greece, and how I feel about repaying the money and you're having yourself a big joke at my expense. Your friends are wealthy, beautiful, sophisticated—so why would you want to

175

take me anywhere, let alone to Scotland for two weeks? You can afford any number of chauffeurs, and chauffeur-driven cars, and probably a private plane, too; you could take your own secretary, or hire ten a day, if you wanted to, so I ask myself, why me?"

"I'm beginning to wonder myself," he said, "the way you go on putting yourself down. I am not setting you up for anything. What happened in Greece is history—except that you keep dragging it into the present, but I'm learning to live with that and next Saturday is payday, by the way, and that was why I wanted to talk to you. Because I'll be in Scotland, not London." He reached across and tugged gently on the hair falling over her shoulder. "And I don't think you're in the least juvenile; that I would find tedious, and yes, you're unsophisticated, but so what? And why the assumption that a sophisticated companion is a personal requirement, or even desirable? Sophistication does not equal interest or enjoyment." She still looked doubtful. "I can only say that I am definitely not having a joke at your expense, and that everything I've said about this trip to Scotland is perfectly true. I'm not going to try to seduce you or humiliate you, or be beastly to you. I need my car, I need someone to drive while I work, I need someone to hold the end of a tape measure, someone to write down measurements in a howling gale, someone to type my notes, someone, preferably unsophisticated, to talk to about perfectly normal things, someone who isn't, for God's sake, on the take the whole bloody time."

She looked astounded.

"Melissa, you've got two weeks' holiday due to you, with apparently no one to go with, and nowhere to go. I know some of it will be working, but I promise you'll have at least a week of it completely work free." He put his hand on hers, stroking the neat nails which never had nail polish on them. "Don't let's do anything so sophisticated as have an argument. You can just plan your answer for later. I won't try to alter your decision." Even to his own ears he sounded

176

resigned. His thumb was gentle on her skin, and he was aware of the charge of attraction and his physical reaction. He was relieved he was on the other side of the table because if she had noticed that reaction she would refuse to come.

"You haven't asked me about Diana Goring that night in The Seashell," he remarked. "Weren't you curious? If not, you're the first woman I've ever met without the curiosity factor."

"I assumed you didn't want your friends thinking you'd gone off your head, and explaining truthfully why I was there would have been embarrassing for me, but quite tricky for you, too."

He looked at her rather sharply. "Diana is an acquaintance who is a tabloid journalist. It's a rather unpleasant combination."

"Ah!" Melissa smiled faintly. "To be discovered feeding lobster to a very junior ugly duckling was a strategical error—the antique buying was quick thinking. You didn't need to tread on my toe."

He gave her a considering look. "You don't read the nasty tabloids, do you?"

She shook her head. "No. Do you?"

"I don't have to. Other people do it for me. You'd be surprised how many people take it upon themselves to be my personal cutting service." He took out his wallet and slid a folded newspaper cutting across the table. "I was sent five copies of this by various people. You might begin to understand why I'm so cautious, and why I gave you a name and a job you couldn't be traced to."

She looked at him in surprised alarm and then opened the cutting to read a circled paragraph under the heading 'City Diary'.

'Dealers Beware! The shy little mouse making the surprise bid in the auction houses may wield more wealth than would at first appear. Multi-millionaire architect Nicholas Thauros tells me that he is tired of people upping

the prices for antiques whenever he appears. He is now using the deceptively childlike Lissa Scott to find and buy his antiques for him. After his very public feud with, and divorce from, the French super model Marie Claude de Rimanac, one wonders just what Miss Scott is providing for him besides antiques?'

She dropped the cutting as if it might burn her. "That's terrifying. No wonder you trod on my foot."

He gave a crack of laughter. "Perhaps I really should use the deceptively childlike Miss Scott to buy antiques for me. So long as you don't repeat the last fiasco."

He saw her shoulders lift nervously and regretted the jokey remark as he slid the cutting back into his wallet.

"Would you like to get back into the art world? Somehow computer software doesn't really suit you."

"The art world doesn't pay and computer software, or anyway HR, does," she said, her voice tart. "For some of us, perhaps not many that you know, it actually matters. What I want is irrelevant. Certainly I'd like to, but I had no success when I tried—my reputation had gone before me—and now I really need a secure job with a good pay cheque at the end of the month, and that's what I've got."

He frowned in sudden suspicion. "You're not still trying to repay Clive Mann, I hope?" He stared at her face in disbelief. "You are! You idiot! What are you paying him every month?"

She shrugged and told him.

"It's none of your business—you made your arrangements—"

"Oh yes, it is!" he interrupted. "It's very much my business. I didn't make my arrangements to line Clive Mann's pockets. I made them so that you could eat without having to eat all your pride as well. How dare you take the opportunity to pay off more to that bloody man!"

"But you wouldn't let me pay you more!"

"And I've just told you the reason! Why have you increased those payments? You told me you paid the same to him as you did to me."

"I didn't increase them—I tried to reduce them," she said, sounding uncomfortable. "Last Christmas. The same time I wrote to you, I asked him to accept less because I'd lost that second job. I had a letter from their lawyers saying that I could reduce the amount but the interest would increase and because of the change in bank rate the interest would increase anyway. I was ending up paying twice as much as I owed." She looked at him apologetically. "I didn't mean to use your—generosity—to fund Mann's, but you wouldn't take any more; and I could save the extra and—" She put her head briefly into her hands. "I'm sorry. The debt was—still is—getting bigger, not smaller." She forced a grin. "I now know what a third world country feels like."

He was not amused. "Didn't you take legal advice? There can't be any way they can legally increase your repayments unless you agreed to do so. What the hell did you sign?"

"I signed what their lawyers sent me. And no, I didn't take legal advice." She was defensive.

"You said you'd sent your grandparents caretaking and house sale contracts to their lawyer. Why didn't you check your own, much more serious, agreement with him?"

"I couldn't afford it."

"Rubbish," he said. "You couldn't afford not to. Or you should have come to me."

"And since when," she said furiously, "have you been any friend of mine?" He looked at her across the table without saying anything. "Sorry," she muttered. "I didn't mean that. I suppose I should have asked them, but I didn't want them to know. I didn't want anyone to know. I suppose they wouldn't have told my grandparents, but I felt—I don't know."

"They certainly wouldn't have told them! What do you think a lawyer is if not discreet? Bring that agreement with you to Scotland. It needs sorting out."

179

"Bring it? I haven't agreed to come to Scotland. This is not your business, Nicholas! You try to interfere in everything, but you're not interfering in this."

"Yes, I bloody well am," he said. "And please come to Scotland. You owe me, remember—next weekend? And Scotland's where I'm going to be, so that means you, too."

"No!"

"Yes. Please. And that book you promised me—Wilbur the Pig, or whatever." He reached across the table again and took her hand, hoping to soften her temper. "You've heard my reasons for wanting you to come. I've promised not to be my usual foul self—and if I fail, I apologise now. I promise to pay you the going rate for services rendered. Oh, Melissa! I love your face when you turn indignant! I promise to tramp round Edinburgh in the rain and visit every nook and cranny of your alma mater. I promise—I can't think what else to promise, but I expect you'll come up with something. Please stop arguing. The thought of Edinburgh and Glasgow on my own is appalling."

"You're mad to be seen with anyone, given you have friends like Diana Goring, but if you insist on it, you could ask any of your friends to come and keep you company."

"You're joking! Most of them have never been north of Bond Street; as far as they're concerned the Scots are tartan-skinned and live on haggis."

"I can't."

"You can. Please."

He sensed that she was beginning to waver, and ran his finger up the inside of her forearm. The soft skin flared heightened awareness through him. His brain shouted warnings and the rest of him ignored them.

*****

The following Tuesday she was driving north, still alarmed by the enormous car which seemed to have a jet engine under the bonnet. Nicholas was in the back with a sea of papers all over and around him. He was on his mobile phone and had been for some time, but as the conversation was entirely in Greek she was at liberty to think her own thoughts. She still couldn't quite understand how she could possibly have agreed to this crazy trip—holiday was too strong a word—and every now and then a dart of apprehension shook her. He was dangerous in every sense that she could think of, not least the fact that she was physically extremely attracted to him, and her terror was that she might inadvertently show it. Whilst she could dislike and distrust him she had felt safer, but it was becoming very difficult to dislike him and the distrust was becoming so diluted that she had to try to remember that he dealt in drugs. It seemed like a figment of her imagination and completely at odds with his character. So why had she let herself in for these two weeks, she thought despairingly. Her abilities as a secretary were certainly nothing special. She shouldn't have been bulldozed into coming, but somehow she had been. She'd packed a bag, given both his and her mobile phone numbers to those who needed to know how to contact her, and had stupidly told her grandparents the truth. Defending herself from their moral objections to two weeks, alone, with a man, had been a struggle. The effort to justify the trip to Brig and Mops had in the end been the deciding factor in her agreement.

Now she acknowledged that he hadn't been making up the work aspect. Between phone calls he dictated notes and letters. She listened quite carefully, suspecting that intelligent questions about his work would be acceptable, but stupid ones would not. Anticipation was beginning to replace apprehension. Was it because their relationship had subtly changed? Eventually he took a break from his dictation and after a petrol stop changed to the front passenger seat. She had asked him if he wouldn't rather drive, but he had shaken his head and not even asked her if she was tired. She asked him about the proposal in Fife.

"It's an idea to convert a large country house into a retirement home so a feasibility study is the first step. It belongs to someone called McNair Watt."

"I was at Edinburgh with a McNair Watt," Melissa said. "Emily, I think. Probably the same family."

"That's a coincidence! You can reconnect with her on Monday."

"On Monday? Am I to come, too?" She felt the familiar stirrings of apprehension again.

"You're driving, and I'm employing a secretary. You will certainly be there, armed with notepad and pencil and measuring tape. If we're going to tender I'll need quite a lot of information. Did you know this girl well?"

"Quite well. She wasn't a particular friend or anything, but I vaguely remember meeting her parents and an older sister. I don't know if it's the same family."

If it was the same family, she wondered what they would make of her travelling with, and working for, a rich, attractive architect. She could already hear the whispers.

"Are they actually selling the house, or do they intend to help run this retirement home and live in the stables or something?"

"I have no idea. This is the first stage and I'm going to have a look because I'm up here anyway on the Glasgow projects. It's quite an effective way of using your house, if you've got to sell up or it's just too big. A fair number get turned into country house hotels, like ours, I expect. Lothian House. I hope there's more on the menu than haggis."

"It's not all that Scotland can manage, you know. We do eat other things. In fact, the Scots eat very well."

"Do they? How encouraging. What for instance?"

"Well. Neaps, for instance. That's turnips to you. Brawn? You'd like it. After all, you like lobster. Brawn is a pig's head, boiled in its entirety, with the trotters thrown in, for the jelly, then it's all picked to bits and the meat and brains and stuff are glued together with the jelly. Aspic."

"Yeugh."

"What else. Kippers. Oh! Capercaillie."

"What on earth is that?"

"It's a bird—quite rare now, but you find them in the Highlands. It's about the size of a turkey, but I think it's inedible."

"What is this? The revenge of the lobster?"

"Something like that."

"Well, no wonder there's no fat on you. Years of pigs' heads and turnips. I feel that Scotland may depress me."

She hadn't really heard him.

"What do you feel when you go back to Greece?"

"What you're feeling now, probably." There was a smile in his voice.

"Do you? It's so odd. When I'm away I feel a bit nostalgic, but when I go back I feel all bubbly and happy, and proud, and Scottish. As if it's all mine. My hills, my rivers, my rain, my city. And it's all right. We have the best steak in the world, and venison, and salmon, and trout, and grouse, and pheasant and whiskies. And as you're so rich, and even richer by next Saturday, I shall eat my head off at your expense."

"You," he said laughing, "are feeling better. Are you also feeling more charitable towards me for forcing this ghastly trip on you?"

"I'm reserving judgement. It hasn't started."

She glanced sideways and saw none of the charm which was revealed when he smiled, but none of the cynicism either. When they reached the Scottish border, she drew in at the lay-by at the top of Carter Bar and showed him the Borders, purple and gold and green, in the fitful gleams of late afternoon.

"There are the Eildon Hills," she said later, pointing them out, "but once they were just one great mountain."

Nicholas stared.

"Say again?"

"Long ago the Devil and Michael Scott the wizard had a competition to see who had the greatest power. The Devil challenged the wizard to split the great Eildon Mountain into three and Michael Scott challenged the Devil to twist the sands of all the world's seashores into a rope."

Nicholas turned to look at her. "And?"

"The next morning, there were the three Eildon Hills as you see them now, but the Devil is still working on his task centuries later." She heard him chuckle.

She drove him through the long shadows towards Edinburgh, and finally the satnav took them to an expensive country house hotel converted from a disintegrating family pile.

Having signed in, they followed an immaculately groomed Ms Thomas up a superb oak staircase, down several passages and round corners. It was quite cheering in a way, she thought. At least this house was still beautiful and the fine pictures and antique furniture looked as if they belonged, even though the original family's possessions must have been sold long since.

Ms Thomas opened a door and ushered them into a spacious drawing room. Comfortable-looking sofas and chairs were ranged round a low coffee table stacked with magazines and books, behind which a real log fire burned. The heavy chintz curtains were drawn across the big windows, their designer tassels and folds spread excessively over yards of pale cream carpet. The whole room, from the painted Adam ceiling to the Persian rug in front of the fire, was expensive elegance, the only jarring note a printer and extension sockets on a modern desk. The efficient Ms Thomas showed her a bedroom and bathroom with every conceivable gadget known to five-star hotels, and a sense of unreality and panic seized her. She could barely see to the far side of the bed, and the cover would take two strong men to fold and lift. Eventually Ms Thomas went away and Melissa sat rather heavily in yet another large armchair. Her small suitcase appeared and was placed reverently on a smart rack. Finally, the outer door closed and Nicholas appeared. He leant against the door frame and regarded her face with concern.

"It's OK. I've checked—there is absolutely no haggis, black pudding, brawn or turnips on the menu." There was a brief silence. "Is everything all right?"

"No! Where do I—sleep? They think we're—we're—what names did you give? Is this your idea of a joke?" She turned in frustration and anger and indicated the bed behind her. "How dare you do this! After all you promised! I'm not sleeping with you!"

"Calm down!" He was trying to control his laughter. "You're booked in under your own name and this is your room, not mine, complete with lock and key. Come through here."

Knowing that she was about to be humiliatingly embarrassed, she followed him across the sitting room and into a bedroom as large as her own. His cases were on the racks, his briefcase open on the bed and already the room looked as messy as if he lived there permanently.

"You obviously don't believe a word I say. I'm not intending to sleep with you either." He looked rueful and amused and led the way back to the central room. She could feel the mortified blush rise and deepen.

"Oh!" She put her hands to her hot cheeks. "I'm sorry. I'm so sorry. It never occurred to me there were two—I thought—the bed was so huge I thought—"

"You've made it clear what you thought," he said. "I can't imagine why as I really didn't think I'd given you that impression. Or had I?"

She felt the blush become, if it were possible, even more radiant.

"No. Of course not. I'm really sorry." Her voice came out as a croak.

"Perhaps your boyfriends have given you the impression that getting a girl into bed is the only thought in a man's head, mmm?"

She shook her head, not as a negative, but to try to stop him.

"Well, now that we've established that neither of us wants or expects a romp on these enormous playgrounds, shall we settle down? We'll be here for a few days and we'll have dinner here tonight. It's been a long day so I won't put your nose to the grindstone until tomorrow. When we've run out of work you can show me the sights." He poured her a gin and tonic and she felt the flush start to fade. "Why don't you go and unpack while I install the laptop and printer. Everything we need is on flash drives and I've got different software for the engineering stuff which you won't need to use anyway. I can print out any calculations and drawings I need."

"Don't you want to get some of that work done tonight?" she said worriedly, but he shook his head.

"Nope, I do not. You can test out the bathroom equipment and change before dinner." He smiled at her over his whisky glass. "Don't look so anxious. You've driven a long way and once you'd got over the surprise of having an accelerator you drove very well and I got a lot of work done as a result. I managed to remain calm, didn't I?"

She was so alarmed by her pleasure at the compliment that she left abruptly to unpack and soak in hot bubbles. She WhatsApped Sarah and called Mops to reassure her that they'd arrived safely and then worry about dinner washed over her. In a hotel like this it would mean dressing up, a perpetual source of anxiety for someone who had very few clothes in the first place and who had brought very few of them in the second place. For a man accustomed to confident, beautiful and desirable women, she must be the epitome of milky feebleness. She wrapped herself in a vast white robe, a towel round her head, and put her head round the door. He was sitting at the computer dabbing figures onto a graph.

"Would you mind if I had my meal up here?"

"Yes."

"Yes I can, or yes you mind?"

"No you can't, and yes I do mind."

186

"Oh. I thought you'd prefer it."

"Did you." It was more a sceptical statement than a question.

"I've got a headache."

"Tough."

He hadn't looked up, and the figures were still going on to the screen. She withdrew her head and shut the door with a snap. Later, when she reappeared, the sitting room was empty and the computer blank and silent. A glass of wine stood on the coffee table. She drank it slowly, sitting by the fire, glancing through the latest copy of Period Antiques, but not really seeing it. Her request had been a mistake, and might well have started the evening off on the wrong foot. His door opened.

"Always punctual. Is it the naval training?"

"Partly," she said, "and partly because my mother was always late."

He chuckled and went over to get the wine from the ice bucket.

"People who are late are so dementing that they make everyone else punctual as a result, is that it?"

"I guess so. My father would get enraged, and it was so scary that all of us would be lined up and waiting. If he got cross with her she just got later."

Nicholas's glance was penetrating and she realised she had made the same mistake. 'All of us' was not 'both of us'.

"That's the illogicality of the female. Has your headache gone?"

"Yes. Thank you." She knew he hadn't been fooled. "I didn't really have one. I thought you might prefer to be alone."

"I know. Thank you for the thought process."

He brought his whisky round and sat in the chair opposite her.

"As it happens, I don't. Want to dine alone, that is. You, of course, think you would like to dine alone, but actually would be miserable doing so." He saw her open her mouth and forestalled her.

"Come on, be truthful! I'm not that tedious a companion. Lots of women think I'm witty and charming."

She was aggravated by the teasing. "I wouldn't know, would I? Being the butt of a joke doesn't necessarily make the joke a funny one. In any case, I'm not one of your women."

"You're not the butt of a joke and certainly not one of my women," he said with mock gravity. "All the women I know would have been extremely put out to find there were two bedrooms, and I was going to be *tout seul* in one of them. All the women I know have only one thing on their minds, which is sex, and they all conveniently forgot that I was married, and all the women I know are late for everything. To find a woman who doesn't have any of those irritants is rare. So rare, that I refuse to pass up any opportunity of making her blush, or making her cross. And I have just succeeded in doing both, which is really very gratifying."

CHAPTER FIFTEEN

On Thursday, the day they went to Fife, the heavens opened. Buckets of water poured out of the sky and down the stone-mullioned windows of Lothian House Hotel and Melissa contemplated the forthcoming site meeting with resigned dismay. Her wellington boots and waterproofs had been unreachable in Hampshire, and she had only a showerproof coat which she knew would behave like blotting paper. It seemed unlikely that a borrowed hotel umbrella would be much use in competition with a notepad, pencil and tape measure.

The results of the previous day's marathon were piled satisfyingly on the desk in transparent plastic folders, the letters already in the hotel postbox. Despite his apparently chaotic working habits, Nicholas's brain was a good deal less scattered, and the reports and letters on various projects and subjects had impressed her. He had specified triple spacing for the first drafts which had then been slashed, circled, arrowed, deleted from and added to, and the finished products were clear and concise. Now, as they waited for his car to be brought to the door, each of them attended by an umbrella-toting member of staff, he was muttering about Scotland and rain and mud to such an extent that she felt personally responsible for her homeland's bad behaviour.

Their first stop had been the hotel sports and leisure shop where he bought her rubber boots and Gore-Tex trousers and jacket. She gasped at the price tag, but one look at his face prevented her from arguing. She drove north, and with the 'Beware Cross Winds' signs gleaming redly, crossed the Forth Road Bridge into Fife, with Nicholas trying to photograph the new half built bridge through the lashing rain.

The McNair Watts were welcoming and the introductions caused little cries of remembrance. Mrs McNair

Watt was keen that, having established a university connection, they should stay to lunch as by that time the family 'should be up'. Lorraine and Emily were at home, unusually, and Emily would be so thrilled to see Melissa, and 'Nick' would want to talk things over further with Angus, wouldn't he? After a morning in the rain they would need something hot and restoring, wouldn't they? She appealed to them both with smiling encouragement bolstered by supportive grunts from Angus who was obviously keen to get started. Melissa deferred to her employer whose eyes had that rather disturbing hard glimmer.

"How very kind," he said. "Lunch sounds delightful, and we will look forward to it."

To her relief Nicholas took charge, the conversation became a meeting and Melissa thankfully retreated behind a hedge of note-taking. Later they donned their survival suits and waded out into the appalling weather. The house stood about 600 yards from the sea, and on a good day might have had a view right across to Leith. Visibility in the driving rain was barely to the shore.

Angus McNair Watt was reasonably well informed about his property, and Melissa wrote dutifully. The notebook was soon sodden and her hands became numb.

Eventually, having picked his way through the stable block, measured and banged and muttered and dictated, Nicholas shoved the tape back into his pocket and packed all his instruments away in their custom-built case. Angus had long since left them to it.

"Come on. That's enough. Pity the poor souls who live out the evening of their lives here."

Lorraine and Emily were both in the drawing room when Nicholas and Melissa, de-booted and to some extent cleaned up, were ushered in. Melissa still felt wet around the edges, her hair damp on her cheeks, cuffs clinging to cold wrists. Compared to the casual good looks of the sisters, she felt disadvantaged, her nose shiny and cheeks wind-reddened. Mother had obviously informed daughters of the coincidence of the architect's assistant being an old acquaintance, and Emily sat her down to a cross-examination on one of the sofas. Lorraine, animated and delightful, joined her father and already held Nicholas in conversation. Melissa was aware of her speculative glance and it dawned on her that her grandparents had been thinking of exactly this scenario when they had objected to the trip. Melissa was careful to be extremely interested in Emily's career.

"Does Mel work for Thauros Associates then?" she heard Lorraine ask Nicholas.

"No," he said. "Melissa and I have very odd working arrangements. It takes a great deal of charm and money to prise her loose from antiques or human resources."

"Lord! What a mixture! It wouldn't take anything to prise me loose from any job," Lorraine said with a laugh. "Next time just ask me—it'll be much easier!"

"But you wouldn't like it any more than Melissa does." His tone was cool. "I'm frequently grumpy. And I expect a lot. Melissa drove me up from London on Tuesday; yesterday she worked sixteen hours and tonight she'll be transcribing today's work into the small hours again." There was a small, amazed silence. "She's doing me a considerable favour, and I'm having to be polite and considerate—quite an effort for me." Melissa smiled faintly and thought it sounded impressive. The four McNair Watts were looking slightly astonished.

"So how did antiques meet the architect?" asked Angus with an attempt at joviality. Melissa kept her mouth firmly shut, but her eyes skewered her employer.

"We met in an argument over buying something we both wanted. It took a while for her to forgive me."

Emily was trying to remember. "You did History of Art, of course. I'd forgotten. How exciting! Were you bidding against each other? Was it a picture? Or a piece of furniture? Were you working for Christie's, Mel?" She didn't wait for an answer. "I sometimes watch those TV programmes and I've often wondered what it must be like to bid at an auction."

"I take it you won the argument," Lorraine cut across Emily. "Was it furniture?"

"No," he said, "it was a book. And yes, I won—of course."

"Why of course?"

"Because," he said gently, "I was using my own money and she was not. It makes a difference. The difference between a whim and a budget."

The rain was even heavier and the windscreen wipers hurled water aside as she drove back towards Edinburgh after lunch. She had been vaguely surprised that he'd told her to drive again, expecting him to take the wheel under the eyes of two pretty girls. She guessed he was underlining the fact that he'd hired a chauffeur/typist.

"So, what did you think of all that?" he asked.

She was silent for a moment or two. "I don't know really. I found it all slightly odd."

"How was it odd?"

She shrugged. "Well, I'm not accustomed to that sort of meeting so it probably wasn't odd at all. I suppose I'd expected them to be more enthusiastic—more interested—in their project. To have more ideas, to ask questions, but instead they were happy to talk antique sales, and things which were nothing to do with why you'd come."

After a pause he said, "Did you like them?"

She said reluctantly, "Not especially, which is unreasonable of me. They were very welcoming, and lunch was delicious."

"Why not?"

"Oh! Nicholas! For heaven's sake! I have no idea why not. I'm your reluctant typist, remember? Nothing could be less to the point than whether I liked them or not!"

"Oh—you'd be surprised. I never underestimate the female instinct."

Melissa refused to let herself be drawn and drove into the city, awash with damp tourists, the air opaque with moisture.

She drove through the New Town, the car purring over the cobbles.

"It's an architect's dream, isn't it?" she said. "Except for Princes Street. Once it was just as beautiful as the rest."

"Little Miss Regency," he teased, "so old-fashioned that you frown on progress."

"It's not progress!" she exclaimed. "It's regression! It's thin tin set in old gold; these horrible glass buildings ought to be blown up. It makes me furious."

He glanced at her curiously. "So I notice. Where are you taking me now?"

"Up to the Castle and down the Royal Mile to Holyrood, and then back to the hotel to get all that stuff down on paper."

"I suppose we should. Does it ever stop raining in this godforsaken city?"

"Not often." She put in a quick burst of prayer for blue skies tomorrow. It would be an unexpected bonus, and she was surprised at how much she wanted him to like Scotland.

The Royal Mile was policed by orange and white cones and she drove slowly and carefully through the clutter of umbrella-toting tourists. Nicholas found himself entertained all the way back to his temporary office. He had to pull his mind back sharply to the morning's work and found he was less interested in the proposed retirement home than he was in Rizzio's murder.

Having ordered tea and given some instructions, he left Melissa to transcribe her rain-stained notebook on to the computer and disappeared downstairs. On his return two hours later, Melissa saw that his hair was wet.

"You look as if you've been walking in the rain," she said, surprised.

He shook his head. "Nope. Squash and fifty lengths in the pool."

"They have a squash court?"

"Two. And indoor as well as outdoor tennis courts, and a gym. And a golf course. And stables. And a lot more if you read the blurb."

"Wow!" she said, impressed. "This is some hotel! I could put up with it for a while, I suppose. I shan't make such a fuss next time you need a chauffeur/typist."

He didn't reply and she looked up from the screen in sudden alarm.

He was looking down at her with that closed speculative expression, as if his mind was somewhere else.

"For heaven's sake! I was only joking! I didn't mean I wanted to use the facilities!" She was embarrassed by her silly comment. "I've nearly finished the notes. What do you want me to do then?"

"Bath? Hair? A nice dress? Dinner somewhere? A show?"

She flushed. "I didn't mean that. I meant—"

"I know what you meant. I know what I meant, too. All work and no play has the makings of a very dull day. You were going to show me your alma mater."

"Not at night, in the pouring rain."

"Such a sensible girl!" he murmured. "So cautious that you're in danger of staying rooted to the spot. Go bath, and put on something decently indecent. And you'd better have some peanuts or something as we won't eat till late. And hurry up. We're due in our seats at seven-thirty."

"Seats? You've got tickets for something?"

Her surprise made him laugh.

"The Usher Hall, Royal Scottish National Orchestra, Gorecki and Tchaikovsky."

"What? How on earth did you manage that?"

"Money," he said succinctly. "It has its advantages. Do stop talking and go and get changed, there's a good girl."

"Who's Gorecki? Russian?"

"Polish. Wonderful."

A man who took unilateral decisions like that, she thought, was high-handed and arrogant, but it certainly

194

simplified life delightfully. When she reappeared, he eyed her over his whisky glass and indicated a glass of wine on the coffee table.

"You've worn that before and it could hardly be called decently indecent."

"Well, there isn't any choice," she said. "Unless you want me to wear what I wore last night, and it's just as decent as this is, I'm afraid."

"Have you only brought two outfits?"

"Yes! I have. I haven't got much more than that anyway, and I certainly wasn't expecting to wear them."

"Amazing!" he said, astonished. "Marie Claude never wore anything twice, and certainly not with the same man."

Still cross, Melissa said, "You asked me—bullied me—into coming. Driving, you said, and taking notes and typing. I didn't expect to need to dress up and I very nearly didn't bring these, so be thankful I'm not in jeans."

"I am," he said. "You look delightful in jeans, but only knee-deep in mud. Tomorrow we will buy some clothes."

"We will do no such thing," she said robustly, "tomorrow or any other day. This is supposed to be a working holiday, not a fashion display and I buy my own clothes, thank you."

He threw his head back and laughed.

"Dear Melissa! That's exactly what you don't do—you haven't got any clothes. What a gem you are! I've never come across a girl who wasn't interested in clothes and jewellery, so it's a new sensation for me. Having been driven mad by my wife's wastefulness, I now find I may be driven mad by a conservative Scot. You cannot go on holiday with just two evening garments—it's ridiculous."

"I didn't expect to be staying anywhere so smart, or to go out to dinner or to concerts."

"What did you expect?" He was suddenly serious. "Did you think we'd sit cosily in a guest house watching television of an evening? Or that I'd take off for the bright lights on my own, or what?"

"I don't know." She was uncomfortable. "I just didn't expect to be wined and dined and taken out. I suppose I thought you'd be meeting clients and having business dinners."

"And where would you be, on these tedious-sounding occasions?"

"Well, working, I thought, and I'm perfectly happy with my own company."

He rolled his eyes in mock exasperation. "You have extraordinary expectations of my work output," he said. "You actually worked quite hard today, got very wet, had a sort of business lunch, transcribed all the notes, and now you want to get stuck into a second draft. What a hard taskmaster you are, just when I want to go out and have some fun in the rain. You may be happy with your own company, but I'm not, so you'll just have to put up with me in the spirit of shut your eyes and think of England—or rather Scotland. We'll finish that report tomorrow, and then I shall get you some clothes."

He ignored her protestations and there was no problem with parking as they were driven to the Usher Hall by a member of the hotel staff. The interval bell had rung when she heard her name called and found herself enveloped in the delighted bear hug of an old housemate. She introduced Robbie Cairns to Nicholas.

"Haven't seen you for ages, Mel. Are you still working in London?"

"Yes, for a computer software company, and now temporarily for Nicholas, who's an architect."

Robbie Cairns looked at Nicholas with sharp interest.

"Ah! Thauros Associates? Thought I knew the name. What on earth are you doing in computer software, Mel? Why aren't you painting, or using your drawing?"

She grinned ruefully. "It doesn't pay the bills, Robbie!"

"Blimey! What a waste!"

The second bell rang and Robbie scribbled his home telephone on a business card and gave it to her with a hug and a kiss.

196

"Call me, Mel. I'd love to see you if you've got a spare evening."

Later, when their tame driver had deposited them at a hotel-recommended restaurant, Nicholas brought him up again.

"An old flame?"

"Well, a spark really. An old friend from my first student digs. There were twelve of us in the house, chaotic, mad, but good fun. Robbie plays the accordion and we had some wild reeling parties in that house."

"Reeling as in alcohol or as in tribal dancing?"

"Tribal dancing."

"Can I see his card? He said he'd heard of Thauros Associates, which is interesting as the only project we have here is the Glasgow one." He looked at the card she handed over. "Yes, he's a surveyor. Did you go out with him?"

"With Robbie? Oh, yes, we all did. But none of us very seriously. He had a soft spot for a politics student who earned her fees being the female half of a fire-eating duo. Every now and then he'd get fed up with the taste of meths or whatever it is they use, and take some of the other girls out."

His eyes crinkled in amusement. "That must have been refreshing. You certainly don't taste of meths."

She had a flash of memory; the pressure of his hands on her body and his mouth on hers. She flushed and picked up her wine glass.

"Anyway, we all went our separate ways after the first year, and I haven't seen him since. I haven't a clue what a surveyor does—I have visions of wooden pegs with bits of string and calculations done on a tripod."

He shook his head.

"A surveyor on a building team is more financial. It's very precise mathematical work."

He looked thoughtfully at his wine glass, twisting its stem.

"He wasn't a serious boyfriend then? But you like him?"

197

"Yes, I do. It was really good to see him."

"And will you arrange to meet him again?"

She stared at him across the table. "I might. Have you got a problem with that?"

He put his head slightly on one side, considering, and she wondered for a mad moment if he were jealous.

"I don't think so. He works for a competitor. You'd need to be careful about what you said."

The mad moment fled and she said, "I can be discreet."

"Very discreet," he said with a grin. "I remember that even when I tempted you with writing off all my criminal charges, you refused to tell me who Mann's clients were."

He returned the card. "If we can finish that report on the would-be retirement home tomorrow, we can have some time off. We don't have to be in Glasgow till Monday."

"Shall I meet you in Glasgow, or what do you want me to do? Do you even want me in Glasgow? If not, I must fix up to stay with someone."

"Yes, I do want you in Glasgow! And no, you won't meet me there because I don't want you going off anywhere. You're here as my driver, remember?"

There was a faint bite in his tone, and she showed her surprise.

"Oh. OK. Where do you want to be driven to?"

"The Borders, I had thought. If this rain ever stops. Otherwise it could be a direct flight to the Skeleton Coast or somewhere dry like that."

"The Borders! Why there?"

It was his turn to look surprised. "It's your country, you said. Beautiful and historical; I assumed I couldn't escape Scotland without seeing some of it. I'm expecting a guided tour."

She was alarmed. "Of where?"

"How do I know? I'm not the expert! I'll go where I'm taken and I'm sure it'll be interesting." He saw her expression and his own softened. "Don't forget, I'm Greek. I know absolutely nothing about Scottish history. I assume they

198

didn't like the English. That gives you a clear educational field, doesn't it?"

She wished she didn't have this suspicion that he was patronising her. He'd persuaded her to do this job for him and now he obviously felt he must make it up to her by being nice and trailing round the dank border landscape after her, pretending an interest he couldn't possibly feel.

"You don't need to be dutifully interested and you can certainly escape Scotland without seeing any of it. And I really am not into guided tours. Why don't you just enjoy yourself and do what you want to do? If you don't need me to work over the weekend I'm very happy to go and stay with friends in Edinburgh."

His mouth tightened slightly and if she hadn't known better she might have thought that his feelings were hurt.

"Why the sudden prickles? I thought you'd like a day on home territory—and I was looking forward to going with you. However, if my company is really that unwelcome I won't force it on you."

She stared at him uncertainly. "You mean you genuinely want to go?"

"What's so odd about it? I'm not going to make you personally responsible for the weather."

"I thought you were just being—polite. I didn't think you really wanted to."

"My dear Melissa!" The mockery was overt. "Since when have I ever been polite to you? If the day ever dawns when I'm polite to you, you can take it that something has gone seriously wrong with our relationship. You must surely know by now that I never do anything unless I want to do it, so you can safely assume that I would like to see you in some decent clothes purely for my own pleasure, and I would also like to be driven around the Borders, see a castle, a stately home, a ruined abbey—whatever. I'd prefer to do it with somebody, and a native would be an advantage, rather than on my own, but I'm not prepared to fight over it if you would prefer to stay in Edinburgh. I'll be coming back to Edinburgh if this

Fife thing comes off and can no doubt discover it for myself, but I doubt I'll ever manage the Borders in quite the same way."

His sharpness contrived to make her feel ungrateful and rude.

"Of course I'll come, if you really want to go," she said feebly. "I just didn't want you to feel you had to. I'd gone a bit over-enthusiastic on the drive north."

"What a very curious girl you are," he said. "It comes in the same category as the headache before dinner, doesn't it?"

She said nothing and concentrated on her plate.

"Somewhere, somehow, on the rocky road to adulthood, you have managed to acquire the most monumental inferiority complex. Did somebody give it to you? Your parents? A boyfriend? Or was it school and schoolfriends? Bits of you stand up and shout back, but not loud enough or long enough. Where did it come from, this assumption that nobody would want your company? That you have no value?"

She remembered the amazing headmaster at her new school in Hampshire battling with those same demons in the twelve-year-old disaster he had inherited.

"You?" she said, half-jokingly.

He shook his head, turning her self-mockery to seriousness.

"No, not me. It was there before I ever started being nasty to you." She looked mulish, and he saw her shoulders hunch as she protested without much conviction. He let a silence rest between them and then asked, "Tell me more about your family. Your parents and siblings."

She looked up, startled. "I'd rather not."

"I know. That's why I asked you. You had several siblings and now there are only two of you, and no parents. After an accident."

She felt extraordinarily helpless. People just didn't say things like this. It was insensitive, an invasion of privacy, and it pulled the scab off a sore she thought had healed.

200

"Are you afraid of crying?"

"No. I'm afraid of all sorts of other things, but not that. I never cried then and I'm not about to start now."

"And when was then?"

He waited while she had her internal debate.

"Twelve years ago. A car accident." He waited again and eventually she sighed in defeat. "Mum drove my three older brothers to a party. We would all have gone but Johnny and I had flu and Dad stayed with us. They were all killed—another young couple, too."

Her eyes were unfocussed, looking back, and her face was just quietly sad. He watched her without saying anything. She spoke again, remembering but not resisting the memory. "You can't help it—the guilt of being the one left—of it being your fault. And please don't say it—" she turned on him fiercely "—don't say it wasn't my fault."

"I wasn't going to," he said mildly.

She relaxed a little. "Everybody does—or did. It drove us wild, Johnny and me. And Dad. Nobody understood—they just kept mouthing these stupid clichés— 'it wasn't your fault', 'you couldn't help having flu', 'time will heal', 'you mustn't feel guilty'. At least we had each other—there was one person for each of us who understood that it *was* our fault. But Johnny—for Johnny it was far, far worse. He's never got over it, never learnt to cope. They were just fifteen, the twins, and James died and he was left. Fifteen is an awful age anyway, especially for a boy. Nobody could deal with him—or me for that matter, and Dad just fell to pieces."

"How old were your brothers?"

He hadn't been sympathetic or commiserated, for which she was grateful.

"Adam was nineteen, Peter seventeen, James and Johnny fifteen and I was twelve."

"And your father?"

Her stomach cramped. "Nicholas, please. I can't. I'm sorry. Can we leave it there, for now? I don't tend to—talk about it much. At all, actually; it's easier to survive that way."

He let a silence settle for a few moments.

"Survival has a big wardrobe," he said. "Different people deal with it in different ways." He smiled suddenly. "You, on the other hand, haven't got a wardrobe at all. I hope there are some decent shops in this city. I've never known anyone with so few clothes."

"Oh, no!"

"Oh, yes! You're not going to fight me, are you?"

He had changed the subject just before the scab came off and the blood ran.

"I can't let you buy me clothes, and I haven't got the money to pay for them. Please don't insist."

He was patient. "I know you haven't got the money. I have. More than is good for me. Think of it as one more example of my self-indulgence. I like beautiful clothes, but as I can't wear them myself, someone has to wear them for me. You're only doing me a favour—is that so difficult? I'm obviously not doing you one."

She went scarlet. "I didn't mean—"

His mouth twisted slightly.

"What didn't you mean?"

Her hand was tense on the stem of her glass. "I didn't mean to be rude—or ungrateful; but it puts me in a difficult position—"

"Does it? I think you only put yourself in a difficult position. What is it you're expecting me to demand in return? What are you afraid of?"

She said nothing, and he continued quite gently. "Do you honestly think I'm capable of that sort of blackmail? You accepted this from me, and therefore you must—do—give? Has everything in life had to be paid for? Is receiving so difficult?"

She looked up at him, frowning, trying to articulate something which had never consciously surfaced before.

"No—not blackmail, I suppose. But people, men, tend to expect something back for giving you a nice time. It's not just that, though, it's more a feeling that I've got to stand on an equal footing. You don't get something for nothing, or you shouldn't."

"What about love and affection? Did your parents demand something in return for loving you?"

"Of course they didn't."

"There are demands, though," he said neutrally. A waiter came and filled their glasses. "One isn't always conscious of them. It can be overt, like having to get good exam marks in exchange for approval—conditional love. Or it can be hidden, like you feel you should make up for surviving when others died. You want to make yourself worth the fact that you exist. Unconditional love tells you that you're loved because you exist, not because of anything you do or achieve."

She thought of her father, who had been unable to survive the guilt of existing, who had thought he had seen accusation in the eyes of his remaining children, and had never recognised the burden of their own guilt.

"I suppose my grandparents are like that," she said, slowly absorbing his words. "They loved Johnny and me through the whole horrible mess, including the fact that our behaviour may well have made Dad—" She stopped abruptly and then started again. "They sold Meath, moved to Hampshire, put us both into a brilliant local school—well, a school with a brilliant and demanding head who saved me from educational disaster. But on the whole I think that people who never demand anything are even less interested in me than those who do."

"Pussycat!" He sounded half appalled, half amused. "I shall demand that you both accept and wear all the clothes I buy you. Is that sufficiently demanding? And that you do a comprehensive tour of the Borders for me this weekend."

"Don't joke about it." She tried to sound cross, but found she was smiling.

As it turned out, Edinburgh was not to be the source of a vast new wardrobe. Nicholas was as precise in his requirements as Melissa was hesitant, and his unerring eye seized on and discarded garments with discerning speed.

"Edinburgh doesn't cater for your shape," he said grouchily, "only for Junoesque ladies with hunting thighs and grouse-shooting calves."

By eleven she was wilting.

"There's an awful lot of work waiting to be done," she said plaintively.

He admitted defeat, and they walked back to the car park in a drizzle that was turning to rain. Suddenly, he took her arm and ushered her into a small boutique they were passing.

"That," he said to the lady in command, pointing to a dress in the window. "In a Size 12." When a Size 12 was produced, she was dispatched into a changing room.

Ten minutes later she had paraded, he had approved, the dress was in a smart bag and they were on their way. Melissa felt stunned. She hung it up in her cupboard at the hotel in horrified pleasure and wondered if she was turning into the kept woman of a drug smuggler, clothes provided out of his ill-gotten gains.

CHAPTER SIXTEEN

At a quarter to one the hotel telephone rang. The voice sounded amazed and Melissa recognised it immediately.

"Mr Thauros's office? My dear, how efficient and brisk you sound! I am impressed! Can I speak to Nick or is he having lunch?"

In the space of seconds, she had managed to reduce Melissa to a typist, and one who wouldn't be lunching with her boss either. Could she speak to Nick indeed! Melissa bristled and straightened her back.

"No, we haven't had lunch yet. He's still working. Who's calling?"

"Lorraine, of course. Didn't you recognise my voice?"

"Sorry to say, no. We have a lot of calls," she said untruthfully. "Hold on and I'll see if he can talk to you."

She rapped on his door and the murmur of his voice stopped with an irritated 'Yes!' He was obviously not pleased to have his dictation interrupted.

"I'll call them back. Who is it?"

"Lorraine."

He lifted his head in a black stare. "Why?"

"I haven't the faintest idea. Personal was the impression."

He switched off the dictating machine and lifted the receiver beside him. Melissa closed the door and replaced her own receiver. She ploughed on down the computer screen. There was a faint ping from the telephone. His door opened and lunch was ordained.

"The McNair Watts have come up with further ideas and suggestions—most of which are almost undoubtedly non-fliers. Lorraine is coming over later this afternoon to deliver her father's notes and discuss the possibilities."

"Couldn't they fax them? It seems a long way to come with a batch of notes."

"Apparently not," he said. She wasn't sure which bit of her remark he was referring to. After lunch, she resumed work immediately, not wishing to risk Lorraine observing that the day's production wasn't enormous. She wasn't going to admit to the morning's shopping and she hoped Nicholas wouldn't either. Nicholas dealt with his emails and seemed pleased about something. Lorraine's visit, Melissa assumed.

Lorraine arrived too late for tea, and fairly early for the whisky she asked for. Sitting down on one of the sofas, she patted the seat beside her.

"The family have been brainstorming. Come and tell me what you think."

Nicholas ignored the invitation but took the proffered envelope. He prowled round the furniture studying the contents and Melissa printed off the remains of the day's work and piled the neat sheets on the desk. She was finding it hard to concentrate on what she was doing as well as cope with Lorraine's faintly barbed teasing comments about her efficiency, and what a lovely office to work in, wasn't she lucky. She was casually dressed, but managed to look beautifully turned out. Melissa guessed it wasn't as casual as it looked. Lorraine picked up the newly printed sheets and riffled through them.

"The computer really does turn out smart-looking work, doesn't it?"

"Yeah, it does a fantastic job. I only press the print button," Melissa said. Nicholas had a coughing fit in the background.

Lorraine had now seen a pile of Nicholas's corrections, the sheets looking as if a demented spider had died spitting blood all over them.

"Good Lord! It doesn't look as if you got them down very accurately in the first place! Still, it was raining, so I don't suppose it was very easy for you."

Patronising bitch, Melissa thought. As there was no way of retaliating unless she criticized her employer's working methods, she just smiled and shrugged. There was plenty more work to do, but she certainly wasn't going to do it with Lorraine peering over her shoulder.

Lorraine flicked the papers in Nicholas's hand. "I told Dad I'd discuss it all with you over dinner and report back in the morning. You can give him a call after lunch tomorrow."

Which was rather arrogant, not to say rude, Melissa thought, mentally leaping to Nicholas's defence. He went on reading and didn't appear to notice.

"Melissa, you need a stiff drink," he said suddenly. "Turn off all that stuff and come and sit down. You haven't stopped all day." Which was not altogether accurate.

He dropped the papers on the coffee table and turned to Lorraine. "We could discuss it briefly now," he said mildly, "but not over dinner, thank you. I do not live to work. Melissa has arranged to show me Edinburgh by night, so I'm afraid dinner isn't possible."

To Melissa's amazement the hardly concealed put-down was like water off a duck's back. Lorraine gave a little gust of laughter.

"How sweet! Showing you all the old haunts! It's like going back to school after you've left—you feel so grown-up, don't you? Can't I come too? Or will I be *de trop*? I certainly don't want to intrude on a romantic evening."

There could be no polite answer to this revolting speech, Melissa thought. Whichever way he jumped, it would be wrong, so she took the decision for him.

"You'd hardly be doing that." She hoped her voice sounded lightly amused. "But in fact, you'd be doing us both a favour in escorting Nicholas tonight. I've had a pretty exhausting few days, and this one hasn't finished yet—I've still got a lot of work to do and I must make some phone calls, too." She eyed her employer somewhat nervously as there was a rather grim look round his mouth. "I'd love to have a bath and a break, and then to try to finish that lot—

though it looks as if you're bringing some changes." She indicated Lorraine's papers on the coffee table. "Don't you think that would be sensible, Nicholas? Then when the Glasgow stuff arrives I can concentrate on that. My old haunts, as Lorraine puts it, can wait, and in any case, she'll be a much better guide than me."

There wasn't a great deal Nicholas could do or say with the two of them standing there smiling at him.

They had drinks together, with general small talk, and Melissa excused herself to bath and change. It didn't sound as if Lorraine was putting forward anything very concrete and she wasn't keen to be the little secretary in front of her.

As they left Nicholas turned and growled, "Don't wait up."

Once, in the heavy darkness, she thought she heard quiet voices and Lorraine's soft laugh. Jealousy flared, even in a dream.

When she appeared in the morning, he was sitting correcting drafts, a cup of coffee in one hand. He had obviously been swimming. She said she hoped he'd had a pleasant evening, to which he gave an abstracted neutral grunt. Room service brought their breakfast and he continued to wield his red pen on the remains of her previous night's typing. Lorraine must have left very quietly, very early, unless she was still in his bed. Which, Melissa thought, was the most likely scenario. Would she suddenly appear, brandishing her amorous victory, or would she stay quietly in his room until they'd left? Or perhaps just until Melissa had left and then Nicholas could say goodbye. Gloom was added to jealousy.

"Shall I retype these now?" She indicated the pile of paper, and he shook his head.

"Certainly not. If you start them now the day will be gone, and you must have been up half the night on them anyway. Let's go."

"You still want to go?"

He gave her a quick hard glance.

"Yes, I do. Are you feeling all right?"

"Yes. I'm fine. Shall I wait for you downstairs?"

He frowned. "No. I only have to collect my jacket. If you get yours, we can go down together."

Lorraine must have left early, although she hadn't looked the sort of girl who liked early rising.

She hadn't been able to keep up her distant manner in the face of his interest and apparent enjoyment of Scottish history and architecture. She drove him down to Peebles, then crossed the Tweed and let him assimilate Traquair. He gazed down the grassy avenue from behind the gates to the tall creamy house, its little windows giving it a smiley, welcoming look.

"A little French château in the middle of Scotland," he murmured in amazement, and proceeded to become headily confused by Border aristocracy, impressed by an entire river re-routed to suit the architect, to get lost in the maze and gingerly, to buy a bottle of the famous beer.

"'The Oldest Inhabited House in Scotland'," he quoted, looking up at the high overhanging walls again from the courtyard.

"They certainly made sure of future generations. Fancy having nineteen children. Poor lady."

"Oh, I don't know. It's all women are good for, after all." He grinned down at her.

"Rubbish—it only goes to show where men kept their brains. Who do you think ran these places? It took a woman to run an army of servants and keep the place fed, watered and defended. She was always pregnant, poor thing. Twenty solid years—plus a few miscarriages, I expect. I can't imagine anything more awful."

"So you don't want children?"

"I didn't say that. I don't want nineteen, that's all. If I ever get married of course I'll want children. What about you? Do you like children? You don't have any, do you?"

The moment the words were out of her mouth, she could have bitten her tongue out. He looked sightlessly at the

209

house and took so long to answer that she knew she'd gone beyond the bounds of acceptability.

"Sorry. Forget I said that." She felt the heat flood her face, and when he focused on her again he saw it and the raw anger subsided as quickly as it had come.

"It's OK. Why shouldn't you ask? I asked you. No, I don't have any, and yes, I like children. I'd like nineteen—so long as I don't have to produce them myself, that is." He smiled down at her and the awkward moment passed. But Melissa had seen something that had shaken her, and found her hands unsteady. She shoved them into her jacket pockets. She had unwittingly trespassed on to unstable ground and was very glad to be back on solid earth.

She drove him down the River Tweed, rolling seawards between its wooded banks. He was again an interested and amusing companion.

"That was my grandfather's mill," she said, pointing it out. "Most of them went bust, including his, but there are a few working mills now." A few miles further on she pointed to a white house deep in the oak woods on the opposite bank.

"That's Meath. Where Mops and Brig lived. We grew up there mainly."

"Would you like to see it again?"

She shook her head. There were too many memories to revisit.

Melrose Abbey held him silent and awed. The skeleton of the rose red abbey stretched bony fingers of gothic tracery into the sky and while he sat on a tombstone and gazed at it, she slid a thin sketchbook out of her shoulder bag and found a patch of sun out of the wind. Drawing soothed her, and she tried to bury the memory of his taut, silent anger at Traquair in the concentration of transferring the dog-toothed window embrasure to the sheet before her. Had that anger been directed at her, and if so, why? Eventually he came to find her, standing at her back until she became aware of his presence. They drove on, past the great viaduct at Leaderfoot, and stopped at Scott's view. The sun had strengthened and the steep valley below was filled with autumn colour, the Eildons rising beyond the silver sheet of the river bend. He sat on the wall and had one of his rare cigarettes.

"It's not grand, or splendid, or magnificent or imposing," he said thoughtfully, "but it's all of them rolled into one and then made gentle."

He got up and stretched. "I'm hungry. Where, in all this lost and lonely land are we going to find anything edible? And I don't mean haggis and black pudding. Your local pubs look very unappetizing."

She had done her online research and drove him a little further to a new restaurant within a mill shop which had burst into the 21st century under the hawk-eyed management of a French designer.

"It's quite expensive," she said, not very apologetically, "but I thought you'd prefer that to poor food."

"How observant of you," he said teasingly. After a lunch enlivened by the turbulent history of the Borders, he bought sweaters for his family, asking Melissa's advice on what they would like. She blinked at the unbelievable cost of cashmere; boat neck for Galina, cable-stitched for Sophie, turtle-necked for Ruth. He held a cashmere polo neck up against Melissa, his strong fingers on her shoulders preventing her from backing off.

"Lapis lazuli," he murmured. "Your colour exactly. The colour you wore when I first met you." His eyes crinkled, and she remembered the bikini and blushed.

"Don't," she said fiercely. "Don't you dare. I don't want it."

"Are you going to make a scene?" His eyes dared her. The shop was full of tourists and the sweater was added to his purchases.

Back in the car, he asked, "Where are they buried? You could go and do your family the courtesy of saying hello."

She shook her head. "This is your day in the Borders."

211

"When are you next going to be here to pay your respects?"

She glanced at him and hesitated. "True. OK. Thank you."

At the church, she sat for a moment staring blindly out into the low afternoon sun, then went away up the hill to the churchyard. He leant back in his seat and grieved for dead children. The destroyed; the discarded; the buried.

Halfway back to Edinburgh she remembered that he had been supposed to telephone Angus McNair Watt.

"I didn't forget. I just didn't," he said casually.

She was taken aback. "Why not? Won't he have been waiting for it?"

"I'm not a tame dog, jumping for a biscuit!" He seemed mildly amused that she was shocked at him. "If he wants us as architects he won't ditch us on the strength of one delayed phone call. I told Lorraine I would be off-duty this weekend. They've thought up some fairly crazy ideas which make me shudder and I don't really want to talk to him about them."

"Like what?" she said curiously, but when he didn't answer immediately she wondered if she'd been presumptuous again. "I'm sorry, none of my business. I didn't mean to pry."

"Don't be ridiculous! You've typed the entire proposal—there's nothing you don't know about. I just haven't given it any thought, that's all. Amongst other things, he's suggesting an underground tunnel between the stables and the main house, and various facilities as part of the underground complex. A cinema; a health spa."

Her eyebrows went up.

"Elderly people hate tunnels. The mind boggles at the thought of a power cut with a dozen old ladies trapped underground. Is he thinking lifts and escalators, or an electric spiral wheelchair ramp or what?"

He was laughing. "What else can you come up with? We could build in an emergency generator."

"Money no object?"

212

"Well, it would have to be, wouldn't it? The gradient between the house and the stables is very steep."

"How about a cog railway?"

He gave a crack of laughter. "That's why I wasn't keen to phone back."

"Expensive," She was dubious. "If he's worried about rain, snow and wind, an enclosed glass walkway would be better. It could be filled with plants to cheer them all up in winter and you could make a tunnel for the cars instead."

"It would certainly be a more agreeable solution. But I doubt any Health Care Trust has that sort of capital investment funds, so it would need to be a private company. These are ambitious ideas which need big investments. Where would you think he might be finding investors?"

She blinked. "He appears to want to give the architect a pretty free rein, so maybe the architect, who is apparently quite wealthy, might go on an ego-trip, might he?"

"I did rather wonder. And I also wondered what you thought about the pretty daughter throwing herself at the architect, and then the poor wretched architect being left to fend for himself last night?"

"Oh!" She drew a breath. "Nicholas—for heaven's sake, I bet you had a fantastic time. Do you seriously think he wants you to invest in this project?" A thought struck her. "Anyway, they weren't to know that it would be you, personally, who would do the feasibility study, were they?"

Nicholas looked thoughtful. "Well, funnily enough I think they did. They asked for me by name. Apparently, they 'liked my work', which is odd as I am quite junior and not a partner, so I don't know what 'work' they liked."

"Well, they don't seem to have thought much of it through or done any proper market research. He'd need to charge vast amounts to get his money back. What happens if he can't get the customers?"

"Dear Melissa. You have been under-estimated, under-valued and under-utilized. You've got a nice, sharp, devious little brain and that very valuable asset, common sense." The

213

compliment made her blush again. "Anyway, it's academic. I have no intention in investing in what amounts to a conversion, which some people enjoy, but I don't. As you've probably realised, as you've typed the report on the stable block, the complications of converting accommodation suitable for horses into accommodation suitable for humans are considerable, and it would be very much easier and cheaper to start from scratch. To return to your inestimable common sense, why do you think we had a visit from Lorraine yesterday? Bringing all these expensive new ideas?"

Melissa turned on the irony. "We? No need to be polite. She didn't come to see me. You were the one who had dinner with her, didn't you discover?"

"Nope. She's far less honest than you are, and can tell lies without a blink, whereas you are quite hopeless at untruths."

Melissa wrinkled her nose. Where did you go for dinner? Was it Lorraine's choice? What did you talk about? Were they different things to the things you'd have said to me? Did you touch her? Kiss her? Make love to her?

"You've gone silent on me," he said.

"You don't like chattering."

"True, but I wasn't expecting you to chatter."

She laughed. "You know perfectly well why Lorraine came with expensive new ideas. Angus dotes on his darling elder daughter who can twist him round her little finger, and darling daughter fancies the architect." And darling daughter came yesterday to seduce Nicholas, and Melissa wasn't sure if she had succeeded or not. Nicholas grinned.

The following morning, she remembered, for no very good reason, that it was Sunday, and that yesterday was Saturday. That yesterday had been Dolphin Day, and that she'd forgotten to pay.

CHAPTER SEVENTEEN

They had had the argument about that payment over breakfast, and as usual she had lost and he had won, his logic being long and his patience eventually short.

They set off for a tourist's visit to Edinburgh in a silence of Melissa's making, which she found difficult to sustain in the face of his interest and curiosity. She put whatever she was feeling, which was unclear in any case, to the bottom of her consciousness and decided to enjoy being driven by a private guide around her own city, discovering that she knew rather less about it than she had thought. There were shafts of wind and vivid sunlight interspersed by occasional showers, and Nicholas was fascinated by their visits to the castle, Holyrood House, and John Knox's house. By late afternoon they both had history overload and sore feet and came reluctantly back to the hotel to pack up and prepare for Glasgow.

The hospital stood in parkland on a hill on the northern side of Glasgow, the surroundings a mess of mud and rubble and heaps of building material. Everywhere there were lorries and men in yellow hard hats, compressors and pumps, cranes and concrete mixers.

The boards listed the firms involved, Thauros Associates, Architects and Civil Engineers, among them. She had asked him whether he had done all the designs and plans himself and had blushed at his laughter.

"A team of eighteen from Thauros, four of whom will be here today."

He showed her the layout from the vantage point of the water tower, and she found herself concentrating on the strong, brown, long-fingered hand, instead of on the black outlines of the plans they moved across.

He looked at his watch. "It's cold. Why don't you come in and meet people and have some coffee?"

She shook her head, feeling shy and out of place. He gave her the set of plans, a hard hat and scribbled his signature on a security lanyard.

"Be careful," he admonished. "A building site is a dangerous place."

She found it fascinating. Without the plans, it would have been a senseless maze of breeze blocks and concrete pilings and pipes and scaffolding. It was hard to imagine wards and clinics, quietness and cleanliness amidst all the clatter and clutter of machinery and drills, the concrete dust within, the mud without. She tried to imagine the rough grey caverns peopled with doctors and nurses and tea ladies, and to fill the rooms with patients. She had a coffee in the main reception area where there were drinks and snacks machines, rough temporary seating and huge boards covered with plans, architects' views and technical data. She was drawn to the internal designs for the children's ward, but they were unimaginative and she studied them with more than a little disappointment.

A surge of voices, clattering feet on the stairs and a gale of colder air warned her that Nicholas's group was about to descend. She went outside and found that it had started to drizzle so she went back to the car, images of her own beginning to crowd her mind.

After half an hour, Nicholas still hadn't appeared, so she closed her sketchbook, and knowing that he had a spare key, locked the car and went for a walk. Beyond the water tower she found the surprisingly small site of the children's hospice on a steep slope. 'Built By The Community, For The Community' the boards announced. The curved frontage already had retaining walls and would have views across beautiful parkland and down over the city. Eventually hunger began to get the better of exercise and she turned away from the busy concrete mixers back towards the car park.

216

Her mind drifted back over the past two days with a relaxed Nicholas as opposed to several days of Nicholas in working mode. There was no doubt that despite all his money he worked extremely hard, and probably to a high standard. Not that she would know, not being an architect. She acknowledged to herself that as well as finding him sexually attractive, she also liked him. It would be so much easier to deal with his refusal to accept the fifty pounds a day late if she disliked him. Only one day, for heaven's sake. Was she being pig-headed or plain stupid? Was he being kind, or unkind? Damn it, she thought, he had been very kind, and there didn't seem to be any ulterior motive behind the kindnesses, although she felt there had to be. He had worked her hard, but had insisted on buying her a dress and a sweater which so far anyway he hadn't used as blackmail for anything. He hadn't made her feel incompetent or inadequate; he appeared to be interested in her life, he had reminded her to ring her grandparents daily, to ring Sarah, and Johnny, he had voluntarily spent two days of his life sight-seeing with her, he had detoured to the churchyard and made her visit the graves. The list was extensive, and made her suspicious, but she wasn't sure why. She struggled to equalize the scales; he flaunted his money, he always got his own way. He had interfered with the repayments to Clive Mann, seizing the agreement and berating her when it was none of his business. In the past, he had been sarcastic and unkind and patronising. He wouldn't let her repay what she owed, and she thought he was sorry for her. And he dealt in drugs. That last was the sticking point. Why, when it was so patently unnecessary, did he deal in drugs? It made her furious.

She had reached the car and wrenched open the passenger door to be met by Nicholas's puzzled and slightly concerned face. *Charlotte's Web* lay open on his knee.

"Oh! You're back!" she exclaimed unnecessarily. "I'm sorry to have kept you waiting."

"I've obviously kept you waiting, but I'm afraid these meetings tend to go on rather, and I couldn't leave it."

217

She looked blankly at him. "You haven't kept me waiting! Of course you couldn't leave the meeting! Why on earth should you?"

He still looked vaguely concerned. "We're all having lunch in a local pub. It'll be shop talk and pulling together this morning's meeting—rather uninteresting for you, I'm afraid—but better than the works canteen."

He waited while she put her sketchbook and handbag on the back seat. She didn't think that she had left her sketchbook in view but then remembered he would have had to move everything from the passenger seat. Not for the first time she wondered why he was making her do all the driving.

"Now. What's the matter?" Nicholas asked as she got behind the wheel.

"Nothing's the matter! Honestly it isn't." She was half laughing. "I went for a walk up to the hospice site, and I'm sorry you had to wait for me."

She started driving. "Tell me where to go."

"Turn right. You came down the road with a face like thunder, looking me straight in the eye. If you'd had a machine gun, you'd have let me have the whole belt. Turn right again. Was it because you forgot payday and I made good on our agreement?"

She really was laughing now, but she was blushing too.

"No, it wasn't. I didn't see you were in the car—the light was on the windscreen."

"The pub on the right. So it wasn't me you were angry about?"

She hesitated a fraction. "Of course not." She turned off the ignition. "Do I have to come to this lunch? If it's all those people from the meeting I shall be a real fish out of water. And how are you going to explain me?"

"You don't have to be explained, and you need lunch." He returned to his question. "If it wasn't me you were so furious about, who was it?"

"I wasn't furious with anyone. And you *will* have to explain me. I'd much rather go somewhere else and I'll meet you with the car afterwards."

"No. Do stop being so feeble. What is so difficult about telling people what you've been doing for the last week? Anyone would think we were having an affair! And you were certainly furious about something, and I want to know what."

"Look!" she said, removing the key from the ignition. "I'll be furious if I want to be, and I don't have to tell you why! Anyway, you're exaggerating. I was only irritated."

"God save us from your fury then! So what had irritated you?"

"Nicholas!" She felt hounded, but then had a brainwave. "If you really must know, I'd been looking at those awful interior designs for the children's ward and was feeling extremely sorry for any child who had to lie in a hospital bed and look at them. I can't think of anything more likely to inhibit recovery."

He looked at her thoughtfully. "I see. Poor little children!" He changed tack. "Why do you mind so much what people think? Especially when it's not true?"

She said nothing, but couldn't hold his eyes.

"You could try calling me Mr Thauros if you like." His amusement was obvious. "It might put them off the scent."

Her sense of humour re-asserted itself. "I'm not dressed for a business lunch; I don't look like a secretary—or a driver." She sighed. "Oh, I guess it's a pretty unlikely scenario, given—"

There was a short hiatus.

"Given—what? My odd sexual predilections? Our respective ages?"

"Oh! Shut up, Nicholas! I just meant that it must be quite obvious I'm not—not your—well, I'm not like your wife."

She could see he was trying to keep a straight face. "No. I think I can safely say you're not like my wife. I've never brought my wife on a business trip."

219

In the Ladies, she dragged a brush through her hair and managed running repairs to her face. She was still apprehensive, but in the event it didn't matter in the slightest as most of the group were liberally splattered with mud and concrete, and there were hard hats on the bar. By the end of lunch, she realised she had not only enjoyed herself, but her prior embarrassment had been quite unnecessary. Nobody had turned a hair at her presence among them. Awash in a genial barracking group of professionals, who tipped a substantial amount of alcohol down their throats, there were only good-natured jokes about the superfluity of architects and how simple life would be without them.

After lunch, he punched a postcode into the satnav and Melissa drove north. He phoned a hotel and confirmed bookings; phoned his office in a flood of Greek. Phoned the McNair Watts and talked briefly to Lorraine. Yes, they'd had a busy day, and no, he couldn't come next weekend. Lorraine obviously pressed him, and he was charmingly adamant. Melissa kept her eyes on the road and her expression neutral. He told Angus firmly that he felt an underground complex was entirely inappropriate, the cost would be prohibitive, as it would be for the staff housing. Perhaps some initial research with the health care company would be wise. Would Angus let his office know whether he wished the design and costings to go ahead—or not.

Melissa's spirits lifted as he finished all his calls and put his papers away.

"Why do you think the interior designs for the children's ward are so bad?" he asked unexpectedly.

For a ghastly moment, she thought that he must have done the designs, but then reminded herself that he was an architect, not an interior designer. Someone he knew, someone in the firm, perhaps. She tried to remember what she'd said, but could only remember that it had not been charitable. This time she kept her opinions as neutral as possible. Ordinary. Not particularly exciting. Cheerful though.

"Can't you come up with anything more precise?"

She gave him a quick sideways look and discovered that he was teasing her again.

"I thought you might have done them," she confessed, "and I'd been rather rude."

"I thought you thought I might have done them. I'm deeply touched that you didn't want to hurt my feelings, and deeply insulted that you thought I was capable of them," he said. "I am not an interior designer. Not only am I not interested, but I have zero ideas. I do know that I think they're perfectly awful. I'm glad you thought so, too."

"But why were they accepted, or chosen?"

"Not my business, that side of it, but I think it was put out to tender locally, so probably not much choice. However, the hospice is a different story. It's not the taxpayers' money in the same way; the finance has mainly been raised by voluntary subscription. The architectural design was chosen on merit more than financial considerations, and I'm hoping that the internal designs will be the same." He paused. "There's a competition for the internal designs" He was silent for a while, and as she had a suspicious mind she said nothing either. "The details are online. I thought you might be interested to see them."

"And why did you think that?"

"Your friend Robbie Cairns said he thought you should be using your artistic skills." He was picking his way rather carefully. "I thought you'd be interested, as an artist, to see the rules and parameters."

"Did you?" she said, tone dry. "Even though you have never seen any of my work? I think, Mr Thauros, that you are a very unprincipled person. I think you opened my handbag and looked at my sketchbook."

"I did not!" He sounded offended. "I wouldn't have dreamt of looking in your bag."

He waited until she had blushed and apologised.

"Your sketchbook wasn't even in your handbag, it was on the seat."

"Oh! Nicholas! You are the pits!" She was half angry and half something else.

"Melissa, you're driving. Do concentrate. Now listen, stop being shirty and listen. I'm sorry if I intruded on—on what? Your sketchbook. I stood behind you at Melrose and watched you draw a lovely architectural feature—pink stone on a pink paper. I could see you have talent. Of course I looked at your sketchbook. It was sitting there waiting to be looked at."

"It was not! It was underneath my bag. I didn't mean to leave it anywhere near you!"

"OK! OK!" he said. "I'm not used to shy young things. Normal mortals want their manuscripts to be published, their paintings to be admired, their sculptures displayed. If they have any integrity they want constructive criticism, if they are arrogant they want acclaim, but people like you are so lacking in confidence they don't want anyone to see anything in case it's a disaster. Right?"

There was an unwilling silence. "Were you going to show me your ideas and ask my opinion?"

"No!" She had to laugh. "I was not!"

"There you are then! You've proved my point. Why not? Because you don't care about my opinion? Or because you do care? Did you think I'd be patronisingly kind or sarcastically critical? Do you know whether your work is good, bad or indifferent?"

"I wouldn't have shown you because they're nothing. I was just filling in time, doodling. I just thought the hospital children's ward could be done better. It's not serious, or thought through, or anything."

"Of course not. There's no need to be defensive. It's too late now to do anything about the hospital, and I don't suppose you were even aware that the designs for the hospice were up for competitive tender, but all I'm telling you is that it would be worthwhile giving it some serious thought. I would think, just from seeing those funny little sketches, that you're good enough to compete should you choose to do so."

She had gone pink and looked rather astonished.

"It would never have occurred to me! There are hundreds of people who are far better at drawing than I am. I haven't a clue what's entailed and I'm not a designer, or an illustrator. I did History of Art, not Art and I'm a failure in my chosen career. I have no qualifications for that sort of thing."

He shrugged. "Perhaps not, but everyone's got to start somewhere. You can draw. I've no idea whether you'd be successful. All I'm saying is, why don't you try? Or are you frightened of failure? If you don't learn how to handle failure, you won't ever handle success."

She heard an echo of Galina Molinaris's words about mistakes. Her philosophy had obviously been passed on to him.

"It would never have occurred to me," she repeated, "but I suppose I could try. I'm not so much scared of failing—I'd be much more alarmed if I got shortlisted or something, but an unknown twenty-four-year-old nobody is hardly going to risk that. Where on earth would I start?"

"How about where you've already started—with a sense of humour? Children, especially very sick children, need to laugh, I'd have thought. Not that I'm a doctor. If you look at the hospice plans and read the interior design specifications, you'd have a clearer idea. Anyway, all these things are worth trying—it's experience. I designed buildings which never got built—and one or two which did get built when they shouldn't have been. My uncle, whose firm it is, used to say that it was better experience for an architect if his building collapsed than if it stayed upright."

"Good heavens! Has anything of yours ever gone wrong?"

He grinned. "Not that badly wrong, no. But design flaws happen sometimes when you want to do something in a certain way, for aesthetic reasons perhaps, or to fit in with some other part of the design. There are temptations, which is why my uncle doesn't employ architects who haven't had enough engineering training. Women make very good architects—and engineers, come to that."

"I noticed your structural engineer is a woman. Is that unusual?"

"Yes, at that level it is. She's very good at her job, but is not hugely imaginative—no frills. You on the other hand have plenty of imagination—"

"—but am not very good at my job—"

"Don't interrupt. Brilliant women are tedious creatures, making men feel inferior. What was I saying about frills? I really fancy some tonight. Have you got something frilly and feminine?"

"You know perfectly well what I've got, as you insisted on buying it. But where am I to wear it? I am driving into the clear blue yonder with no end in sight except a postcode."

"If only it was the clear blue yonder! Shall we do a U-turn and fly to the Caribbean? White sand, blue sea, sun, sex— sorry, no sex please, you're Scottish. How about it?"

"No." She laughed. "You're a coward."

"*I'm* a coward? You're the one saying no."

"You're scared of Scotland in the rain. You're scared you might get bitten by a haggis, you're scared of black pudding and turnips. You're scared that you'll melt." She peered into the downpour. "Nicholas, where are we going?"

He laughed. "Oh, she of little faith! Stop fretting, you'll get dinner, unless we drown first. This really must be the wettest country on earth. I suppose people live in Glasgow because it has the Clyde running through the middle of it, like a drain. Still, I rather like Glasgow. I hope it won't go the same way as Athens, the city of dreams, which poisons you as you're dreaming."

"All that pollution? Does it really? I've never been. I'd have liked to have seen it."

There was a note of wistfulness.

"The Acropolis will be there for a while longer, so I expect you've got time."

"Time maybe, opportunity doubtful."

He was amused. "You won't be poor for ever. You're going to be at least fifty pounds a month richer from now on."

"I wasn't thinking in financial terms. Thanks to you I'm *persona non grata* in Greece."

He was puzzled. "What on earth do you mean? Of course you're not!"

"I think I am. The good Inspector Kiprionidis said so. Don't come back, he said. Or words to that effect."

"Rubbish! You must have misunderstood. You were upset and got the wrong end of the stick."

"I don't think I did. He said I would not be welcome in Greece."

"He couldn't have. He didn't speak English. Anyway, they wouldn't have a clue whether you came back or not."

"I'd rather not risk it," she said. "I escaped incarceration by a whisker and I don't fancy ending up in custody again. And he spoke perfectly good English."

"Good heavens! Did he really?" He sounded truly startled by this revelation and not for the first time Melissa wondered how accurate his translations had been. "No wonder he was biased towards you and against me. I bet he wouldn't have been so concerned if you'd been a spotty youth with greasy hair." She smiled at the thought. "Anyway, did they stamp something rude in your passport or blacklist you?"

"Nothing in my passport, but I bet I'm on some computer somewhere."

"Greeks are hopeless with computers, and Kiprionidis was definitely on your side. He followed up every detail of your story to his entire satisfaction, with your landlady Nina giving you the best possible references and the waiter, too. No doubt Kiprionidis is still trying to nail Rambiris on your behalf."

"I don't expect Rambiris will ever reappear, and even if he did there wouldn't be a hope of getting Mann's money back."

Nicholas grinned triumphantly.

"I think Mann's have already had it from the insurers. I emailed my lawyers about your agreement and they said that he was wriggling like the worm he is as a result of their enquiries."

There was a prolonged silence, and her hands tightened on the wheel.

"His insurers have paid? When? You're making that up—you're guessing!" She was incredulous.

"I'm not, and they're pretty sure they have. I didn't say anything because they haven't had it in writing yet. If it does turn out that Clive Mann has been accepting your repayments when negotiations with the insurers were in hand, he won't be on a very secure legal footing. To put it mildly."

She found herself short of breath and her heart galloping, as she tried to digest the implications.

"How could he do that?" she gasped. "He would have to be mad to be so dishonest. To risk his reputation for that!"

"Well, it looks like he did. Probably it would be sensible to wait until we're one hundred per cent certain before suing him for millions, but it certainly sounds as if the insurance has come through. Hadn't it occurred to you that Clive Mann would have had some insurance policy in effect? After all, you might have absconded with the goods, or the money."

"I wouldn't have known how to!"

"Well, he probably knew *you* were quite incapable of doing either, but he would have an insurance policy in place as a matter of course. Fire, water damage, theft, all that sort of stuff." He paused. "And I now know for certain that Clive Mann was buying for Marie Claude."

"But how did she know that you were trying to buy it?"

He sighed. "She could have seen papers on my desk, or even on the computer. I was unwisely careless, looking back on it. After—" He broke off, his face set. "We had a fairly

226

major row and she wanted to inflict some damage in retaliation. I never thought she'd come back to the house, but she still had her keys. I knew she'd been there. I could smell her perfume." He took a breath. "It's water under the bridge. She told Clive Mann what she wanted and where it was. He must have known there was something not quite right about the deal—perhaps he'd dealt with Georgio Rambiris before and therefore didn't want to go himself. He set you up very neatly. You can bet your life he had his safety nets in place, and he couldn't give a damn about the risks he exposed you to, or the situation he left you in. And then like many a man before him, he probably succumbed to the financial temptation of having his cake and eating it as well. The insurance money and your monthly repayments. Yours are disappearing into the accounts without a trace and the auditors would probably never have picked them up. Even if they did, it would be easy to plead forgetfulness or even no knowledge."

She was shaken. All those months struggling to find the repayments, the worry over her rent, the second job, the exhaustion, the shame of it all.

"Oh God! How stupid I've been! You must think me an absolute fool." Her voice cracked.

"No, I don't," he said gently, "but I think you can now tell your bank to stop paying that standing order. I'm getting my lawyers to draft you a beautiful letter." She opened her mouth to protest. "Be quiet girl! One more word from you about not being able to accept dubious favours and I shall get really cross and announce to the world at large that you are a shameless courtesan milking me of all my earthly wealth."

She gave a choking laugh, grateful that he had lightened the tone.

"Tonight, I shall insist you wear that quite nice dress, and tomorrow it will probably snow and you can wear cashmere. Do stop being ashamed of thinking the best of people— though it would be nice to be included; it really is better to err in that direction than the other."

How can I think the best of him when that wretched case full of drugs hangs like a red danger flag in the back of my mind, she thought. It had been hanging there for so many months, through the changing nuances of her feelings for him, from fear to dislike, to liking, to attraction. To full scale desire.

As they had a pre-dinner drink that evening in a small, but comfortable, hotel on Loch Lomond, she asked him how he had got bookings at such short notice.

"The office travel agent did it, and suggested a sightseeing route."

"I'm amazed at your influence," she said. "I bet there were tourists flung out of their rooms into the heather to make room for us!"

It didn't snow, and instead they got an autumn heatwave. The route took them north and west, via the ferry from Mallaig to Skye, taking in Eilan Donan Castle and an enormous prawn and crab lunch at a famous fish restaurant.

"I am truly impressed," Nicholas said as they drove through the Torridon mountains. "Scotland is definitely what it says on the tin."

"I'm impressed, too," Melissa said. "Even the midges have given up."

They tramped bare granite and the forests above Loch Maree, with its little mysterious humpy islands floating in grey silk. Nicholas took photographs and occasionally her hand, hauling her across tumbling burns or up boulders twice her height. They both tanned in the sun and wind and Melissa's hair had gone the colour of a ripe conker.

Their old-fashioned rooms in the fishing hotel were quite separate; Nicholas had not so much as put his nose inside her door and she felt secure and obscurely piqued. But often she found his eyes on her and wondered with a tightening in her throat if he was entirely indifferent to her. His peaceful companionship and humorous teasing were as far removed from the man in Greece as it was possible to imagine. One evening he found an ancient backgammon board in the hotel.

"Can you play?"

"Yes, Brig taught us."

"For every fifty points you win, I'll pay you a dolphin, and for every fifty points I win, you pay me one of your drawings."

"I'm going to lose, am I?" she said, nettled. "For that I shall throw a series of double sixes every game and accumulate a shoal."

But to her annoyance and his laughter, she barely won a single game, and had to draw him his winnings.

"I shall teach you Racing Demon," she said crossly, "and this time, *I* will win."

"That's not fair!" he said. "I've never played it."

"No gambling then, until you've beaten me."

The hotel playing cards were dog-eared but serviceable, and she won every game.

"Determination will get you everywhere," he said, grinning, "even on to private yachts and into trouble. Do you know, I will really miss your monthly paydays."

She leaned back in her chair and inspected the ceiling. "It depends what you mean by 'miss'."

She tried to analyse her own feelings of loss, because she was sure that he would not be in touch with her again after their return. There would be no need for him to do so.

"You aren't going to miss fifty pounds a month, I guess." But those dolphins would remind her of him every day.

"No," he agreed quietly. "No, I won't miss that. But I will miss your visits." He paused, swirling his whisky round the glass. "And who is going to feed the cat?"

She sat upright.

"I'll catch my own fish."

He looked at her thoughtfully. "Yes, I think you'll do that now." He put the glass down. "On the whole, my little Greek cat stands her ground, but just occasionally I scare you off, don't I? A long memory of how I treated you?"

229

She gave him a straight look, and nearly had the courage to challenge him about the drugs. But not quite. She just nodded.

"It's not an excuse, I've said that before. But there was a reason for my—" he paused. "—my insanity. My nastiness. Marie Claude and I were at rock bottom just then."

"You were certainly nasty. I was really scared." The little smile was an effort to lessen the reproach, but the tone was still cool.

He looked remorseful. "I'm sorry. Nastiness really is not my default character trait."

He thought for a moment, frowning. "On *Joanna*, before I said a word, you were really frightened, and I assumed it was because you were in Marie Claude's pay. But you weren't. I'm still mystified as to why you were so frightened that you tried to escape through the hatch. Then the knives. That shook me, I can tell you. I thought she'd been telling you her lies about my wife-beating habits, but she hadn't, so why were you so frightened?"

Melissa remembered putting the black case on the bunk, and opening it, expecting the book, but instead being confronted by the drugs. She still couldn't bring herself to face up to him.

"I thought you'd stolen the Bible. If you'd done that, you could do anything. Like drown me. I certainly was frightened. Anyway, I'm a coward."

He looked at her searchingly. "Even if I had stolen the Bible, I still find it odd that you were that scared. And you're not a coward. A coward wouldn't have swum round to search my boat. A coward wouldn't have dropped that coffee tray."

She looked away, knowing that she was indeed a coward, because she hadn't the courage to challenge him about that case.

He rubbed his face ruefully.

"I am sincerely sorry." He took a deep breath. "You didn't know it, but you picked a really bad moment to retrieve your lost property. I am unable to explain my

230

blindness about Marie Claude. I'm unable to explain a lot of things."

He sounded grim and looking up she saw his eyes had lost focus again and his face was taut. He must have loved his beautiful wife very much, she thought. She wondered if he was now divorced.

"You don't have to explain anything. Your marriage is a private matter."

"Private! It's not private. And it hasn't been much of a marriage," he said bitterly. "She splashed our private lives across every tabloid and international gossip column—or her version of it. And as virtually none of it was true, I do mind what people think. I mind what you think. Apart from anything else, it is very much your business. Your life has been totally disrupted because of it."

She shrugged and smiled a little crookedly, "You've made atonement—several times over. You don't have to feel sorry for me."

"I wouldn't dare feel sorry for you," he said with a wry smile. "You'd bite my head off."

CHAPTER EIGHTEEN

Back in London the real world reasserted itself. Mr Emmett welcomed her back with relief, commenting on how fit and tanned she was. Melissa, however, felt depressed. Nicholas had said goodbye with a lingering kiss on her forehead and an unmistakeable finality.

Poor sales, reduced turnover and plummeting profits had brought the unwelcome news of forthcoming redundancies. The atmosphere was tense and bad-tempered, and there were discussions in low undertones about who pulled their weight or not. They had stopped recruiting. It was unsettling, and her office was avoided as if the plague leaked from under the door.

A gigantic cheque arrived from Thauros Associates, pinned to the time sheets Nicholas had made her sign daily. Further discussion over a monthly fifty-pound payment seemed ridiculous, and in any case, she had already lost the argument.

An impersonal communication from Nicholas's lawyers contained a draft letter to Clive Mann bringing her repayment arrangement to an end, and firmly asking for a refund of the moneys she had paid. Nervously she typed, signed and sent it and told her bank to stop the payments.

Completion on the Old Rectory went through without a hitch. Her grandmother, she realised with a pang of anxiety, had forgotten that the house no longer belonged to them.

With no monthly appointment with Nicholas and no more dolphin receipts she felt dejected and rejected, although she knew she should feel relieved. Looking back, she was mortified by the fuss she had made about those repayments. However, as he had made her promise, she downloaded the interior design specifications for the children's hospice and found time, first to think and doodle and then to draw designs to fit, loosely, the hospice specifications, and after an anxious internal debate finally sent them off. After all, they could only turn them down. There was a note of acknowledgement of their receipt and then a deathly silence. She heard nothing from Clive Mann either, but she had stopped the payments and her bank account began to look positively healthy.

One flatmate left, replacing herself with a resting actress who had chaotic arty friends who smoked: and not just tobacco. They also drank endless cans of beer and pints of coffee, and given the chance, ate anything they could lay their hands on, regardless of who it belonged to. That, and the fact that the dole never seemed to stretch to the milk or utility bills, finally enraged Melissa to such a degree that she went flat-hunting for somewhere more amenable.

Mr Emmett, on hearing at least some of the dreary saga, reminded her that Elizabeth Forbes, one of the systems managers, had a space in her flat. Her twin sister, with whom she'd shared the flat, had just married.

To her surprise, her diffident approach was seized upon, and she was borne off the same evening to a charming attic flat off Kensington Church Street.

"I don't particularly need a flatmate, though the rent is welcome, but it's probably unhealthy living on my own," Elizabeth said, unscrewing a bottle of wine. "Most of my friends have their own flats, and the rest can't face the stairs and no lift. And I can't face interviewing total strangers." She gave a glass to Melissa and lifted hers in salute. "Can you afford the rent?"

"Yes. Just. I'd love to come, and I'm pretty tidy-minded and clean about the house." She hesitated. "I thought you'd feel I was far too young."

Elizabeth wrinkled her nose. "If one's talking about irresponsibility and untidiness, you can get that at any age. I got the impression from your desk that you were clean and tidy, and from Mr Emmett that you were conscientious. No extended lunch hours or leaving early!" She had a glinting lop-sided smile. "Well, do you like it? I'm offering you the room."

Melissa's heart lifted. She liked Elizabeth, but more to the point Elizabeth must like her if she really didn't need to fill her sister's place. They went to the local Italian, had a pasta and developed the beginnings of a friendship.

It was December before she had found a replacement for her old flat and could move. In the spirit of starting a new life she changed her email, informing her friends, but not Nicholas Thauros, of her new addresses. The same week she received a letter from Clive Mann's lawyers. Enclosed with the letter, which made only a passing reference to her own, was a cheque for a vast amount of money, which transpired to be a repayment of the total amount she had paid them, with interest accruing. After reading it through carefully several times, it appeared that they no longer required her monthly remittance.

Oscillating between triumph and relief, it then occurred to her that the insurance company might not have paid Mann's at all, but that Nicholas might have done so, to make amends. She could, of course, ask either Clive Mann or Nicholas Thauros to clarify this. Her courage failed on either count.

The flat in Kensington Church Street was as delightful as it had at first appeared. Elizabeth introduced Melissa to her sports club, where for a fee, which a few months ago she could not have contemplated, she could now swim and play squash on any evening she had the energy to do so. It was there that she met Dr David Allison, whose fair hair waved unmanageably in the slightest of breezes and whose plump cheerful face lit up at any sight of Melissa. In his adoring company, she expanded like a flower opening. He admired everything about her, liked her sense of humour, the expressions on her face when something amused or upset her; he thought her intelligent and beautiful. He liked Elizabeth and the flat, and in due course he liked her grandparents. Rather disconcertingly, her grandfather did not return the compliment.

"Nice enough, I suppose," he said dismissively, in his brigadier's putting-down voice. "Bit of an old woman and quite awful hair. Needs a decent barber."

"Character is more important than looks," she said crossly. "At least he doesn't pounce all the time, like everyone else does."

"Including that Greek chap?" he asked rather sharply.

"No, of course not. He didn't come into that category. He wanted a typist and a driver and that's what he got. Anyway, his wife is considered one of the world's most beautiful women." She hadn't been completely transparent about the wife.

The old man grunted and reverted to David. "Young whipper-snapper. Thinks he's cleverer than he is. Always bragging about how well off he is."

It was true he didn't pounce, and there wasn't too much pressure to sleep with him until he was sure that Melissa didn't make a habit of sleeping around. As a doctor, he had said a shade pompously, it was more than his career was worth to be careless. He was slightly taken aback and, furthermore, offended when Melissa expressed the same reservations. The male pride had amused, but not upset her, and he was, on the whole, an easy companion who made few demands on her. He owned a spacious flat in Lexham Gardens, was safe, reliable and perhaps not quite as attractive as he thought he was. When he kissed her, she was certainly stirred to attraction, if not to passion, but it was Nicholas's face that tended to interpose if she shut her eyes. He liked her clothes, to which there had been a few additions lately, but never offered to buy her any, which saved arguments. He knew little of Greece or Scotland or of Nicholas, nor any details of her past financial struggles, and she had no wish to extend his knowledge. It was old history which she almost managed to ignore except when her eyes drifted to the dolphins which leapt and dived along her window sill, gleaming in the sunlight as if slicked with a thousand multi-coloured water particles. She had arranged them so that she couldn't see the permanent ink of those receipts. She missed those Dolphin Days. She missed Nicholas.

Both she and Elizabeth knew that the company was losing money. Staff who left were not replaced and the demands for higher output from the already unsettled ranks of the pimply youths who devised the software led to an escalation of unrest. Melissa was growing used to typing bad-news letters, so it was no great shock to receive, two weeks before Christmas, her own interview with Mr Emmett. The letter lay whitely under his hands, clasped on a grey space on the peripherally cluttered desk. The only surprise was that she hadn't been asked to type it.

Despite expecting it, she felt a bit shaken, but it wasn't as bad as being fired, she remembered.

On the way back to the flat in the evening, she bought an *Evening Standard* and leafed unenthusiastically through the Situations Vacant. Waitressing wouldn't pay the rent. She looked at the clean paint, the comfortable furniture and the sparkling kitchen and thought fiercely that she didn't want to give it up one bit. Why couldn't life have at least six months smooth running before being upheaved? She posted her employment problems on her Facebook page and morosely made lists of agency telephone numbers. Three months' pay. That would take her into March. She could earn extra with temping while looking for a permanent job and she was not paying anything to either Clive Mann or Nicholas Thauros and that was a distinctly good feeling. She dreamt of Nicholas and in the morning tried to replace the memory of his face with David's.

Elizabeth was still employed, but anxious not to lose her flatmate. She had been encouraging about the hospice designs and kept Melissa focussed on the project.

"You were going to contact the hospice. Have you done it?"

"No. I've had a few other things on my mind. I'm still uncertain, and it was a case of 'don't call us, we'll call you'. I never expected anything to come of it, and I expect by now they've thrown them away."

"They wouldn't dare do that, and you should get your designs back, otherwise someone else might use your ideas. You ought to get copyright on them."

"Can't think who would want to use them. It was a pretty silly idea to send them anyway."

But she was wrong. Three days later an envelope was forwarded from the old flat. The governors of the Angel Children's Hospice were pleased to inform her that her interior designs ideas had been shortlisted for final selection and were to be placed before the board on January 15th. It was slightly longer, if no warmer, than the acknowledgement of their receipt. Melissa glowed, amazed. She and Elizabeth celebrated with a bottle of wine in front of the electric fire. To be on a shortlist (how short?) of such a project was immensely flattering. She wrote and told them her change of address and asked them to return the designs in due course. She didn't say 'if she wasn't successful' as it seemed presumptuous to use 'if'.

David hugged her when he heard.

"That's brilliant! And really good for your confidence! You could do design as a sideline, and that would use your artistic abilities a bit, wouldn't it? Of course, only one in a million make a living out of art, but quite fun to have a go now and then." She asked him whether she should get copyright on the designs as Elizabeth had suggested.

"I don't think so," he said after some thought. "Bit of an unnecessary expense, isn't it? Who would want to use them?" The glow faded slightly in the light of his common sense.

She went to John Lewis with a Christmas shopping list and as she passed through the outer glass doors heard her name called. It was Lorraine McNair Watt. Melissa hadn't seen or heard of her since Scotland and didn't much wish to now. Their only point of contact was Nicholas. There was nothing for it, however, and they stood between the two sets of doors and 'caught up'. Melissa said untruthfully that she mustn't be long as she was meeting a friend.

"Not Nick, surely?"

Which was a funny way to phrase it. She pulled herself together. "Nick? Nicholas Thauros? Good Lord, no. I avoid him like the plague in case he tries to get me to do the travelling secretary bit again. How are the retirement home plans coming on?"

Lorraine shrugged. "Slowly. Nothing will happen till March or April apparently. The Trust is being difficult about the plans."

And the finance, I bet, Melissa thought. Lorraine's face took on a faintly calculating aspect.

"When I was with Nick recently he told me that you'd sent in some designs for a hospital or something. He says they're not bad at all." She smiled conspiratorially. "You needn't worry about getting the job. He'll make sure you get the contract. He's terribly kind, isn't he, as well as being incredibly sexy!" She smiled broadly and virtually winked. "Such a nice man. Clever you, having such good friends in high places."

Melissa felt winded. She said feebly, "Well, I don't know about that. Look, I must dash. I've got to get various things before my coffee date."

"Emily's meeting me here—she's already late. Can't you wait and see her?"

She summoned a smile of regret. "Give her my love, but I really can't."

She plunged on into the crowds and when she got back to the flat found that all her Christmas purchases were completely inappropriate. At least John Lewis would take them back.

238

CHAPTER NINETEEN

"**I** never told you that I've been shortlisted for those designs I did for the children's hospice in Glasgow."

She was with her sister-in-law Sarah for the weekend. She had always got on very well with Sarah, whose blunt Yorkshire speech disguised a soft heart and hard head, and she adored her four-year-old nephew Sam who was free with his uncomplicated kisses and matey hand-holding.

Sarah stared. "You got shortlisted? How utterly brilliant and fantastic! You clever, clever girl! Not that I'm surprised. Have you seen the other ones on the shortlist? How many are there?"

"Haven't seen them, and haven't a clue what the competition is."

Sarah frowned. "You don't seem very upbeat about it. What's wrong? Aren't you thrilled to bits?"

"I don't know. I was, but now I don't know. I heard—"

"Heard what?"

There was quite a long silence. Melissa felt a real need to pour out some of her dismay and confusion over Lorraine's revelations.

"That job I had in Scotland, you know, for Nicholas Thauros, the architect. His company is designing the hospice, and it was him that encouraged me to try some interior designs. Someone told me that he was pushing my submission. Trying to influence the judges in other words. They said, 'he'd see to it that I won'. I don't want to win unless it's by merit, and even being shortlisted may mean— probably does mean—that it's because of who he is, not because they think my work is any good. Perhaps to shortlist me is a way to get him off their backs, and I'm not really in the grid at all, but now I really don't know whether my ideas are any good, or whether they've just gone along with a guy

239

who's got influence. And if I actually won, which of course is highly unlikely, it would—" Words failed her.

"Take the gilt off the bloody gingerbread," Sarah exclaimed indignantly. "What a stupid, interfering wally! Men are so patronising, so effing pleased with themselves, they can't see talent when it's staring them in the face. I hope you've told him what you think of him, but of course you haven't," she rolled her eyes in disgust, "you're too bloody nice and well brought-up. Give me his number and I'll do it for you."

"Don't be daft! But it was a bit of a downer, I must admit."

"Who did you hear it from? Someone reliable?"

"Someone who couldn't possibly have known unless he'd told them. Why say it if it wasn't true? It's hardly something you'd make up. It was another client of his. I suppose they thought I'd be pleased."

"And he thinks he's doing you a kindness." She shook her head in disbelief. "How come there are so many stupid men around? I guess you've got two choices—you can either leave well alone and forget you ever heard the suggestion, or you can tell him to lay off the unwelcome assistance and hope he doesn't scupper your chances instead. If you win, which you ought to, take the accolade gracefully, with becoming surprise and humility."

Melissa laughed, feeling better to have shared what had been a devastating blow to her self-esteem. Sarah dropped the subject of Nicholas. She wanted to hear about David, and asked all the wrong questions.

"Marry him!" she said succinctly.

"He hasn't asked me."

"When he does, say yes. Don't believe all that rubbish about eyes across a crowded room. That's me and Johnny. That's sex. You say he turns you on a bit, and I say you can make a bit go quite a long way. He's qualified, he's honest, he can support you, he's got a job and not an impoverished NHS one either. He sounds dependable, kind, punctual,

240

generous. For heaven's sake, Mel, what are you waiting for? Go get him!"

They both got the giggles and Sam grinned and then pealed with laughter, too.

Back in London, David said he'd missed her. He helped her go through the ads, and enquired about how interviews had gone. He was kind and encouraging. He kissed her more often, and more passionately, and said he worshipped the ground she walked on. It was a welcome sensation.

There was not a word from the Angel Hospice, even though 15th January came and went. She had been offered two or three jobs, but none had appealed in the long term, so she continued the temporary work, aware that a cold and dreary January had run into a cold and dreary February, and that her next pay cheque would be the last.

David brought up the subject of marriage obliquely. Security versus insecurity, a desirable environment for children, in due course. The single life tended to pall after a certain age. To her dismay, Melissa found herself stifling a desire to laugh, to prick the pomposity. Even so, what he was hinting at was more than a bit tempting, and her common sense told her that romantic love was every girl's dream, but few girls' reality. Nicholas Thauros was certainly not reality and the attraction was because he was totally unattainable. Reality was less than perfection.

For perhaps the first time, Melissa was tempted by the idea of living with David to see whether it would 'work out' and as she returned on the tube to Kensington High Street from another hopeless interview, the thought of a man taking responsibility, being the bread winner, was good.

A voice, a little hesitant, spoke her name. "Melissa?"

She looked round, surprised. The young woman had a baby in a pushchair as well as two small children, and they looked like a small crowd. She also looked a total stranger.

"I thought it was you. You don't remember me though. I'm Sophie. Sophie Newington." She smiled and gave Melissa the needed connection. "Galina's birthday—my brother-in-law Nicholas brought you."

"Oh! I'm so sorry! Of course I remember. How very nice to see you again." She smiled too. "You were a rather different shape." She turned to look at the baby. "And here she is. Hello, gorgeous! She's lovely."

The baby regarded her solemnly, out of a cocoon of pink fleece.

"Are you about to challenge the tube with this lot?"

"I am. Bus queues a mile long, pouring with rain and not a taxi to be seen! How are you? It's ages since that party. Charlotte is a year old now. This is extraordinary to meet you!" Sophie had a look of pleased astonishment. "I've been trying to get in touch with you recently, but with no success."

Melissa thought that was rather unlikely, but wasn't going to be rude. "I've moved," she said briefly, and turned back to the children.

"Hello. You look damp and tea-timish. What are your names, or is that asking too much at this time of day?"

It was asking too much. Sophie introduced them.

"This is Fiona, known as Fifi, and this is Robert."

Robert had the end of a grubby plaster cast sticking out of his anorak.

"And I'm Melissa. I'm usually called Mel. It's easier. You've hurt your arm, Robert. Whatever did you do?"

Robert was evidently proud of his cast.

"It's broken," he said with relish. His gaze was steady on Melissa who had hunkered down to their level regardless of the crowds surging past. She glanced up at Sophie in surprise and sympathy.

"I am sorry. Poor little mite. I thought it was almost impossible to break a young child's bone—they're so flexible."

Sophie's mouth twisted slightly. "The nanny thought so, too." Her eyes held a warning which Melissa didn't understand at first. "Anyway, she's gone, thank God, even though she's left me holding the babies as it were, rather unexpectedly. But we've had a lovely time, haven't we darlings? We've done all sorts of wonderful things together."

Melissa was perturbed at what she thought Sophie was saying. "I'm so sorry, what a dreadful thing to have happened. Look, I mustn't hold you up. You need to get this lot home and dry and fed, too, I expect. And it's such a horrible evening. I'll come down and help you on to the train. I can't see how you can possibly manage alone."

"With difficulty," Sophie said, grimacing as the waves of humanity pushed past. "Someone usually helps, even if it's only to get us out of the way. I'd be really grateful if you've got the time. Do you live near here now?"

"In Kensington Church Street."

"I'm sorry to hold you up when you're just getting back from work."

"No problem," Melissa said. "I'm temping as I've been made redundant, and I see no reason to prolong the day's agony further than the official working hours. And I've just been for another job interview." She had taken Robert's unplastered hand in hers, and Fifi was attached to the pushchair. "Right, everyone, shall we tackle the escalator?"

But Sophie was scrabbling in her bag and produced her mobile.

"Do give me your phone number. I really would like to get in touch. I sent an email but it pinged back and your Facebook settings are private. It was fascinating what you told us about that bible we gave Madame."

Melissa thought it was probably unwise to renew contact with the family after Nicholas had broken it. However, on the spur of the moment she couldn't think of a very good reason for refusing, without an outright lie.

"Well, I don't suppose I'll be in the flat much longer. It's pretty expensive without a proper job."

Sophie's expression seemed faintly hopeful, with an element of speculative enquiry.

"Well, let me take it anyway. It's been really nice meeting you again."

Melissa could hardly refuse, and with some misgiving provided it and her new email address. Sophie accepted her renewed offer of help into the tube and they all waved to her through the window, crushed beside the doors. It was only one stop after all.

She walked back to the flat, trying to dispel her sense of uneasiness. Nicholas was only a stepbrother-in-law and probably hardly ever saw them. There was no reason why Sophie should tell him of this chance encounter and even if she did, Nicholas would hardly be interested. Will had given up long ago, and it was unlikely that Sophie really would contact her. It was a kindly intention, nothing more. Melissa felt the disquiet that came from not knowing what Nicholas had told them. Whether the family knew all or part of what had happened in Greece. Whether they knew about Scotland. She tried to put it all out of her mind by concentrating on David and the film they were going to, but the film was slow and intellectual and David irritated her. She drew away from his kiss when he took her home.

"PMT?" he said teasingly. "You've been very silent tonight."

She said coolly that she really must have a night in tomorrow. She had a lot to do.

"Hair-washing, I suppose," he said, rolling his eyes.

"That, and paperwork, and telephoning. I have a job to find."

"No need to be snappy."

She didn't ask him up for coffee.

Unlikely or not, Sophie telephoned the following day and asked her to come for coffee on Saturday morning.

She was taken by surprise. Sophie pressed her.

"Do come. I want to ask you something."

Like, 'What do you mean by going to Scotland for two weeks with Nicholas, a married man? Have you got some ulterior motive? How could you let Nicholas pay for that fine, and the air fare and Michael's doctoring, and a dress, and a

cashmere sweater, and all your hotel bills and all those meals?'
Surely not.

She should have said no, but somehow she didn't. Idiot,
she told herself. Don't get involved again. She knew nothing
of Sophie and Michael except that Michael had been kind
when she'd had the flu, and that, too, was embarrassing;
called for by Nicholas to attend some silly girl with a cold.
She liked Sophie, in so far as she could like someone she'd
only met twice, and both times briefly. They didn't know her
from Adam. Or did they? Had Nicholas told them about her?
Had he, perhaps in a fit of conscience, given them the
impression of a tragic life; death and poverty, a poor
unfortunate. Maybe he had even told them how he was
influencing the Angel Hospice board in her favour. Was
Sophie doing her charitable best for someone she felt sorry
for? Melissa's discomfort deepened as she tried to do some of
the things she'd told David she was staying in for. She needed
to think.

She went to Stanhope Gardens rather nervously, as if
Nicholas might somehow have read her mind and be lying in
wait for her. Unsurprisingly, he was not, and Sophie seemed
genuinely pleased to see her. The house was full of children
and animals, as Sir Richard had described it, and the kitchen
floor was covered in saucepans and lids which made highly
satisfactory timpani.

"Sorry," Sophie shouted apologetically, "but they have
long since learnt to bypass the cupboard locks. Anyway,
they're as good a toy as any. Mug?"

Melissa nodded to save shouting back.

"Tell me about being made redundant. You worked for
an antique shop or auction house, didn't you? Nicholas gave
me a telephone number, but it sounded like a business, and
they said you didn't work for them any more and the email
didn't work either."

Nicholas had given Sophie her old work number. Why?
Her heart thumped uncomfortably.

"I did work for an antique dealer, but subsequently I worked for a software programming house. It was much better paid, but sadly they've now made me redundant."

The children scrambled noisily amongst the saucepans. "It'll be better if we adjourn to the nursery. Do you mind?"

Melissa smiled. "Of course not."

The nursery was upstairs, a big sunny room with a cork floor. A large grey Persian cat lay curled up on a pink corduroy bean bag in a patch of fitful sun. The floor was a sea of toys and books.

"Everything was on the shelves and in the cupboards this morning," Sophie said with a sigh. "I can't keep pace."

Melissa laughed. "It's like cooking. All that effort and then there's nothing to show for it. Still, toys are for playing with and books are for reading. Have you got help?"

"Once a week, and I scrabble round trying to tidy so that she can clean. It doesn't work of course, cos by the time you've cleared one room and started the next, these mobsters have wrecked the first one."

The mobsters were rolling over each other, taking the baby with them with screams of laughter. The cat rose, stretched and jumped to a safer perch.

"Are you going to get another nanny, or an au pair?" Melissa asked. "Three is a real handful, and I thought you worked—wrote books?"

Sophie nodded, a little wearily. "I do—primary readers, for children with special needs. I've got to have someone to help, but the thought of all the interviewing is awful, and so time-consuming. And that's part of a trickier problem— which is why I wanted to get in touch with you. I've got a deadline to meet on the latest series of books, and I'm way behind because of Delphine leaving." A prickle of unease of a different sort crept up Melissa's spine. Sophie lifted the baby on to her lap.

"You said you were job hunting. What sort of job are you looking for?"

"Anything really. Secretarial, PA, office management, HR. That sort of thing." She helped Fifi slot in pieces to a puzzle.

"But you're an artist, Nico said."

Melissa's hands jerked, and the puzzle pieces fell out. She started to replace them.

"No. Not now—it doesn't pay and I just can't find anything." She was aware of being terse. "I ought to go. I'm holding you up."

"No, you're not. Please don't go yet. I want to ask you something. I told you I have a bit of a problem. The publisher wants this book by the end of next month—it's the first of a series—which could be fine, but the illustrator they've allocated me is just not up to scratch and I've been trying unsuccessfully to find someone else—which is incredibly stressful and time-consuming, as well as embarrassing. It's not that he can't draw, exactly, but he's desperately slow and doesn't see how my mind works—how I tick—and honestly, for children, especially for primary children and books for special needs children, it is really important that words and pictures work in tandem."

Melissa felt uneasy again. "Well, I quite see how important it is, and how it's obviously a problem for you, but I don't see how I can help."

"Well, the family obviously heard about the nanny leaving and that I had no help, and about the illustrator problems, and Nico showed me some little drawings which he said you had drawn and was that the sort of stuff I needed?" Melissa's heart began to thud. The only drawings Nicholas could have had were his backgammon winnings, and they had been scribbled jokes on rough paper: Nicholas punted high in the sky by an enraged highland cow and hooking the Loch Ness monster from a tiny rowing boat. That rough paper had been the Scottish hotel's notepaper and she had assumed he would throw them away. A wave of alarm washed through her.

"I loved the way you drew," Sophie went on. "Very precise, and accurate, but full of humour. I've only seen a very little of your work and only drawings without colour and I'd love to see more, and I wondered if you might consider working with me? Nico gave me your work number and email, but I'd given up when I couldn't contact you. And then I saw you at the tube station. An extraordinary coincidence!"

It certainly was, Melissa thought rather grimly.

"Obviously, we'd have to have discussions and you'd have to consider the books and whether the thought of illustrating them was of any interest, and whether there was enough money in it for you. And you'd have to meet the editor and publisher, and they'd have to approve and all that, but I thought it was worth asking you, and when you said you were job hunting, well, I thought that it might be something that might fill a gap."

Melissa was thrown off balance and didn't know how to reply. There was David to consider. And Nicholas! Was it so obvious that she was such a failure that he just had to 'help' yet again?

Sophie saw her expression and was immediately apologetic.

"I'm putting pressure on you, and I really didn't mean to do that. It's terrible cheek of me to even ask, so of course if you'd rather not, that's fine. I quite understand. You must have a very busy life, and after all, you don't know us at all." She sounded so contrite that Melissa was penitent in her turn.

"No! It's not that! It's just that, well, I don't know really. How did Nicholas—how can you know from a few drawings that I could do it? I'm not an illustrator—not trained. I've never done anything like that."

"Well, I don't know for sure, but I did like the few Nico showed me and thought we could possibly work something out, but honestly, if you don't want to consider it that's absolutely fine—I won't be at all offended!"

A door banged downstairs and a man's voice called up.

"Soph?"

"In the nursery," she shouted in the direction of the door. The uneven steps came upstairs and Michael (why on earth should she have thought it might be Nicholas?) came in. He looked faintly surprised at seeing a strange girl in the nursery.

"Hullo! Sorry, didn't realise you had company." He addressed the excited children. "Hello, mob."

"This is Melissa," Sophie said, "Melissa Scott-Mackenzie. Do you remember? She was at Galina's birthday party."

He turned to her, smiling. "Good heavens, so it is. Last time I saw you, you had pneumonia and didn't look nearly as pretty as you do now! No wonder I didn't recognise you. You look a picture of health." He heaved two children off his legs and into his arms. "Just like you two, eh?" He made faces at them, bumping noses.

"Clever Daddy! Made Melissa better! Isn't he brilliant?" They giggled, wriggling, and he let them slide to the floor, picking up the baby instead.

"Hullo, Miss Charlotte. Good grief, you've put on two pounds since breakfast" He passed her over to Sophie. "I've got a visit to make, so see you later, darling. Goodbye, Melissa, nice to—"

"—I've asked Melissa if she might think about collaborating on the books—the illustrations."

He turned and focused on her. "Oh yes, I remember Sophie was having problems finding you! How very nice. If you draw, and Soph thinks you're OK, Soph could do with some help. You heard about our drama with the au pair?"

"Yes," Melissa said. "I'm really sorry."

He shrugged with a little grimace. "Not very good. But these things happen. It could have been disastrous, but it wasn't, but it has taken up a lot of time and now Soph is up against her book deadline."

He ruffled Robert's hair, kissed Sophie and was gone, thumping unevenly but efficiently downstairs.

249

"You had pneumonia?" Sophie asked as the last of the footsteps died away.

Melissa blushed. "It was very embarrassing. Your husband had to treat me for flu last winter. He must have thought it so odd; I didn't ask him to." She was grappling with how to explain.

Sophie looked perplexed. "Well, he's a doctor. It's his job! What do you mean, you didn't ask him to?"

"Nicholas rang him—asked him to come to see me, because Will had taken me for a pub lunch and I was coughing—it was all Will's fault really. He asked Nicholas to ask your husband to come. Oh! It's just rather mortifying. Nicholas had to—I couldn't—pay the bill, but I never asked your husband to come."

Sophie's face was cautiously amused and confused.

"A real family affair by the sound of it! I expect that if Nico asked Michael to go and see you, then Nico would expect to pay the bill. I really wouldn't worry about it."

"But I think Nicholas wouldn't like me to—"

Sophie frowned. "To what?"

"To be here. To be involved here." Sophie looked at her shrewdly.

"It's not Nico who doesn't want you to be here, because it was him who tried to help me get in touch with you. I'm guessing you don't want to be here because you'd like to avoid him, is that it? Was it something to do with the Perissos Bible we gave Madame? Was that why you were there?"

Melissa swallowed wordlessly and Sophie went on, "His marriage went on the rocks and he's been desperately unhappy. He was foul to everyone and I'm guessing that may have included you, though I have no idea why. There were all sorts of undercurrents swirling about at Madame's party, and I noticed that although you were his guest, you didn't spend much time together."

Melissa still said nothing and concentrated on Fifi's puzzles as Sophie continued. "He's much better now and the divorce has come through. I think it's a huge relief somehow.

250

It seems sad, and I'm not at all pro-divorce, but it really was disastrous."

Melissa took a breath. "We had a mutual misunderstanding. I'm sorry, I really can't explain. Sophie, would you mind not—not telling him I've been here. Or that we've met? I can't take on these illustrations, much though I'd like to help. I really don't think he would like it."

Sophie's eyebrows twitched together. "But it was him who suggested you as an illustrator. Don't be too hard on him. His wife behaved really badly and made him utterly miserable, and because the whole family had tried to warn him off her and prevent the marriage, when it fell apart he was furious—about his own bad judgement, I think. I've known them all for years and they're all lovely—Richard, Madame, all of them. A really nice, sane family, which is pretty surprising, given their money."

She got up. "Let's have another cup of coffee. Can I bring the book for you to see? Have a look, anyway, before you give it a final thumbs-down. I can promise you that both Nico and Michael would be really pleased if you were able to help me out on this."

CHAPTER TWENTY

Sophie shut the little book with a satisfied snap.

"Yippee! Done and dusted." She squeezed her eyes shut on a huge grin. "And before the deadline!"

"Just!" Melissa grinned, too. "That was a roller-coaster month! Thank goodness for acrylic crayons."

"Thank goodness for a super editor, too."

"I couldn't agree more. I've learnt so much about illustrating and the process of telling a story in drawings. I really have loved it."

Sophie gave her a hug. "You are wonderful! And a real brick to agree to do the whole series. I am so thrilled. The next ones won't be nearly such a rush." She went to the fridge and took out a bottle of prosecco.

"Come on, let's celebrate before the children come back. Talking of celebrating, Nico got his driving licence back and celebrated by buying a new car. I expect he'll be caught speeding again and lose it for another six months."

She poured two glasses.

"I didn't know he'd lost it," Melissa said, trying not to sound as shocked as she felt. That explained Scotland and why he had needed a driver. Nothing whatever to do with wanting unsophisticated company or talking about normal things. She felt hurt and angry and exploited.

*****

At the end of April, when the cherry blossom carpeted the pavements in sad, battered drifts, she felt even more hurt and angry. A letter had arrived from the Angel Hospice telling her that the governors were now pleased to inform her that her designs had met with the overall approval of the board. *However*, it was felt that they were over-complex and would be time-consuming and expensive to carry out, which had initially put them above the allocated budget. It was felt the award should be given to a simpler design.

However. It transpired that a budget increase had now been made, along with extra private donations and they could now confirm the award to her, on her agreement to the alterations listed overleaf and her signed acceptance of the general terms of the award. They apologised for the delay.

Overleaf were some architectural and structural changes which affected the size of certain grids, and the number of designs had been reduced. Discussions would be required on some of the actual drawings. Please sign and date the enclosed agreement.

She read and re-read the dry prose, and with each reading saw ever more clearly a board who had been persuaded, perhaps bullied, by the architect into accepting designs it felt were unsuitable, over-complex, far too expensive and encompassed a humour which they probably thought was tasteless. When the runners-up saw the winning entry, they could, with perfect justification, demand an enquiry and declare the results void. Nicholas's powerful and wealthy hand was also clearly behind the private donations. At least, she thought bitterly, there wasn't any moral alternative. She didn't have to pretend he might not have interfered. She realised there was no way to know whether her ideas had any intrinsic merit or not, spoilt as they were by Nicholas's misplaced ideas of patronage.

Dithering for about a week, she began to craft her reply and after polishing up a few well-chosen phrases, sent it on its way to Glasgow. After a further lengthy delay, the governors of the hospice returned her designs, as requested, deeply regretting her decision to withdraw rather than reconsider the minimal alterations they had suggested. There was a note of genuine dismay and disappointment in the tone of the letter, and Melissa had a moment of stomach-churning uncertainty as she read it. Could she have been wrong about the board being pressurized to give her the design contract?

253

If so, she had thrown away a seriously prestigious job for no reason.

She had kept her head above water financially with temporary secretarial work together with the book illustrating and occasional babysitting for Sophie and Michael. The fact that sometimes David had to be put off, or an arrangement changed, did not distress Melissa, although David himself suffered a certain pique.

His oblique references to the married state were becoming clearer, causing more panic than pleasure. Her unidentified sense of unease countered by the many identifiable advantages only served to confuse her more.

One morning, working on the next series of drawings, Sophie surprised her with an invitation.

"We're going to Madame's house in Greece in July, for a month, when Robert's school finishes, and we wondered if you'd like to come with us? Partly to help with the children, but mainly because we'd love to have you. We might get some more ideas for books and illustrations too. What do you think? It's a fabulous place."

"Oh, Sophie! What a lovely idea, and such a kind invitation!" She had a fleeting memory of Inspector Kiprionidis telling her not to come back. "Can I think about it? I don't know that I can afford it, and I suppose I'd better discuss it with Brig and Mops and with David, too—he wants me to meet his parents, but I don't think there was a specific date."

"Forget the affording!" Sophie exclaimed. "We'd definitely do your air fare, and pay you for hours worked. We'd love you to come for the whole month, but we'd understand if you couldn't stay that long. It'll only be us lot in the beach house, and Madame and Richard will be in the main house."

"It sounds really wonderful, so long as I really could be useful. I mustn't say I will, until I've cleared it with the family, though."

Sophie laughed. "You're always being useful! It's time you had a holiday! The beach house is great as it has direct access to the sea and no dangerous steps. But it would be nice occasionally for Michael and me to spend some evenings with Richard and Galina in the main house so a babysitter would be great. You really would be doing us a huge favour."

Anywhere but Greece would have been just perfect, she thought unhappily over the next few days.

Taking courage in both hands, she telephoned Lady Newington and asked if she might have a meeting with her. There had been a moment's silence after Melissa's initial explanation of who she was, and then pleasant recollection and a consultation with her diary. She did not ask the reason for this strange request, but calmly made an appointment for Melissa to come to see her.

They lived in Richmond, in a big house set back from the street, the woodwork painted a glossy dark blue. Terracotta containers full of bright flowers surrounded the door which Galina opened herself, elegant in a deep blue silk dress. Her brown eyes smiled an easy welcome as they shook hands.

She led the way through the house and Melissa passed pictures she would have liked to stop and look at. Comfort and money were discreetly apparent.

"Today is warm enough to sit on the terrace. We must make the most of what may be the only day of summer. Richard is out fishing on the Test, hoping for a mayfly hatch, or some such thing."

A blue-tiled fountain on the terrace had a life-sized ceramic dolphin scything up from the water, droplets spraying off the turquoise and silver glaze. It reminded her of Nicholas's dolphin receipts.

"Oh! How beautiful!" Melissa exclaimed. "It looks as if it's alive!"

"Yes, I love it. We commissioned this piece from my brother-in-law, Carlos Thauros. He is a wonderful sculptor, but, sadly, he is very ill, and I don't think he will ever create anything like this again."

255

On the white iron terrace table there was a tray with tall heavy glasses and a matching jug of iced drink.

"We will have some tea in due course, but first a cool drink. Yes? It is home-made lemonade," Galina said, "but here the lemons are so acid, it is not as good as when I make it in Greece." She sat back smiling, her eyes steady on Melissa. "And I think it is about Greece that you wish to speak to me, yes?"

"Yes, Madame. About Greece. I'm sure you know that Sophie and Michael have invited me to come with you in July and I would love to come and help with the children, but I don't think I should come back to Greece and I don't know what to tell them. They don't know that I was there two years ago and I didn't think it was for me to say anything, if you hadn't."

"So why have you come to see me today? Do you want me to tell them you don't want to come?"

"It's not that I don't want to come," Melissa said, rather desperately, "and I really don't want to let them down, it's just that after what happened I feel I shouldn't go back, and that you wouldn't want me to. Also, I got the feeling that the police would rather I didn't go back either. I may be on some computer black list, and they might refuse to let me enter Greece, or even arrest me."

Galina's dark eyebrows went up. "What is all this about the police? It is unbelievable! You know, Nicholas told me very little, and only from his own perspective at that time, which was that he thought you were a—how do you call it? A honey trap, I think. Someone that his wife had sent to tempt him into indiscretion. I think perhaps you need to tell me what happened from your point of view, from the beginning, and then perhaps I will understand. I think it had something to do with the Perissos Bible that Nicholas found for me, did it not?"

There was no disapproval or hostility in her voice, so Melissa told her the whole story from Clive Mann's commission to buy the bible to Nicholas's payment of the fine and her airfare. The only thing she left out was finding the drugs. Eventually lifting her eyes to Galina's thoughtful gaze, she felt emptied and raw.

Galina gathered up their glasses on to the tray in silence, her head slightly on one side, thinking.

"Well," she said lightly, "I shall go and put the kettle on and digest all that a little, while you enjoy the sun. I shall have coffee, but there are all sorts of different teas you could have. I have a passion for sweet sticky things, so we will indulge ourselves, yes? Coffee or tea?"

"Coffee, please. Can't I help?"

"No," she said firmly, "you will sit in the sun and feel better in a little while, and then we will laugh, and talk, and sort out what is probably not so very dreadful after all."

And later she had indeed sorted out most of Melissa's confusions with brisk common sense, and the inspector's perceived threat was dismissed out of hand.

"You would not be going on business, but on holiday, with a family. And Greek bureaucracy does not run to computerised blacklists, I can assure you. So, if that is what was preventing you from accepting Sophie and Michael's invitation you need not give it another thought."

"It wasn't the only thing!" protested Melissa. "It's your house, and I couldn't not tell you after what happened there—I mean I didn't get the impression that Nicholas had told you any details."

"Well, no, he didn't. And so you decided you had to confess all this to me before—before what? Accepting or refusing?"

"I felt I should refuse, but I didn't want you to think—I was a coward. Before their invitation there was no need—no opportunity—to tell you. That's not quite what I mean either. No right moment, really. To come, out of the blue, to tell you, seemed presumptuous somehow. As if I was asking for something. Which I'm not."

Galina waited, smiling. "And now?"

Melissa looked at her hands and tried to relax them. "I suppose I wanted to apologise."

"My dear child! To apologise for what?" Her voice was almost sharp. "To apologise for doing your best in circumstances beyond your control, in a strange country where you neither spoke the language nor knew the law? In a situation you should never have been in, in the first place. Your employer had no business sending you to do that job, whether it was legal or illegal, just as Nicholas had no business taking revenge on his wife through another young woman, whatever misapprehensions he may have been under. You were unwise to be so trusting of an unknown dealer and of course if you had been older and wiser you would have insisted on a proper receipt and kept it separate from the bible. But trust and inexperience is the prerogative of youth. Nicholas, I'm afraid, trusts few people now." She sounded sad for a moment, and then a more severe look crossed the mobile face. "It was unwise, too, not to say dangerous, to go searching an unknown yacht for this book. You might have been murdered."

"I thought I was going to be," she said without thinking. "I thought he was going to push me overboard." She shivered. "Nicholas wouldn't want me to go to Greece, but I can't tell Sophie why."

"But it is neither Nicholas's house, nor anything to do with him. So far as I know he has no plans to join us. Sophie asked me if she could invite you to help with the children so that she and Michael could have a bit more freedom. I said I was very happy for you to come. The children like you and you appear to like them, do you not?"

"Yes, of course. I love them—they're adorable. But it's different now—you know that I was there, in your house. You know what happened."

Galina laughed. "Well, I certainly knew you were there because both Zena and Nicholas told me so. What I didn't know was *why*—of course he could not tell me about the

Perissos Bible before my birthday. But now you have filled in all the remaining gaps, and Zena told me much more."

"That only makes it worse," Melissa said. "Zena was very upset about the whole thing."

"Not perhaps in the way you thought. Zena has been close to me for many years, and she is concerned for my privacy. She was much more upset by Nicholas than by you. She told me that he treated you very badly." Galina smiled mischievously. "And that you were very tidy and clean. High praise from Zena! And she admired your disappearing trick when Marie Claude came, which so unnerved my son. I understood from her that he was not at all grateful."

Melissa blinked at recollected ferocity. Galina's hands were clasped round her coffee cup, long-fingered like Nicholas's.

"I wanted to forget the whole thing, and I had really, until Sophie asked me to come with them. I don't want to hurt their feelings, but I can't bear to dig it all up again."

"If we don't dig up our own bones, we can be pretty certain some other dog will," Galina said. "But there is no meat left on this particular bone after two years and if I were you I would accept Sophie's invitation at face value. She has been very grateful for your help with her books, so come and enjoy the sun and a family holiday—it won't all be hard work! You have blown this up out of all proportion and I have not the slightest doubt that Nicholas would be perfectly happy for you to be there, not that he has anything to say in the matter. As I said, it's not his house, nor his invitation, nor any business of his. So, you will come with us, yes?"

Melissa was not nearly as certain of Nicholas's perfect happiness as his mother was.

"If I do, would you—could I ask you not to tell him?"

Galina didn't answer at once and Melissa flushed uncomfortably.

"No, Melissa, I don't think you can ask me that. This is not a conspiracy against Nicholas, and if the subject comes up naturally in conversation, as I'm sure it will, then he will know. In any case, we are a big family, and we talk and communicate even if we do not see each other very frequently. Nicholas is thirty-six and you are—what? Twenty-four?"

"Twenty-five."

"Twenty-five. You are two adult people who had a mutually unpleasant experience two years ago, but you can surely behave in a civilised way now. In any case, you would find Nicholas very different now. Two years ago he was a deeply unhappy man, angry and bitter. Much of that has gone, and the scars of his disastrous marriage are healing, but it has taken a long time because it was entirely his own—" She hesitated. "Fault is too strong. Bad judgement perhaps." She twinkled. "Men hate to admit they have bad judgement, or make mistakes, don't they? So now poor Nicholas is wary about his judgement, and he must learn to trust again. Are you able to forgive him for what he did?"

"Oh!" Melissa exclaimed. "Of course! And he has apologised. I mean, he has been—very kind. It's just that his way of trying to make amends was rather humiliating—for me." Galina frowned, not understanding. "Well, he paid that wretched fine which was huge, and my air fare back to London, but then he wouldn't let me pay it back, or at least only very little and we always ended up having rows about it." Melissa took a deep breath. "He meant to be kind, I think, but it didn't feel kind to me."

Galina's mouth pursed in a little smile. "Well, I think you will have to forget that. He has plenty of money, and I expect he felt very guilty about how he treated you. As far as Greece is concerned, I only want Sophie and Michael to have a proper holiday. After Robert's broken arm she went through a difficult time, and the book illustrations were a great anxiety and they would like to thank you in some way. I have seen the books and the illustrations are delightful and very clever, I think. I would be very pleased if you will come with us."

Melissa capitulated with a smile. "Well, thank you. If that is really how you feel, and if you think I won't be refused entry, then I'd like to come."

"Good!" Galina said briskly. "Now we can leave all that aside, and you can tell me about your life, and work, and family. I am very curious. I like to know what people like, about their jobs, why they do things."

And she was off, genuinely interested, and totally unEnglish in her frank enquiries. And again, Melissa found herself not minding so much, but instead coping with the explanations of why she was brought up by grandparents instead of parents, and why she had fewer brothers than she had started with. Only that last secret, about her father, she couldn't bring herself to confess, and as always it festered, like a boil which will not burst, tender to the touch, yet needing to be pressed.

"And now, how are your grandparents managing? Coming from Scotland to Hampshire was a big move, leaving all their friends and having to start over again. And they must be in their eighties now?"

Melissa nodded, fingering the pretty flowered coffee cup. "My grandmother has developed a clinical depression and is becoming—confused, I think is the word." She glanced up at her hostess. "Brig is a darling, but Mops has become very negative and emotional. Her glass is always half empty, never half full. It's rather wearing! Still," she said, more cheerfully, "things are rather better now. Johnny and I are out in the world and the house is sold, and the creditors are paid off. Their debts were like a millstone for them, poor things."

"But if the house is sold, where do they live?"

"Well, it's extraordinary really. They still live in it, and nothing much seems to have changed. A company called Cathedral Properties bought it, apparently as an investment for when house prices rise, and they kept my grandparents on as, well, as caretakers. Mops is rather unreliable now and I wouldn't have thought that two elderly people would make very good caretakers. The estate agent seemed to find it

261

reasonable, and I had it checked out by a lawyer, but I must say, I thought the arrangement was extraordinary."

From Galina's astonished expression she clearly thought so, too. She frowned and began to say something, and then changed her mind.

"I don't know what will happen when they do sell it on," Melissa continued, "but there's three months' notice on either side, which seems very generous, so I'm not complaining. It would give me enough time to get them into sheltered housing of some sort. We'll cross that bridge when we come to it."

"Very sensible," Galina said slowly. "And they don't mind the change of status from owner to tenant?"

"Seemingly not. The company pays them a little salary to caretake the house! And pays two-thirds of the running costs as well. There must be good business sense behind it as well, I suppose. I minded much more than them. Now they seem conveniently to have forgotten that they aren't the owners."

"And you and your brother? You don't mind losing your home?"

Melissa wrinkled her nose in thought and shook her head.

"It's never really been home, not like Meath. There aren't any memories—or at least not particularly happy ones. They moved to break with the past. To give Johnny and me a fresh start. I think." She smiled at Galina. "I'm only guessing. They don't talk about it."

"New beginnings don't always eliminate the past, do they? Nor should they. How else are we to learn about life, and indeed death?"

She looked at Melissa pensively and began to talk of other things. It was a long time before Melissa realised how long she had been Galina's guest, and made embarrassed apologies which were charmingly dismissed, and thanks which were as charmingly acknowledged. In the train, she thought there was very little that she had not told Galina, although a case of drugs on Nicholas's yacht and a fortnight in Scotland with him were substantial omissions.

Sophie was genuinely delighted with her decision, but David, to her initial surprise and then subsequent irritation, was furious.

"You didn't even ask me whether I minded, or if it would inconvenience me in any way. How about my plans? You didn't ask if I'd arranged anything—I could have booked a surprise holiday for us both, and then I'd have lost the deposit."

"But you haven't—"

He ignored the interruption. "You never even mentioned the possibility of this—and a month! I thought Michael Newington was supposed to be a doctor? How can he possibly take a month?"

"He's not. He's coming out for the middle two weeks."

"Pretty poor support from his wife then—leaving him to cope on his own for two weeks."

She sprang crossly to their defence.

"He'll only have to cope for a few days at each end, and it was Michael who insisted. She's had quite a tough time, with Robert's broken arm and the nanny leaving, and he wants her to have a proper rest."

He looked at her with patronising pity.

"You're deliciously naive, Mel. That woman is cushioned from all life's bruises by money. A tough time! Nanny left her to look after her own children, poor little thing! No one looks after their own children these days, of course! I can tell you now, the mother of my children will look after them herself." He forestalled any possible interruption with a wave of his hand. "She'll be lying tanning herself on the beach while you sweat your guts out on her children, and her husband runs a practice and that huge house, and feeds himself on his own in London. Charming. She sounds a selfish little madam, and if you don't mind my saying so, I think it's catching."

"I do mind you saying so!" she said coldly. "You're being absolutely idiotic, and the last thing she is, is selfish. They're

263

being very generous. I could never afford to go to Greece myself, not outside a package, which I'd loathe, and I'm getting all my fares paid, and getting paid as well. And I love the children. And frankly I need a break, and you haven't even thought about it, let's face it. And even if you had, I wouldn't let you pay for me."

"But you're letting them pay for you!" He was unreasonably angry, she thought. "Money! Money! Money! They think it solves everything, don't they? Well, you don't need it from them. They'll use you like a skivvy."

"They won't," she said wearily. "They treat me like family. I will be looking after the children, but with Sophie and Michael most of the time. I like them, and they won't 'exploit' me, for goodness sake. And they do not think money solves everything. I feel I can accept their invitation because I can do something for them, although it will still be a real holiday for me."

His voice took on a pleading note. "Mel, it's a whole month! I'd got lots of things planned for us to do, and I'll take you on holiday myself. You don't have to go with them."

"Sweet thought, but you'd never told me you had things planned, or asked me whether I'd like to do them with you." She was hurt and angry at his reaction. "We'd never discussed a holiday together, and as I said before, I wouldn't let you pay for it."

"Why not?" he demanded. "We're going to—" He stopped, looking at her face.

"We're going to what?" There had been a definite note of proprietorship which had raised her hackles, and he took a more conciliatory tone.

"We're more or less engaged."

"More or less engaged! Are we?" She put as much astonishment as sarcasm into her voice. "You never said! You never asked, for that matter."

"My intentions were completely clear," he exclaimed hotly. "You know that perfectly well, and you're certainly clever enough to put two and two together. We've talked about marriage hundreds of times!"

"Marriage, yes," Melissa said, "but not *our* marriage. Don't you think it would have been presumptuous on my part to have read that intention into our rather generalised discussions?"

"Oh! Come on! Of course not! If you weren't sure you could have clarified it." Speech forsook her and he took her silence for agreement. "Surely our relationship is such that we should have discussed the Newingtons' idea together? It would have been kinder—more courteous—to me, wouldn't it?"

His use of the old-fashioned phrase was, she thought, designed to make her feel guilty, and her reply sounded petulant.

"As I didn't originally intend to go, there was no point in discussing it, and then you were away at that conference in Brussels."

"So what made you change your mind? The money? Honestly, darling, I would have lent it to you—given it to you if I'd thought you'd accept it—if you were short."

"I'm not short." Her voice had gone up a pitch and she lowered it. "And I prefer to earn it anyway. I changed my mind because Lady Newington asked me to come as well. They want me to, not just because I'll be a help but because they like me. As a person. For myself."

He looked dubious, which hurt.

"Of course they do, darling, but not as much as I do. I'm upset because if you go I shall miss you horribly. It'll be very lonely without you, and I'd hoped to take you up to meet the parents. It was such a shock, I suppose. A month!" He did look appalled and she felt the first genuine prick of remorse.

"I'm sorry. I hadn't realised you would mind so much. You never gave me the impression—that you'd be devastated without me." She tried to joke. "How flattering!"

"You don't like me getting too keen," he said with perfect truth, and then spoilt the effect by adding somewhat archly, "but I suppose you felt that absence might make the heart grow fonder, is that it? Well, the heart couldn't be more fond, darling Mel, but I can understand your impatience with this dilatory chap who hadn't quite plucked up the courage to pop the actual question. And I'm going to take courage in both hands, right now!"

He slid off his leather sofa on to his knees, capturing her hands and bringing them to each side of his face.

"Darling Melissa, I love you, and I'm really, really sorry not to have made it absolutely crystal, brilliantly, unmistakably clear." He took a deep breath. "Will you marry me?"

She looked at him. Stared at his clear eyes, his clear conscience, his basic kindness and his justified hurt. She stared at the love and security he represented, the sharing of problems and triumphs; she stared at a home, children, a future. She stared in the mirror of her own indecision.

He was waiting for her to say yes. To throw herself into his arms, waiting to kiss her. She wished he wouldn't wait, but illogically, when he drew her forwards gently, reaching with his mouth to hers, she resisted the pull and heard herself say, "David! Wait!" And then justifying it. "This is so sudden. Give me time to think!"

"Sudden? Think? Haven't you been thinking?" He laughed up at her, not able to take her seriously. "Women! Indecisive creatures! One minute you're blowing hot, and the next minute cold!"

She didn't say, though she fleetingly thought it, that neither of them had ever blown terribly hot.

"I'm not indecisive, but this is a huge decision, and I honestly wasn't expecting the question. Is this really a good idea? Are you sure? I haven't even met your parents, or your sister, or been to your home."

"You're not marrying my family, or their home. You're marrying me and this will be our home. You like it, don't you? I suppose you'll want to make some changes." He looked round as if he couldn't conceive what she could want to change. "I'll take you to meet the parents soon—as soon as the ring is on your elegant finger, my sweet. And you'll tell the Newingtons the good news and that will be a wonderful excuse not to go to Greece."

She was horrified. "But I must go. I said I would, and I'd be letting them down."

"They've money to burn and can take someone else to nanny their kids. Of course you don't have to go. You're engaged!"

She shook her head frantically. "No, I can't do that." She thought of Galina. "There are other reasons—it's not just a job."

"Melissa! What other reasons?" She shook her head again. "Are you saying you're going even though I don't want you to? Darling, I'm asking you seriously not to go to Greece—not even to think about going—just at the point of our engagement when we need to meet people, my family and friends, and make arrangements and plan for the future—" In a more humorous situation she would have described his face as registering shock and horror. "I'm sorry, but you really can't."

Melissa saw he had a point, and in a brief flash of self-understanding knew that she would indeed not think of going to Greece for a month were she truly in love with him. She took a decision she knew was despicable and hated herself for it.

"Are you saying, David, that your proposal of marriage is dependent upon my instant obedience and decision now? Because if so—"

He retreated immediately. "No! No, of course not. I just thought you wouldn't—I mean—to go away for a month, just when we've got engaged, well, it's pretty extraordinary. What will people say?"

"Who will know? You don't have to tell anyone yet. And you don't appear to have noticed, but I haven't said yes."

And you haven't asked if I love you. You didn't wait for an answer. You just assumed it. Assumed I'd be flattered,

267

thrilled, over the moon. Assumed I'd leap into marriage with such a catch as David Allison. She was horrified by the coldness of her thoughts.

"But you will, won't you?" He was looking shell-shocked, alarmed. And also astonished.

She touched his face gently. "I think so, but I'm not sure. Thank you for asking me, but I want time. Time to be completely sure. Neither of us wants to make a mistake, do we? Please give me time to think about it—to make sure about a lifetime's commitment. That's not too much to ask, is it? And maybe you need to do the same thing—after all, you need the right wife just as much as I need the right husband!"

Her attempt to lighten the atmosphere fell flat. He looked uncertain, as if he didn't know whether he should insist on her bowing to his wishes, or whether it was a reasonable idea after all. She hastened to hammer home her decision.

"Darling, I'm afraid I'm going, because I feel it's the right thing to do. I won't let the Newingtons down, and I do mean it when I say I want to think about your proposal."

He heard an unaccustomed steeliness in her voice and gave way.

"Well, if I let you go, and I really will miss you, will you wear an engagement ring?" and added with sudden boyish enthusiasm, "I do want to buy you a ring. I want to cover you with diamonds and pearls and buy you clothes, and spoil you to bits."

He kissed her hands and she smiled at him, grateful for the change of mood and his capitulation.

"OK. A ring, if that's what you want. But no announcements. Promise?"

He only hesitated for a moment. "OK. I suppose. Not even my parents?"

"Especially not your parents, you idiot!"

On returning to the flat, Melissa looked again at her dolphins, dusting them in turn and running her fingers over the illegible indented symbol on the base of each. There had been a similar discreet symbol at the base of Galina's fountain. She googled Carlos Thauros, noted the address of his London outlet and after work the following day took a bus down the King's Road.

The shop was delightful, bursting with the rich colours of the glazes reflected from mirrored shelves. Geckos, seals, lobsters, tuna, sea urchins, lemons and pomegranates. Little Greek cats. Dolphins. The assistant brought out the dolphin she pointed to and told her the price. Melissa smiled regretfully.

"I'd love it," she said, "but sadly I can't afford it."

CHAPTER TWENTY-ONE

This time she knew where she was, having looked at a map, and discovered that two years earlier Nicholas must have sailed a very long way round. But this time Mixos was heaven, not hell.

The days had drifted past in busy indolence; morning walks along the beach with the baby in the backpack, the two older children picking up little treasures as they went; coloured stones, tiny shells or driftwood that took their fancy. They threw pebbles into the rattling shingle and tried to float cuttlefish shells, mottled like a tortoiseshell cat. Their bedrooms silted up with sandy souvenirs.

After a fortnight of paradise, she realised there were another two glorious weeks to go.

She was sitting on the patio trying to push back the thong of one of Robert's broken flip-flops, while they slept off the afternoon heat. Michael and Sophie had gone up to the house in the morning and the two older children unhesitatingly decided to stay with Melissa and Charlotte.

"*Yassoo*, Melissa," Nicholas said.

Her shock was followed by the shifting emotions of embarrassment and anger and back to a flush of acute uneasiness.

"When——? How did you——? You weren't coming——they said——you wouldn't come."

He said nothing, not smiling.

She stood up abruptly. "If I'd known——"

"Yes," he said, "if you'd known I was coming you wouldn't be here. You'd have started swimming for the mainland probably, leaving Sophie in the lurch. I thought it was better not to give you any advance warning."

He moved then, and she took an involuntary backwards step away from him. But he went into the kitchen, returning

270

with a can of Sprite. He came and sat down at the table, taking the flip-flop out of her nerveless hands and applying himself to the problem. He let the silence settle.

"I told Madame," she said sturdily. "I told Madame everything. I had to because Sophie and Michael wouldn't have understood why I couldn't come."

"Everything?" He waited but she didn't respond. "But you came, even so."

"Yes." She took a breath to explain, but then didn't and he noted her obvious discomfort.

"And has it changed much, in two years?"

She shrugged. "I don't know. I haven't been to the house. Your mother and Richard walk down here every morning. I came to help, which I hope I have and I've enjoyed it very much until now. I'm perfectly willing to leave now that you're here. I told Madame and Sophie that you wouldn't like me to be here, so they won't be surprised."

He looked at her mildly over the temporarily mended flip-flop.

"Your reasons for being here are nothing to do with me."

"Why did you come then?"

"Oh, I came because of you. You have some explaining to do."

"*I* have some explaining to do? What about you!"

His brows lifted. "What about me?"

"Well, firstly, that utter rubbish about wanting me to drive in Scotland because you had to work. That was a lie. You needed a driver all right, because you'd lost your licence. I thought it was odd that you never drove at all. I was just a convenience."

"I am so sorry for your hurt feelings. It wasn't a lie, as I did have to work, and you'd have refused to come if I'd told you." He sounded coldly matter-of-fact. "Is there anything else you want explained?" She was more hurt than she could even admit to herself.

"Clive Mann. You paid him off."

He looked briefly startled.

271

"I did not," he denied calmly.

"You must have." The flat assertion held a hint of uncertainty. He shook his head.

"Not me. I don't believe in rewarding the ungodly. As I told you in Scotland, if anyone paid up, it was the insurance company. All I did was set the lawyers on him, and he didn't like that at all. Did he pay you back?"

She nodded, reluctantly.

"All of it? Plus interest?"

She nodded again, her certainty beginning to wilt. "Why did he pay it back then? Your lawyers must have threatened him with something."

He nodded.

"Sure they did. Reputable dealers do not send young and naive secretaries—or even junior members of their profession—to make unspecified financial deals in foreign countries with dubious gentlemen of unknown background. Unfair dismissal, putting young persons at risk, negligence, illegal payment, no export licence. Taking repayment whilst negotiating an insurance claim."

She was silent.

"Now," he said. "It's your turn to do some explaining." He appeared to notice her left hand for the first time. "You're wearing what might be an engagement ring."

"So?" she said sharply. "That's not your business, nor does it need explaining."

"Of course not. I was only going to congratulate you," he said, mildly enough for her to wish she hadn't been so sharp. "When are you getting married? And who is the lucky man?" His eyes held something more than polite enquiry and she suppressed an inward quiver. He shrugged in the face of her silence.

"Poor man. A month out of jolly engagement time seems a bit hard." He dismissed the subject and his voice took on a steelier tone. "Now, having established my innocence of your latest fantasy, back to my particular bone. You are accusing me, yet again, of something I haven't done. This time,

272

however, it is a rather more serious accusation and you have done my previously impeccable reputation considerable damage." She felt her heart thudding. He was neither laughing nor teasing. He had to be referring to her letter to the Angel Hospice governors.

"I believe it's you that needs to make an explanation." She was aware that her voice was not at all steady. "I assume you're talking about the designs for the hospice."

"You assume correctly," he said, his face grim. "Specifically, I'm talking about your letter to the governors." His eyes speared her. "By what gigantic leap of logic do you accuse *me*, a mere minor architect, of manipulating the design competition results in your favour? Why the hell should I, for a start?" When she did not reply he continued. "I encouraged you to enter. Not a criminal offence, I don't think. The competition results come in. They're probably all averagely awful and the shortlisted five go for final selection. A process," he said savagely, "which the humble architect is not only not privy to, but is not remotely interested in." She still said nothing, held in some numbing paralysis.

"In their wisdom, they choose yours." There was a slight pause. "Later I learn they are complicated, expensive and so far outside the actual specifications as to be laughable. What the hell were you playing at? Didn't you read the specs?"

She shook her head helplessly, her throat closing. "Well, answer me," he said sharply.

"I did them for—for fun. I didn't think I had a hope so I just—did what I wanted—and sent them off."

"You just did it for fun, and sent them off. I see. How amusing." The sarcasm was biting. "So then they had weeks' worth of song and dance and delay and argument, and I gather you were asked, not entirely unreasonably, as your efforts should have been declared ineligible in the first place, to resubmit your entry within the specifications and the budget, or make some alterations, or something. And then, not content with having caused mayhem among the other entrants who did keep to the specifications, you write a snotty

273

letter accusing *me* of manipulating the results in your favour—"

"I didn't accuse you," she said, her voice trembling, but he silenced her savagely.

"Yes, you did. That was the effect. And then you took the opportunity of withdrawing altogether, leaving bad feeling and accusations flying around like bloody confetti!"

Shocked, she said, "I didn't mean that to happen! I thought—"

"You thought! I should be interested to learn exactly what you did think, and why you thought it. But I'll tell you what I thought. I thought we'd had a good time in Scotland—both work and play—at any rate I wasn't aware that I'd deserved this particular form of revenge—but I guess your memory is much longer than I'd imagined. Was all this a payback for what happened here two years ago?"

"No! Of course not!" she said in a defiant anger. "I thought you were trying to—to help, but I didn't want you to. I didn't want to be shortlisted because you asked them to. As if that might make up for what you put me through here, and you never bothering to communicate after 'the good time' you think we had." His face hardened. "I sent in some ideas because you made me promise to. I don't know what I expected, except that someone might have said if the ideas themselves were any good, or along the right lines. I was totally amazed and thrilled to be on the shortlist. But then I realised it couldn't have been on merit and that they'd done it to get you off their back." Nicholas now looked furious, but she persevered. "I couldn't have been shortlisted because I hadn't kept to the specifications, or completed the estimated time schedules, or the cost estimates for materials, or anything. I hadn't a clue how to, so I just left them blank." She gulped slightly. "So when they wrote and said I'd won the award, I knew I couldn't possibly have won it fairly, and it was just proof that what she said was true—that you'd make sure that I won."

He stared at her in astonished anger.

"What do you mean 'proof that what she said was true'? Proof that who said what was true? What 'she' are we talking about? Lady Beith?" Melissa suddenly felt unsteady and sat down. "OK. Not Lady Beith. What 'she'?"

"Who's Lady Beith?"

"Never mind." He was savage again. "What 'she', Melissa? Who the hell are you talking about?"

She felt the universe shift sideways, but tried to keep anger as her defence.

"A friend. Someone I met said that you'd make sure I won. I didn't want to believe it, but it was obviously true." She tried to keep her voice sharp, but the tremor was audible. "And then the letter from the board came, and it just confirmed everything she'd said. It had to be true because I knew I couldn't be the winner, and I was so disappointed and angry that I wrote—"

"I know what you wrote," he said furiously. "You virtually accused the panel of judges and the board of governors of taking bribes, and the architect of illegal lobbying—and you tell me *you* were angry! It's nothing to how angry I am. You accused the lot of us of malpractice, for God's sake!"

"I didn't!" Shamingly, she could feel tears on her cheeks.

"Yes, you did! You told them to get lost. You told them to take their award and get lost! It's unbelievable! And all because some mythical person, who if they exist at all other than in your fevered imagination, responded to an imaginative story you'd just told them. So, who is this female, and how does one of your so-called friends presume to know what I do or do not think?"

She was aghast. "If it's not true, I shouldn't say."

"Don't be ridiculous! If it's not true you bloody well *have* to say! Have you any idea where this has led? My chairman had complaints and nearly fired me, and I've had to go before the board of governors to defend myself, with everyone picking up every off-the-cuff remark and chance opinion I've made for the last year, and accusations have been flying amongst the judges' panel about how they made the decision and whether it was partially my fault or just entirely my fault."

Robert came and stood in the doorway of his bedroom. He was stark naked and knuckling the sleep out of his eyes.

"You're being horrid to Mel," he said.

"Yes." Nicholas was standing over her, his hands flat on the table. "Go away, Robert, until I've finished being horrid. Who, Melissa? Or have you just made up the whole thing?"

She choked. "No, I didn't. I'm sorry. It seemed—"

"Who was it?" She wilted under the implacable eyes.

"I met Lorraine, in London." It came out in a croak. "She said you'd told her my designs were 'quite good'," she tried to parody the two words into contempt, but they came out as a sob, "and you'd make sure I won. I wasn't to worry."

"You're being so horrid you've made her cry." Robert hadn't moved from his doorway.

"Go away, Robert." He was staring down at her, bemusement in his eyes.

"Lorraine? Lorraine McNair Watt?" There was a small intake of breath. "Bloody little bitch. I said nothing of the sort. You can't possibly have believed a word she said."

"You shouldn't swear," Robert said disapprovingly.

"Robert!" He swung round ferociously and Robert ran for his bed.

"Don't!" Melissa said furiously through her tears. "Don't frighten him." She tried to get up to go to him, but Nicholas pushed her down again.

"He'll survive. Sit down." He rubbed a hand through his hair. "Lorraine came to see me, to discuss that damn retirement home." And for what else, Melissa wondered miserably. He paused, recollecting. "She asked after you. She asked if you were a good secretary, and I told you were pretty efficient, but an even better artist and she was so patronising about that, that I unwisely sprang to your defence. I won't do that again," he said. "I told her you'd sent in designs for the hospice and that from what I'd seen of

276

them they were very good." He looked slightly uneasy and Melissa deduced it had been pillow talk.

"But why—why would she tell me that you'd make sure I won if you hadn't said it?"

"I don't suppose she did," he said bitterly, "but you're so paranoid about my motives you probably just assumed it."

"She did say it. And that I needn't worry about getting the job." She sniffed. "She said you'd make sure I got the contract. Thank you so much. Why should she say that if it wasn't true? What possible reason would she have for making that up?"

After a little silence, he shrugged. "I'd made a point of putting a pin in her self-conceit. This was revenge. Mischief. She's not a fool, and you're obviously the sort who'd be insulted by that sort of help. I expect she was jealous and wanted you to feel insulted. I don't suppose she thought a passing comment would have such spectacularly successful results." His anger was abating. "The fact is, I didn't say it, or even think it, and I most certainly didn't discuss the design applications with anyone or try to influence the results. Ridiculous though it may seem, you won without any help from me. As usual, you made stupid assumptions and jumped to the wrong conclusions."

And lost the award as a result, Melissa thought wretchedly.

Aware that his anger had been reduced from boil to simmer, she got up and went into Robert's room. He was curled into a small heaving ball in the farthest corner of his bed. She touched his shoulder.

"He's stopped being horrid now. And I'm not crying."

There was a noisy silence. "Are you sure?"

"Yes," Nicholas said behind her. Robert sat up slowly and looked at Nicholas angrily. He had been crying, too.

"You shouldn't have been horrid. You shouldn't say bloody. You shouldn't shout."

"No, I shouldn't," said Nicholas, looking penitent. "Sorry."

277

"You should say sorry to Mel as well as me. You were horrid to her first."

"Yes. Sorry, Melissa." He didn't sound sorry at all, she thought. He looked at Robert gravely. "OK? Shall I kiss you better?"

Robert nodded.

"Where do you hurt?"

Robert leant back in the attitude of a dying soldier and clutched the general area of his heart. Nicholas duly kissed him on the chest.

"And you should kiss Melissa better, too." Robert was still angry on her behalf.

"OK." Nicholas grabbed her arm as she tried to escape.

"You don't kiss ladies' chests," Robert said informatively.

Nicholas's bad temper dissolved into laughter. "No? If I can't kiss her chest, what do I kiss?"

"You kiss ladies' cheeks. First one side and then the other."

"It's not just Melissa's cheeks that need kissing," he said wickedly, eyeing the two flaming items, "it's her mouth that hurts." It was quite some time before Robert observed that Melissa's mouth must be feeling better by now.

CHAPTER TWENTY-TWO

He seemed to have enjoyed that kiss, and as a result was distinctly less cross. Nevertheless, he cajoled Robert into continuing his siesta and propelled Melissa back to the patio.

"I'd really like my personal reputation cleaned up as soon as possible, so a letter to that effect by tomorrow lunchtime, please." It was not a request. "Completion on the hospice is behind schedule and withdrawing your designs has not been helpful. You've already caused untold delay and argument, so you can tell them you'll get back to work on them immediately."

"I will not!" she exclaimed. "And it's not true I caused any delay. I withdrew weeks ago, so they could have used whoever was next on the shortlist, and it's a separate issue as to whether or not you gave my designs an unhelpful boost."

He looked startled and then outraged.

"Whether or not—? I thought I'd made it quite clear—I did nothing of the sort."

She was angry, too. "All right, I've got the message. But I can't have caused any delay," she repeated. "I withdrew unconditionally, and there can't be any argument or even a huge disappointment about that. You said yourself all the designs were awful."

"I said no such thing!"

"Well, averagely awful then," she said and added sarcastically, "I don't see the problem in accepting one of the other designs which is also averagely awful, but must have the added beauty of being within the specifications and within budget. I'll get you off the hook of trying to influence anyone, but she made it sound as if it was the obvious thing you'd do, and that you'd actually said it. How was I to know she wasn't telling the truth? How do I know now, just because you deny it? You admit you discussed me and my

279

designs with her." She ignored his protest. "The board must have known whether any of them had been 'got at' by you or not. They could have accepted one of the other designs, or if they had all withdrawn in a huff, they could have started a new competition by now. So what was their problem, beyond dithering?"

Nicholas looked disconcerted.

"The problem," he said slowly, "is that there really was no contest."

She was mystified. "What do you mean, there was no contest? You said there were several—"

"That's not what I mean, no. There were sixteen submissions and four finalists. I apologise for the averagely awful description. Your ideas were apparently the best, and it was your ideas they wanted. Your ideas they still want." He paused and added crossly, "They want you to reconsider your withdrawal."

"You have to be kidding! No way!" She was horrified. "Even if I did reconsider, which I definitely won't, and David won't agree either, it would take me weeks to rework them and get them into grids, and work out the figures. I told you, I wouldn't know where to begin, and by the time I'd discovered, your precious schedule will be even more months behind. Aren't there penalty clauses for late delivery?"

"Yes," he said grimly. "Happily, the architects delivered roughly on time. It's the rest that's completely up the creek."

"Well, they took months to shortlist me and months more to award me the contract. I don't see that's my fault."

"Of course it's your fault! It's all very well for you to stand on your dignity and withdraw your designs, but you leave the hospice in a very difficult position."

"Tough," she said, still stubborn. "They never said so. They wrote me a horrid letter. They wrote me two horrid letters. What would have happened if I hadn't sent them in at all? They'd have had fifteen applications and three finalists, at the very least. And they'd have chosen one and been perfectly happy." She suddenly remembered something. "And there's another thing! They said that extra funding had been specifically given to allow the designs to qualify. After what Lorraine had said, perhaps you can imagine my thought processes." She was on the offensive after that kiss.

Nicholas leant back and put his hands up to fend off her verbal assault.

"The designs weren't kept secret. They were all on public display. The fundraisers went into overdrive and the extra funding came from multiple sources." He didn't deny that he had been one of the sources, she noted sceptically.

He went on, his tone dry. "In theory, I thought that your designs shouldn't have been shown at all. But they were, and everybody thought they were exactly what was wanted, and they bent the rules. And then you opened a can of worms by withdrawing, and the board is in a complete uproar, and blaming me for something I *have not done*." The last three words were emphatically separated. "Along with exonerating me, you can now tell them you'll do the damn designs and try to make some sort of amends for the damage you've caused."

"No!" Melissa said, but this time there was a note of pleading. "Absolutely not!"

"Yes," he said. "A letter. To my satisfaction. By tomorrow midday."

After a tea of cucumber hunks and Marmite on crusty bread, Nicholas, Robert and Fifi had gone along the beach to do essential maintenance on the wind-blown sandcastle. Melissa cleaned up the kitchen, propped Charlotte on her hip and walked slowly down the beach. She watched the two children patting and scraping at the sagging sand walls, their golden bodies perfect flexing curves in the slanting sun, Nicholas cross-legged between them, hard gleaming angles, his natural dark skin darkened further by the hair on legs and arms and chest. There was no question but that he was a pleasure to look at; another irritation to Melissa who wished fervently that he was bald, fat and ugly.

She sat in the tiny wavelets, balancing Charlotte between her knees so that she could splash in the water. The baby screamed with pleasure.

David's ring caught the light and she twisted it round her finger, sliding it to and fro over the knuckle. It was an opal, flecked with pretty greens and blues. But pale, like a fish's eye, she thought in sudden distaste. He had chosen it and had not observed her lack of enthusiasm. It was different, he'd said. Everybody had boring old diamonds and sapphires. He had been so pleased and proud of her, so obviously longing to tell the world of his latest acquisition.

She put a stop to the disloyal thoughts, but the disloyal action remained heavy on her heart. It had been Nicholas making trouble, but she could have prevented it, if she had really wanted to. Nicholas had seized the opportunity; that long kiss had been briefly deep, and deeply disturbing.

She felt the sand vibrate faintly and knew he was there. He sat down in the warm water beside her.

"Penny for them?"

After a pause she said, "I wish you hadn't."

"Kissed you? No you don't. I don't either." There was a slight hesitation. "I'm sorry I'm so bad-tempered." He kneeled to pick up Charlotte. "I'm going to teach her to swim."

"Don't you dare! She's not a puppy!"

He lowered the baby into the sea and she let out a piercing howl which changed into a shriek of laughter when he threw her up into the air and caught her. He did it again with the same results.

"You see? She loves it." He held her with her legs in the water and sat on the bottom, laughing into her face. Getting up he held her to his chest with one arm, and hauled Melissa up with the other.

"Go and have a swim. I'll babysit. Hurry up, or I'll kiss you again."

She swam out, over the smooth clean sand, the water turquoise about her; her own shadow, like her thoughts, following her like a shark. She swam back towards the two older children who, seeing her coming, leapt up and into the water, coming to their usual abrupt halt at the waist, jumping up and down screeching at the sudden chill on sun-warmed skin. Further down the beach Charlotte was rubbing sand into Nicholas's mouth as he lay on his back on the hot beach. He really does like children, she thought, and children like him. Children always know.

Fifi took the plunge and clutched her round the waist, gasping. Melissa held their feet as they did handstands and swam between her legs, thrashing like beached whales. Their bodies, slick with cream, flashed and gleamed and twisted and curled, and the sudden cramping delight in them seized her again. David did want children—he had plans for school fees insurance, for the schools themselves. Would it be enough?

Nicholas had gone back to the beach house and was returning with Charlotte on one lean hip, and a huge inner tube which he was endeavouring to firm up as he walked.

"It's got a leak!" Fifi yelled at him.

"So I'm discovering," he said, blowing valiantly.

He handed Charlotte to Melissa and she sat on the sand watching him tipping the children off as they fought for supremacy, the shrieks of laughter increasing in direct proportion to the decreasing air in the tyre.

Michael and Sophie were walking back along the water's edge and Sophie gave her a concerned look.

"You OK?"

Melissa gave a wobbly smile and relinquished the baby to her. In the kitchen, she grappled with a mixture of spaghetti bolognese and the Angel Hospice governors. Chopping onions, sniffing and blowing her nose alternately, she wished she had never heard of the hospice, at the same time wondering what the other entries had been like. She swept the invading sand off the tiles and back on to the beach while the sauce cooked. She could see Michael's ugly caliper abandoned on the beach and the two men being half drowned by the children. The shock of Nicholas's arrival and the angry words between them had shaken her. The fact that she had lost the hospice job because of her stupid mistaken assumptions was a very bitter pill to swallow.

The children came running up the beach, shedding salt water and sand. She and Sophie bundled them under the shower and returned them desalted, dried, brushed and still bursting with energy. Sophie had had no opportunity amidst the noise to do more than say, "I'm sorry. I had no idea he was coming. Are you all right? He said he wanted to talk to you alone."

"It's OK," Melissa had said. Nicholas had given her less than twenty-four hours in which to draft a letter to the governors which would satisfy both them and him. No, it was not OK at all.

After Charlotte was in bed, the others played dominoes in the soft evening light. The click of the tiles and the children's sharp light voices mingling with the deeper adult ones came to her clearly in her room as she tried to draft the letter. Although it wasn't all her fault, she thought miserably. She hadn't mentioned his name, although she supposed it had been quite clear who she was referring to, but the panel should have declared her entry void from the start, and Nicholas shouldn't have been talking about it to Lorraine McNair Watt. She guessed Lorraine had gone to his house, not the office, and she guessed she'd been in his bed when they'd had that conversation. Maybe there was still truth in Lorraine's gossip, despite his denials.

Normally after the children had eaten, they would have a last scramble along the beach, or up the path to gaze in fascination at the huge ants' nest by a rock. The denizens of this underground world would be popping busily in and out of their hole, intent upon the urgent business which would be the basis of the evening's saga from Melissa. Sophie had decided that the ants would be the heroes in a future book and in preparation for the illustrations Melissa had sketched shells, grasses, flowers, leaves and stones. There were intricate drawings of driftwood, birds, geckos, and ants and gradually these acquired characters, expressions and actions.

Tonight, however, Nicholas was with them, and Melissa had not ventured out of her room.

Sophie knocked on her door and came in quietly, closing it behind her. She looked worriedly at Melissa and the mass of papers on the table.

"He's gone back up to the house, and says he intends to stay for the rest of the holiday. I'm sorry about whatever it is that's happened. It's not like him to be unkind, but we can see he has been. Can we help?"

Everyone said he was kind. It was such an irritating virtue, kindness, making everyone else feel not kind. Melissa shook her head. "No, but thank you. I'm going to have to sort this out on my own."

It was a revelation that she could have, indeed apparently had, damaged his reputation, but she got no satisfaction from having done so. I wish, she thought fiercely, that just for once he could be completely in the wrong and I could be completely in the right. I wish that the people I really like didn't like him. There was no way she could leave without letting down Sophie and Michael, but her heart sank at the thought of him staying.

The ring on her finger reminded her of kind, normal David. At this moment, he seemed infinitely desirable and his love and solicitousness would be balm to her bruised soul. She texted him saying how much she missed him. Underneath was the faintly guilty knowledge that the longing had not been very deep for the first two weeks. The ring was a constant reminder, the white band of skin more obvious daily as her hands grew browner, but she did not ache for his presence as she had ached for Nicholas in those silent months after Scotland. Did David ache for her? She had WhatsApp-ed daily at first, but latterly it had seemed an effort to find anything she hadn't said before, and she was not, she told herself, the sort of person who spilled feelings and emotions all over a text message.

She knew she didn't really love David, and if he loved her, was it enough? Was it enough to have all the things he was offering: a home, security, companionship. The fumbling lovemaking, the consideration of his well-judged kisses.

She wondered why she was being such a coward, and so unfair to David by putting off the evil moment. The phrase in her mind upset her: getting engaged should not be termed 'the evil moment'. Sarah's extensive list of his attributes echoed in her memory. The downside was shorter; the only criticisms she could come up with was that he was a bit domineering and a bit patronising. Nicholas, too, had those downsides, only more than a bit. And sometimes she was irritated by David for no very good reason—or at least for reasons which she wouldn't even think about if she really loved him. She sighed. It was better to know now that David had faults. No one was perfect and eternal love existed only between the pages of romantic novels.

She should eliminate Nicholas from her thinking once and for all. He was far too old, he was divorced, he was not interested in her, let alone in love with her, and he was very angry.

In her letter to the hospice governors she had tried to exonerate Nicholas while at the same time trying not to sound as if she was reapplying for the project. The following day he looked it over, and altered the wording to a definite agreement to do the designs.

"I am not going to agree to do them!" she exclaimed desperately. "I can't do it in the timescale and I won't. How could I possibly agree after what's happened?"

Nicholas heard the obdurate pitch in her voice and realised that he wasn't going to win the battle quite yet. He watered down the wording slightly.

"You're worse than a bloody client," he grumbled as eventually she wrote a final fair copy which was scanned and emailed to the hospice governors that afternoon.

Prior to his coming she had enjoyed the Newingtons' relaxed and amusing conversations. Now, when Nicholas was present, she found herself silent and edgy. There had been no mention of the events here two years ago, nor of the two weeks in Scotland. The threads which connected Scotland with her present predicament and discomfort over the hospice were thin but strong.

She had been over and over her meeting with Lorraine, remembering her acceptance of Lorraine's words, and now remembering too that sideways look, sly in retrospect. Her anger, the bitter disappointment of thinking that her success was due only to Nicholas's interference, had cheated her of a triumph, lost through nothing but stupidity. She felt certain that there could be no second chance, despite what Nicholas had said.

She had made assumptions about Nicholas ever since that terrible day she had tried to steal back the Perissos Bible, and almost all of them had been proved wrong. There was just that case of drugs which seemed less and less characteristic. But she still could not account for it. She churned in mental discomfort for having, on this occasion, punished him for something which it turned out he hadn't done at all. Or so he said. The memory of his kiss caused her cheeks to burn and made her skin prickle with unwanted desire.

CHAPTER TWENTY-THREE

That evening Sophie and Michael went to the main house for supper and Nicholas appeared at the beach house. She'd been expecting it and had tried mentally to prepare herself, but even so she could feel her heart beginning to pound.

"You and I have got some business to finish," he said, putting wine and glasses on the table.

He didn't waste time on social niceties. "I hope you've been getting your mind round the hospice designs. There's very little time now."

"No, I haven't," she said, anger stirring again. "I told you I can't possibly do it. It would take weeks even if I knew how to do it, which I don't."

"You could do the preparatory work in a week with some help. They could find people at the Glasgow School of Art." He made it sound the simplest thing in the world.

She was exasperated. "Nicholas, I just can't. I have to find a job. I'm engaged, and David can't be expected to agree to this."

"Look, this *is* a job!" he said crossly. "I was bloody angry to be accused of professional misconduct, but I suppose it's only caused a temporary hiatus which hopefully will be cleared up by your apology, so perhaps we can put aside my feelings about what you charmingly call 'a misunderstanding'. The hospice is built and I'm very pleased about it, but it needs to be finished and begin work. There are terminally sick children out there who need the respite care, and they need an environment which is happy and positive. The other designs are crass and patronising—all clowns and carousels. Old-fashioned. Primary colours. There's no humour, no peacefulness, no curiosity, nothing educational, nothing original. I'm telling you that what you've produced is right for the building, right for the nursing staff and, most importantly,

288

right for sick children. Can't you try to make something out of this? If you don't want to seize the chance of a lifetime, could you possibly think about the children who have no chances left in their lives at all?" He put a brown hand across the table and put it on hers. "Please?"

She stared at him with tight lips. "You are a rat."

He shook his head. "I'm not." Touching her face lightly, he refilled her glass and went away to the kitchen where she heard him inspecting the contents of the fridge.

She felt confused. Nicholas was not in the habit of asking, let alone pleading, and the change of tactics left her without an anchor. Part of her—a large part—was flattered and astonished. She wanted the recognition this project would bring her, but at the same time she was terrified by it. She had, it seemed, a tiger by the tail.

"I just can't believe the governors can really want to use my ideas," she said, when he came back.

"Apparently they do."

She sighed. "How many of them are there? And who are they? Are they unanimous?"

"I doubt they're unanimous—no committee of that size ever would be, but it'll have gone to a vote. The Chairman is Sir Norman Westerman who is head of Paediatrics at Glasgow Infirmary, and a cancer specialist. I should think there are about twenty-five of them probably."

"*Twenty-five!* Who on earth are they?"

"Financial, legal, medical, social, psychologists, local government. All sorts. And of course, fundraisers."

"I wouldn't have to meet them or anything, would I?" She was twisting her fingers together in anxiety.

He hesitated. "I would think meeting with them, or some of them, would be a priority. For one thing, a personal explanation is called for—"

"But I have written!" she exclaimed in dismay. "This whole thing is now horribly embarrassing. Even if I did agree to redo them, and I haven't agreed, I can't just hop up to Glasgow every time the bell strikes. I haven't got the money for a start, or the time. I must find a proper job—Sophie's illustrations won't last forever—and David will expect me—to, well, be around. I'm engaged—he won't want me disappearing."

His eyebrows went up. "Melissa! The penny simply hasn't dropped, has it?" He spoke quietly but emphatically.

"This is a prestige contract we're talking about. The project is worth millions in total. National bodies are looking at it carefully. Children's hospices are a new departure, and there are still very few facilities specifically for teenagers or young adults. The architectural designs were important—very important—to us. It was champagne and smoked salmon in the office when this one came through. There will be interviews, articles and photographs in national and local newspapers and in specialist magazines. Your name will be known to anyone and everyone who has even a peripheral interest in these things, as will Thauros Associates and every other involved company. You will be paid to do this as well as getting the design award. You do know how much that is, don't you?"

"No," she said weakly.

"Good grief! Didn't you read the contract? Your expenses, travel and accommodation, will be paid—oh, there's a limit of course, you won't get Hilton rates. You won't need a job—this is a job. And a very big one. It doesn't come to an end with finished designs, you know, that's just the beginning. You'll be seeing to their execution for a start, and, I sincerely hope, doing all the detail yourself."

Her mouth formed an 'O'. She said, even more weakly, "I can't possibly. All that media stuff—I'd loathe it and—"

"You'll learn to deal with it. You'll get used to it." He smiled thinly, thinking of Marie Claude. "Learn which profile to present to the cameras."

"No!"

"Yes. Don't be such a wimp."

She was indignant. "I'm a complete amateur and this is not the sort of job I can cut my teeth on. It's one thing to do

290

the designs, produce the ideas, and perhaps even to work those designs to specifications and budgets, with a lot of professional help, but it's quite another to physically carry out the work. I don't know what paints to use, how much would be needed, how I would even apply it over huge areas."

"OK, OK. I realise all that, and I expect the governors realise it, too. Stop imagining the bogeymen and start thinking positively. For one thing, the hospice is not a vast building—it only has ten units and not all the rooms will be decorated. If you allow your designs to go forward but don't oversee the work, you'll find they don't come out as you visualised—or how anyone else visualised them. You've got to have more input than that. It's like designing a house and then leaving it in the hands of the builders. All the details will go wrong—doors hung on the wrong side, sockets just where you didn't specify them, skirting boards too narrow." He looked sympathetically at the genuine alarm on her face. "Look. Everyone has to start somewhere, and you'll be able to get help and advice."

She blinked and hunched her shoulders in denial.

"It's scary, but you'll love it. You have talent, but it will never develop unless you're forced to use it. You're one of those people who need to be dropped in the deep end because your self-confidence is virtually nil. You'll get commissions after this which you'd never have got otherwise."

"But I can't *start* with something like this. It's too big. I had no idea—it never occurred to me."

"Pussycat, has it never occurred to you that your mind teems with unusual ideas? Did no one ever tell you?"

She stared into his eyes, astonished. This was horrible Nicholas saying complimentary things.

"Not really. Everyone else seemed to be so much better than me. I worked hard because I wanted to prove I could stand on my—" She decided not to embark on her grandparents' attitude. "I just didn't believe what I did was particularly special."

"Well, you can believe me. You know from experience that I'm the most critical person alive."

"You're only saying it now because the hospice needs to be finished. It's a rather unsubtle form of blackmail, backed up by flattery. David won't like it. He won't agree to it. I know he won't." Her tone was tougher.

Nicholas ignored the accusation of blackmail.

"David," he said carefully, "will be exceedingly proud of you. Any man would be thrilled to bits to have his future wife admired and respected for her work and talents."

She felt doubtful. David believed a wife should be home-loving, a good cook and a proper full-time mother. She wasn't at all sure that he would like a successful career woman who might take the limelight. Nicholas was watching her, a frown creasing his forehead.

"Shouldn't you try to use your gifts? If he really loves you, he'll encourage you. Don't be so afraid of trying, otherwise you'll never know whether you can do it or not. You didn't believe you had a hope of winning that competition, so you didn't even try. And then you won, in spite of deliberately messing it up. Doesn't that give you belief in yourself?"

When she didn't reply, he continued almost irritably. "I never knew anyone so lacking in self-confidence as you. What does it matter even if you do fail? What happened? Was it the accident?"

She looked away without answering, hoping he would back off. He didn't.

"What happened to your father if he wasn't killed in the accident?"

She blinked. He had asked the unaskable again; tactless and invasive.

"I don't think I—"

"I'm not just being curious. I'm guessing that losing your family hasn't helped your confidence, so what happened to your father?"

She stared at him blindly. Why was she even debating in her mind whether to answer? Perhaps it would be liberating to tell him, just so long as she didn't fall to pieces, which was unlikely after thirteen years.

Nicholas was still waiting and she sighed wearily.

"He killed himself." After a pause, "A year later."

Nicholas looked at her without any obvious sympathy or indeed anything else. He just waited.

What was possessing her, she asked herself, to embark on this difficult psychological exercise with this particular person at this particular point in time?

She glanced at Nicholas, angry that he was tearing the scab off again.

"Go on," he said quietly. "Tell me about the accident. You might find you feel better telling someone."

She stared at him and then at the moon path on the sea, debating the truth of that. After a long moment, she heaved in a breath.

"We were at Meath for the Christmas holidays. Mops and Brig were out for New Year drinks with neighbours, and the rest of us had been invited to a party. But Johnny and I had raging temperatures, flu I think, and Dad had just driven down from some naval event in Rosyth so he was tired and Mum said she'd drive the others if he stayed with us."

She stopped briefly, her eyes unfocused and then squeezed shut on the memory of anger and denial and guilt.

"She looked so pretty and I was foul. She was really hurt that I wouldn't kiss her goodbye and I wouldn't speak to the boys and I said it wasn't fair. And Johnny didn't want James to go without him. As if he knew."

She stopped again, staring into space. Nicholas didn't move in the long silence.

"The boys were in their kilts, and they all had assorted kilt jackets, second-hand down the family. They said that's why their bodies weren't completely burnt. The wool was so thick."

293

When the car had been winched out of the ravine, her youngest brother's pockets had had the remnants of what boys' pockets have always been full of: rubber bands, bent nails, forbidden chewing gum and rusty razor blades, a dented ping-pong ball. Dented before or after, no one would ever know.

She swallowed. "It was frosty, but not snowing or anything, and only about half an hour's drive. Nothing special. Nothing unusual. They said they thought the motorbike was on the wrong side of the road, coming round the corner. They were on the short cut, to save time, and its only single track really, but at night you can see headlights coming so you can drive faster, but maybe with a motorbike you wouldn't see its headlight so well. They couldn't really tell what had happened. There were no witnesses. No survivors. A boy and his girlfriend. They all went over the edge. Our car, their bike."

She paused, almost dreamily, but her arms were wound tightly round her body.

"Funny things survived. The dockyard pass, a shopping list. You'd think paper would have burnt. Peter's Swiss Army knife that we'd all given him—all us children—for Christmas. It was the biggest and the most expensive. Masses of gadgets. He'd spent the week learning how to open them all up so that it looked like a porcupine. He was really pleased with it. He'd taken it to the party to show it off."

She smiled faintly. "That was a success anyway. He enjoyed it for a week; opened bottles, sharpened pencils, cleaned out the ponies' hooves, cut his nails. Johnny's got it now." She paused, remembering. "The police came. Johnny and I slept through it all, and Dad never woke us up. I expect we were full of paracetamol or something. It was New Year's Day in Scotland. Nothing happens. The world just—stops. By morning Dad wasn't functioning at all. There was a policewoman—quite young—too young, poor thing. Eventually people turned up, the doctor, naval people, the minister from our church. I was at my worst with the flu, a really high temperature, and Johnny wasn't much better. Brig and Mops were there, people arrived with food and things, I think. Johnny and I never even cried. I don't think any of us took it in. They just never came back, though we went on expecting them every time a car came—I hear the car coming back in my dreams. And the funeral was just extraordinary. All these people crying and Johnny and I did nothing. I didn't feel anything at all. Dad didn't do anything either. He replied nicely to people and said thank you when they said how sorry they were and there were the three of us, behaving like zombies and everyone else in pieces. It wasn't happening to us—it was like a film and we were directing." She swallowed.

"And somewhere inside me there was Mum screaming, 'You wouldn't even kiss me goodbye.' And I still hear her. In nightmares."

Again, there was a long silence and then she said, almost conversationally, "I might as well finish. Do you mind?"

Nicholas shook his head. He had his back to the light of the sea and she couldn't see his face, only his silhouette.

"Brig and Mops looked after us, even though they were just as—they'd lost a daughter-in-law and three grandsons. Johnny and I resented Brig and Mops terribly and behaved really badly. Mops didn't run things like Mum and we were rude and bolshie about food and clothes and discipline and everything. And Dad became more and more hopeless—listless, and not bothering about anything much. I think the Navy did what they could, but in the end, he had to leave. School was better really, it was boarding; no one raked it up after a while, but I went right off the rails. I didn't do any work, and was rude to the staff. I sneaked out at night, stole pocket money, bought alcohol, went to the cinema with local boys, experimented with weed. It made me sick as a dog, so I didn't do that again. They expelled me eventually. The holidays were awful. Both Johnny and I were really horrible and disruptive and I have no idea how Brig and Mops coped with us."

295

Nicholas silently topped up their glasses and Melissa realised the dam had been breached and the memories would keep coming until the reservoir was empty.

"The nightmares were so bad I would keep myself awake so as not to have them. I went downstairs one night that first Easter holidays, and I heard Dad and Brig in the sitting room—or at least I heard Dad talking to Brig. About how he should have gone that night, and how exhausted Mum was from looking after Johnny and me and if only we hadn't been ill it wouldn't have happened. They'd left late because I'd been making a fuss and whining and if only they'd left on time she wouldn't have taken the short cut, and wouldn't have met the motorbike, and she wouldn't have been driving so fast. And if only he'd driven it wouldn't have happened and he'd have gone if we hadn't been ill—and on, and on and on, over and over and over again. And Brig never said anything. I thought then it was because he thought the same, but later—years later—I wondered if he was just letting Dad talk to get it out of his system. I never asked Brig, so I don't know. I think I've always been afraid of the answer. I used to go downstairs at night often after that, and they were always there, and Dad would be saying the same thing, night after night, and Brig would say nothing, just let him talk."

Another silence. Nicholas didn't move.

"Johnny knew. Johnny and I fought like crazy, but we still stuck together. Like a conspiracy. He just knew. He and I knew it was all our fault."

Again, the pause.

"Dad swallowed a whole bottle of pills. A year later, on New Year's Eve." She sighed. "I think it was guilt that she had died and he hadn't. It was a long time ago. Poor Brig and Mops."

After a long time, Nicholas spoke.

"Why don't you walk down the beach."

She nodded. After a while she got up and went down to the water. Then she walked along where the sea foamed at the edges and sat down on the rocks at the end of the beach.

Much later, exhausted from the strange raw weeping, she found that he had left tsadziki and bread and her tumbler of wine on the table. There was a trace of his cigarette smoke hanging in the still air, but Nicholas had gone.

When Michael returned to London, he and Nicholas sailed back to Skiathos together. Nicholas was away for one night and the last week slid away like fine sand in an hourglass.

CHAPTER TWENTY-FOUR

David was at the airport to meet her, as was Michael to collect Nicholas, Sophie and the children. Madame and Richard would have another month on Mixos. David's greeting was physical and public and she extricated herself from his arms rather pink-cheeked. She didn't feel quite as ecstatic as he did and when he seized her trolley and started for the car park she found herself telling him sharply to wait so that she could say goodbye to the Newingtons. He had the grace to look slightly abashed.

"Sorry, darling. I'm just so thrilled to have you back. I've missed you to bits. Hurry it up and I'll wait here for you."

"Don't you want to meet them?" she said, amazed.

"Not a bit. I came to meet you."

"I think you should." Her voice was cold. "I've just spent a month with them and they're my friends. It's rude not to, and they're expecting to meet you."

"I suppose they must be, as your fiancé."

He was very civil and gracious and accepted Sophie and Michael's congratulations, and their thanks for Melissa's help. Nicholas had inexplicably disappeared.

She hugged and kissed all the Newingtons and allowed herself to be dragged away. David noticed her preoccupation with the people around them.

"What's wrong, darling? Are you looking for someone?"

"No," she said quickly. "I hope they'll manage all right with all the children and luggage and everything."

"Of course they will," he said soothingly. They would be, she knew, because Nicholas would be back to help them. "Let's get to the car and then you can tell me all about it."

In the car, he turned her towards him and kissed her. She clung to him rather desperately, staring at the engagement ring on her brown hand six inches from her eyes

"It's lovely to see you. It was quite a journey—it's taken all day."

"Air travel is always a bore—all that security and waiting about. But you can forget it all now—I've got a surprise in store for you."

"A surprise? What?" She was cautious.

"Don't sound so suspicious! It won't be a surprise if I tell you."

"Well, is it a nice surprise?"

He looked hurt.

"I'm hardly likely to give you a nasty one, am I?"

After a momentary pause, she said, "How lovely. I'll look forward to it."

The drive into London was slow in rush-hour traffic. He told her he'd come second in the squash competition, that his sister had shingles, that two of his practice were away on holiday and they'd been rushed off their feet with a spate of the usual summer skin problems.

"I hope you took care and used those products I gave you. You look a lovely colour, but it wouldn't be the thing for a skin specialist to have a wife with melanoma," he joked.

"I took care," she said quietly. "Michael's a doctor, too, and we all used sun blocks, especially the children. Anyway, I didn't sunbathe as such—there wasn't really the time."

"Poor old you. Were you desperately bored looking after those kids?"

"Bored! Of course not! They're delicious. Hardly any clothes to wash and lots of salads and fruit and cold food. The children are very easy and if we weren't in the sea, it was sandcastles on the beach or walks or Ludo on the veranda. I told you all that in my texts and on the phone." She sounded reproachful, but he didn't notice.

"Talking of holidays, my darling, my good deed of working through July has been rewarded. I've got two weeks in mid-September when all my colleagues' children have gone back to school. I thought we'd go off to somewhere hot and romantic for a pre-honeymoon swan. To give us energy for the wedding and all that. Bet that tickles your fancy, doesn't it?"

He obviously thought it should. Melissa suppressed an unworthy desire to slap him.

"Is that the surprise?"

"What? Oh no! I wouldn't have told you if it was."

"It needs some discussion," she said. "There are just one or two points which we need to talk about."

She was on the verge, she realised, of having a row within ten minutes of seeing him.

His eyebrows lifted. "Are there? Like what?"

"For a start, I don't think I'll be free in September. I think I'll have a job."

"Darling Mel, a temporary job is a temporary job, didn't you know? You just tell them you can't work for two weeks in September. And if it's money you're worried about, you needn't. Now that we're engaged I'll look after all that side. But, unlike you, I can't just take my holidays any old time—I have to think of the practice and my patients and September it is."

She kept her temper with difficulty.

"I may have a big job to do then, which I won't be able to leave once I've started. It won't be secretarial. And I'm quite capable of paying my own way, thank you for the offer."

"But we're going to be married and therefore of course I'll be looking after you and paying all the costs."

"We're not married yet," she shot back. "Don't you want to know what job I'm talking about?"

He looked taken aback by her ferocity.

"You don't need a job. I don't want a working wife—I can support you very well. It's not as if you'd got a career or anything."

"You don't think I should use my qualifications then?"

"It's not a serious degree—not vocational, like medicine or law. I mean it was great that you did it, and proved to yourself you had the intellectual capacity, but it's not exactly

300

useful or financially valuable, is it? Clive Mann was the one and only art job and from all accounts it wasn't an overwhelming success, was it?"

Anger and hurt rendered her speechless for a moment.

"Do you want to hear about it or not?"

"Of course I do, darling. I didn't know you had a job in mind." He was trying to be soothing. "I'm sure we can work it out. Tell me about it."

She tried to ignore the patronising tone.

"I did some interior designs for a children's hospice in Glasgow."

"I remember, but you said the Greek man had put a spoke in the wheels by promoting your application. You turned it down, quite properly, I thought."

"Well, it turned out that he didn't. He didn't endorse me, or my designs, and although I withdrew my application, it appears they still want them."

"How perfectly extraordinary!" He looked completely amazed and she could see the cogs churning. "How on earth do you know?"

"He told me."

David rolled his eyes back in a parody of surprise. "Well, well! He'd hardly admit to lobbying on your behalf, would he? But he must be soft on you if he's still trying to get your application through to the top."

"Thanks a bundle for the vote of confidence." She was fuming, but tried hard for irony instead.

David took a second to realise what she meant. "Sorry, darling, I didn't mean that I don't think your efforts were brilliant."

"You never looked at them, so you can't know."

"For goodness sake, you can't have it both ways," he said irritably. "But he would deny trying to push your application, wouldn't he? What with your trouble in Greece a couple of years ago, and now this Greek architect, I'm surprised you don't give all things Greek a very wide berth. Touch not the Greek and all that."

301

She had a fleeting thought that the original lack of explanations might have future consequences, but pushed them aside for the moment.

"I believe him. He was furious—very angry indeed. He said the reasons I gave for withdrawing from the competition damaged his reputation."

His eyebrows rose in amusement. "Naturally they did, and in my opinion quite rightly so. I hope it will teach him a lesson not to try that sort of thing in the future. I don't suppose he expected to run into an honest girl like you, but thought you'd fall into his arms with gratitude."

She sat firmly on her bubbling irritation. "Well, it appears I won on merit and he had nothing to do with it."

"But you can't have won on merit!" he said, puzzled. "You said you sent in some ideas—some drawings—for fun and hadn't bothered with the competition rules. Come on, Mel! He must have pulled strings—though why on earth he should bother I simply can't imagine. Perhaps," he said archly, "this Greek builder fancies you." She didn't bother to reply. "So what's the problem, you've turned it down and that's that, I assume?"

"No, it isn't. I've had to write an apology and explain it was all a complete misunderstanding, and now I've got to redesign within the specifications."

He was cross and puzzled. "Apologise? You'll do nothing of the sort! Why should you apologise or redesign?"

Somewhat tartly, she said, "Because they like the designs. They think they're the best."

"Good grief! How amazing!" A bit tardily he added, "But that's wonderful!" and still managed to express considerable doubt.

"And if I do that, Nicholas Thauros says it will be a big and important and prestigious job and will take some time."

"What does 'some time' mean? Surely you can't mean it will take till September!"

"Well, yes. In fact, probably well into December. I've never done this before—it may take me a while to get the hang of it."

He said decisively, "It's completely out of the question then. We've got a wedding to organise, and I thought we could fix a date around the end of November. I've found out my parents' local church is free then. Not too near Christmas—people don't find Christmas weddings very easy. That's a cast-iron excuse for telling them to get lost. Nicely, of course, but they'll just have to find another artist or painter or whatever." An idea struck him. "If they like your ideas so much, why don't they get someone else to paint them? Then they'll be up on the wall and you won't have had to do it. Brilliant or what?"

Melissa wondered if the early start, a long journey, two airports and three children had made her unreasonably grumpy. She tried to control her fraying temper.

"Can I take some of that in order? Firstly, I had no idea there was a wedding to organise—let alone in November. As far as I knew there wasn't even an official engagement and even if there was, November is far too soon. And perhaps I might remind you of the convention that girls get married from their own homes, not their future parents-in-laws', and weddings are organised by the bride's family not the groom's. We haven't even discussed weddings, and in case you'd forgotten I agreed to wear your ring on condition that you didn't tell anybody." He wasn't at all used to the tough tone. "Nobody does know about it, do they?" She instinctively knew from his body language that he'd been incapable of keeping it quiet.

He looked uncomfortable. "Well, they do actually. I mean, it was quite impossible not to drop a hint."

"A hint to whom?" she said ominously. "You specifically promised not to tell your parents." The look on his face told her she was right. "David, you promised not to. I wore your ring on condition that you told no one, especially your parents." The anger took hold. "If you can't keep a promise

303

like that, about something really important, how can I trust you? You pushed me into this, and just assumed that I was as certain as you are. Well, I wasn't. I'm not. That's why I needed to go away and think it through. I'm not certain at all, and especially not now, after this. I went to Greece to sort myself out, to have time to think, without you push, push, pushing. And in the meantime—"

"Look," he said hastily, "calm down, darling. If I've jumped the gun a bit, I'm sorry, but it's only because I adore you so much, and you really had led me to believe that you felt the same way about me, and you accepted an engagement ring."

"On condition that you wouldn't tell anyone."

"You're naturally unassuming and modest—but honestly, no girl accepts an engagement ring and then doesn't want the world to know about it! If November's too soon, let's discuss it. Nothing's set in concrete—of course it isn't, but I don't want to put it off too long. I don't think long engagements are very wise, do you? Too much time being neither single nor married. Very uncomfortable! And I am only a man, my darling, and it's not that I don't think you're wonderfully strong-minded and everything, but there can't be another girl in the kingdom who isn't living with her boyfriend, let alone her fiancé, and frankly there is a limit."

She took a hold on herself. "Oh! For goodness sake! I would have thought a long engagement was very wise if one of the parties isn't certain. That's what engagements are for." Marry in haste, repent at leisure, was the cliché she thought but didn't say, feeling treacherous. "Anyway, November is far too soon. I would still be working on the hospice." Odd how it had hardened into fact.

"But you can't!" He was genuinely aghast. "You can't keep popping off to Glasgow during our engagement. There'll be arrangements, and parties, and your wedding dress—Mum wants to give you the wedding dress, by the way—as her present. She's dying to go shopping with you—

and we'll have to do a wedding list. People will expect you to be here—it'll be a really busy time."

"Not if you explain that I'm working, and how important it is, and not if the wedding isn't until the spring. And I'm afraid I wouldn't be 'popping off' to Glasgow. I shall have to live there. I suppose I could 'pop off' to London occasionally." She knew she was deliberately making it worse for him and was ashamed of herself. "And parties are hardly a good excuse for not doing something as worthwhile as this."

"But it's not important!"

"It jolly well is!" she interrupted fiercely. "It is to me."

"I think you're being extraordinarily selfish. It's not important compared to our future life together. You're saying you don't care about this first bit of us together as—"

"As an 'item'?" she said bitterly. "What about me as a person? Don't you think I should seize this chance now it's been offered to me? On a plate, what's more, as I really didn't deserve a second chance. If I make a success of this—which maybe I won't, but I won't know without trying, will I? Nicholas said I might get commissions. Wouldn't you be pleased about that? Would you be pleased for me?"

"Nicholas said? Commissions? What on earth are you talking about? Why should anyone give you a commission, and what for?"

He wasn't being deliberately unkind; he simply didn't understand and she was too tired to try to go on explaining. But he went on worrying at it like a dog with a rat.

"It's not the job that bothers me, though you won't either need one or want one when we're married. It's the timing. Now is not the time to start doing something that is a) miles away from home and b) going to take months rather than weeks. It's dotty. After we're married, if you insist, though I shall be sad. You know I believe in breadwinning and homemaking, and each of us having those roles, but I can assure you, my darling, that I am not the homemaker, and I have a career which can and will support us very adequately, together with what my parents have and will provide. This

305

sounds a fun idea, and I do see that you must be terribly pleased they liked your drawings. But let's leave it there. I'm sure my idea of somebody else painting them would work, wouldn't it?"

"I don't know," she admitted, exhausted.

He sensed the beginnings of acquiescence and pressed on.

"You could redesign them here in London, and get all the prestige for the ideas and everything, and then someone else could paint them. But it really is out of the question for you to get more involved than that just now."

"Are you saying you won't let me?"

He put his head on one side, considering.

"I think I have to insist, yes. I know what's going to be involved here, and I don't think you have any real idea at all. There's too much to do." In a jokey little falsetto he parodied, "So much to do, so little time."

There was silence between North End Road and the Earls Court junction. Melissa shook herself mentally and said decisively, "David, I'm very tired. We got up at four this morning and the children were pretty restless on the flight. Let's discuss things in the morning. I'm just not thinking straight, and talk of holidays before I've even got back from this trip is a bit much. If you don't mind, I think I'll just unpack and go straight to bed."

To her surprise he was horrified.

"But you can't! Definitely not! Darling, it's only six-thirty. Have a bath and a bit of a rest and I'll collect you at, say, quarter to eight. No later."

"Collect me? Are you mad! I'm not going anywhere tonight." A suspicion entered her mind. "You weren't thinking of taking me out, were you? Cos, if so, forget it. Rebook for tomorrow." She peered at him, suspicion rising. "David, you haven't organised something, have you? My first night back?"

He looked guiltily disappointed.

"Yes, I have. I never thought you'd be tired. You've just had a month's holiday."

"Working, if you don't mind. I wasn't lying about, you know. And travelling with children is exhausting. How could you think I could face going out!"

"For heaven's sake! Where's your get-up-and-go? You're only twenty-five, not sixty-five. You can't not come. I've organised the whole thing around you."

"What whole thing?" Her suspicions deepened. "Is this your surprise?"

"Yes, it is." He sounded sulky. A cross little boy. "Please don't spoil it. It's all for you. I wasn't going to tell you. It was a surprise."

His anxiety and disappointment were too much for her and she gave in. His delight in how she looked with her golden tan, in her best black dress with the low back, his pride in her as his future wife, the congratulations, the raised glasses, the admiration of her ring, the engagement presents in little gift-wrapped packages. She had to be touched by the trouble he'd taken, a cake with sparklers, the fact that he'd invited some of her friends as well as his own. Melissa decided that an all-out public row with her fiancé in a London club was not an option. She caught her flatmate Elizabeth looking at her worriedly.

Even later, she simply could not bring herself to hurt him. His boyish delight in his 'surprise' and his certainty that she was equally thrilled was a powerful inhibitor. She leaned back exhausted in the taxi, the parcels overflowing the carrier bags in a welter of shimmering paper and shiny twisted ribbons and bows. She said it had been a wonderful party, and what an amazing homecoming, and how kind and generous he had been, and wondered how on earth she was going to have the courage to tell him she didn't love him at all.

Her cowardice increased in the face of his solicitous care. She must sleep in, he wouldn't ring till late morning. How stupid he'd been not to arrange it for the following night, how thoughtless of him not to realise how tired she'd be. How beautiful she was, and what a lucky man he was, and how proud he was of her.

She lay awake for a long time. Five dolphins swam across the windowsill and her guilt pounded in her head. She felt trapped and panicky and miserable and knew that she was not in love with David.

She was in love with Nicholas Thauros, but Nicholas Thauros was not in love with her.

CHAPTER TWENTY-FIVE

Glasgow was a welter of wind and rain. The streets and buildings were alien and confusing, and now she was faced with a room full of board members, many of whom were not altogether satisfied with her reasons for withdrawing. She could feel herself sweating, even though she had practically bathed in anti-perspirant.

"I still don't understand why you assumed Mr Thauros had intervened on your behalf," said a governor whose name she had forgotten.

"Because the person who told me said he had," she said, tired of explaining. "That person had a business connection with Mr Thauros. It appeared quite plausible."

No, she would not specify who this person was, and yes, she was satisfied that Mr Thauros had not lobbied anyone on her behalf. She apologised again to the board members and judges panel.

They continued to ask questions, and she knew instinctively that some of them disapproved of, or at any rate did not like, the designs.

Her drawings were pinned up on boards behind the big table. Copies were scattered across the polished surface.

"And this," said the large and domineering woman who Melissa had eventually established as being the Lady Beith whom Nicholas had mentioned, "strikes me as being not only silly, but rather smutty."

Melissa stared at her, and then at the drawing she was pointing to. She was suddenly, wonderfully, liberated by anger. She picked up a ballpoint pen, leaned across the table and drew in two lines.

"Is that better?" she asked politely.

There was a crack of suppressed laughter from a man with a mad head of curly hair. Lady Beith looked startled.

309

"I suppose it is," she said.

"I daresay," the curly-haired man said, "but I fear the humour is now lost." Melissa looked at the speaker, surprised. "Smut is not something that terminally-ill children have at the forefront of their minds. Nor is it in the minds of their carers. The hospice is a potentially terrifying place for children and in my opinion, as a clinical psychologist, the original idea will make them laugh. Laughter is a great healer."

She nearly got up and hugged him, and he dropped one eyelid at her almost imperceptibly. She knew the drawing wouldn't have made sense with Lady Beith's improvements. Why should a prim little Miss Octopus be wide-eyed and holding a tentacle to her mouth when the water baby in question was decently clad in a pair of swimming trunks?

Of the whole group, it was Lady Beith and the treasurer, Philip Lockley, who were most censorious. Lady Beith of the designs themselves and Lockley of the potential for escalating costs.

"We've been through all this, Philip, at the last meeting," the chairman said irritably. "It was agreed to increase this budget and we have raised a good deal of the extra finance already."

"And I still maintain we should raise all the money first, before embarking on something we don't know we can pay for."

"And it was agreed that we cannot delay that long, as we're already far behind schedule. May we please return to the subject in hand." He turned back to Melissa. "Miss Scott-Mackenzie, the Board agrees that these ideas for the public areas are too complex, delightful as they are. Can you give us your opinions, and indeed suggestions, for simplifying the designs for these spaces?"

And completion dates for each area, and paint specifications, equipment requirements, number of assistants, time schedules, accounting procedures, security, accommodation, hours per day, time off, transport.

Her head spun as she tried to answer questions she didn't even understand, and to remember what she'd said before; she said, 'I don't know' far too often. There was a man taking fast and detailed notes in the background, and she prayed that she'd get a copy. She felt totally inadequate and out of her depth, and with a sinking heart knew that David had been right, and Nicholas had been wrong.

She descended the grandiose stone staircase of the Institute of Clinical Studies feeling like chewed string, and hesitated at the doors in the face of a torrential downpour. She turned back to the elderly gentleman behind the reception desk and enquired about buses. After a time, it was clear that walking would be quicker. A voice spoke behind her.

"May I assist, Miss Scott-Mackenzie? It sounds as if you are contemplating a wet journey." It was the mad head of curly grey hair. She remembered he had said he was a clinical psychologist.

"Perhaps I could give you a lift." He beamed at her. "I'm quite sure you cannot remember eighteen names. Mine is Robert Bryn. What hotel have they put you in?"

He said it in such a tone of voice that there was instantly a 'them and us' distinction. The wink came forcibly to mind and she smiled back.

"That's very kind, but I'm sure I'll manage. I wouldn't want to take you out of your way."

"I'm quite sure you'd manage," he said, amused. "You managed to hold your own up there." He indicated upstairs with a tilt of the curly head. "But I think you'd get as wet as one of your own water babies. Look not a gift horse in the mouth, and they simply can't have put you in Gourock."

Before she knew it, he had swept her away out of the heavy doors and into his ageing Rover.

"I must try harder with umbrellas," he said cheerfully, shedding drops of rain from the curly mane. "Now, I don't suppose you're installed in the Hotel du Vin, so where are we going?" She told him the address and he kept up a gentle flow of entertaining small talk as he drove through the heavy traffic, giving her little snippets of information about members of the board, and Glasgow life in general, before coming back to the hospice designs.

"This award is a substantial coup for someone of your age and you should be very proud of yourself. You don't want to worry too much about all those budgets, and requirements and specifications. Remember you're an artist, not a functionary. Artistic licence will take you quite a long way—within reason of course. But I suspect you are a cautious soul, and not used to taking licence, artistic or otherwise, quite yet." He changed conversational direction without drawing breath.

"Did you really think there was skulduggery and inducements going on?"

She bit her lip. "Yes, I did, but it was a horrible and embarrassing misunderstanding. Mr Thauros was extremely angry, and I'm sure all the judges and the board were, too. I was so amazed to be shortlisted, let alone to win, and then when somebody told me—that well, I hadn't won it on merit, I believed them."

He was quiet for a moment, concentrating on the traffic.

"It probably didn't do much for your self-confidence at that moment. But you did win on merit, so be encouraged! Don't be overawed by our august board. None of us have a creative thought in our heads, so you have us over a barrel anyway!" He roared with laughter.

"I'm terrified by the whole thing," she admitted, looking at her lap.

"Once you get going, you'll be all right. You've got the right ideas for children—not juvenile and not patronising. I can't bear children being patronised. Sick children have immense strength and dignity—and can see a joke better than most."

She looked at his kind, round face and felt warmed and heartened.

"Have you got friends in Glasgow?" he said abruptly. "It's a big city—can be lonely."

"I don't think so, but I graduated from Edinburgh so some of my contemporaries may be here. I've lived and worked in London for ages, and have a flat there, so I'm quite a city girl really. I think I'll be too busy to be lonely."

"And where do your parents live?" She was used to coping with the question and didn't flinch.

"They were killed in an accident. We came from the Borders originally, so Edinburgh was my home town, and now my grandparents live in Hampshire. It's odd that I spent most of my life in and around Edinburgh, but hardly ever set foot in Glasgow."

He frog-leaped the waffle. "I'm so sorry about your parents. How very sad. But I'm glad you've got grandparents, and they must be glad they've got you." He navigated round a chaotic roundabout. "And yes, we can be very unaware of our own country. I have a clinic in Edinburgh twice a week so I'm always running between the two cities, but you're right, most people tend to stick to one or the other. I have an affection for Glasgow; it's more down to earth, but has an enormous amount to offer. As an artist, you'll enjoy it. The galleries and museums are excellent. Here's your hotel. It looks very unprepossessing, I must say. If I didn't have a clinic I would take you to lunch."

She laughed. "They have bar snacks, which is all I need. And they'll get me a taxi to the airport, and my fiancé is taking me out to dinner when I get back to London."

"Glad to hear it." He drew up outside 'Clydeview Hotel' and fished in his wallet for his card as she got out into the rain.

"My wife produces good home-cooking. We'll get you over before too long," he beamed again. brushing aside her hesitancy, "and if you can't stand the paint a minute longer, just give us a ring. I am after all a psychologist and I love having someone new to practise on!" With which disarming amiability he waved away her thanks and drove off.

313

*****

Later, eating a hasty lunch at home, he instructed his hospitable wife to make a note to invite Melissa Scott-Mackenzie to Sunday lunch in about a month's time.

"She's twenty-five," he said, emptying his briefcase of Angel Hospice documents and refilling it with clinical files, "and looks about seventeen. She hasn't a clue about what she's taken on."

"Did Lady Beith eat her?" his wife enquired.

He put his head on one side, like a bird listening for a worm.

"No. She tried to. I rather think little Melissa took a bite herself." He grinned at the memory. "As lovely a put-down as you'd care to see. Have you seen my appointment list?"

CHAPTER TWENTY-SIX

She cleaned her brushes with an automatic thoroughness, and gazed, frowning, at the day's work. The open windows and doors let in such a howling draught that the clean brushes stirred in their jars like bullrushes on a river bank and the dust sheets that protected the floors from paint lifted and billowed. A large manta ray, she thought, and then suppressed it. Already she was behind schedule and couldn't afford to add any more of what some of the governors had termed 'flights of fancy'.

She was in a room on the lowest of the three levels and therefore under water. On the ceiling above her floated the underside of a rowing boat, barnacle-encrusted and with an inquisitive floating seagull gazing at a broken strake just above water level. A fishing rod jutted over the gunwale and the slack line went to a red and white striped float painted on to the ceiling light fitting. The anchor rope, or rather two ropes knotted together, descended the wall to an anchor lodged between boulders, where an octopus was busy trying to pull it up.

The walls were a riot of coral and fish and squid; sea anemones, and starfish and sea urchins. Seaweed waved, shells, pebbles and stones littered the painted sea floor, along with one of the boat's rowlocks, a frayed piece of old string still attached.

The trestle table kept the dust sheets from taking off, and was itself laden with books, magazines, photographs and drawings, in turn held down by paint pots, jars of brushes, rags, stones, shells and other bits of nautical flotsam and jetsam.

Melissa finished cleaning the brushes and closed the windows on to the security latch. There had to be thorough ventilation or she went home with a pounding headache from the paint fumes.

As she locked the latches, she heard Liam's returning steps in the hallway and turning, saw not Liam, but with heart-thumping surprise, Nicholas Thauros. She felt her cheeks redden.

"Oh! Hello. What on earth are you doing here?"

She hadn't set eyes on him since their return from Greece, although she knew that he had visited the hospice for two site meetings in September. As the meetings were scheduled in advance and posted on the notice board, she had absented herself on expeditions to collect more paint, visit the library, and discuss scaffolding with the foreman. She had not only felt cowardly about these manoeuvres but also rather silly. There was no indication that Mr Thauros had so much as come looking for her, or indeed that he had looked at the progress of the interior designs. This visit was unscheduled and inexplicably embarrassing. She wished fervently that she was not wearing a woolly hat and that her heart would stop banging.

Nicholas looked at her and laughed.

"You don't look at all pleased to see me. Like I'm a nasty shock or something."

"A surprise, certainly. What on earth are you doing here?"

"I'm one of the architects. Remember?"

Her flush deepened. "I didn't mean—Sorry. I thought all that was finished. I just wasn't expecting you." On which idiotic statement she scrubbed her fingers savagely on an oily rag.

"I like the mittens. Very fetching."

"I tried gloves but I can't paint in them."

"Glasgow weather is certainly chilly," he said, eyeing her layers of sweaters and quilted waistcoat. He turned away to look at the ceiling and walls while she recovered her equilibrium.

"What an astonishingly wet environment! It's brilliant. There won't be any need to buy expensive educational toys; it's all here on the walls."

She found she'd been holding her breath and was cross with herself for minding whether he approved or not.

"Are you pleased with your building?"

"Not particularly mine, but on the whole, yes. Are you pleased with your paintings?"

"I don't know. I wake up in the night in a panic."

She pulled off the mittens.

"Panic about what?"

He was wearing a dark suit and looked expensively smart, tired and rather cold.

"Oh. How little time, how vast the space. That sort of thing." She frowned. "You're wearing a black tie—have you been to a funeral?"

"Yes. My uncle Carlos. He's been ill for a long time. It wasn't unexpected."

She was puzzled. "Here? In Scotland?"

He shook his head. "No. It was in London—but there was a meeting here and I went directly to the airport and haven't had time to change. He was married to Isabella, who you met at the birthday party, and you met their daughter, my cousin Angeliki, too." He was walking slowly round the room, taking in her paintings. She remembered the introduction to the glamorous lawyer on his doorstep on one of the fifty-pound appointments. She also remembered the ceramic dolphins.

"I'm sorry about your uncle. I thought they lived in Greece."

"They did. Originally, he was in the family shipping business, but when he retired he went back to his first love—sculpture—and he and Isabella lived in glorious isolation on an island quite close to Mixos. He got cancer and eventually the drugs stopped working and he had to come to London for treatment."

317

She was silent. A slow and vague comprehension began to infiltrate her brain. She remembered that hot little cabin on the yacht, the figure of a limping woman coming down the track towards him, the black case on the ground, their embrace, the white envelope given in exchange. She stared at Nicholas without seeing him.

He had turned and was looking at her in frowning perplexity. "What's the matter?"

She was still processing memory.

"Isabella is lame, isn't she?"

"She has a bad hip." He still looked mystified.

"It was her, wasn't it?" Melissa closed her eyes and felt her shoulders sagging in relief.

"What was her? What is it? What are you talking about?"

"The drugs. The drugs stopped working." Her voice was just a whisper. "The drugs were for Carlos."

He was still at a loss.

"The drugs. The case of drugs. They were for Carlos, not you." The relief seeped into her physically, as if she were suddenly boneless.

Comprehension began to dawn on Nicholas.

"Oh, my God! Did you find his drugs when you searched *Joanna*?" She nodded wordlessly. "And you thought what? I was an addict, or drug running or something? Is that it?"

She nodded again, helplessly, her head dropping, and tears spilling down her cheeks. He stepped across to her, pulling her against his shoulder.

"And you saw me delivering them to Isabella? Pussycat, I'm so sorry. How horrible for you. I only locked you into the cabin because I didn't want to complicate her life, or mine, by having you scream for help. I didn't think you could see and it hadn't occurred to me that you'd looked in the case. I assumed it was locked, not having tried to open it. No wonder you were so terrified. No wonder you took the knives." She was crying in earnest, raw jagged breaths, and he held her to him more tightly, his face against her woolly hat.

"And all this time you've thought I was involved in illegal *drugs*?"

She took a deep breath and sniffed. "Yes—no. I couldn't understand. It wasn't—it didn't seem to be in your character, you were rich so it wasn't necessary for you, but then I thought your money might have come from drugs. And you talked of cameras and recorders. I didn't want to think it, but I couldn't think of any other reason."

"But you knew my money was inherited, and that my concern about cameras and recorders was because of Marie Claude, didn't you?"

She sniffed again, pulling out a tissue. "Yes, but later. And it still didn't explain the drugs."

"Your reluctance to have anything to do with me takes on quite a new dimension," he said slowly. "No. I don't do drugs, never have—unlike you! Even in my reprehensible youth. I collected Carlos's drugs in Perissos to save Isabella from having to do the trip herself or having to organise their collection, and I had to get them to her quickly as the case wouldn't fit in the fridge. I couldn't afford to hang around waiting for the police to pick you up, so you had to come too." His face twisted a little with regret. "I am really sorry you've been living with that suspicion. Carlos had lung cancer which spread everywhere and eventually he had to come back to civilization for treatment and pain management."

He put a finger under her chin and lifted her face. "No wonder you tried to exit by the hatch. And no wonder you told the horrible Jeremy you were in the hands of a criminal. Why didn't you ever ask me about it? You accused me of lots of things, but not that!"

Melissa swallowed. "I didn't have the courage. I didn't want to hear you confess to it."

He looked down at her with a frown and cupped her face in his hands.

"Would you have minded?"

"Your family would have."

"Yes. But would *you* have minded?"

319

She brought her lips together in wry acknowledgement. "Yes, I'd have minded."

He laughed and slid the woolly hat off, the coppery hair falling loose. "Well, thank God for that!" He leant his head on hers gently, hands sliding through her hair. "Now, I want to ungum you from the paint pots, not talk about poor Carlos and Isabella, though it's a good thing we did." She thought he was going to kiss her, and lifted her head in anticipation, but he stepped back and released her.

"There was a filthy, incomprehensible, pony-tailed young man on the way out who said you were still cleaning up. I've done most of my checking, but there are one or two more things on the snagging list which I want to look at. And I wanted to see how you were getting on and hoped if I came at the end of the day you wouldn't have absconded as you usually do and I wouldn't interrupt the painting muse. You could show me the rest of your masterpieces, couldn't you?"

Her heart lifted. He had noticed her absences and he wasn't a drug dealer. She remembered how Isabella had seemed familiar when she met her at Galina's party. Perhaps it had been a subconscious recognition of shape, or gestures, or movement.

"Are the upper floors finished? I want to see them."

She was heartily relieved to have some achievement to admit to. "Yes, and Liam has nearly finished the background on the hall. He's been brilliant, I couldn't possibly have done them without him. For one thing, he's much taller than me and doesn't have to move the scaffolding so often." She knew she was chattering to cover her nervousness.

"Liam being the pony-tailed young man, I presume?" He ushered her out and switched the lights off.

"Yes, he's an art graduate and specialises in paint media. He's in charge of the paint, thank goodness, and he mixes the colours for me. We had a dreadful time at the beginning—all the colours looked hopeless when they were on the wall—not at all like the samples. He's concocted some extraordinary mix which he swears is non-toxic, even if the children lick the

320

walls, and as tough as the white lines on the roads." She didn't add that she'd mixed a good many salty tears into those pots in the first few days.

"Well, come and show me the opus as far as it's gone. I must look at the showers on the top floor. I know the lift works, so let's try the stairs."

They climbed the wide, shallow, curving treads with the glass up-stands. A smooth round white pine rail ran an inch below the level of the translucent glass wall and a second rail ran below it, the right height for a small child to hold on to.

"That's so annoying," she said, tapping the upper rail. "If it was on the top, you could slide all the way down."

"Precisely," he said.

"Oh! Safety! When did you last hear of a child falling off a banister? It comes in the same category as removing diving boards from swimming pools. No danger, no risk, no excitement."

"Just the danger, risk and excitement of being sued for millions. Keeping our reputation is a powerful incentive to invest heavily in safety, I can tell you."

Their footsteps rang hollow on the uncarpeted floors. Opening the door to the first room, he switched on the lights.

"My God!" He stood surveying an empty space bursting at the seams. It was peopled—no, not peopled, for there were no people—but full of air and treetops, birds on the wing and birds on nests. On the ceiling was the underside of a green and white balloon and wicker basket, spilling with detritus, a net shopping bag stuffed with bread, baked beans, chocolate bars and tins of Coke; a tatty anorak covered in badges, a penknife and can opener on a string hanging out of one pocket. He tore his eyes away from the incredible details and looked at the walls. A fat pigeon shot past with a smug expression on its face as a disappointed eagle back-pedalled with a lone tail feather in its beak. The flying birds were all totally different; all plumaged; characters; busy or pleasure-bent. The trees were in spring leaf, a red squirrel hurtled from its perch and concentrated comically on landing on a whippy branch below; some other furry animal slept in the fork of a branch, and a large hairy blue caterpillar was negotiating its way over the fluffy tail.

"It would take half a dozen visits to see everything you've put in!" he said in astonishment. "It's incredibly precise, almost photographic."

He found himself without adequate words and turned abruptly to the adjoining room and shower, to inspect the drains and tiling.

He came back into the room.

"I can paint things out. If there's too much," she said, anxious for his approval.

He took two steps and took her in his arms again, looking over her head at some large bird trying to pluck a fish out of a waterfall with no success. "On no account paint anything out. It's quite, quite wonderful. Extraordinary. I'm sorry to be so wordless, but the last time I saw this it was just roughed out. It just wasn't what I was expecting. I mean, it's all terribly alive. Your drawings were good, but they didn't give this impression. I feel we might fall out of the trees." He was shaking with laughter. "No wonder Norman Westerman said he hadn't the energy to describe it."

He put his head into the small room designated for accompanying family which was plastered, but for financial reasons would remain undecorated, before returning to the child's bedroom.

"Poor parents without anything to look at! But this is unbelievable. How long did this take to do?"

She bit her lip, reluctant to admit the truth.

"Um—about a fortnight. It was the first one. I'm faster now, honestly. I kept getting the perspectives wrong and having to repaint, so it took a bit of getting used to. Having to paint the ceilings lying on my back was awful. Michelangelo must have had permanent backache. I found I couldn't do it for more than half an hour at a time, because my hand began to shake, and the paint dripped in my eyes and in my mouth. I look unbelievable after ceilings." She wanted to reassure him. "I can manage much longer now, and Liam paints in the backgrounds for me. I'm much faster altogether. I can do a room this size in about a week." He hadn't said anything and she was worried again.

"Is it all right? Will they be cross it's not the same as the drawings? I mean, the ideas are sort of the same, it's just that I seem to change the details as I go. There was such a row over the water babies that I thought it was better without them."

She tailed off rather uncertainly. He looked incongruous standing there silently in his suit amongst all her flying birds. The hug had been comforting, but now she was unsure again.

"Don't be daft. Of course it's all right and no, they won't be cross. They'll be utterly delighted. Electrified! It's truly amazing."

He was gazing in fascinated awe at the extraordinary botanical detail. "I can't wait to hear the public and media reaction! I know Norman Westerman has seen some of it, but have the rest of the board?"

"I don't know," she said. "I don't think so."

"It's extraordinary," he said, "the children will never want to leave. Come on. I want to see the rest and I must check the other showers. Then I'm going to feed you best Aberdeen Angus to celebrate your *tour de force*. Did you have any lunch?"

"I expect so, I can't remember. Liam usually force-feeds me. Yes, I had a cheese and pickle soggy. You don't need to feed me, Mrs Norton—my landlady—is expecting me for supper."

"No, she isn't," he said, disappearing into the next unit where perforce she had to follow him. "She said it was ox-tail stew, whatever that is, and that it would keep nicely till tomorrow. I shall think of you tomorrow night with sympathy."

"No need for sympathy. It's delicious and frightfully sustaining. She's a brilliant cook."

"I'm delighted to hear it. Is she nice as well?"

323

"I love her to bits. They come from Rainham, and there's a splendid whiff of Essex via the flock wallpaper and frilly bed hangings."

He'd checked in the office for the phone number and rung Mrs Norton up. And he'd come here to find her. And he'd noticed that she had gone absent during his visits. She felt short of breath again. "I can't come out like this. I'll have to go back and change."

He put his head out of the shower room and grinned at her.

"And a bath in paint remover as well."

Crossing the landing he looked up silently at a painted bi-plane held together with leather straps and bits of string. There were treetops here, too, but bare branches under snow and conifers full of different birds, cosied up together in fat fluffy winter plumage. The little jokes were there, a wedge of falling snow dislodged by a mischievous mouse was about to fall on an unsuspecting sleeping owl. A horrified beetle was sliding helplessly down an icicle.

He went to inspect the side room destined for relatives and Melissa stared critically at a woodpecker peering out from a hole in a gnarled tree trunk.

"Are all these creatures definable?" he asked curiously, rejoining her. "Can you put a biological name to them?"

"Oh yes. They're mainly British, but some things I just couldn't resist, like parrots and coral. I've copied them from pictures and books. The Glasgow City Library has been most obliging." She parodied the last sentence in broad Glaswegian. "See, woodcock, great spotted woodpecker, tawny owl, robins, buzzard, magpie, jay, big hairy caterpillar—he's got a wonderful Latin name which I've forgotten. Do you think it's too chilly, all this ice and snow? Will the children hate it?"

"Getting cold feet, are you?"

"Oh! Nicholas!" He was making her laugh and she felt warm inside.

324

He hugged her again. "The children will love it—they love snow, and the heating will be excessive. They need to design a biology treasure hunt. Come on, I'd better have a quick look at the rest."

She accompanied him through the other rooms. Each was similar in the sense that this upper floor was the top layer of an overall picture, mountain tops, treetops, castle battlements, roof tops, cliff tops, all inhabited by a multitudinous population of different creatures and flying machines, from ants to zeppelins. Ground level was ground level, and Level One below sea level.

"I'm not at all sure there won't be a roar of disapproval when the furniture and equipment goes in," he said, "but I notice you have cunningly managed to keep a lot of the detail higher up the walls."

Eventually he was finished with his checking. The remaining backgrounds had already been painted in by Liam, and awaited the welter of detail at sea and ground level. She wanted an ancient oak where the handrail went round the corner and was considering plaster to make it really bulgy.

"Paint is so flat," she complained.

"Not your paint," he said firmly. "This is not Hundertwasser House. And you have a schedule and a deadline."

The anxiety returned at once.

"You're worried about it, aren't you?"

"Concerned. Yes. I think you should try not to get side-tracked."

"By my flights of fancy?"

He smiled as he held the front doors open for her.

"By your flights of fancy," he agreed. "Come on. Hot bath and a large steak for you."

*****

The evening was relaxed and amusing and fun. She told him about the interview with the board of governors, of Robert Bryn's kindness and subsequent hospitality, of the chairman's encouragement, of Lady Beith's disapproval, of

325

finding Liam and various assorted helpers and how they had experimented with paint that clogged and paint that dripped, of the additives which had turned out to be hallucinogenic giving them both nightmares, and of the day the rope broke on the painting cradle. Nicholas laughed and enjoyed it all and noticed that she did not wish to talk about David.

"You're not wearing opals," he said, "which would go with that shirt. Has it fallen off into a paint pot?"

He was fascinated by how easily he could make her blush. He didn't think Marie Claude had ever blushed in her life.

"Um. No. I don't wear it during the day—it would get encrusted with paint. I forgot to put it on tonight."

"I hope you don't forget when David comes. What does he think of your work here?"

She hesitated. "He hasn't seen it yet. He's very busy."

He feigned surprise. "I didn't realise skin specialists had to work such long hours and weekends, too. Strictly ten till four, I thought, but how wrong I was."

She suppressed a smile. "Nicholas, you are absolutely horrid. Why are you being so unkind about David? You haven't met him and you're behaving as if I wasn't entitled to have a boyfriend or get married. He hasn't seen the hospice, but he was very encouraging about the original designs."

"Why hasn't he been up to see you then?" he demanded. "I can't believe he hasn't got the money." She looked uncomfortable. "He's still furious about you doing this, isn't he? You've gone against his wishes."

"He was upset and I can't blame him. He wanted the wedding in November and we had to postpone it and now I'm not there to do anything—wedding lists and guest lists and all the arrangements." He said nothing and waited for her to go on, but she wouldn't.

"So, if it's not November, when is it?"

"We haven't decided on a definite date. David now wants February, but it's such a ghastly month; horrible for my grandparents and horrible for guests."

326

"Horrible for the bride, too, I should think. I can just see you with your skirts blown over your head and the veil flying away in a blizzard. What's the raging hurry? Most couples can play house together for years." She was silent, shredding the remains of a roll on to her side plate. "Sorry," he said. "Out of court. Do you like your future in-laws?"

"They're very pleasant. Very generous."

He put his head on one side.

"I'm guessing you didn't take to them much."

After a moment, she giggled. David's father was an older, fatter version of David; faintly patronising and distinctly pompous.

"Not much. His father kindly promised to take the whole burden of the wedding arrangements off my grandparents' hands, though sadly he didn't mention the financial burden. He said that as he'd married off two daughters, he knew organising a wedding was not for the faint-hearted. He patted my hand and thought he'd made a joke. His mother is stout and submissive and said weddings needed organising down to the last detail and her Andrew really was a man for detail." She hesitated. "The detail included wanting to know—about everything." Her shoulders went up in that familiar sign of discomfort. "They're very kind—just rather bossy. I think they feel that an art student and general failure in the careers market is incapable of taking sensible decisions about anything, let alone her wedding, and as I am motherless I must therefore need managing."

"Not mothering?" He laughed in his throat, angry for her. "You must practise self-assertion some more." He gave her a straight look. "I'm going to say something which I admit in advance I've no particular right to say." She tensed at his abrupt change of tone.

"You mustn't, you simply mustn't marry him if you're not sure. He doesn't appear to understand you or build you up in any way. He'll squeeze all the essence out of you—all your gifts, all your sensitivity. He'll make you conform and sap your confidence. He should have been here, encouraging

327

you, allowing you to achieve something special of your own before tying you down to marriage and home and children. If he's as selfish as he appears to be, it will rot your life before it's even begun."

Her voice caught. "You don't know. I'm the selfish one—I insisted on coming here and doing this."

"Come to that, I'm the selfish one, I exerted the pressure on you. Blackmail, you said, talking about those poor little children who wouldn't get treated unless you came and painted your pictures."

"Wasn't it true?"

"They'd have got their hospice, but a second-best environment. I'm selfish because I want the best for them and that meant you being here and to hell with your plans. I'm not making myself out to be anything very nice, but I think David is treating you like dirt, and he ought not to if he wants to marry you."

She looked devastated at his words and he put a hand across the table and laid it on hers. She tried to withdraw, but he felt the movement and his fingers tightened, trapping her hand.

"I'm sorry," he said. "I didn't mean to make you cry again. Am I completely wrong about him?"

"You've never met him," she muttered, holding back the tears with difficulty.

"May I?"

"Do you want a wedding invitation?" She was drier and fiercer.

Unsmiling, he withdrew his hand. "Not much. I assume he'll be coming to the opening and I'd rather meet him there—and find out that I'm wrong."

"And when you do—?"

"Then send the invitation and I'll come to your wedding," he said.

CHAPTER TWENTY-SEVEN

After the official opening, and the photographs and speeches, Nicholas joined her, putting a glass of champagne into her hand.

"Congratulations on a fantastic achievement!" he said, smiling. "You never believed you could do it, and here you are, the toast of the Angel Hospice! They look absolutely wonderful, and so do you."

She felt extraordinarily warmed by his words, and a wave of gratitude and affection swept over her. After David's cold disapproval when she had felt treated like a rebellious child, she had been terrified that everyone would hate the designs. Instead, there had been genuine compliments.

"It *all* looks wonderful and the building is beautiful, too. It's brilliant to see it finally finished and the first children due next month."

"Yes. It's a good feeling, after all the hold-ups, but financial and logistical problems are a given for a project like this." He glanced round. "Where's David? You were going to introduce me."

David's decision not to come had been devastating. "He's not here," she said shortly. "He couldn't come."

He wasn't here because she had ignored his feelings, and his wishes. He had been hurt by her actions and her absence. He said he was saddened by her childish and selfish behaviour. It wasn't a case of couldn't come; he had refused to come.

Nicholas frowned in incredulity and she was mortified by his displeasure.

"I'm really sorry about that. He should have been here to see your hour of triumph. Why couldn't he come?"

She shrugged. "Oh, it's mid-week. His clinics." She tried to shake off her bruised feelings.

He put a comforting hand to her shoulder. "Silly man. It's his loss, though. He could be wallowing in reflected glory." She smiled in gratitude and thought he might have given her a hug, but he glanced at the photographers and reporters around them, and dropped his hand.

"My flatmate Elizabeth sent me your uncle's obituary from *The Times*." It had come with a scrawled message. 'Isn't your Greek chap called Thauros? Perhaps a relation?' "The dolphins you gave me were his, weren't they?"

Nicholas nodded. "He had an outlet in London, both for himself and for various other Greek artists."

She nodded. "I know. I went there."

He looked slightly uneasy. "Did you? When?"

"After I visited your mother before going to Mixos with Michael and Sophie. I realised when I saw the signature mark on the dolphin on your parents' terrace."

She laughed at his apprehension.

"Yes, I was quite horrified at the time. But more because you'd ruined their value by writing on them in indelible ink. Now I can't even sell them," she teased.

He grinned in relief and clinked his glass to hers. "Enjoy them." She clinked back with a smile. "I do."

Later, when he said goodbye, it was with a finality that made her heart sink. He was not intending to take their friendship any further. Why would he? She was engaged to another man, and should have no feelings for Nicholas, nor he for her. He kissed her very gently on the forehead and wished her a happy future, shutting the door of her taxi and standing on the pavement until it turned the corner and she couldn't see him any more. A vast desolation swept through her, extinguishing all the pleasure and excitement of the evening.

The triumph of the opening and the plaudits of many had not taken the sting out of David's non-appearance. It was all in the past, not even mentioned now, and he appeared to have forgiven and forgotten. Melissa was unhappily aware that she had done neither. Brig and Mops had been pleased and proud of her, Johnny had said an astonished 'Well done!', Sarah had pored over the photographs in flattering amazement and Sam (obviously under Sarah's direction) had made her an enormous and colourful congratulations card.

Since then, there had been three interior design job offers. Brief discussions with David, who was disapproving and unenthusiastic, ensured that she turned them all down. Just as well, she thought later, given the complexities of David's attitude, Mop's broken hip and hospitalisation, Brig's care, earning a living, Christmas and wedding plans. With the help of Johnny, Sarah and David, she began to look at alternative accommodation for Brig.

She got out the Cathedral Properties paperwork, knowing that she would soon have to give them notice. Staring at the headed notepaper and the little logo of a cathedral, she was reminded again of its vague familiarity, and focused more sharply. Where had she seen that logo before? Nothing came to mind and she dismissed it, beginning to re-read the correspondence and the agreements.

Mops was still in hospital for Christmas and the only plus point to the holiday, and even that made both Johnny and Melissa highly nervous, was that Sarah announced that she and Sam would come to the Old Rectory on Boxing Day for three nights. Melissa knew that Brig was delighted at the news, despite his criticisms of the modern parent and child, and she also knew that Sarah, apart from wanting to help Melissa cope with the complexities of juggling home and hospital, was also making a real effort towards reconciliation with Johnny. At the Christmas service Melissa prayed fiercely, if incoherently, on behalf of her brother, and virtually pointed a shotgun at the Almighty.

In the small hours of Boxing Day morning, for no reason whatsoever, she woke and knew that she had seen the logo of the cathedral on one of the brochures in Nicholas Thauros's office reception. Then she remembered telling Galina about the sale of the house to Cathedral Properties, and how she had looked amazed and astonished. At this distance in time her reaction had obviously been due more to Nicholas's involvement, and less to surprise at the business methods. Melissa felt a fool, even so long after the event. He had obviously thought that she wouldn't accept his help if he offered it, so he had helped without telling her.

It was Sarah, with her down-to-earth Yorkshire common sense, who metaphorically rapped her knuckles and told her not to be so irrational.

"Count your blessings," she said sharply. "Just think how difficult the situation would have been if he hadn't done it. You got the wrong end of the stick about the guy last time and had to eat humble pie. You've probably got the wrong end of the stick again, so for goodness sake don't go off the deep end and make a fool of yourself. All these months you never realised, so another few weeks won't matter. Don't ruin everybody's holiday—life's complicated enough just now without you putting more spokes in the wheels."

Johnny was equally adamant. It seemed to him to be a perfectly reasonable business transaction which gave the speculator valuable investment opportunities. Johnny and Sarah's disapproval of Melissa's attitude did at least have the benefit of bringing them into unity with each other, on that subject if on no other. David spent Christmas and Boxing Day with his parents, somewhat out of charity with his fiancée who had refused to accompany him, and when he rejoined the Scott-Mackenzies, his opinion on the matter was ignored.

CHAPTER TWENTY-EIGHT

Nicholas sat at his desk in Eaton Square gazing morosely at the pile of mail he had just opened and in particular at the letter in his hands. He could disregard its contents and do nothing further at all, which was what he would like to do, for his own good. Even though his divorce was now absolute, what his lawyers were suggesting could open the proverbial can of worms, and he shrank from the publicity that would inevitably come with it. He sighed and checked his mobile for a number before dialling it.

A minute later he felt reprieved, but oddly disappointed. Melissa's phone was turned off.

He reminded himself that he had been a fool ever to embark on that strange relationship which could never have worked even had she wanted it to. Which she hadn't. His age, his wealth, his marriage and above all his divorce had all conspired to scream out both the dangers and the unsuitability of any connection. He remembered standing in the icy wind, watching the taxi carry her away from the hospice and feeling the deep regret for what might have been if he had made different life choices. He had had the strength of mind not to contact her again after the hospice was finished.

Now, his strength of mind was considerably weakened both by the requirements of the letter and by an aching desire to see her again. He guessed she was with her grandparents for the Christmas holiday and perhaps for the anniversary of the family deaths.

He was uncomfortably nervous as the satnav brought him to the brigadier's drive. His decision not to try her mobile again, to say that he was coming, had seemed perfectly sensible this morning, but she would probably be furious for not having had any warning. He looked with tepid interest at Cathedral Properties' investment and found it a reasonably pleasant but unexciting-looking brick house, the damp garden extending away behind it, wet leaves blown into untidy piles against the shrubs and hedges. On, or rather in, one of these piles was a small child, rotund in shape, stiff with hooded yellow oilskin and grubby blue wellingtons, gender unknown. The hood turned towards the car and watched it draw to a halt. Nicholas dragged his coat off the back seat and got out. He hadn't expected a child, and couldn't guess why it should be here, or what connection it might have with an elderly couple. Where there was a child, there would be a parent, if not two; already his explanations were becoming more complicated.

The child was advancing on him, although not him, he realised tardily, but his car.

"Thassa Jaguar."

Nicholas felt unaccountably comforted. This was boy's talk and straight to the point. No messing about.

"Yes. Do you like it?"

A pair of extremely blue eyes swivelled towards him. "Yep. Wanna get in. Exkayate, innit?"

A voice said, "No, Sam." And then, "Can I help you?"

Nicholas said, "Yep. XK8" and turned. The Yorkshire voice's owner had the same very blue eyes, and white blonde hair straggled damply out of a beanie. Sam. The nephew. This then must be the sister-in-law; Samantha? Sally? Sarah.

He smiled at her.

"Hullo. You must be Sarah if this is Sam." He extended his hand. "I'm Nicholas Thauros, a friend of Melissa's." He saw her frown slightly as she shook it. "I apologise for just turning up, but wondered if I could have a quick word with her."

The child said louder, "Wanna get in!" and Nicholas put his hand on the driver's door.

"Fine by me. The ignition is locked. He probably knows more about the car than I do."

334

The young woman's eyes smiled, but the rest of her face was still.

"Thanks. He's car mad. Take your boots off, Sam."

After a pause she stated, "Melissa's out."

The child had clambered in behind the steering wheel, boots abandoned on the gravel. Nicholas had a fleeting thought for wet oilskins on leather seats.

"When will she be back?"

Sarah seemed reluctant to tell him. "About half past twelve, maybe later. Her grandmother's in hospital. Mel helps with her lunch and that."

There was no invitation to wait, but Nicholas was in no mood to give up on his original intentions and was prepared to be inconvenient.

"I'm sorry to hear that. But do you mind if I wait? Sam and I could have a long conversation about the car—is he just a Jaguar expert or can he recognise every make?"

Her mouth puckered in a faint smile. "Every make and most sports models. I suppose you'd better come in then. David's with the brigadier."

Was that a warning? He wondered how much Melissa had told her sister-in-law about him. More to the point, he wondered how much she'd told her fiancé about him. He was going to meet the fiancé at last.

Sam was extracted from the car with difficulty, and she led the way round the house to the back door where the child was revealed as a normal wiry five-year-old as the layers were peeled off. Sarah swatted a tabby cat off the table and Nicholas noticed another one on top of the Aga. He rubbed its head and engaged Sam in car talk while Sarah took off her own boots and coat, filled the kettle and rattled mugs. She offered him coffee rather brusquely and he wondered if she was nervous or just shy. He made easy conversation, located the milk in the fridge and, taking the tray, followed her through the house to the sitting room where two men sat either side of a log fire. He was introduced to the brigadier and noticed that Sarah did not hesitate over his name, which must mean that she was familiar with it. The brigadier didn't get up, but he had the upright posture and firm handshake of a military man. The faded eyes were sharp and bright and he looked perfectly happy about the interruption.

David Allison got to his feet and was introduced as Melissa's fiancé. The old man waved Nicholas into David's vacated chair and Nicholas made vague explanations for his visit. In the background, he heard Sarah ask David to put more logs on the fire as she went briskly away. The child appeared, carefully carrying a large box which clinked. They drank their coffee, and Nicholas passed his biscuit to Sam, who in exchange pressed a battered Dinky model of a yellow Lamborghini into his hand. Sam went into raptures about the Jaguar, which amused the brigadier.

Nicholas was relieved to discover that David was far more interested in talking about himself than in remembering someone called Thauros who had been responsible for Melissa's involvement in the Angel Hospice. On the other hand, the brigadier was struggling with his memory and eventually it came to him. He interrupted David's sporting history with the fact that Melissa had worked for an architect called Thauros in Scotland, and it must have been him, mustn't it? Nicholas agreed that it had indeed been him, and yes, his firm had designed the hospice and she'd won the interior design award for it. He turned to David with a smile.

"Lucky man! You have a very talented fiancée. They were brilliantly conceived and are much enjoyed by staff and children. I hope there have been plenty of subsequent commissions for her? It should be the start of an excellent career."

David flushed faintly. "We've decided that she doesn't want that sort of career—it wouldn't be very conducive to family life. In any case, as far as I'm aware there have only been a few enquiries, so it's hardly arisen."

Nicholas expressed surprise at the lack of commissions, and contented himself with embarrassing David by apologising for not having recognised him, as of course

David must have been at the hospice inauguration to share in Melissa's triumph. David grappled with the admission of his absence on that occasion, and the finding of excuses which didn't criticise Melissa. Nicholas managed to look puzzled.

He had never liked the sound of this fiancé and on meeting him he liked him even less. Pompous, he thought, and more in love with himself than Melissa. Slightly horrified by his own thoughts, he asked about their wedding plans in the manner, he hoped, of an ex-boss, or perhaps an old family friend. While David embarked on dates and churches, receptions, best man and ushers, Sam hunkered down beside Nicholas and laid out the contents of his clinking box in serried ranks of cars and lorries. Sam told him the make of every single vehicle in his car park and David seemed content with his occasional responses. Some quite nice smells began to emanate from the kitchen and the brigadier announced that it was time for a drink and dispatched David to do the honours in the dining room.

"What's this business all about?" he said crisply, as David disappeared. "Melissa doesn't tell us much, but I can put two and two together, even if young David can't. You're Greek, she had some ghastly upset in Greece some years ago, financial if I'm not mistaken, and you were involved, and then there was that trip to Scotland, and that decorating thing in Glasgow and now you're back again rocking the boat. Melissa doesn't need her boat rocking just now. I could see you setting the boy up." His disapproval was obvious.

"I assure you I'm not intending to rock any boat," Nicholas said, slightly alarmed by the brigadier's perception. "Melissa was cheated on a business deal by a man in Greece. The Greek customs agents have arrested this man on another charge, but they want to close the file on her case as well." The door opened. "That can't be done without Melissa."

David put the tray down. He had heard her name and his ears were metaphorically pricked.

"What can't be done without Melissa?" He sounded suspicious.

337

There was a small silence and then Nicholas said firmly, but he hoped without rancour, "Something that only she can decide—and I can't discuss it without her, I'm afraid."

"You seem to be discussing it with Brig," he said rather petulantly. "But as I'm her fiancé then I'm the one you can discuss it with. What Melissa does or doesn't do isn't really a matter for a stranger, but for us as a couple. We make decisions together."

"Of course," Nicholas said politely, feeling that a well-planted fist on David's nose would be satisfying, "and when she gets back, I'm sure she'll want to make those decisions with you."

Pompous, arrogant little doctor. She must be mad to think of marrying him.

He passed his host his dry sherry and asked after Mrs Scott-Mackenzie

who, it transpired, had slipped and fallen on the damp York paving outside the back door.

"It was a bad break and they won't discharge her until she can manage stairs," the brigadier said gloomily, "And there are a lot of stairs in this house. The family are talking about a small bungalow and though we don't like the idea, I can see it might be sensible." He sipped his sherry. "At least the house is already sold, so we're cash buyers."

The selling of the house was rather dangerous ground, as indeed were Greece and Scotland. He changed the subject back to David and his career as a skin specialist, endeavouring to be pleasant and interested in his work and ambitions. Sam grew restless and wandered off, leaving his cars scattered like potential banana skins all over the floor. Sarah returned and asked Nicholas if he'd like to stay to lunch. He sensed her anxiety and smiled reassuringly.

"An unexpected guest! The cook's nightmare! Thank you for the invitation, but I really won't. If I can talk to Melissa privately for ten minutes that's all I need and then I'll be off and leave you in peace." Her relief was obvious.

At last there was the sound of a car and he rose to his feet. David followed him out of the room and as soon as the door closed behind him, said aggressively, "It was you, wasn't it? That bought the house?"

"Sorry?" Nicholas said, his heart sinking. "You've lost me."

"Mel said—I'm sure she said it was you—the architect. It was you that bought this house. She's furious."

Nicholas blinked. "I am an architect. I design houses—I don't buy them—and I can assure you that I haven't bought this house." Which was perfectly true.

"OK, not you, your company bought it. Church, or Abbey or something like that."

Nicholas frowned in well-simulated confusion and had a nasty feeling that the past was going to unravel into the present unless he could put a lid on it.

"I have no idea how Melissa has arrived at this conclusion, but I would suggest that possibly you have got the wrong end of some stick? Why on earth would I buy a house I don't want when I have a perfectly nice one of my own?"

He gave David what he hoped was a look of baffled contempt and preceded him back to the kitchen. Melissa had linked Cathedral Properties to Thauros Associates; he was acquainted with Melissa's dislike of unasked-for assistance and hoped that David would leave it alone.

He was nonplussed by the fact that a good-looking young man followed her into the kitchen, but then he saw the similarity between the two of them. This must be her brother Johnny, Sarah's unemployed husband. Melissa looked at first astounded and then apprehensive, and after introductions to her brother, Nicholas made a graceful plea for a few minutes of her time. What a tricky family reunion, he thought, as she led him reluctantly into her grandfather's study. There were all sorts of undercurrents swirling about. "How's your grandmother?"

"Fine," she said tersely. "Why didn't you ring to say you were coming? Why are you here? Is it the house?" She was sharp with anxiety.

"The house? No, of course it's not the house. I thought you might refuse to see me, or abscond at the last minute. I need to explain a letter I've received from my lawyers in Athens."

He produced the envelope and watched her face as she stared at the closely typewritten Greek. She looked up at him, puzzled and concerned.

"The Egyptians have arrested our friend Rambiris in Cairo, for illegal export of Egyptian artefacts to Greece. But the Greek police want to nail him for illegal exports out of Greece and have him extradited to stand trial in Athens. His theft of the bible in Perissos is still on the books, as it were, and basically they're asking if you will be a witness."

"But he didn't export it—he sold it to you, and you, I assume, exported it legally. And in any case, didn't your mother return it to the monastery?"

"Yes, that's true, but it was still stolen from you, and the money has never been recovered."

She looked confused. "It was actually stolen from Clive Mann—it was his money."

"Your case, though. Clive Mann apparently washed his hands of it. You made the complaint."

"Good grief, Nicholas! *You* made the complaint!" She was almost laughing, but not quite. "How can I possibly be a witness? I'd have to go to Athens, wouldn't I? To a Greek court? I don't understand one word of Greek, and as you pointed out at the time, I had absolutely no proof. Nothing in writing, no bill, no receipt, no export licence, nothing. I'd be shot down in flames. And I can't see Clive Mann helping much. In fact, I wouldn't put it past him to deny all knowledge of my being there, or of having sent me to buy it."

"He couldn't do that. Your phone conversation with him

was recorded. And you wouldn't be accusing Rambiris of anything in one sense—just reporting what happened to you. And everything would be translated into English in court. Don't think I'm trying to persuade you one way or the other—it would be entirely your decision, or rather yours and David's."

"What's it got to do with David?" she said belligerently. "He hasn't any idea about what happened. I've never mentioned it, and I sincerely hope you haven't either."

He couldn't resist the entirely childish desire to make trouble for David.

"No, of course not. Only he was upset that I wanted to speak to you privately. He said all your decisions would be taken jointly, and I respect that."

She looked annoyed, but also undecided. "I don't know what I should do." She chewed her lip. "I don't want to get involved again one bit. The whole thing was ages ago and I've tried to forget it. It would mean telling the family." She meant David, he thought. "I don't want to open it all up again. But perhaps I ought to. He was a horrid little man, and he's obviously been doing it for years and ought to be stopped, and maybe he'll get away with it if I don't do my bit to help." Nicholas was unhelpfully silent. "Look, I'm getting married in a few weeks. I can't get into this now, David would have a fit. I don't have to make a decision this instant, do I?"

"No, not this instant," he said with a shrug. "The case would have to be put together—all the different charges, and witnesses and everything. Talk it over with David and let me know what you want to do, but I'll need to let them know within a week or so."

"I don't need to talk it over with David to know what he'd say." She rubbed a hand over her face. "What should I do? What do you want me to do?"

"I can't decide for you." There was something in his voice which made her look up with a frown. "I can't decide for you, and I can't advise you."

341

"It's never stopped you before," she said with enough crispness to bring a smile to his face. "Why didn't they write direct to me about it?"

"The police wrote to my lawyers, because they dealt with the case at the time. My lawyers naturally wrote to me. It's in Greek," he pointed out. "How would you have read it?"

"Lawyers like yours either speak beautiful English or have translators," she said. "It's a very long letter—two full pages—what does it actually say?"

"I could translate it for you," he said, but was relieved of the need to do so by a sharp knock and David walking in.

"I don't know what's going on," he said, "but perhaps this *tête à tête* could be terminated. Sam is starving and getting bad-tempered, and Sarah wants to dish up lunch. You're welcome to stay," he directed this to Nicholas without any welcome at all, "but we really must eat." Nicholas saw that he was angry at having been excluded, and knew Melissa wouldn't want a row with him. He made his exit rapidly, shaking the brigadier's hand, and thanking Sarah for the coffee.

"Bye, Sam. Shall I buy a Lamborghini next time?" Sam grinned and said that he liked the Jaguar. Melissa came out to the car, shrugging on a jacket against the wind.

"Nicholas—can it wait till after the wedding?"

He shrugged. "Probably not. Do what you think is right."

She said despairingly, "I don't know what's right. There's something more, isn't there?" He said nothing. "If I send you an invitation, will you come to the wedding?"

"No," he said neutrally. "I can't come. I'll be away." He took a breath as if he was going to say something else, and then opened the door, throwing his coat across to the passenger seat.

"Why did you really come?" She sounded desperate. "What do you want, Nicholas?"

He slid into the driving seat. "What do I want?"

He spoke in Greek, so she didn't understand, a long emphatic sentence, and then he smiled at her.

"Goodbye, pussycat. If you think you should do something about Rambiris you'll have to contact me, and if you don't want to, then that's OK, too. I hope they'll nail him anyway, with you or without you. I wish you a lovely wedding, and a very happy future with your David."

He let the brake off and drew away down the drive. He could see in the mirror that she watched the car until it turned on to the road.

CHAPTER TWENTY-NINE

When the doorbell rang, he dropped Cat on to the floor and put his glass on the desk, irritated by the interruption but having no expectation of surprise.

"Hello, Nicholas."

She was clutching a tartan umbrella as if her life depended on it. He was so startled that he immediately reverted to the chilly sarcasm that had served him so well in the past.

"Well, well! If it isn't Mrs David Allison! And how is married life? You're looking good on it, I must say, so the married state must be all it's cracked up to be. Did you have an idyllic honeymoon on some romantic island in the sun?"

She shook her head. "No." She took a deep breath, as if gathering her courage. "I was passing. I saw your lights were on." It sounded as if she knew his house had been dark and empty for weeks.

"So you dropped by. How lovely. Passing from where to where? Destination Lexham Gardens? Is that right?"

She shook her head again. "I go to lectures on Wednesday nights." He cocked his head in interrogation. "Near Waterloo. Design and Illustration."

"More books? Is Sophie needing an illustrator again?"

"Yes. But I wanted to tell you—"

"—all about the wedding, and the reception, and the lovely flat, and how wonderful it is to keep house, and cook delicious dinners for when he comes home tired, and about how brilliant he is in bed, and being the perfect little wife to the great skin specialist." He was laughing, leaning against the door jamb, a hand holding the door. He saw her face tighten at his derision and the familiar defensive lifting of her shoulders was like a punch in his ribs.

344

"No," she said, and he could hear the tremor in her voice. "I wanted—" There was a distinct hesitation and he raised his brows questioningly before she finished, "to discuss the Rambiris thing."

"You wanted to discuss it?" He put plenty of regret into his response. "Too late, I'm afraid. I told them weeks, months ago, you wouldn't—couldn't—help." He smiled without amusement. "It's OK—I knew what the answer was anyway, the moment I met him. There was no way he'd let you get involved in the case, before or after your wedding, so I told the Greeks they'd have to do without you, and let Rambiris off that particular hook. I just had to let you know about it, that's all. Don't give it a second thought." She seemed silenced by his assessment, and he let the moment lengthen before making a slight movement as if to begin closing the door.

"I'd invite you in out of the rain, but I'm expecting guests."

She stiffened in anger. "I don't want to come in, thank you. I'm on my way home."

He sighed dramatically. "Ah! Home! The cosy nest awaits, the slippers and the pipe laid ready, the bed turned down. You'd best get a move on if his dinner isn't going to be late."

"Oh, I'm moving on, Nicholas," she said coldly. "I've suddenly realised just how much I'm moving on. Sorry to have disturbed your busy social life, but it won't happen again. Goodbye."

She turned away, down the wide rain-slicked steps, the tartan umbrella tilted, hiding her head. He watched her until she was obscured by the hissing traffic and then he closed the door and leant back against it with his eyes closed. But closing his eyes didn't stop him seeing, or hearing, or remembering, or regretting. As he stood there, the door cold against his back, something was scratching at his memory. He tried to recall her words.

345

'I wanted to tell you—' He'd seen something but hadn't seen it; heard something but hadn't heard it. Why had she come, damn her? She'd wanted to discuss Rambiris. Had she? And that wasn't the same as *telling* him something. What had she wanted to tell him? He'd been so quick with the sarcasm that she had changed her mind, he was sure. Damn his tongue, he thought, squeezing his eyes tighter, seeing the moisture clinging to her hair, seeing the taut muscles in her face, seeing the nervously tight grip of her hand on the umbrella. In his mind's eye, he looked at that hand again, white in the halogen street lighting. Her left hand, holding the umbrella. Ringless. No opal. No wedding band.

Nicholas opened his eyes and swore aloud. He pulled the door open, the force swinging it back against the wall and as he started running towards Sloane Square, he heard it swing back and close with a solid thump.

There were scores of people in the square, most with umbrellas, but he couldn't see a tartan one. If she'd taken the tube she'd be long gone. He turned away from the Underground and thought desperately that he might find her somewhere in Lexham Gardens. But if what he thought—hoped—might be the case, she wouldn't be going to David Allison's flat. She could be going anywhere. He searched the King's Road bus stops, then crossed the square and hurried up Sloane Street, scanning the queues, seeing the lines of buses turning north and the crowds pushing to get out of the rain. He was too late and a terrible choking dismay filled him.

And then suddenly he did see her, crowded under a bus shelter, nearing the front of the queue, the umbrella folded now, staring unfocussed at the oncoming traffic, her mouth tight and her shoulders high and stiff. His heart lurched and he pushed through towards her.

"Melissa!"

The people about her turned their heads, but she paid no attention. "Melissa!" he said again, loudly, urgently. She turned her head slowly, frowning, and looked at his dripping figure in disbelief, as if he were a figment of her imagination.

346

"You haven't got a coat," she said stupidly.

He reached for her wrist and pulled her out of the queue and across to the railings.

"And you haven't got a ring." He took her left hand and stared at it. "You haven't got a wedding ring." He raised his eyes to her face as she tried to withdraw her hand and gripped it tighter. "You didn't marry him, did you?"

"It's being altered. It was too big." Her voice was cold and he thought she was lying, but all his old certainties about her were dissolving and the feeling of helplessness was back.

"Tell me you didn't marry him." He was almost shouting.

"Go away, Nicholas." She sounded distressed. "I can't take any more of you."

A bus was about to leave, the last passengers climbing in, and Melissa tore her hand out of his and ran for it.

Nicholas just managed to squeeze through the central doors as they swished shut and was trapped in a tight knot of standing passengers. By Knightsbridge he had managed to work his way back to where she was pinned in to a window seat by a large Jamaican lady.

"Melissa." He sounded desperate, even to himself.

She turned her head in shock. "Why are you still here?" she hissed angrily. "Go away."

"Did you marry him? He can't have been that inefficient to get a wedding ring that didn't fit."

She turned away and stared out of the window again and Nicholas burnt his boats.

"I hated him. I disliked him before I even met him, and I hated him when I did. I was jealous, and angry, and very sorry for myself." The Jamaican lady was shaking her head in a melancholy way. "I couldn't have come to the wedding—I couldn't bear it, I went away." He willed her to look at him, but she refused. "Did you marry him?" Several interested heads began to turn towards him.

She didn't answer, her face averted, rigid with tension.

"I am very sorry. Really sorry. It was unforgiveable, what I said." She still didn't speak. "Did you marry him?" he repeated in desperation.

"Nicholas! I am not having this conversation with you. Let alone on a bus. Go away." She said it quite quietly but with enough force for him to recognise how angry she was.

"Can we have it somewhere else, then?"

"No."

"If you married him I'll go away. For ever. I'll go now." He swallowed. "But it was you that came tonight, to tell me something. Did you marry him?"

She held herself very still and then shook her head a fraction.

"Is that what you came to tell me tonight?" She shrugged, taut as a bowstring.

The Jamaican lady cackled gently. "You need this seat, boy." She heaved her bulk up and pushed him into her seat. He said a fervent thank you, and Melissa glared at her.

"Why did you come to tell me?" He could hear his own anxiety.

She neither moved nor spoke and for a long moment he couldn't formulate any of the questions he most wanted to ask.

"OK. Well, why did you call it off?"

She still didn't answer.

"Melissa, please. It matters. Damn it, I've been bloody miserable. Why did you call it off?"

"*You've* been miserable?" She looked confused and startled, and then her shoulders dropped. "There were lots of reasons." She sounded quite matter-of-fact, but he knew she wasn't.

She tensed again. "Anyway, I didn't call it off. David did."

He drew in a sharp breath. He hadn't been expecting that and experienced an immediate protective indignation.

"Self-defence. He must have known that I would, so he sensibly got in first." She gave him a quick, wry glance and

348

relaxed fractionally. "Well, I'm getting off, because I'm on the wrong bus, going in the wrong direction. You'd better go home if you've got guests coming."

He felt a bubble of relief.

"I lied, as you very well know. Time for both of us to get on the right bus, and go in the right direction, don't you think?"

As they extracted themselves from the bus he took her umbrella and held it over them both. He asked her again, "So, tell me, what happened?"

She shrugged, feigning indifference. "Oh, it just wasn't going to work. Mops died and Brig needed me. I couldn't cope with weddings as well." She looked at him seriously. "Different buses, I think. You're a man who takes taxis, anyway."

Nicholas shook his head. "I'll take a bus anywhere, so long as it's with you. Anyway, I've got no coat, no wallet, no phone, no house keys and no wife, and I need you, in every sense." Standing still and silent, the rain rattling down on the tartan, she looked vulnerable and uncertain, and he knew she was unsure of what he meant.

She indicated his sodden T-shirt. "What happened?"

He said tersely. "After you'd gone I realised you didn't have a wedding ring, and I'd just thrown away the one thing I wanted. I just ran after you." He scrutinized the evening traffic. "We'll get whatever comes first, bus or taxi," he said. "I'm frozen and I shall die of pneumonia shortly." He remembered a more painful death for Melissa. "I'm really sorry about your grandmother."

She hunched her shoulders a little. "She never recovered from the broken hip and died in hospital about a month after you came." She paused. "I'm sorry I didn't help about that court case. Did Rambiris get off? I felt so bad, but I just couldn't bear having it all made public, and the family finding out. I'd never told them the whole story. And at that moment, with Mops so ill, and David and I going through

349

rather a tough time, I simply couldn't face it." She looked miserable and ashamed. "I'm sorry I was such a coward."

"Don't," he said gently. "I was a complete coward, too, if that makes you feel any better, and for essentially the same reasons. I was very relieved you refused to be a witness, because although my divorce was long finalised, it would have been horrible publicity, and tongues would have wagged—not just about me, but about you as well, and my family and yours, and frankly, that whole episode in Greece was best forgotten, I thought. Rambiris was found guilty of various things, but not of stealing the Perissos Bible."

"So why did you come that day? You didn't know that I would refuse to give evidence, did you? You could just have buried the letter and not asked me at all."

"I could have. I very nearly did." Suddenly, seeing a taxi pulling in to drop its passengers he took her hand and they ran, dodging the traffic, arriving breathless and triumphant before anyone else had got to it.

The relief of being out of the bitter wind and rain was enormous. He took her hand, running his thumb along the finger that wasn't wearing a wedding ring. She so nearly caressed him back that she snatched her hand away in panic.

"So why did you come?" she said again, as the taxi stop-started through the heavy traffic. "You needn't have driven all the way to Hampshire to show me a letter in Greek. You could have written, or phoned."

He sighed. "I don't know. I wanted to see you and the letter was an excuse, I suppose. I'd hoped to spend a bit of time with you, and I hadn't expected David to be there, or your brother and Sarah and Sam. David and I didn't hit it off, I'm afraid, and I thought I should remove myself before I made real trouble."

"When you came, you said something. In Greek. Were you warning me off David? What was it you said?"

He exhaled sharply. He had seldom been so nervous.

"I'll tell you," he said rather unsteadily, "later, if you still want to know. But I need to tell you something else first. It's

350

sort of an explanation, and an apology, and I suppose I'm using it as an excuse or justification for how I behaved towards you—a temporary insanity. It nearly destroyed me, and you, and the people I mind most about, but I need to tell you because—" He broke off. "If we have a future—relationship, friendship—I don't want it lying there, a horrible secret. And if I don't tell you now, I won't ever have the courage."

"You're gay?" she said. She looked at his face in the flickering street lamps. "No? A polygamist? A murderer? No. And not a drug dealer. OK." Her relief was obvious. "So what is this horrible secret?"

He leant forward and ran his hands through his wet hair, trying to gather his words coherently.

"Marie Claude didn't want children and, to be honest, she would have said so from the start had I asked. But I didn't, I was so bloody besotted. After we married, she refused to even contemplate starting a family. What with that, and her general absence on catwalks all over the world and her affairs with the rich and famous, I got—angry. And eventually malicious. And devious. I organised, to suit her work schedule, a very private holiday on a very private Caribbean island, threw away her pills and set out to make her pregnant. Successfully." His mouth was hard. "I don't come out of this at all well. She called it rape—which it certainly was not—and said it would ruin her career and she would have an abortion, so I hired twenty-four-hour bodyguards to make sure she didn't. The cost of that made even me blink. In France, the legal limit for an abortion is twelve weeks, but in Britain it's twenty-four." He hadn't looked at Melissa. "I had her accompanied and watched for twenty-four weeks." There was a long silence which Melissa didn't break. "She was six months pregnant, and she found a clinic in America and had the abortion. She paid for it with my money." The taxi had crawled as far as Queensway. "Love can turn to hatred so quickly," he said quietly. "I don't think she would have done it if I hadn't behaved as I did. I

351

was responsible for the conception of the baby, but even if it had lived, what sort of a life would we have given it? Two warring, hating parents. Both of us guilty and both of us responsible for its death." He rubbed his face; the moisture could have been tears or rain. "I don't even know if it was a boy or a girl."

In the silence, he was grateful for the wet darkness and intermittent street lighting. His clothes seeped damp and cold into him, along with fear about what she was thinking. The traffic passed in relentless streams, tyres hissing on the wet tarmac, spraying water from the puddles.

Melissa eventually broke the silence.

"Had that just happened—the baby, the abortion—when I came to Greece?"

"A few weeks earlier, yes. No one knew what had happened or why I was behaving so badly, and my parents were so appalled they sent me to Mixos to get out of everyone's hair. My uncle gave me leave of absence, because I was so awful in the office as well. I think I was—" He took a deep breath. "I don't know what I was; half-crazy I think. Getting the Perissos Bible was one way of keeping sane—of thinking of something other than myself. I was unbelievably angry."

She made an affirmative sound and his mouth tightened.

"Melissa, I'm so sorry. For what happened, for how I treated you. I truly thought you'd been set up by her in retaliation for what I did. I thought you must have been involved."

After a long silence she took a deep breath. "So now that you've told me your not-very-nice story, and you know mine, tell me what it was you said, in Greek, that day you came to Hampshire? It was important, wasn't it?"

He ducked his head uncomfortably. "Yes. I couldn't say it in English. I'm not sure I can, or should, say it now, after what I've just told you." His confession had appalled him by its selfish viciousness, the spoken words stripped of the dubious excuses.

"What did you say?" She was insistent.

He took a deep breath. "You asked what I wanted, and I said I wanted to kiss you, to make love to you, to marry you and to have children by you." Into the silence he added, "And I still do. I love you."

She looked astounded, almost frightened. "You can't!"

"I can. I do." He sighed and rubbed his face again. "I know you find it hard to believe. I've been jealous and resentful of your boyfriends. I've treated you incredibly badly, I've said and done awful things. But the fact is, ever since we met again in London I've been falling in love with you. But I didn't think you could possibly love me. Why would you? I've behaved so badly."

Melissa shook her head disbelievingly. "Your wife was, is, so beautiful. I'm not hideous, I know that, and I know I'm not stupid, but I'm not exactly the most stunning, wittiest, funniest girl around. You come from a completely different background. We're from different planets. How could I fit into your social environment, or get used to the way you use money and influence? You would be bored by me within a year, and I'm not willing to go through the process of being chewed up and then spat out again, and you really don't need a second divorce."

He shook his head in frustration. "I can't prove anything now—but I honestly believe you're wrong. Those are arguments we've both used, but I simply don't think they stand up. I know I got my values all screwed up with Marie Claude. God knows," he said, raking his fingers through his hair, "enough people tried to tell me. I messed up my marriage and my life and in the process messed up yours, too, but what I feel for you is honestly not me trying to make amends for what I did to you, or trying to get rid of my guilt. I know the values you live by and they're the same ones that Richard tried to instil in me. We're not from different planets at all; both of us can make an effort to give and take and discover where the other is coming from. And to suggest that I'd be bored by you is ridiculous. There's nothing wrong with

353

your brain, only with your self-confidence." His mouth quirked. "I don't think boredom would be our problem." He became serious again. "You'd be more than entitled to hate me, I know, but I think you came to tell me you didn't marry David, and I'm hoping like hell that was because you felt something for me." There was another long silence from her as the taxi sat in sodden gridlock. "You haven't said anything about what I did to Marie Claude."

She thought for a few moments. "It seems to me that guilt is like a big, heavy sack dumped on us and we can't put it down. I didn't choose to be the survivor in my family and you didn't choose to have the abortion. Of course, we both did things we're ashamed of, but—well, I felt better when I'd told you about the accident and how horrible I was both before and after it—telling somehow puts the past into perspective and takes the sting of guilt out of it. What happened between you and Marie Claude was dreadful, but did your family disown you? I think not."

He took a sharp breath. "They don't know. Nobody knows. Only you."

"So you didn't use it during the divorce?"

"No, I didn't. I threatened to and maybe I would have if she'd forced my hand, but I didn't want to because I was ashamed of what I'd done and washing that particular dirty laundry in the public domain was so shameful. It would have reflected on my entire family, not just me. No. Nobody knows except you."

"Well, I know perfectly well it wasn't my fault that I survived, and you know perfectly well that the abortion wasn't your fault either. We have to deal with our shameful peripheral actions and then dump them, otherwise they'll haunt us forever."

Her reaction was so different from his own anger and self-accusation that he felt almost robbed of the disgust he had expected, and at the same time an overwhelming sense of relief swept through him.

"So how do you deal with them? And where do you dump them?"

"I think you've just done it," she said slowly, "and I did it on the beach in Mixos. You hadn't told anyone about what you and Marie Claude did and I had never actually admitted how badly I behaved after Mum and the boys were killed — although everybody knew, of course. I think perhaps it goes rotten inside one unless you let it out. But once it's out, somehow it loses its power. Somehow, you've dumped it. Well, I guess we can pick it up again, and then you have to go through the dumping process again. I think I'm going to have to apologise to Brig if I'm going to get rid of my guilt completely—that's not going to be easy. I would have liked to say sorry to Mum and Dad and Mops, but maybe Brig is a start." Hesitating, she added, "Perhaps you'd feel better if you explained to your parents, and said sorry too?"

Nicholas said nothing for a long moment and then he turned her towards him, drawing her head into his shoulder.

"Somebody put a wise head on your young shoulders. Who was it said that?"

"Miss Jean Brodie. In a film."

He tried to imagine apologising to Marie Claude as well and, for the moment, failed.

"I love you. I've loved you for a long time, I think. I love you in a completely different way. I feel like I'm coming home after years of being in exile. My wife was beautiful to look at, but she had a rotten core which I was completely blind to. It was the blindness of obsession I suppose. Everyone else saw it—Madame, Richard, my various siblings, my genuine friends. I saw it eventually—she was unfaithful from the start, and it became clear, even to me, that all she wanted was my money, and I suppose, my name, because I was rich. She didn't need my name—the de Riberacs come from the French aristocracy."

He cupped Melissa's face, rubbing back damp dark strands of hair from her eyes.

"Now I happen to know that you despise my money, and you haven't given a very good impression as a nymphomaniac. I like you as well as love you. I like your company and your conversation. You're intelligent and talented, and I haven't been bored yet and I've given myself plenty of opportunity."

She frowned, not understanding.

"You haven't had any opportunity."

He laughed. "Yes, I have. What about Scotland? And those months when I made you come and hand over fifty pounds in cash? Or Mixos, come to that."

"I don't know—I never did work it out."

"Apart from anything else, I couldn't drive and I really did need a driver. I was annoyed and embarrassed about it and I didn't tell you because you'd think exactly what you did think when you found out—that I'd only got you to come for my own convenience. You certainly wouldn't have come with me. But you were under my skin with a vengeance by then. I thought perhaps a prolonged time together might cure me, but instead I enjoyed your company, found you hard-working, full of common sense, knowledgeable, you never complained once about the weather, and looked enchanting with rain dripping off your nose, which you still do." He brushed back a tendril from her forehead. "I was furious that you spent your time trying to avoid me, was jealous when that creep Cairns talked to you, livid that you dumped wretched Lorraine in my lap."

She blinked. "You didn't give me the slightest idea! You hardly even touched me!"

"I can assure you I wanted to. But I'd promised not to, so I didn't." He pulled her close to him again, his mouth at her temple. "I thought I was trying to get you out of my system because I knew that you were too young for me, too innocent. I was too old for you, in every sense. I had done an unforgivably awful thing to my wife, I was partly responsible for the—the death of my own child, my marriage was on the rocks, and a steamy media divorce is a recipe for a rebound disaster. As you, and various other people, have told me on more than one occasion, I have too much money, and I drive too fast, and I'm untidy and bad-tempered and sarcastic and antisocial, and all in all, not a very good bet as a lover, let alone a husband."

His hands tightened on her shoulders.

"And it didn't work. And you were still under my skin, and I had fallen in love much against my better judgement. After Marie Claude, I promised myself never to do it again, and I genuinely did try not to, and to fall out of love again, and not to see you." He took a deep breath. "I kept away all those months, thinking that you didn't even like me. Thinking that I'd get over you. And I didn't. I missed you coming every month, and kicked myself for not reminding you to pay that day in the Borders. You were in my mind biting like a bloody mosquito. And then you accused me of pulling strings over the hospice designs, which was the one thing I honestly never even thought of doing because it was so totally unnecessary, and that made me furious. I was completely, stupidly, besotted about you. And you couldn't stand being anywhere near me." Melissa shook her head in denial. "Every time I came to the hospice, you weren't there. You knew I was coming and you avoided me like the plague."

Melissa protested. "I avoided you because I thought you wouldn't want to see me. I couldn't believe you had any interest in me, and I was terrified you would see how I felt." She gulped. "Terrified you'd see how I reacted when you touched me. You'd see a silly girl, with a crush on a rich man. I was mortified by my own reactions." He realised she was crying and ran a finger under her eyes to wipe away the tears.

"Pussycat! We have both been very blind, and very foolish." He pressed her gently against him, wanting to reassure and be reassured and then held her slightly away from him to look down at her face.

"And David Allison was absolutely the last straw and how you could have even contemplated him I can't imagine! And I could have killed him for making you so unhappy."

"Oh, Nicholas! He didn't! I wasn't!"

"He did, you know. You were almost afraid of him. I know I'm not your ideal man, and I've been more than horrible to you. I'm sorrier for that than you could possibly imagine, but you did come tonight and you didn't marry David and I can't help hoping—well, that perhaps we could start again?"

She looked up at him and her mouth moved in what might have been a very small smile.

The taxi turned into her street. "Go in the same direction, you mean? We both seem to have been pulling on the same rope, but in different directions." She extracted herself from his arms. "We have arrived."

Melissa paid for the taxi and Elizabeth Forbes grinned at the edited version of why Nicholas was wet to the skin and locked out of his house. She waved a hand in the direction of a hot shower and went on her way out to supper with friends.

Melissa, between his kisses, tumble-dried and ironed Nicholas's clothes. He could see she was deeply apprehensive in spite of the way she reacted to his kisses.

After his shower, he kissed her again very thoroughly, until she dragged herself out of his embrace and made him sit down to sort out the problem he'd created by shutting his own front door, while she herself went to shower and change. Without his phone and wallet, he was aware of uncomfortable echoes of Melissa's situation in Mixos. He would be happy to stay in her bed, but didn't think he'd be invite. He sighed and turned on her tablet, logging in to his account.

He found the number he required and solved his problem using her mobile. Getting up, he stood at Melissa's bedroom door, contemplating her tidy kingdom. There were photographs in frames on the chest of drawers, and a pair, portraits, hanging on picture hooks. Her parents, he guessed. A naval officer in formal pose, hat under his arm, looking straight at the camera. A pleasant, intelligent face with a definite likeness to Brig. The other was less formal, a pretty woman with shoulder-length hair, looking away and laughing at something over the viewer's shoulder. Melissa would be like her when she was older. He picked up a frame containing several snapshots of, he assumed, her brothers in various boyish situations; bikes, ponies and trees, another of Johnny and Sarah on their wedding day, another of Sam standing on top of a large round hay bale. Five ceramic dolphins leapt along the window sill. He picked one up, remembering how he had missed those monthly visits. When Melissa returned, wrapped in an ancient towelling robe, she saw he had a frame in his hand and that all the photographs were in slightly different positions.

"Do you mind me looking?" he said. She shook her head.

"David never showed much interest in my family, dead or alive. Of course I don't mind. Have you sorted your key out?"

"I hope so. I eventually got Paulina's number and I've sent a courier to get her key." He watched in amusement as her mouth opened and failed to formulate a question.

"Who is Paulina?" he prompted teasingly. "That's what you should be asking. Who is this mistress in the wings who has a key to his house?"

She grinned, the shadow of doubt fading. "If it was a mistress I imagine you'd know her number."

"Ah, but my memory is in my mobile, not in my brain. Paulina is my cleaner cum housekeeper, and without her I'd be in total chaos. I meet her when I leave Cat with her, and pick him up." He put his arms round Melissa and held her close without moving. "I'm going to have to ask you to pay the courier—the tables are turned, aren't they? I promise to pay you back."

"Thus are the mighty fallen, if only temporarily," she said, with a small smile. "Go away so that I can get dressed."

"You don't have to get dressed," he said, without great optimism.

"I do," she said, putting a bemused hand to her head. "I can't believe this is happening. I can give you a glass of very cheap wine while you're waiting."

"I wouldn't normally take that for an answer," he said glumly, "but you seem to have got the upper hand at the moment. But when the courier comes, will you come back with me?" He saw her hesitation and put his arms around her again, his cheek against hers. She smelt cleanly of soap. "I know you think that leopards cannot entirely change their spots, but will you give me a chance? I promise to bring you back later if that's what you want."

Later, sitting on the sofa, his arm around her and her head on his shoulder, he asked about her grandmother's death in hospital.

"She just never recovered from the hip fracture, and Brig was so sad when she died, he simply couldn't cope. Johnny and Sarah helped me move him into sheltered housing. There was stuff we both wanted to keep, and a friend put a few boxes in their barn, but most of the house contents went to auction. It was a bit of a nightmare, really." She made a little comic face and he tightened his grip in regret.

"My darling, I'm so sorry I wasn't there. I would have helped, not that you'd have wanted me to, I know. Didn't David help?"

"He did try. But it felt like he was always telling us what to do, and how to do it. Neither Johnny nor Sarah ever liked him and all three of us got scratchier and scratchier with him."

Nicholas laughed. "How I sympathise! I never liked him either."

"You only met him once!"

"Once was quite enough. So, what happened?"

"It was awful. Endless rows. It was my fault. Well, your fault really. If I hadn't gone to Scotland, and you hadn't come to Mixos, I think I would have tried to make it work. But I fell in love with you." She turned in his arms to face him. "I had no expectations of you, I still don't. But I knew I'd never love him and that I'd rather be single than unhappily married."

"Thank God for that," Nicholas said fervently, his hands sliding down to her waist and under her sweater. Melissa's nerve ends exploded as his fingers stroked up her back and across her shoulder blades. "I went through hell thinking you'd married him, thinking of him making love to you, making you the submissive wife, stopping you fulfilling your potential. All that creativity going nowhere." His fingers caressed her skin and then released her bra hooks, before slowly easing the straps off her shoulders. As he cupped her breasts in his palms, the nipples hardened into fierce peaks between his fingers and his groin tautened. She gasped, her back arching as her eyes closed at his touch.

Her phone rang.

CHAPTER THIRTY

"**D**amn!" said Nicholas softly, into her hair. He withdrew his hands reluctantly as the ringtone persisted. Melissa pulled herself together and answered.

"It's Paulina," she said, handing it to him, trying to recover her equilibrium. Her skin felt hot. How had he reduced her to such an uninhibited state in just a few moments? That had never happened with David.

Nicholas cut the call. "The courier has the key and should be here in about twenty minutes." He leant to kiss her on the forehead. "Twenty minutes is not long enough to do all the things I want to do with you." He traced his finger along the bones of her face, under the eye socket and down her jaw, smiling as she closed her eyes at his touch.

He topped up her glass while she did her bra up.

"So how did it all happen? When I came, just after Christmas, it all felt very uncomfortable. David was very tetchy and your brother and Sarah very on edge."

Melissa sighed. "Oddly enough, as David and I fell to pieces, Johnny and Sarah's marriage sort of came together. Mutual disapproval of David, I think."

"I'm afraid I behaved pretty badly," she went on guiltily, "but he seemed to become more and more demanding and domineering and I thought he'd turn into a replica of his father." She sighed again and he rested his face against hers.

"He resented the success of your hospice designs and Sophie's book illustrations. A successful wife was not to his taste. I was furious he had pressured you to turn down commissions."

"How did you know that?" she asked in surprise.

"I asked him. He said 'there had been a few enquiries' and you'd taken the decisions together, but I knew it wouldn't have been a 'few enquiries'. After the hospice there would have been a great deal of interest! They were his decisions and you'd gone along with it. But you kept this flat on, even though it must have been a drain on your finances. Didn't he want you to move in with him?"

"Yes, he did, long before the hospice even, and I refused. I don't know why. A sixth sense perhaps, of what was to come! He thought I was mad to keep the flat."

"But you weren't. It's nice," he said glancing round the low-ceilinged room. "Cosy. And you needed a home."

Which reminded her. "Did you actually buy The Old Rectory?" she said hesitantly. "It was only at Christmas I remembered that Cathedral Properties was part of your company." He looked down, feeling more than a little guilty.

"No, I didn't, but I have to confess that I mentioned your difficulty to one of the directors who saw no problem in obliging me." He stroked her cheek. "You were so miserable about the sale falling through, but I knew you'd be furious if you found out I'd interfered again."

Melissa gave a half laugh and then said, "How well you know me! But thank you. It was a huge relief and they were very efficient. I'm sorry about my misplaced pride." She smiled a little crookedly and Nicholas kissed her with great relief, his hands again drifting under the hem of her sweater to caress her skin. She again became instantly breathless at his touch; the nerve ends on fire.

The doorbell rang, long and hard.

"Someone is conspiring against me. That must be the courier." He sighed and removed his hands. "What bad timing." She heard the frustration and took a deep breath.

"Here's my wallet. Go pay the courier and get your key."

"Will you come back with me?"

"I need to think. Without you interfering in the thought process."

Nicholas went down to the street door and Melissa sank back on to the sofa. This could not be happening. Too much in too short a time. Emotions could not swing from such misery to such intense hope. From such fury to such intense desire. She thought of his sarcastic, unkind words on his doorstep. Did leopards ever change their spots? Nicholas came back into the room and looked at her. Neither spoke for several moments.

"Pussycat, your silences speak louder than words. We are two people with a wealth of mutual misunderstandings to sort out, and, hopefully, a new relationship to embark on. And I shall cook you a steak. Shall we just start with that?"

She smiled a little, choosing to believe him. He called a taxi, stopping it to buy supper with the last of her cash on the way home.

Using Paulina's unfamiliar keys, he fetched his wallet and paid the driver. Closing the door behind him, he leant back against it with his eyes closed.

"An entire lifetime has passed since I was last here," he said. "A hundred years of emotional roller coaster. I feel completely exhausted."

"I feel hungry," Melissa said, picking up Cat who had trod delicately down the stairs to welcome them.

He snorted with laughter and kissed her firmly on the mouth, Cat floppy between their bodies.

"That's my pussycat. You always did need food at the crucial moment."

She followed him downstairs and stared in awe at the kitchen.

"Designer kitchen for my wife, who never cooked a single meal in it," he said, seeing her expression. "Designer house as well, but she hardly lived here." He took two glasses from a shelf. "I must feed my other pussycat, too. You do the salad, I'll get us a drink and do the steaks. What would you like?"

"That's the first time you've ever asked," Melissa said. "You used to just give me something, whether I wanted it or not."

"You might not always have wanted it, but you always needed it. How often did I get it wrong?"

"Not often." She grinned and extracted the salad ingredients. "You choose."

He put Cat's dish of food on the floor before opening a bottle of good claret, and poured them both a glass. "I'd have had champagne on ice, had I known." He raised his glass and toasted her before turning back to the contents of the bags.

"Richard told me once that wealth like mine was a weight that could crush me—and others—if I used it irresponsibly. He's a rich man, too, and I always admired how lightly he held it. But I thought I did hold mine lightly, and responsibly. I got my engineering degree and trained as an architect. I worked, I had a few extravagances, like cars. Marie Claude certainly did her best to spend what was in her power to spend, but I wasn't behaving responsibly—looking back at what I did to her and to you, what I put you through, I saw how I had misused the power that my money gave me, and what Marie Claude and I had done to each other wasn't relevant to how I treated you—it wasn't an excuse."

The seasoned steak went into a hot grill pan.

"I saw it a long time ago, and though I tried to put right what I had done to you, it was all too late. I called your self-respect stubborn pride, but it was all my fault that you went on hurting yourself struggling to repay Mann and me, and looking after your grandparents and working yourself into the ground." He tipped in the sliced mushrooms. "You hated discovering that I had paid that fine, and the result of that was that you thought I had meddled with getting the Angel Hospice project. Oh! And a million other things." He rubbed his hand up his face. "I wanted to protect you and all I did was to damage our relationship further. I'm sorry," he said helplessly. "I'm sorry to have made such a total mess."

She hesitated. "But it's not all one-sided, is it? It wasn't all self-respect on my part; most of it *was* stubborn pride, and I wasn't sure about my motives—all those months coming here with fifty pounds in cash. What on earth was I doing? Ever since you kissed me, when the police took me away, I've been wondering about my motives." She flushed painfully.

365

"It was just worse because I thought that I was absolutely nothing but a very faint blip on your life, and it made me angry, I suppose, and bloody-minded, because I thought everything you did was to get me out of your hair." She felt tears on her lashes. "Every month, I swore I wouldn't come again, but I did. Like a—like a child coming back for more punishment. Every time I looked at the dolphins I thought of you, and wanted you, and knew that David wasn't even second best. But I didn't want pity either. David, and his parents, pitied me. None of them thought there was anything I could contribute, to life, to them. You never did—you said that pity wasn't in your 'repertoire of emotions'."

He was startled. "I said that? When?"

"Oh. I can't remember. I think you were asking what had happened to Mum and my brothers."

He caught her against him with one hand and turned the steaks with the other. "I didn't pity you because I thought you were really tough underneath; you refused to tell me Mann's clients, or to accept my dubious favours, but I suppose I tried to find the weak spots and use them. I wanted you to break, but I didn't want you to break, if that makes any sense." He kissed the top of her head. "I really did try not to fall in love with you, and I just couldn't help it. I love you very much. I've loved you for ages."

He turned her to face him and lifted her chin to look into her eyes.

"In spite of all the negatives, would you give me a chance?" His hands were gripping her so hard it almost hurt and there was real urgency in his voice. Both of them were aware that in the space of one evening their relationship had swung from antagonism to much more than friendship.

She looked at him seriously. "The whole idea scares me to death. How can we have reached this point in just a few hours? I still don't know you, although I've been in love with you for so long."

He relaxed his grip, just holding her against him. At that moment, his feelings were of tenderness and protection

366

rather than sexual hunger. He recognised his own confusion as well as hers.

"You kept that a dark secret," he said quietly. "I never had any idea. You always looked excruciatingly uncomfortable whenever I turned up and I assumed you disliked me as much as you did when we first met." His fingers were in her hair, stroking, running down her skull behind her ears. She pressured her head back into his hands, half delirious at his touch.

"I *was* excruciatingly uncomfortable. I was terrified that you would know. I dreaded your reaction to this silly, green girl who had a crush on you. Too young, too naïve, too ordinary. And for weeks and weeks I walked past this house, hoping to bump into you, but terrified that I might, thinking that you'd sold it, that the lights would never be on again, that I'd never see you again, that everything you'd ever done for me was to relieve your conscience, and you were lying on some yacht in the sun, with one of those gorgeous, elegant women like your wife and that I wasn't even the glitch I had been once. Just a nothing, a non-thought." His grip on her had tightened, his cheek hard against hers.

"My darling pussycat! All these presumptions! We have both been idiots. I did know I wasn't old enough to be your father, but I thought a fourteen-year age gap was still too big, and then my divorce, and I'm Greek not British, together with a whole mountain of other negatives—I really did not think you would even have contemplated me. When I saw you after Christmas it seemed as if your wedding was a certainty and I just couldn't bear to be in England. Thauros Associates had a new project at the university in Singapore and I asked to be transferred on to it. I've been there ever since."

"Until when?"

"Until four days ago, and then only for consultations. I'm due to go back next week. The house has been empty, except for Paulina keeping an eye on it, and it would have been empty for another two or three months. I kept meaning to sell it, but it was too much hassle. I can only thank God that I was here tonight and that you saw the lights. And that you had the courage to ring the bell." He could hear the relief in his own voice. "I suppose Sophie knew the wedding didn't happen, but I've hardly been in touch with the family since I left and I didn't mention you, and nor did they. I was being cowardly. I thought I'd have had to pretend I didn't care about your marriage, and I knew that you would have asked Sophie and Michael to the wedding. I just kept clear, and didn't ask. If I had, I would have saved myself, and you, quite a bit of grief."

Melissa felt the weight of his regret. "Sophie and Michael did know, but not, of course, that it had anything to do with you. I'm still illustrating her books so I see them often." She smiled. "The most recent one is based on the letters D and F. Called Daphne the Dolphin."

She felt him chuckle. "You know more about dolphins than most girls do, but I'd like to show you lots more." He turned her face up to his and gently kissed her forehead and then her eyelids. "Would you consider it?"

"Well," she said, her eyes closed under his lips, "As I seem to collect dolphins, I suppose I might consider it. I'll consider it further after a steak which won't be rare if you go on kissing me like that."

He turned the hob off and moved the pan with one hand, while relocating his mouth to hers for a long moment.

"Salad, vinaigrette, mustard," she said eventually, withdrawing reluctantly.

"Steak knives and forks, plates. Eat, for pity's sake, before I lose my mind and all control."

Not too much later he observed, "Steak and red wine have to be the way to your heart. You obviously haven't eaten properly since I last fed my little Greek cat."

She sat back with a sigh of satisfaction. "It was utterly delicious, but I think only because I feel happy. Steak when you're miserable doesn't taste of anything. It might as well be—"

"Capercaillie?"

"I was thinking brawn."

"I was thinking of something quite different."

"Like?"

"Like getting to know each other better?" He hesitated, elbows on the table opposite her. "I know I said I'd take you home if you wanted to, and I will. But I am hoping, very much, that you don't want to."

He watched her smile, loving the crinkles at the edges of her eyes, and knew the answer before she even came round behind him and slipped her arms round his neck.

"I think it's about time we did start getting to know each other. So far, there has been nothing but misunderstandings which definitely need clearing up." She leant her head against his. "Where were you thinking of starting?"

He grinned and taking her hand, led her up the stairs.

END

Dear Reader

Thank you for reading Dolphin Days and I hope you enjoyed it.

The island in Greece—renamed Perissos in Dolphin Days—is where we built a beautiful house twenty-six years ago and we still spend a lot of time there. I am originally from the Scottish Borders, and my husband is a Highlander, thus the locations in Dolphin Days.

I write because I love writing, but my reason for publishing Dolphin Days is to raise funds for a charity called 'An African Dream'.

'An African Dream' dates back to 1997 when Mark Wynter felt a call from God to go to work in Western Uganda. In 1998 Mark married my daughter Sophie and while in the UK for the birth of their first son, Mark was re-diagnosed with cancer. He died aged 31 in 2005 just after their second son was born. Sophie set up 'An African Dream' in his memory and although she now lives in the UK, she is still much involved with the charity and visits Uganda regularly.

'An African Dream' built St Mark's Primary School and provides education for orphans and funds the teachers' salaries. It sponsors a teen development ministry, provides training and micro-enterprise opportunities for widows and funds training for Christian pastors, all in partnership with the local church.

If you would like further information, (or if you'd like to sponsor one of the gorgeous children!), please contact:

Email: info@aaduganda.org
www.aaduganda.org
Registered Charity No: 1123231

My next book has a working title of "Come In From The Cold" and tells the story of three generations of two very disparate but strangely connected families, and the secret sacrifice of the merchantmen and sailors who sailed on the horrific convoys from Loch Ewe in Scotland to Russia in the last war.

https://www.facebook.com/pg/charlottemilnewriting
https://charlottemilne-author.blog

About the Author

I grew up in lots of places, being a naval daughter, but home was always a fabulous house buried in the woods above the Tweed valley in the Borders of Scotland. My grandparents lived in the same house which I thought was wonderful, but now I wonder if my mother thought the same! It seemed to be a childhood of summer sun and winter snow and ice, of rough ponies, cats, dogs, the river and huge amounts of *risk*. I have three elder brothers who I just love to bits, along with my sisters-in-law. How many people are lucky enough to have that sort of family! One of the best times was in Malta when I was a young teenager. We lived in Fort St Angelo, in the middle of Valetta harbour, and there is a fantastic novel to be set there. I just haven't written it yet.

I trained as a secretary at The House of Citizenship and worked for a software house—early days of computers—before going, in 1966, to live in Kampala, Uganda, working as a secretary first for Caltex Oil and then for the Dean of Makerere University.

Forty years later my daughter went to Uganda with her husband Mark and 'An African Dream' was born. Any royalties from the sale of Dolphin Days are going to that charity.

I have never, so far as I can remember, been bored. The world inside my head is a seething mass of characters and conversations. I see people passing by and give them much more exciting lives than they could possibly have. I've always written stories (mounds of loose manuscripts and all the pages are muddled up) and as I'm now 70, there are lots of them, those that haven't been burnt or shredded.

I now live with my patient, supportive, but travel mad husband in a retirement village near Southampton, about half way between our son and daughter and seven grandchildren. We divide our time between Greece, Scotland, Southampton and far flung destinations around the globe. To my relief, I no longer have to garden two acres or try to keep an Elizabethan farmhouse from disintegrating around our ears. I don't miss the spiders who inhabited it, but I do miss digging my own potatoes and picking my own beans.

Charlotte Milne

Printed in Great Britain
by Amazon

30706494R00212